TARGET 91

TARGET 91

by

Kerry Cue

www.PenmorePress.com

ISBN-13: 978-1-946409-80-5(Paperback)
ISBN :-978-1-946409-81-2 (e-book)

BISAC Subject Headings:
FIC000000 **FICTION** / General
FIC055000 **FICTION** / Dystopian
FIC031060 **FICTION** / Thrillers / Political

Editing: Chris Wozny
Cover by The Book Cover Whisperer:
ProfessionalBookCoverDesign.com

Address all correspondence to:

Penmore Press LLC
920 N Javelina Pl
Tucson AZ 85748

Publisher's Note

Publishing a humorous story about such unfunny matters as gun laws and mass shootings is, admittedly, a risky undertaking. But in Kerry Cue's outsider's view of our homegrown issues we found not only humor, but compassion and profound insight into the motivations of peoples on all sides of the struggle over gun laws and gun usage in our country.
We ask our readers to take this story in the spirit is was written; it is not a diatribe nor manifesto, it certainly is not a call to arms; it is a slightly warped mirror held up to show us our very human nature.

I am your 2nd Amendment President. With me in the White House, you will NEVER have to give up your GOD GIVEN right to own guns. NEVER! OK!
@TheRealPresident

Acknowledgements

When some authors write their thank-yous the list goes on and on. This makes me feel overly slack on the gratitude front. Should I invent contributors to boost my gratitude rating? Back when my first book was published in the eighties, I realized the 'Other Works' page would be blank. So I made up a genuine list of other works, namely Chem 1 Prac Notes (unbound), 5 Christmas Cards (3 yet to be posted), and so on, for a dozen works. Unfortunately, interviewers did not read the list and introduced me on radio simply as 'the well known author of 12 books ...'

Now that I've managed to fill an appropriate acknowledgement space I would genuinely like to thank my dedicated readers Donna Jones, Matt Hales, Ruston Hutchens, Roland Ebringer, Geoff Meehan and my husband, Donald Cue. Special thanks to Donna for her knowledge of New England; my brother Geoff for his operational knowledge of guns; my husband Donald for his prodigious knowledge of gun history (Truly, darling, you can stop now!); my daughter George for her knowledge of Boston, NYC and Bed Stuy; and my son, Jules, who couch-surfed across 25 US states and provided insights into anarchist houses and other groups. I'd also like to thank Constance Renfrow for her invaluable comments.

Special thanks to my editor, Chris Wozney, whose comments were not only accurate but hilarious and Michael James, who read the manuscript of TARGET 91 and rang me the next day telling me I had a contract although 7am was a little early for an intelligent conversation.

Chapter 1

Kee

Friday, the 15th of September

Kee wanted to feel sad for Brodski. Closer to the corpse, she could recognize those traits that made Brodski, well, Brodski. His scraggly ginger hair. His matching scraggly ginger beard. His red-and-black checked lumberjack shirt. The tattoo of a snake up his neck and around his left ear. She should feel heart-sick sad for Brodski. Harmless, hapless Brodski. She had joked with him only two days ago when he stood smiling at her with his bent, broken-toothed grin as he pumped gas into her car, the 1969 Pontiac Firebird that she adored as if the Vintage V8 convertible were a trusty steed she could whistle up if danger threatened. She wanted to feel a totally-empty-inside sadness looking down at cold, dead Brodski. SAD, however, just wasn't registering on her mood meter at that moment. She was a journalist and this was her first, ever, crime scene. This was real news. National news. The usual stories she covered for *The New England Gazette,* a local paper which ran 5 days of the week, Tuesday through Saturday, were animal rescue reports, library events and school fairs, did not generate grab-you-by-the-eyeballs headlines. It was unfortunate that Brodski was the victim. But this was click-bait news. A murder. A strange, film noirish, freeze-frame murder.

The path that had led Kee to this pivotal moment in her career was long, meandering and hard-won. Following graduation, it had taken eight years of internships and waitressing, along with an astounding news-focused track record of blogging, tweeting and Facebooking to score her first job, a real job as a journalist, with *The New England Gazette.* Almost no one reads *The New England Gazette.* Certainly no one she actually knew. And she'd had to move to Ridgefield, Connecticut, which according to her then-boyfriend, Reece, was the "ass end of nowhere." Which was a trifle harsh. But he couldn't handle her geographic relocation, so, they split. But honestly, if she had to pick between Reece-plus-waitressing and a job in journalism in, say, an underground bunker in Siberia, there was no contest.

At her first interview, Kee sat her boss-to-be down and explained the voice you put on for each type of social media. "Twitter," she explained, "is all hot currency and hysterics. 'OMG. My cat just dragged in a rat with slippery guts spewing everywhere!' Add image. Blogs are more chatty, like you're talking to a friend. 'The less appealing side of cats is their habit of bringing dead animals into your house.' Add a nice cat pic. While the actual print media account is much more formal and written in a more detached—call it authoritative—voice. 'CAT BRINGS DEAD RAT INTO HOME.' Interview a vet. Upload a picture and video to the website of the vet blah-blahing on about cats. Although," Kee amended, "I wouldn't say 'blah-blahing on' as that would undermine the expert opinion." Her future boss sat blank-faced with his arms crossed, nodding his head. He'd hardly understood one word. She got the job.

Kerry Cue

After only 3 months, her @KeeHasSpoken Twitter feed had 3,000 followers, her *Inside Out New England* blog had 14,000 hits, and her *Ridgefield Rocks* Facebook page had an amazing 25,000 likes, which was the population of Ridgefield. She also tapped out hard copy at a rate that would exhaust journos of the old school of hard drinking. Of course, those journos were an endangered species now. They were either being given the gold watch and the royal boot out of the office, or they were long dead from flat-lining with liver failure. It wasn't Kee's prodigious output that impressed her boss, but the fact that she would sit at her computer, tie her shiny black hair into some top-knot arrangement and then proceed to Tweet, blog, post on Facebook and upload to the newspaper website all at the same time. Her recent feature on "Gun Packing Mamas" about mothers carrying handguns into children's daycare centers had been picked up by a number of mainstream newspapers. She was currently working on the open carry laws that allowed licensed gun owners to take guns into the ten Texas state-run psychiatric hospitals. Her piece appeared under the banner heading "One Who Flew Over the Cuckoo's Nest Found Shot Dead". Even though the focus of *The New England Gazette* was local news, Connecticut readers could not get enough of critical comment about the gun laws of those southern states. Connecticut represented a conundrum for gun manufacturers. Colt, Ruger, Mossberg, Stag and some other manufacturers had their headquarters in CT, due to a historical link reaching back to the Civil War; but post-Sandy Hook, Connecticut introduced some of the strictest gun control laws in the country, banning assault weapons, limiting the capacity of bullet magazines, and demanding strict gun owner permits.

Getting herself to her first crime scene had been three parts miracle and one part good luck. Earlier that morning, she had been sitting at her desk at *The New England Gazette* tweeting: OMG! OMG! They're putting parking meters in Catoonah St. Time to protest, peeps.@KeeHasSpoken.

Kee smiled as she put her cell phone with its blindingly brilliant fluoro-green visibility jacket down on her desk. The whole visibility concept worked. She didn't lose her cell phone. Ever.

Smiling came naturally to Kee. Her irrepressible exuberance beamed out of her like a child's drawing of the sun's rays. She smiled so often she was accused by more somber types, such as her life-is-all-shit-and-ass-wiping boss, Graeme Bradstreet, of being mentally disturbed, or on drugs. Or possibly both. But the last few months had given Kee many good reasons to beam.

Firstly and finally, she had managed to dump her first name, the name, Kee felt she had worn, or more accurately, dragged through her entire life like an antique metal-and-leather leg brace. Her parents, Kim and Vinh Le, were South Vietnamese bureaucrats who had fled a collapsing Saigon in the early seventies. After several attempts, they won US residency and settled in, of all places, a rundown Tribeca, New York—well before gentrification drove the price of a cup of coffee up to four dollars. There were, however, many skeletons dancing in the Le family closet. One was Le's maternal grandmother, Kim Cuc. She'd fallen pregnant to a French official when the French reclaimed the colony from the Japanese after World War II. These matters were *never* discussed. Kim Cuc married. She gave birth to a daughter, Kim, in 1948. And in 1985, that daughter gave birth to Kee in that beacon of democracy, the United States of America. So thankful were Kee's parents for their good fortune they gave their daughter the most English sounding name they knew: Agatha. She was named after the British crime writer Agatha Christie. Agatha Kitchi—pronounced Keet-chi—Le was teased mercilessly in middle school after one of her teachers told the class that their newest classmate shared a name with a prominent English mystery writer. The teacher effused at length that she adored one of the characters, a certain little old lady detective called Miss Marple. The class assumed that Kee was really meant to be called Miss Marple.

Kee felt she shouldn't really complain. It could have been worse. One of her mother's friends learned English by watching old American TV sitcoms. This friend adored *Petticoat Junction* and duly named her two daughters Billie Jo and Betty Jo. Billie Jo and Betty Jo had an older brother Robert, but everyone knew he was really Bobby Jo. "What if my mom had washed *My Mother the Car?*" Kee-but-actually-Agatha had slurred to three girlfriends during a post-exam drinkathon at a beer hall called Harry's Place in Soho. "It wash a shixtiesh shitcom." Kee-but-actually-Agatha was unable to continue, for her companions pig-snorted and hooted with laughter. They loudly debated whether Kee-but-actually-Agatha should be renamed Edsel from that moment on, and, more importantly, if all sitcoms should be rebranded shitcoms. The gaggle of giggling girls insisted that each of them should be named after a car, and gave each other the names Edsel, Pinto, Corvette, and Dodge. This conversation, however bizarre, set the seed in Kee-but-actually-Agatha's brain. Maybe she *could* change her name someday.

Kee had put up with the name-of-endless-torment for too many years, so when she started her new job—her real job—at *The New England Gazette,* she promptly dumped her first name, trashed all her social media sites along with her old identity, and started afresh under the shortened version of her name: Kitchi Le, or Kee for short. The timing seemed right, and her girlfriends agreed. The changeover was seamless, disturbing no one except her father, her brother, a few aunties, and those jerks from DeWitt Community High School, whom she never wanted to see again anyway. It didn't take long before she was shocked whenever a letter arrived addressed to Agatha. She no longer felt like an Agatha. She never really had.

The other reason for her beaming countenance was that she had actually scored a real job in her chosen profession of journalism. She, Kitchi Le, worked for *The New England Gazette,* with runs 5 days a week, Tuesday through Saturday. Kee looked at her phone again. She read her Twitter feed and retweeted the latest comment.

"@ZombieBoy87 says don't pay to park in Catoonah St. They use the money to buy more parking meters" @KeeHasSpoken.

She picked up another item, but this time it was on her private Twitter feed.

"Body of Ridgefield Man found in a quarry near Hawley. Suspicious circumstances" @PoliceBizz.

Kee retweeted the news and ran, clip-clopping into her boss's office in her overly high black heels. She was also wearing excessively tight black jeans under her loose-and-sloppy burnt orange woolen sweater, and a knotted black scarf with orange spots. She had a slight build and the height of a catwalk model, but she packed too many curves to be a professional coat hanger. Her impish good looks gave Kee an eye-catching yet indefinable beauty, and her personality was the feature that lit up any room. She was not aware of these blessings. An animator would surround her in a cartoon with rainbows, frolicking unicorns, and twittering birds, but she was no lame storybook

Sleeping Beauty. Kee had a determination honed from steel. She could, at any time, step into the role of a slightly maniacal, sword-wielding, head-lopping princess.

Growing up in a minority among minorities in New York had formed Kee's attack-first-and-look-sweet-and-innocent-after skill. "Yes! I had a Vietnamese heritage. Deal with it, douche bag!" had been her attitude long before she even knew what a douche bag might be. She first came up fighting against the stereotypical putdowns in kindergarten. A white-trash-in-training redheaded 4-year-old boy with beady eyes which were too close together to garner a cuteness rating had come shuffling up to her, bowing and chanting "Ching Chong Chang, Chinaman."

"Honestly," she mused years later to her college bud, Annalise, "what little kid thinks twice about another kid's color? Hell! They think Smurfs are blue and Bart Simpson is bright yellow. I reacted in the only logical fashion. I hit him over the head with the Tonka tractor I happened to be holding. Why not? They do arm you with these heavy-duty weapons in kindergarten. He screamed. I dropped the truck and just stood there looking angelically innocent. When the teacher asked me if I'd hit the boy with the tractor, I said, "He tripped and fell on it." At first I felt all squirmy inside for telling a lie. Má would have killed me for lying. So I felt all squirmy, then smirky in a shove-that-up-your-butt-you-no-neck-gnome sort of way! It felt so good." Kee learned from this encounter that a lie can be used as a weapon. She wasn't a good liar, but she could, when push came to Yikes!-I'm-gonna-get-the-shit-beaten-outta-me-here shove in grade school, aim a hollow-point lie at any beady-eyed kid with the precision of an assassin.

The philosophy that Kee adopted early in life, namely, that she was no better than nor worse than anyone else in the world, was, in fact, the same "equal in the eyes of God" code of belief written into the American Constitution. When her mother refused to pay for canteen lunches at high school and insisted Kee take Vietnamese food for lunch, she had to put up with the endless "Yuck! What are you eating? Dog?" teasing. Kee just rolled her eyes and retorted, "It's better than that fat-ass muck on your tray."

Kee had inherited, and learned, this feistiness from her mom. She could remember the time when two bent cops came into their family run business, Vinh's Saigon Bakery in Tribeca, trying to pick up some spare cash on the side. Kee's Ma worked the front of the shop and organized the books, while her father did all the baking. Kee helped out in the shop after school. Vinh's work day began at 4 am and ended when the baking and prep work was done. One day, after Vihn had gone home, Kee was helping her mother close up shop when two short, wise-guy cops wandered into the otherwise empty shop and started poking bread loaves with their police sticks and knocking them off the shelves. Kee didn't understand her mom's game plan at the time, but it was brilliant.

"Look what we have here," sneered Cop 1 to Cop 2, "food on the floor. This is definitely against health regulations."

Flick! Thud! Flick! Thud! More bread hit the floor.

"Those fines cost a lot of money," warned Cop 2.

Flick! Thud!

"Do you understand, lady? Big fines. Or you can just give us a bit of cash every now and then and your problems just go away," said Cop 1 to Kee's mother.

"You want money?" shouted Kee's mom in a heavy, put-on Vietnamese accent—the shouting was central to the performance.

"More money. No worry! I do this for you. I ring up your boss, Mr. Policeman 31256 and Mr. Policeman 34768. I ask more money. Okay? MORE MONEY! I write down. Mr. Policeman 3-1-2-5-6 and Mr. Policeman 3-4-7-6-8. MORE MONEY!"

The bent cops looked aghast. They backed off, saying, "Thanks, ma'am, but no thanks." "Crazy bitch!" one muttered as they left the shop. Kee's mom had smiled. Maybe even smirked. And Kee smiled at the memory. She really missed her mom. Mostly, however, Kee operated on light entertainment, funny-girl setting because it made people laugh, and laughter, along with heavy metal music, is an energizing soundtrack to accompany your life.

"Mr. Bossy!" she called out to her boss while looking at more Tweets on her phone.

"Don't call me that. It sounds like I'm the star of the Mr. Men books for children."

"Mmmmm," rejoined Kee, "would you prefer Mr. Grumpy?"

"Why are you here?" he grumbled, but Kee knew her boss appreciated her exuberance, especially in an office otherwise staffed by a cynical, borderline alcoholic grandma; a thick-as-a-plank sports jock; and a part-time, sleep-deprived mother of 3 under 3. That was it. *The New England Gazette's* budget only extended to four-and-a-half employees.

"Boss," she hissed, "they've found a Ridgefield man in a quarry near Hawley. Dead. Suspicious circumstances."

"Who?" he demanded.

"The name's not out yet. Can I go? It's just up the road."

"Hawley? Just up the road? I assume you're talking about Hawley, Pennsylvania. That's hours away," protested Bradstreet.

"No, no. I checked Google maps. It's a one hour-ish drive."

"One hour-ish? Are you on La-La pills again?" grumbled her incredulous boss.

"Well, one hour plus, say, another hour. But, Mr. Bossy, it's early. I can be there and back in no time. File copy on time just the same. And nothing ever happens here in Ridgefield. No one even runs a red light."

Ridgefield was, tragically for a wannabe-star-Watergate-style journalist, an idyllic New England town, all heritage buildings, old style redbrick shops, picturesque tree-lined streets, replica vintage street lamps, and stars-and-stripes a-flutterin' in the breeze. It was voted into the Top 50 tourist Villages of America. The highlight of the week for many residents in idyllic Ridgefield was wheeling out the mobile trashcans for their private garbage contractor. There was, however, a county ordinance on the books that forbids trashcans from being left out all day. Keeping up an idyllic village ambiance took effort.

"And," enthused Kee breathlessly, "this could be a real-life murder, Boss."

"No!"

"Think about it. I can Tweet live from the crime scene. And do an interview. Get a video for the website," Kee continued. "I've already finished the 'Ridgefield High Student Urinates on Wilton High's Football Field Prank'—sorry, 'Outrage'. Plus the Route 35 upgrade debacle. All tweeted and blogged with copy in your inbox for tomoz's paper."

"No."

"And I'll pay for my own gas."

Bradstreet threw his hands in the air.

"Go, go!" he huffed, adding, "Put me out of my misery. And if a Ridgefield man has been murdered, or simply died of a heart attack, don't you release any name via your Tweeter thing until you get the official okay from whoever."

"You're a legend, Mr. Bossy," Kee cooed, adding as she ran out of the office, "And don't worry! It's all under control."

"Hmmph!" snorted Bradstreet, as Kee grabbed her bag, phone, and laptop and headed towards her car, the mighty Silver Beast, her pet name for the monster silver convertible with the blue racing stripes. The car was as un-PC as clubbing baby fur seals for a living, yet she loved that gas-guzzling grunt-machine. This wasn't a car that you drove. You sat behind the steering wheel and wrangled it to your destination. Her bicycle riding and Prius-devout friends thought she'd gone all redneck now that she'd immigrated to the wilds of New England. Some even harangued her that by driving that car she would single-handedly raise the temperature of the earth by one degree, thus causing the melting of all the arctic ice. She rejoined that she would refrain from starting, say, a nuclear war in the near future as her contribution to saving the world. At that moment, as she fired up the ignition of the Silver Beast, she felt a surge of superhero power rippling through her veins as if she were Batman on a mission to save the world. Hell, she even owned a Batmobile.

The euphoria didn't last.

"Just up the road" turned out to be a nightmarish drive negotiating bridge works on Route 35 and manic crisscrossing commuter traffic on the 3-lane Interstate 84. Then there was the idiot driving a camper van with an "Adventure before Dementia" sticker on the back. He kept cutting in front of Kee on the 84 and then slowing down. She wanted to yell "Too late, buddy. The dementia's winning!" out her window each time she passed him in turn, but she figured he was probably deaf anyway. There was a lane closure on the Hudson Bridge, slowing traffic to my-grandma-can-cartwheel-faster-than-this stop-start speed; then she had to sit huffing as she drove at a limping-dog pace along the Owego Turnpike behind a logging truck. She arrived at the Boneridge Quarry outside Hawley, PA, at 1:30 p.m. The trip had taken Kee two-and-a-half grumbling, cussing, steering wheel thumping hours across three states.

"Darn you, Google Maps. Every minute counts here!" Kee shouted at her cell.

The picturesque red and yellow foliage set against the vivid green pasture en route across upstate New York could make a viewer's eyes water on this sun-blessed Fall day, but failed to register a single Oh-my-gosh-it's-amazing light bulb thought in Kee's brain. She was concentrating on the road ahead and the freeway exits. There was no time for mistakes. Kee was terrified she'd arrive too late at an empty crime scene and find nothing but ends of police tape flapping in the breeze.

"Freaking freak hell!" she cursed under her breath as she drove past the entrance to the quarry. Firstly, the quarry could not be seen from the road. It was hidden behind a screen of thick Fall foliage. Secondly, the quarry entrance was blocked by two police cars, with state troopers casually redirecting any interested parties away from the scene. Kee hadn't driven across three states to be stymied by a couple of Pulitzer-Prize-neutralizing, grey-shirted troopers in Smokey Bear hats. She pulled to the side of the road and checked the quarry layout online. It was huge. Maybe a mile long and half a mile across. She could see another entrance off a sidetrack. So Kee drove back past the entrance, dropped a left turn, bumped along a washed-out unmade road and pulled the Silver Beast to a jolting halt in the forest by the unused back gate.

Luckily, I'm not an idiot, Kee thought to herself when she contemplated the scale of the crime scene. She kept a spare pair of sneakers in the trunk. The quarry site was, according to Google Images, all grey dust, dirt roads and gravel mountains dotted with big dirty-yellow machines and grey rock-crushing equipment. This broad and flat southern part of the quarry was flanked to the north and north-west by blue-grey rock cliff faces waiting to be blasted into smithereens and reconvened as tomorrow's garden path. Kee pulled on her sneakers and looked at her phone again. She grinned and text-replied,

"I love you, @PoliceBizz. Buy you a drink sometime." @KeeHasSpoken.

@PoliceBizz had just tweeted her the exact GPS coordinates of the crime scene. She suspected @PoliceBizz was an unemployed, overweight 35-year-old porn addict living at home with his mom and dad, who spent his days listening to Police radio bands. It didn't matter. He—Yeah, it would be a he—was a star to her. He'd previously provided her with several hot-to-rock news tips.

With the GPS coordinates in her cell, Kee hit Get Directions. She was looking at a 12-minute hike. She crunched for five minutes over some dried leaves from the remnant forest edging the unused quarry road, looking intently at her cell phone screen, and tripped into a mountain of dusty grey gravel, which Google Maps obviously thought she could walk straight through with her superhuman powers. She felt as if she'd just stepped onto a mock moonscape maze. She spent another five minutes kicking up dust, walking the length of the dirt wall then cautiously poked her head around the corner. Bingo! She could see some yellow crime scene tape, maybe 300 yards away. She snapped a few photos. Police tape photos didn't make the best crime scene pictures, but Kee was worried that the cops might confiscate her phone and wanted to get all the shots she could before that happened. "I'm not stupid," she mumbled to herself. The crime scene tape ran around a monster yellow tractor, aka a John Deer 844, then wound about a digger thing, aka a Komatsu Excavator, and was tied at different ends to spades shoved into another grey dirt mountain behind the crime scene. Kee could see three police cars parked near the digger thing, and she could hear CSI officers coughing now and again. This was not surprising, as, periodically, dust eddies geniied out of an invisible lamp and danced across the crime scene to add nostril-itching discomfort to the background quarry stink that made Kee suspect she'd just stepped into an oversized outdoor boys' urinal.

Kee snuck up behind the monster tractor, crouching as she moved for no logical reason other than the watching of too many TV crime shows, and arrived at her first crime scene sweaty, dusty and hyperventilating with excitement. As she peered around the yellow monster, blood pumped so fast in her veins she heard swooshing in her ears, but not for long. Kee quickly clicked into professional mode. She took a few more snapshots, pocketing her cell as she moved around the tractor, and approached the crime scene tape. She tried to make some visual notes of the scene. Rocks. Dirt. Digger thingies. Then she noticed the body. There was something familiar about the body, but she couldn't quite pin it down at first. She quickly moved on to more general observations. *Right. Body. Cops and some technicians in crime scene suits. There are six stiffs plus the real stiff,* thought Kee. She clicked a few more photos on the sly from elbow level as an officer approached her. The haunting, unnerving imagery of the crime scene wasn't the corpse, but the fact that the police officers were all sprinkled with light grey dust, echoing images of New Yorkers fleeing the collapsing Twin Towers during 9/11.

"This is a crime scene, Miss. You shouldn't be here!" snapped the state trooper as he grabbed her by the elbow and swung her away from the scene.

"I'm with the media, Officer Oroza," she said, taking advantage of his name tag and taking out her press pass.

"I don't care if you are with the New York Philharmonic Orchestra. This crime scene is off limits."

Then she uttered the words that would lead step by painful step to the very edge of her undoing.

"I know him," she lied. "He's from Ridgefield."

She really hoped she knew him. She couldn't see much from her current position, but there *was* something about the corpse she recognized. What was it? What Kee didn't know and couldn't know was that the victim had no ID on him other than a Tazza Cafe napkin from Ridgefield. The victim had no wallet, no license and no vehicle parked in the vicinity. The CSI officers were contemplating ID-ing him from his tattoos when Kee appeared from nowhere like the Celestial Clerk of Death verifying the paperwork. The officer let go of her elbow and returned to talk to an overweight black guy wearing gold-rimmed glasses, kitted out in a flash, light grey suit—an excellent choice for the day—with a baby blue shirt and a snappy pink paisley tie. With his cropped grey hair and trimmed grey mustache you wouldn't call him a fashion plate, but he was presentable for an old guy. Early sixties, Kee thought. After she'd waited half a lifetime, which may have been closer to five minutes in real time, the presentable old guy turned and looked in her direction, then came over to introduce himself.

Chapter 2

Kee

A Familiar (but Dead) Face

"Hello. My name is Quincey Washington Booker. I'm from the New York office of the FBI," he said.

"Wow!" gasped Kee, "that's awesome. The feds are here. WOW!"

"What's your name?" he asked.

This was the moment she'd been waiting for ever since she started her journalism studies all of 12 long years ago.

"My name is Kitchi Le," she announced, holding out her hand. "I'm with *The New England Gazette*."

Booker replied, "Glad to meet you, Miss Le," while heartily shaking her hand. *He's got quite a grip*, she thought.

"I understand that you know the victim."

"I better have a closer look," Kee suggested, "but I'm pretty sure that is Hayden Brodski."

A significant detail hovering in the shadowlands of her mind had suddenly leaped into the light of her conscious thoughts. She'd seen a rag sticking out of the trouser pocket on the corpse. It was a Barbie sweat towel. That rag allowed her to nail the ID of the body. Only two days ago she'd joked with Brodski, saying, "I can't wait to see you in your matching pink sneakers and yoga pants." Her mind flashed up an image of Brodski holding the gas pump nozzle, giving her his trademark bent, broken-toothed grin.

"He works at a gas station just on the edge of town. He's had a few bolters of late. Customers who, you know, fill up with gas and don't pay. I go there. Fill up with gas myself and get a story out of him."

"Come and have a closer look. But you must not ... hear me ... you *must not* write or Tweet or whatever it is you do about the way the corpse has been staged," Booker insisted.

"I won't. I swear," said Kee, spitting on her hand and placing it over her heart. Booker lifted an eyebrow, then lifted the yellow police tape so Kee could step into the crime scene. She followed Booker to the corpse. This was a hauntingly weird scene.

Firstly, the victim lay on his back with some sort of rifle jammed barrel first into a seeping, gaping wound in his chest. And secondly, there were no pools of blood. The loose dirt acted like a blood sponge keeping the murder scene dry and neat.

"What type of gun is that?" asked Kee matter-of-factly. She was curious.

"It's an AK-47, Miss," replied Officer Oroza, who had decided she was now on their side.

"Was he shot with that gun?" Kee asked. The all-male crime scene crew responded with synchronized laughter.

"Was that a stupid question?" protested Kee.

"All options will be considered," replied Booker, "but this execution is, well, meant to send a message." And unlike the run of the mill gangland murder, the message in this case was clearly spelled out. Attached to the rifle butt and gently flapping in the faint breeze was a piece of paper. The half sheet, Kee noted, had a flag-like quality. This was obviously intended.

One side of the note sported an American flag. The other side was more confrontational. It displayed the words BAN THIS WEAPON.

"Do you recognize the victim?" asked Booker.

"Yes! That's Hayden Brodski for sure. He lives in a trailer behind a gas station out of town. I can text you the details if you like. But you have to tell me one thing. Why are the feds involved?"

"Mmmm!" rumbled Booker. "I'll answer that question, Miss Le. And that's it. My responsibilities within the bureau involve organized crime, including gangland executions. There are fairly obvious signs, as you can see, that this is an execution-style murder."

"Whoa! Ridgefield has become newsworthy at last!" Kee chortled.

"Not so fast, young lady," warned Booker. "For now you can only report that a male Caucasian from Ridgefield area has been found dead in the Boneridge Quarry near Hawley."

"Gangland execution!" enthused Kee, adding, "I'd better get your number to text you the victim's address. Oh! And I'll need to check with you to find out when I can publish the victim's name, too."

Reluctantly, Booker took a card out of his pocket and handed it to Kee. *Mmm*, she thought, taking the card, *he wears aftershave cologne. Nice.*

Within 10 seconds she'd texted him the victim's address and her contact details, pronouncing "Mr. Booker, you've just got yourself a stalker."

Chapter 3

Kee@KeeHasSpoken

Once she'd ID-ed the victim Kee left the crime scene, calling out as she ducked under the police tape, "Thank you, Mr. Booker. I'll get back to you pronto if I find any useful information about the victim." As soon as she was behind the first dirt mountain and out of sight she tweeted five news headlines.

"Body found in a quarry near Hawley is confirmed as Ridgefield resident. Kitchi Le reporting from the scene." #ridgefieldmurder @KeeHasSpoken.

"Ridgefield man murdered. Body found in Boneridge Quarry. Name not released yet. Sadly many will know the victim. Kitchi Le, *New England Gazette*." #ridgefieldmurder @KeeHasSpoken.

"Police confirm that body found in Boneridge Quarry Hawley PA was killed in an execution-style murder. Kitchi Le reporting from the scene." #ridgefieldmurder @KeeHasSpoken.

She was temporarily interrupted by a foghorn blast announcing a new text message.

"HEY BB GIT YR LAZY ASS DOWN HERE. JO"

Kee laughed. Joe Lyman was the public relations officer at the mayor's office. He wasn't exactly THE PR officer, as he only worked 2 days a week. And he didn't really work in the mayor's office. Ridgefield didn't have a mayor. This historical village, where you could almost hear the painfully slow creaking sound of the cogs of local government at work, was governed by the First Selectman. It sounded as if he was the first pick for a Little League Baseball team. Kee could not get this Selectman tag into her head. She called Ridgefield's chief honcho Your Honor the Mayor, and got away with it. Lyman's texts were always written in capital letters as if he was shouting. She shouted back. They bonded via TEXT MSSG joke banter. BB stood for Bimbo Brains. Lyman was an Iraq vet who'd returned with one less limb than he'd had when he first deployed. He sported an artificial leg below his left knee. She called him Ironman.

DEAR IRONMAN SOME OF US HAVE REAL WORK TO DO. WATCH MY TWITTER FEED. REAL BODIES. IN REAL TIME. KEE

Kee pressed the send button on her cell phone, then returned to her Twitter feed.

"Murder may be gang related. Watch for updates on *The New England Gazette* Website. Kitchi Le" #ridgefieldmurder @KeeHasSpoken.

"Police will not release details of the execution-style murder of Ridgefield Resident. Kitchi Le reporting for *The New England Gazette*." #ridgefieldmurder@KeeHasSpoken.

By the 5th Tweet, Kee noted the number of followers of @KeeHasSpoken had jumped to 19,263. She also updated her boss via text naming the murder victim and noting that the feds were on the case.

She'd hit, Kee felt, the right tone on her Twitter feed stream. No OMGs or WTF?s *This one had to be low key,* Kee thought, rolling her eyes at her own name-based pun. She returned to her car, tethered her laptop to her cell and uploaded some discrete crime scene photos to her *Inside Out New England* blog and one serious-reporter style at-the-scene selfie to Facebook, commenting, "This is a murder scene. One Ridgefield resident is dead in an execution-style killing. Details to follow as soon as they are available."

She did a quick Google search on Hayden Brodski, checking for unusual associations, links, anything. She typed in a few keywords related to the case. AK-47. Execution. Gangland. Murder. Then she tweeted @PoliceBizz.

"Hey, Buddy we have some real police bizz. Check out Quincey Booker FBI. And give me a heads up on any cop talk re: the murder." @KeeHasSpoken

"Yeah. Right." @PoliceBizz

Kee turned the key in the ignition of her Pontiac Firebird. It coughed and spluttered. "Come on, you big bruiser. Get me home pronto. There's some Pulitzer Prize reporting to be done."

She did a 6 point u-turn in the narrow side road and then drove, or wrangled, her beloved Silver Beast along the Owega Turnpike, urging her gas-guzzler to "Take me home, my loyal steed!" She turned onto the I-84, slammed her foot on the accelerator to kick her speed up to 65 mph—a challenge to her limited abilities—while glancing every few seconds at her cell on the front seat. The traffic didn't bother Kee on the return trip. She was watching her Twitter feed and cruising. When @PoliceBizz tweeted an update she nearly ran off the road.

"You won't believe this. There's been another one." @PoliceBizz

Kee slewed the Silver Beast back into her lane as her brain raced, no, quantum leaped, at hyperdrive speed in three different directions at once. "This is big! Bigger than big. So huge it's freaking me out!" she shouted at the road ahead, slapping the steering wheel with excitement.

Later, just past the Middletown turnoff, Kee saw Booker's name pop up on her cell. She nearly ran off the road a second time. "Note to self: Stop the freaky freaking out," she instructed herself as she pulled the Silver Beast into an emergency lane stop on the I-84.

"Tell me more about this Brodski character," Booker asked without preamble.

"There's not much to tell," answered Kee. "I've checked out his Facebook page, Date-a-Dude online, Tinder, and any clubs/organizations he might belong to in Ridgefield. The only thing that leaps out is his love of guns. He's got the classic Gangsta shot on Facebook. You know, crossed arms holding two handguns. Tattoos everywhere."

"Mmmmm," replied Booker, thinking.

Kee leaped with all guns blazing into the gap in the conversation.

"Mr. Booker," she pressed, "I know another body has found. And I hear the body was, ah, staged. Your description. Just like the other one. Any comment?"

"Now you listen to me, young lady. I don't know how you got that information, but it is confidential. You jeopardize this entire investigation if you release that information to the public before we have a chance to properly access the situation."

Whoa! He sounds really angry that I have up-to-the-minute intel on his case, thought Kee. *But it isn't just me, it's, like, me and half the online world.*

"Mr. Booker. All due respect and that. But this is not an era when the FBI can block information from getting out there. It is out there already on the web. Google AK-47 execution. You'll find it in gun-nutter chat rooms," Kee explained as if she were talking to a little child.

"I will not confirm or deny any facts, Miss Le. But I ask you *not* to publish either victim's identity at this stage. This is a courtesy to their relatives. And if you come up with any information relevant to this case, I'd appreciate you passing it on to me *before* you go online or into print. You may get the facts wrong. Are you listening?"

"The thing is, Mr. FBI"—she was getting her customary exuberance back—"Online you may be wrong, but not for long. That's how Twitter works. Out there somewhere someone knows something, and they let you know quick smart. Or hundreds of them let you know!" Kee continued triumphantly. But she still wasn't sure how to play her hand. Go for the big story or sit on it?

"Thank you, Miss Le, I'll try to remember that." Booker pressed the red end-call button on his cell.

"Oh," Kee observed, "so there are no Bye-Byes or Catch-you-laters with the FBI. Fair enough."

Kee didn't waste any time. First she called her boss.

"Mr. Bossy, we have a big, big story." She summarized the details.

"What the beJesus?" exclaimed her boss, when she got to the "And there is a second corpse, and the chat room gun-nutters are talking about AK-47 executions. American manufactured. 2014. Must be important. They're all going on and on about it. How much do I tell?" She was watching the chat room talk scroll on her laptop screen as she spoke. "Oh, shit! My cell battery is low. Give me an answer. Quick!"

Kee suddenly realized her relationship with her boss had moved up a professional notch to the okay-to-swear-in-front-of-you level of intimacy. Great.

"Okay. 2 rules. We've got news. But we want to sell newspapers. Put out your Tweet things. But promise details in tomorrow's *Gazette*. Then get your ass back to the office. It's 3 p.m. We've got some real reporting to do."

Kee tweeted.

"Another body found in gangland killings. Exclusive report. *New England Gazette*." #ganglandexecutions @KeeHasSpoken

"Same bizarre MO used in gangland executions. Details in tomorrow's *New England Gazette*." #ganglandexecutions @KeeHasSpoken

"FBI fear more killings possible. Kitchi Le for *The New England Gazette*." #ganglandexecutions @KeeHasSpoken

Kee struggled with the last Tweet. Was she being too tabloid, whipping up a "serial murders" scenario? And should she say "police fear" or "FBI fear"? There was no rule book. She had to wing it. In the end Kee went with the higher authority, even though it might piss Booker. She had battery power enough for two more Tweets. Loudly remonstrating, "Note to self: You idiot. Get a cell recharger for your car!" she tweeted:

"Dramatic turn in events involving gangland execution of Ridgefield resident. Full details in tomorrow's *New England Gazette*."#ridgefieldmurder#ganglandexecutions @KeeHasSpoken

Then she tapped out a private Tweet to @PoliceBizz:

"You are my hero. You were so totally on the money. FBI confirms. Do you know location of 2nd stiff?" @KeeHasSpoken

Target 91

Chapter 4

Kee

Shock! Horror! No Wifi!

Kee sat in the Silver Beast at the side of the road for 10 whole seconds, blankly staring out the windscreen. She shook her head slowly in disbelief. "This story is really, really big time freaky," she muttered, "especially for someone who for the last three months has been covering animal rescues, library news, and the mayor's yawn-inducing edicts."

She gave herself a quick get-on-with-it-girl lecture, turned the key in the ignition, shifted into gear, planted her foot on the accelerator and gunned the Silver Beast toward Ridgefield. Her mind, she felt, was racing at Warp Speed 8. With her phone out of action and a long drive ahead, Kee had time to think.

She was occasionally irritated by the speeding SUVs, pickup trucks and 24-wheelers rumbling past the Silver Beast on the 3-laned I-84.

"It's not a race, you morons!" she yelled into the traffic thrum.

Mostly, however, she was oblivious to the thundering river of traffic. Her mind was elsewhere. *There is some sort of deeply weird something going down*, she thought, *but what? AK-47s. Bodies. Notes. Gangsta photos. Freaking Jesus!* Brodski's Facebook gangsta portrait haunted her every thought. She might start musing about what to have for dinner, and the next instant there was Brodski: skinny, tattooed, but as far as she knew harmless Brodski posing like some biker gang enforcer. This cocky self-portrait of Gangsta Brodski morphed into an image of Dead Brodski, Brodski skewered and staked to the ground like a wild boar, not with a feathered spear, but with an AK-47.

"Freaking hell! I've got it!" she exclaimed. "It's about guns. The link is guns, I bet! Absolutely, I bet that some crazy anti-gun group has decided to pop off some gun nutters. That would mean we've got one lot of crazies killing another lot of crazies. I've gotta get my head around this."

She automatically reached for her phone. "Freaking freak hell, it's dead!" she fumed. "Next town. I'll hook up my laptop. Next town. NEXT TOWN. Hurry the freak up, next town. Where have all the towns gone? Isn't small town America meant to be the heart and soul of the Nation?" Kee turned off the I-84 towards Danbury. She drove down an endless Avenue of Honor paying tribute to soulless drive-in commerce. There was, she noted, a Super Shop 'n Stop (how can you shop without stopping?), a Fort Delta Self Storage, a Lawn Mowing Supply Center, a Honda Dealership, an outdoor furniture emporium, a gas station, a Fitness Center (how can we be the Land of Fat 'n Flab with so many fitness centers?) and a pizzeria.

Kee turned off Mill Plain Rd into a strip mall of half-a-dozen small outlets with parking space out front and a diner at one end named The Diner. *Some folk have no imagination*, she thought.

She parked the Silver Beast out front and hot-footed her way into the eponymous diner, a sixties retro refit. The Diner decor showcased black and white chessboard floor tiles, red vinyl booth seating and round red chrome and vinyl counter stools. The whole retro-viby thing definitely wasn't working; there were only two other customers. A scrawny old timer sat on a stool at the main counter, regaling the unimpressed waitress about his "ostrige-arthritis" and bunions. There was one other customer, a young mother, who sat in a toy-strewn booth grappling with a fractious toddler. The mid-forties waitress wore a red retro-diner uniform dress with a white collar. She sported a luxurious ponytail of Afro-American braids and long, fake tangerine nails. She also bristled with underutilized vitality and attitude. Those devoted to James Bond movies might imagine how, activated by a single phone call, she could leap on the counter and take out the old timer's throat with one swipe of those tangerine talons. Kee looked around for the coffee machine; one handle, two handles? No luck. This was a retro-diner. There was a single filter coffee pot and warmer. A non-retro flat TV screen mounted on the far wall hosted smile-afflicted presenters jabbering a constant stream of advice about weight loss instruments of torture. But it was the chalkboard sign hanging above a dish-cluttered stainless steel sink behind the front counter that caught Kee's eye:

NO WIFI. TALK TO ONE ANOTHER. CALL YOUR MOM. PRETEND IT'S 1973. LIVE.

"Freaking freak-town," Kee muttered under her breath, wondering if you can insult a town that is not a town. She claimed a booth and plugged in her phone, mumbling "OMG! They got that newfangled E-lec-tricity connected right up here."

Kee strolled over to the counter with the white laminate top and ordered a soy latte. The waitress ambled over to Kee, tilted her head sideways and gave her a bemused look.

"Honey, we got coffee, or we got coffee."

"Right. I'll have coffee then," enthused Kee with a dumb-and-dumber grin, "and a low-fat, gluten-free donut."

"Honey," replied the waitress, who despite her blank expression was in on the joke, "we got donuts or donuts. Deep fat fried. Sugar loaded donuts what come with heartburn guaranteed."

Kee laughed. "If you put it like that, I'll just hafta have one of them gourmet donuts."

Kee carried her "gourmet" chocolate glazed donut and mug of coffee back to the booth. She sniffed at the donut. It came straight out of grease central, possibly a hundred years ago. She looked at her phone. There was barely a flicker of charge on it. Kee bit into the donut and chewed it with some difficulty. To a kale-and-quinoa-chomping-vegetarian, it tasted like chocolate-flavored Play-Doh. Swallowing hard, she concluded that a past-its-prime "gourmet" donut needed a bucket of lukewarm coffee to wash it down.

"Can I leave my cell charging for a minute while I see if I can catch some WIFI outside?" Kee called out across the diner.

"Sure, honey," replied the waitress.

Kee stood outside the diner checking for free wifi on her laptop. She wandered around the car park moving her laptop up, down, sideways. Nope. She positioned herself on the verge of the non-sidewalk holding her laptop in the air. Zilch. She walked to the edge of Mill Plain Rd. Bingo! She picked up some free Wifi from a nearby Starbucks.

"STARBUCKS!" she groaned. "How could I have missed a Starbucks?" Kee shook her head. The Starbucks was located right next to the strip mall, but set back from the road and hidden behind some of those damn-blasted annoying New England trees. Kee laughed. "How could they let trees block a beautiful view of a picturesque Starbucks? It's criminal." A born and bred city girl, the clean country air smelt like room refresher spray to her. "They must need a very big spray can out here," she joked to herself.

"Starbucks. Bless," she muttered, using one-hand to tap out a quick Tweet to @PoliceBizz.

"Any location yet on that last execution?" @KeeHasSpoken

No reply.

"Come on, PoliceBizz. Pick up your phone, pleeeeease." @KeeHasSpoken

"Gotchya" @PoliceBizz

"Location on last CS looks to be a car park in the Seminoe State Park, Wyoming." @PoliceBizz

"Name?" @KeeHasSpoken

A horn blasted. A thick-set bruiser with a shaved head and a Z Z Top beard yelled, "Fucking bitch!" out the driver's side window as he swerved his truck around Kee, who had inadvertently stepped onto the road. She glared at the rapidly receding 1997 Dodge Dakota, which sported a back window sticker with a pistol silhouette and the slogan "If you can read this you're in range."

"And won't you be surprised when they come for you, you halfwit!" she yelled back. She continued to type and read as she retraced her steps back to The Diner.

"Got some buzz on ham radio. Talk of execution-style gun death. Wyoming. Name Desmond Colt keeps coming up." @PoliceBizz

"I'm thinking. Have you heard of any anti-gun groups?" @KeeHasSpoken

"You mean anti-gun folk who shoot gun lovers?" @PoliceBizz

"Not sure about that one. Got any intel on your Ridgefield victim?" @PoliceBizz

"I'll get back to you on that when I'm back in the office. Keep me up to date." @KeeHasSpoken

Kee grabbed up her phone and called out to the waitress, "Thanks for the gourmet donut."

The waitress replied, deadpan, "May the heartburn be with you." Kee leaped into her car, fired up the Silver Beast, picked up the I-84 again and took the turnoff to Ridgefield. She muttered to herself, "Gotta think. How do you write about anti-gun crazies shooting gun nutters without sounding crazy yourself?"

Kee's cell rested on the front seat as usual as she cruised down Route 35. "My only friend," she joked to herself, "and my cat, Harold. I'm his friend when he hears the rustle of the cat food bag." She was just 6 miles down the road when her cell lit up. "Ignore it. I'm nearly there," she told herself. As if! She had to peek. For a third time, she nearly ran off the road. Folks say that when you are not paying attention to the road, you will always steer in the direction you are looking. She was looking at a high impact relationship with a Northern Red Oak. She wrangled the Silver Beast to an abrupt stop on the side of the road. The Tweet read:

"There's been another shooting." @PoliceBizz

"Where?" @KeeHasSpoken

"Looks like S Carolina." @PoliceBizz

"Name? Location? Anything? @KeeHasSpoken

"There's a lot of talk online and on ham radio. Name Carl Koober Jr. 28. Car park. Cesar's Head State Park." @PoliceBizz

"Don't forget to get the intel for me on your Ridgefield guy." @PoliceBizz

"All good." @KeeHasSpoken

"There's a link somewhere!" Kee yelled at the steering wheel. "Arrrrrgh!" She held her hand down on the horn. It didn't blast. It squeaked. "Poor baby, you don't have much of a roar, do you?" she laughed. The rubbishy horn was the reason why Kee'd bought the Silver Beast in the first place. It had been for sale at a ridiculously low price. Apparently no one wants to buy a grunt machine with a horn that sounds like a hysterical squirrel. No one except Kee. And she was very happy with her squeak-mobile. Out of sheer frustration, Kee thumbed the three victims' names into Google, expecting a hotchpotch of intel. But one acronym kept leaping out from the search results. Over and over. NGSA. National Gun and Shooters Association. "OMG! OMG! The victims are all members of the NGSA!" she yelled, "I'm going live with this. Have to. In three minutes this news will explode across the blogosphere."

Draining the last bit of juice in her cell she tweeted:

"Gangland execution news. Now three victims. Seems anti-gun activists, the AGB Anti-Gun Brigade, is shooting NGSA members. See *New England Gazette*" #ganglandexecutions #AntiGunBrigade @KeeHasSpoken

Chapter 5

Kee

Victim or Villain?

Kee cruised the Silver Beast down Ridgefield's village-quaint Main Street as a scattering of locals and tourists strolled along the tree-lined sidewalk. There were young mothers in puffy coats, pushing babies in strollers while clinging desperately to their take-out coffees; seniors in tracksuits and white sneakers walking with an age-denying purpose; and real estate agents in bland and predictable you-can-trust-us realtor suits returning from house inspections. Main Street was the epicenter of tranquility. Photographs of this Main Street vista could be used as calming computer desktop images for years to come. It was 4:30 p.m. on Friday, the 15th of September.

She parked the Silver Beast on a nearby vacant lot—finding a space was a life-and-death battle with tourists during peak season—grabbed her cell, laptop, and one squashed coffee cup and sprinted toward the office. The *New England Gazette* was housed in a featureless white block-shaped shop just along from Purple Frog Gifts and Hutton's Fine Men's Wear. "Fine Men's

Wear," mused Kee every time she passed the shop. "Yes. I'm looking for a fine man ... maybe I should stake out the joint." The office was marked by one distinguishing feature, the gold lettering on the glass door announcing *New England Gazette est. 1867.*

Walking in the door, Kee tweeted @PoliceBizz.

"Update. Just been searching thru women's chat rooms. Talk is Brodski may be asshole/creep." @KeeHasSpoken.

There was no time to check for a reply, for the office erupted into excited chatter as soon as she entered the door.

"Way to go, girl! Real grab 'em by the balls news," Hollis called out across the office from her cluttered, file-littered desk. "There may be some life left yet in this here old rag. Love this stuff. The boss has taken me off funeral notices—Yay!—and put me on research. You've gotta look at this."

"Well-upholstered" Hollis—a description she'd devised and owned with confidence—was a 66-year-old grandmother who, adopting a style sense inspired by her African sisters, wore a combination of charity shop clothes that were so loud and colorful it could blind innocent bystanders. Today she sported yellow polyester slacks, a floral top *cum* massacre of purple and pink flowers, and an electric-lime-green jacket with gold buttons. Hollis held back on parting with her hard-earned cash for clothes. She had a mortgage, a daughter-with-young-children who couldn't quite make ends meet, and an up market taste in liquor to support.

Kee skipped lightly around the wood-paneled front counter. The *New England Gazette* needed a front counter to serve those customers who brought in hard copy personal notices. Obituaries were often handwritten in—according to the texting generations—an ancient script with loopy gees and deformed effs. Only someone over 40 could read those missives.

Before Kee arrived at Hollis's desk, she was accosted by Chivonn LaRoux, 34, mother of 3 under 3. Chivonn worked on real estate copy three days a week through a hormonal, sleep deprived fog. Sometimes her brain was set on a 7-second delay like live radio broadcasts. Others in the office would make a comment. Wait 7 seconds. Then Chivonn would answer "Right! Got it!" But today—the boss had called her in on her day off and her mother was on child wrangling duty—and right now all her neurons were firing. "Kee! Kee, this is amazing! Look. Wait. Come here, quick!" exclaimed Chivonn.

Kee didn't get a chance to see what Chivonn wanted to show her before Bradstreet stepped out of his office and yelled, "Get your ass in here, Le." She jumped at the brusqueness of her boss's command and scurried into his office.

"This is what's happening. Time is the killer. Deadlines must be met. I want all copy put to bed at 6 p.m. for tomorrow's edition. I'm doing a special print run. 20,000 copies. God, thank you for killing a Ridgefield local. Now *that* is news." He raised his eyes heavenward. "We might make a profit this week."

Kee stood wide-eyed, watching Bradstreet in his newsroom Commander-in-Chief mode. *This real newsroom viby-thing,* she thought, is *freaking fantastic. Let me see. Friday. I would normally be writing up the latest edict from the Town Hall. Not today. The mayor's State-of-the-Trash-Cans speech can go take a leap into oblivion.*

"I've sent Shidfa out to interview Brodski's buddies," continued Bradstreet. Shidfa was actually Aron Whittle, 22, a boy born to drink beer, eat pizza and watch football on tv, known in the office as Shit-for-Brains, or simply Shidfa. "He can do sport-speak. That should help. I've got Chivonn doing a ring-around profiling Brodski. Hollis is researching past murders using AK-47s and mass shootings with assault rifles." He shook his head in disgust. "You'd think we'd learn. How many lunatics running around with assault rifles do we need before we do something?" He sighed in despair. "I'll do the 2nd Amendment and Connecticut gun laws. You do crime scene, local news—LOCAL RESIDENT GUNNED DOWN—and national news—LOCALS DEATH LINKED TO HIT SQUAD MURDERS."

He glanced over his half-moon glasses and looked directly into Kee's eyes, capturing her full attention with his forceful glare. "And I'll do an editorial. So you are this minute in an editorial conference. We have to make a call. Is Brodski a victim, a villain, or a hero?"

"A hero?" said Kee, taken aback. "How could Brodski be a hero?"

"Say, ah! say he was in a state park with his AK-47 to prevent armed maniacs from slaughtering little, big-eyed Bambis and fluffy state park critters. The maniacs get to him first. BAM! He's toast. They dump his body in the quarry as a warning to others. Hero."

"Maybe, I guess, but I don't think so," Kee said hesitantly.

"That's what we have to decide now. Victim or villain? We can't afford to look like a don't-know-shit-from-silver-dollars quaint village daily tomorrow morning if the latest updates swing the story in the opposite direction."

"Hmmm," Kee pondered, remembering the chat rooms. "He's a victim, but a sleazy one. That's my take on it," she said cautiously.

"I'm with you on that. So we go with TRAGIC DEATH OF TROUBLED LOCAL. That covers us every which way. Now one more thing. I hate to admit this, and you will not hear these words again, but you are right. The feds cannot suppress names anymore. Hollis checked. The rumor about Brodski's death is all over the web. But *we* know the truth. So the first thing you do before you even sit your ass down is get that news out there. Make it official. Put a hold-no-punches piece on our website. Do your Tweet thing and bloggy chitchat. Now get to it. The broadsheets and TV crews will be all over this in no time flat. But *we* get to break the story."

"Right, Mr. Bossy. Consider it done already."

Kee knew the website post had to be quick and dirty to beat the opposition.

She started with TRAGIC DEATH OF TROUBLED LOCAL, naming Brodski and cutting and pasting copy into Twitter.

"Freaking Hell," she muttered to herself, "I need to update PoliceBizz." She tweeted "Brodski creep asshole angle confirmed." Suddenly, she realized she should ring Booker. Her journalism lecturers had told the class, "Your relationship with officials is always a you-scratch-my-back-and-I'll-scratch-yours setup," which made Kee think all officials were orangutans living on free-range fleas. Which reminded her. "OMG. Harold!" she gasped. She hadn't fed Harold. "What time is it? He can last until 6:30 p.m. I'll have my feature story written by then."

She scribbled a reminder on a yellow Post-It note and stuck it on her laptop keyboard: BOOKER, FEATURE, HAROLD.

At 6:30 p.m., precisely, she yelled into Bradstreet's office. "Mr. Bossy, I have to go and feed my cat. I'll be 20 mins. Tops."

Nighttime was inching its way into Ridgefield, leaving ominous shadows across the ordinary streetscapes. *It's this freaking weird day,* thought Kee, *it makes everything look creepy.* Despite the "olde worlde" ambiance of a town that hosts a Nutmeg Festival, Ridgefield had its seedy underbelly. You can buy into the American Dream in Ridgefield with a S2 mil 5-bedroom classic Victorian clapboard farmhouse with wrap around porch, antique reclaimed floors, wainscoting, high end appliances and superbly landscaped acreage. But the dream costs and can quickly turn sour. There are foreclosures here, too. Ridgefield hosts both financial meltdowns and drug-addled breakdowns. These, however, are discretely handled. There are drug, alcohol, and gambling addiction recovery centers here, and one "olde worlde" brothel. The sex workers—their preferred term—aren't olde worlde. The brothel is housed in an out of town heritage farmhouse with a wrap-around porch. You have to wonder if the old rocking chair on that particular porch ever gets a thorough work out.

Kee jumped into the Silver Beast, but before she fired it up she checked out the back seat. You never know. A knife-wielding assassin ninja might be hiding there. Nup. Nothing there except three weeks of take-out food boxes and umpteen old copies of the *Gazette*. Even too-busy-to-chuck-out-car-trash Kee had to admit the Silver Beast had acquired the *odeur de* pong of a V8 trashcan. She drove to her box-like apartment over Pampered Pooch Snip 'n Clip on the far end of town. It only took 8 minutes. She parked out front of the old past-its-prime redbrick heritage building with the dilapidated blue and white awning. She groaned. The only appealing feature of the apartment was its price. It was, as the ad had said, "Priced for birds. Cheap. Cheap. Cheap." You had to be barking mad to live over a shop of barking mad dogs. But all the coiffed Labradoodles and dolled-up toy poodles were home by 5 p.m. It was only Harold who had to put up with the 9 to 5 whimpering. He seemed not to mind. He may have enjoyed it. Harold was a big cat, a Maine Coon. He was a longhaired miniature grey lion with a majestic silver-grey mane. He was a dog-cat who liked to hang around his people all the time. If Kee went for a walk from home, she'd often turn to find Harold following her. He was also a curious cat. If she was in the bathroom drying her hair, he'd come and watch the performance, trying to work out why someone might want to blow hot wind all over their head. He had the freedom to slip in and out his cat door and was sometimes seen looking in the front window of the Pampered Pooch at all those caged canines. Kee swore she saw him smile once.

Kee pushed, lifted and fought with the old wooden gate with the coat of faded and peeling green paint at the side of the property. This daily wrestling match really wasn't something you wanted to do in the cold and the dark, or in the slushy melting snow, or anytime. She climbed the wobbly—possibly illegally so—open wooden staircase at the back of the building, calling, "Harold, baby, you there? Where's my baby? I haven't forgotten you."

As soon as she opened the door Harold turned up, wrapping his body around her legs with great affection, or possibly hunger.

"Alright, my little darling. Dinner's coming."

Kee ran her hand up the inside doorframe looking for the light switch, peering into the gloom of her apartment looking down the walk-through that separated the open kitchenette on her left and the small bathroom on her right. She switched on the light. Kee was stunned. Her one-room apartment looked as if vandals had trashed it. There were clothes, coats, shoes, books, dirty plates and empty food packets littered all over the floor, the coffee table, the single charity-shop couch, the kitchen table and the kitchen sink.

This was, of course, the usual state of things in her apartment, but it was as if she were seeing it for the first time. She also noticed a reek of stale orange peels, old thread-bare furniture, and damp cat. She looked around her little abode in amazement. "My freaking weird day has changed the way I see the world," she said aloud. "But the annual Cleaning Up Day will have to wait. I only have time to feed Harold and bolt." She opened the fridge. It contained three cartons of off-milk, a drooping bunch of celery, some mixed berry yogurt, and an open can of cat food.

"What gourmet treat have we for you tonight, Mr. Harold? Why, it's real beef and liver! Yum!" That was a generous concession from someone who was a moral vegetarian.

"Here you are." She filled Harold's food bowl, topped up his water and explained to him that she might be a little late, but she'd leave the light on.

Kee had a quick shower. She was suspicious that she might be emanating an *odeur de* pong herself. Showering was a battle in this apartment, as the old and rusty monster showerhead over the antiquated stand-alone bath had a tendency to fall off and hit her on the head mid-shower. Dried and dressed in her bra and bikini panties, she picked some jeans and a sweater fresh off the floor, smelled them, wrinkled her nose, but decided they fitted the 2-more-days-wear-left category and got dressed. She pulled on some sneakers. Comfort was the dress code if she were to pull an all-nighter at the office.

She patted Harold, who had wolfed down his dinner, very undignified behavior for a cat, closed her apartment door, turned the key, rattled it a few times to make sure it was locked, then headed down the creaky staircase and wrangled the Beast back to the office, which was lit up like a luxury cruise ship in full glory docking in the dark. Those lights gave her the same cozy feel as a warm, open fire in a stone fireplace. She was home. Kee parked the Silver Beast out front, in a not exactly legal spot. There'd be no county officer trying to book her tonight.

"You won't believe this," called Hollis from her desk, "Aron has done some real reporting."

Aron sat at his desk, typing at the rate of three words a minute. He could text so fast you couldn't see his thumbs, but he typed at the painfully slow pace of a two-fingered sloth. Aron looked up and gave her the thumbs up. Poor Aron, he was too thick to understand sarcasm.

"What's he turned up?" Kee asked Hollis.

"Well, according to Brodski's buddies at Billy Bob's Let 'em Buck Bar outa town, way outa town, the person known as the victim never owned an AK-47. He was strictly a handgun man. Mostly 9mm Springfields."

"What does that mean?" asked Kee.

"That the AK-47, and I am becoming quite the expert here, the one sticking out of Brodski, was not owned by Brodski. So we can assume there are lunatics out there willing to donate AK-47s to the FBI. I looked up the price of an AK-47 online at Atlantic Firearms, and the discounted sale price was $599.00. Ain't that sweet. You could buy one for your liddle old grandma for Christmas."

"So... Brodski has been done in by a hitman who then left his rifle at the scene?"

"Yeah!" replied Hollis. "Looks like it."

"Well done, Aron!" enthused Kee, walking over and slapping him on the back. Aron just nodded. Earbuds were blocking any higher level of human communication.

Now for some back scratching, thought Kee. She rang Booker.

She told him about the NGSA connection between the three victims, about Brodski not owning an AK-47 and about the Brodski creep/asshole information.

"That's good intel Miss Le. Keep it coming." He hung up. Kee couldn't get used to this abrupt axing of a conversation. Her friends took half-an-hour to say good-bye. What are you watching on the Teev? What're you doing Saturday night? You're on a diet? What diet? You don't have to lose weight? Does it work? All of these questions and more had to be worked through in order before you could say "Better run. There's someone at the door" or "The chili tofu is burning" (or equivalent).

Kee tweeted the same intel to @PoliceBizz. This time she got a reply.

"Yeah! Thought that might be the case. Makes sense." @PoliceBizz

"How so?" @KeeHasSpoken

"I'm thinking the note. It was a statement. So the rifle is making a statement too. Not sure what." @PoliceBizz

Kee updated *The New England Gazette*'s website and shot out a few Tweets.

"Believed that Hayden Brodski resident of Ridgefield executed by AK-47 did not own rifle that killed him. See *New England Gazette* tomorrow" #AntiGunBrigade @KeeHasSpoken

"AGB Anti-Gun Brigade kills victims with AK-47 then leaves the weapon in the body. Details in tomorrow's *New England Gazette*." @KeeHasSpoken

She looked at her Twitter feed. 42,675 followers. "I'm going viral, I'm going viral," she sing-songed to herself. It was almost

8:30 p.m. when Kee made the phone call that would skyrocket her to national fame.

She rang Gig DeKant, CEO of the National Gun and Shooters Association. Bradstreet, she assumed, had managed by some conniving newshound method to lay his hands on DeKant's home number. Actually, he knew someone on the board of the NGSA and promised them several bottles of Kentucky Vintage Bourbon for this one little favor. Gig was not happy when Kee rang. He talked and ranted and talked some more. Kee had the smarts to record her interview with DeKant on her cell. It was tricky setting up her phone before the call, but doable. When he finally hung up at 8.48 p.m., Kee was spent, too tired to Tweet. It had been a monster weird as all hell day. No two ways about it.

Chapter 6

Booker

Friday, the 15th of September

When the state trooper who'd found the body rang through to the Organized Crime Unit at 8:30 a.m. Friday morning, Booker answered the phone. Officer Oroza explained that he thought they should call in the feds because there were obvious signs that the murder was an execution-style job and therefore an FBI case. He'd called the Philly feds first, but they told him that the NY Organized Crime unit was best equipped for this type of (assumed) cross state kill. This sort of behavior was called "cooperation between the law enforcement agencies", or "play our cards right and we can dump this shitload of crazy on the feds"—according to the state troopers—or "...on our esteemed colleagues in NY" according to the Philly feds. If shitload dumping were included in a psyche assessment test, psychologists would find it gave the dumper far more satisfaction than mere cooperation did. In other words, it won out every time.

Booker listened carefully to Officer Oroza, adding "Hmmph!" every few words. Finally Booker remarked, "That's a new one on me," and "Hold the crime scene, will you, until I get there." He did a quick check on Google Maps. "I should be there by 10:30. Can you manage that?"

"Not a problem, Sir," Officer Oroza replied, trying to suppress a deeply satisfied grin.

Booker could have sent a member of his team to the crime scene, but his intuition told him that he should see this one for himself. Besides, his team had some serious paperwork to do to tie up the loose ends in a case against 7 members of a Chinese Triad they had recently arrested for running a money-laundering-sex-slave-prostitution-and-God-only-knows-what-else racket out the back of a chain of—would you believe?—shoddy laundromats called Miss Bubbles. He called out to Perez in the next office.

"I'll be out of the office all morning. You can get me on my cell."

"Right, chief," she replied, adding as she stared at her computer screen, "Do you want me to add illegal firearm charges or pass them on to the ATF?"

"Give it to the ATF. Call Agent Mike Belle. He knows what's going on."

"Okay, Chief," acknowledged Perez. This was another fine example of "cooperation" between the agencies.

Booker caught the lift down the 25 floors to the lower basement of the FBI's New York head office and climbed into his battered, slime green—his wife's description—Jeep Patriot, puffing.

Puffing? Really? He flogged himself with knotted-whip thoughts. *You only walked down 2 corridors and across a basement, and you're puffing. Quincey, 62 ain't old. Weight is your problem, my man. Too much of it under your belt, and ... puff ... over it.* He turned the key in the ignition and, as he backed his Jeep out of the car space, recalled his lithe young body of his childhood. Growing up on a farm in Jackson County, Kansas, he could run for miles carrying a rifle. He'd jump fences in his stride. Shoot rabbits. The family needed those rabbits. His father's wage as a farmhand didn't stretch to feed a family of five. It was military service that swirled Booker up and out of Kansas, like Dorothy's tornado in the Wizard of Oz. He never returned. Booker shook his head. How things change.

"The two-hour-plus drive to the crime scene won't be unpleasant," he mused, and chuckled to himself again. *You have to tell yourself these little lies.* If you admitted it was a mind-jarring, near death experience with 24-wheelers buffeting your car on the three-lane NJ-7 as they thundered past on either side, you might just scream out the window like that actor, what's his name, in the film, what was it called? Sometimes he thought his mind was going. But he remembered the actor's rant. *"I'm as mad as hell, and I'm not going to take it anymore!"* He was only in his twenties, maybe, when he saw that film, whatever it was called. Even then it had resonated with him. *"Mad as hell!"* He had been an angry young man. He'd turned 19 during the Vietnam War and "won" the draft lottery. "You, Sir, are the lucky winner of 13 weeks of boot-camp, Drill Instructor inflicted physical torment and verbal humiliation, and near on two years in a steamy, leech-riddled hellhole in the tropics trying to avoid getting your ass blasted half-way back to Kansas." When he arrived at Camp Lejeune in Jackson, North Carolina, he'd had a chip on his shoulder the size of Boulder, Colorado. But boot camp suited him. He could focus, burn off the rage-fueling testosterone, meet other "crack heads, retards, dumb asses"—their DI's terms of endearment—from across the country. And instead of getting his ass blasted halfway to Kansas, he ended up in the relatively cushy role of Marine MP, supervising mobility ops and earning a ticket into the FBI.

The white-hot rage was still there. But if he had learned anything in this life, it was that screaming "I'm as mad as hell and I'm not going to take it anymore!" only gave you high blood pressure and changed jot. But you don't have to "take it" either. You sort of move around "it" when you can, whatever "it" might be. That was Booker's MO. He remained quiet and calm even if he was churning so much on the inside he wanted to rip off arms. His outer calm bought him time to think. And thinking could highlight a path around the trouble spot like one of the alternate routes on Google Maps. He turned the Jeep onto the NJ-7 towards Newark.

"What was that film called? Come on. You know it!" he berated himself.

When Booker arrived at the Boneridge Quarry he had been off wandering around in his thoughts for so long he couldn't remember any of the photo-perfect sightseeing vistas he must have passed on the drive. The state troopers at the quarry entrance directed him to the crime scene. As he parked the car and walked to the police tape, Booker realized he was painfully desperate for caffeine. He should have stopped somewhere. Now he was standing in a desolate, grey, caffeine-deficient expanse of nothingness and his brain was screaming "Coffeeeeeeeee!" Fortunately, he was soon distracted by Officer Oroza, who greeted Booker like someone who was about to donate him a kidney, and then walked him to the corpse.

Kerry Cue

Booker was fascinated by this murder scene. He thought he knew death and all its grotesque cameos. He knew the smell of death. He could rate a murder scene like others ranked wine. Pungent, ripe, a dash of ox blood. Or stale, cloying, barnyard overtones. This murder scene was sharp, earthy with a hint of gasoline, yet the presentation was precocious. Booker had seen enough 8x10 prints of executed crims to wallpaper his entire apartment 3 times over. The thought amused him. He imagined his apartment wallpapered with photographs of bullet-riddled, blood-spattered, dismembered or garroted bodies of lowlifes, punks and thugs, then shook his head. The job had its costs. He'd sold at least part of his soul to the devil. But didn't we all do that? Sell a piece of our soul for cash with any job or handout? Not caring was the only way he held onto his sanity.

This crime scene was different. Those other slayings were quick, crude, messy. There was a precision to this execution. Booker took off his gold-rimmed glasses and polished the lenses on his silk tie. The gesture suggested that he was wondering if the smudged lenses had somehow distorted reality. He slipped his glasses back in place. Reality remained grotesque. The crime scene looked ... he was searching for the word ... Uncanny. Yes, that was it. Uncanny. His specialty was organized crime, gangland executions, and online hit men. He'd had to deal with more than one hireahitman.com site. This execution did not fit any category he knew. The body, the AK-47, and the note were all arranged in a brilliantly-back-lit artistic composition, staged against a stark washed-out grey backdrop. The crime scene reminded Booker of those dioramas you see in the museums of, say, the Pilgrim Fathers greeting a majestically feathered Indian Chief. The crime scene looked ... fake, though the bullet-riddled corpse were real enough. Booker muttered the word "Uncanny" out loud as he walked slowly around the body.

"What do you make of it?" Officer Oroza finally asked.

"I don't know," said Booker, shaking his head, then saying out loud for the first time, "I've never seen anything like it."

Booker's attention slid back to the corpse and the BAN THIS WEAPON in Arial font. He walked around the corpse. Studied it for some time.

This has all the symbolism of a turf war, thought Booker, *but what turf are we talking about?*

Officer Oroza coughed. "Sorry to interrupt again, Sir, but that girl over there claims she knows the victim," the young officer pointed in Kee's direction, "and we're a bit stumped on the ID." Booker turned and looked at the young woman standing by the crime scene tape. Fashion conscious. Young. Maybe mid to late twenties... but anyone under 40 looked young to him. Itching to get involved. Booker could read the enthusiasm in her face. He walked over to introduce himself.

Chapter 7
Booker
Best in Show

The young reporter ID'd the body. Booker chuckled to himself as he held the police tape aloft for the girl as she left the crime scene. "So I've got myself a stalker now." He shook his head as he walked back to the corpse. Anything was possible with this unusual case. The MO was bizarre and the crime scene surreal. He looked down at his polished brown loafers. Classic shoes. Covered in grey dust. He had dust in his hair, in his mouth, and on his glasses, but his thoughts were elsewhere. "There is some detail missing," he kept thinking. He obsessed over detail.

"I'm not seeing something," Booker grumbled to himself. He left instructions for the crime scene officers and headed back to his car. He needed that caffeine blast. He felt as desperate as any street crackhead needing a fix. Booker drove 7 miles along the Owega Turnpike towards Hawley with no a glimpse of a café or other eatery. There was no MacDonald's. No Pizza Hut. No Dunkin' Donuts.

"How do people live out here?" he complained. He was a hardcore New Yorker accustomed to finding a deli or a fast food joint three steps away at any point in the city. The thought of actually having to search for food was pre-prehistoric. "Here's all these little vintage clapboard shops selling whatnots, antique rocking chairs, and artisan candles but where's the food? A man's gotta eat!" He was feeling so curmudgeonly that the thought entered his head that he might have to shoot and devour one of the locals. Raw. Then he saw the most beautiful sign he could imagine. *The Best Breakfast in Poconos* banner was strung across the shingle roof of a quaint little café decorated with corn husk wreaths and other corn craft whatnots. They looked delicious.

Booker ordered a breakfast burger and coffee to go, but before he could hit the road his phone rang and there he was, standing in the open door of his Jeep in Main Avenue, Hawley, talking on his cell as he desperately gulped down his—ah! ah!—hot coffee.

"But Mom, you went to the wedding. I took you.... No. It wasn't my wedding. I'm married to Phillis. It was Nikki's wedding.... Our daughter. Your granddaughter .... They are not trying to poison you in the home.... Alright, I'll drop by and investigate .... Yes! It will be a full police investigation. Gotta go, Mom. Look after yourself."

That was lame, thought Booker. *How can I ask an 83-year-old with dementia to look after herself?* He took a deep breath and sighed. His cell rang again.

"Booker.... Right.... When?... You've got to be kidding. Another one! Are you sure it's the same MO?... AK-47. US manufactured. 2014. Was there a note attached?... Email the official crime scene photos.... Yes! All of them. Don't put them in one email. Send me 20 emails. Whatever it takes. I don't use the bureau Dropbox. Thank you."

The FBI classified a mass shooting as four or more deaths, and Booker's gut-feel told him this crime was linked to a mass shooting. But how? And why?

Booker rang Kee. The young reporter had already unearthed some interesting intel on Brodski by simply sitting in her car and doing a Facebook search. *I must get up to speed on all this social media business and not leave that part of the investigation to all the young just-out-of-short-pants agents in the office. Do young folk even wear short pants these days?* he wondered. *And how the hell did she pick up the info about the second corpse?* He hung up, annoyed to hell. This was not good. The media was one step ahead of the FBI, and the killers appeared to be crime scene artists determined to win Best in Show Arrangement of a Corpse. This made Booker feel uneasy, like one of those vacationers who stood stunned on the beach as the sea withdrew dramatically, leaving vast stretches of sandy seabed just before the tsunami hit. Booker knew he was about to be hit by one massive tsunami of trouble. He knew it was coming. But damned if he could work out from which direction it would come. He checked his phone. It was 3:30 p.m. already. Unbelievable. Where does the time, where does your life, go?

The return trip took three butt-numbing, frustrating hours. "Doesn't anyone stay home anymore?" Booker grumbled to himself as he inched his Jeep Patriot along the Essex Freeway towards Newark against the outbound rush hour traffic. The inbound traffic was also moving at a glacial pace. *Or do glaciers move faster than this traffic these days?*

He was still cursing the traffic when he had an epiphany.

"Network!" he exclaimed. "That was the name of the film. With the mad as hell news reader. *Network.* Where the sweet Jesus did that name come from?" Booker shook his head, adding, "Thou shalt not take the name of the Lord thy God in vain." He was constantly chastising himself for his unholy slip-ups, but—goddamit!—giving up his sinner's MO was hard.

Booker had to pull into the emergency lane to take a call from his wayward daughter, Charlotte, 22. Warm gusts of noxious fumes puffing across his face with each passing vehicle. He and Phillis did the best they could with Charlotte. She'd never fitted in high school. She'd graduated. Just. She'd had a string of dead-end jobs. "Stop being a judgmental asshole," he corrected himself. "A job is a job. It puts food on the table." But she never settled on anything for long. She'd disappear for months, then return home broke and broken.

She'd had ADHD as a kid. He and Phillis had sought help. Drugs were the only answer back then. He and Phillis didn't like it, putting an 8-year-old on amphetamines, but Charlotte was tormented by school. A little pixie that wanted to sit under the table or dance on top of it, she just didn't understand how a school operated. And school goddamn didn't understand how she operated, that's for sure. By 18 years of age, Charlotte had been through a few drug regimes, amphetamines for a while, then hooch, weed, cones, skunk, whatever. Booker was never quite up to speed with the current street name for marijuana, and now, of course, it was legit, a medicinal used, so it seemed, as a cure for sad and lonely lives. *Maybe that's a good thing,* thought Booker.

Every time Charlotte turned up at home, the apartment was thrown into bedlam, literally turned into a madhouse of screaming, sobbing, and zombiehood. Some days Charlotte couldn't get out of bed; other times they just hoped she wouldn't get out of bed. In one screaming match, she swore she would hide her weed stash in the family home and call the police. "Then you'll be on the news, Dad!" she'd yelled. Booker called in some favors and had the dog squad go over his home. They found the stash in the bottom of the ragbag under the laundry sink. Booker showed Charlotte the plastic bag with enough medicinal weed in it to cure the sad and lonely lives of half the neighborhood, and then he flushed it down the toilet. Charlotte gave up her stash-and-trash-Dad's-reputation plan. Too risky. Too expensive. At least now he and Phillis knew Charlotte came home to dry out. And they tried to keep the Charlotte-versus-mom-and-dad battles to a minimum for Jarrel's sake. He was only 12 years old. An after-after-afterthought. Phillis had assumed she was going through early menopause when her periods stopped. Then she found out to her amazement she was pregnant. Jarrel was the high-energy blessing that countered the black clouds of misery that trailed behind his sister. He deserved a stable home. Although, Booker had to admit, a "stable" home life hadn't really worked for Charlotte.

"What is it, baby?" answered Booker. Despite everything, she still was his little, lost, girl.

"Hey, Daddy-O," she chuckled, "can I have some money for the bus?"

"Where are you?" he queried.

"Ah, like, I'm not sure ... ah, Brooklyn."

Booker could hear some thudding electro-dance music in the background. Charlotte could be anywhere. That hideous *doof-doof* beat blasted out of every funky-fashion boutique in New York.

"How much?"

"Fifty would be sweet," she chirped.

"You know I don't do that, baby. Ten bucks. That's the limit. I'll put it on your card now."

Booker figured that $10 could not cause too much damage; besides, she really might need money for the bus.

"Okay. See ya." Charlotte signed off without sounding angry or grateful. She just sounded like... like Charlotte. The $10 Charlotte Card deposit only took one minute as all the details were preset in his bank account.

Before he threw himself back into the glacial traffic, Booker managed to snap out a few orders over his cell phone to his team. They needed to move fast on this one. Media sensation was written all over the case.

"And," contemplated Booker, "what would they call these murders? The Best in Show Murders?" Booker chuckled. At least he could amuse himself.

Chapter 8

Booker

In the Incident Room

Booker arrived back at the office at 6:15 p.m. He parked his car under the New York FBI's Federal Plaza headquarters and caught the lift to the 23rd floor. His team had already set up an Incident Room with whiteboards displaying up-to-date intel.

He had a good team. Vince Cogliano, Criminologist (gang crime MOs were his specialty); Mary Skule, Profiler; Lucia Perez, Liaison Officer—her role was really to stop the other agents from shooting the local or state police incompetents who got in the way or corrupted-evidence in federal investigations. She was so good at her job she could sweet talk confidential information out of a cactus—and Kendrick Volkman, Online Intelligence and Money Wizard. Money Wizard. was not exactly an official title, but Volkman could trace money buried under three stories of cement. Denney O'Shea and Joe Godbold rounded out the team. Both had street smarts. Both were ex-military. Five tours between them, including Afghanistan and Iraq. They knew handguns, assault rifles and ballistics inside out. More importantly, they could think like a crim. That's how they'd survived their active service. O'Shea, an easy-going yet self-contained loner, had been a sniper; Godbold, a conman's conman (he could sell Bank of Bozo bonds to a Nigerian scammer), had run an intelligence unit collecting intel from local Iraqis, who were, supposedly, sympathetic to the coalition cause.

So good was his team, there was a hot pizza waiting for him in the Incident Room. They could not only read his mind, they could read his stomach too. Booker was bite-the-south-end-off-a-north-bound-donkey starving. He looked in the box. Meatlovers. Again. Sigh. He loved meat as much as the next Neanderthal, but he craved some greens. A humble sprig of parsley would have done the job. Thank God Phillis kept him part-human with salads. Some days when he'd consumed meat mains followed by meat dessert, he thought he'd have to howl at the moon. Booker gulped down a slice of pizza, picked up the hot coffee that had, miraculously, appeared beside the Sammy's Sicilian Pizza box, and looked around the room.

It was a conference room repurposed for this case. An oval-shaped conference table surrounded by a dozen comfy padded blue office chairs held center stage in the room with some desktop computers set up at the far end. Three freestanding whiteboards dominated the front of the room, and another three stood at the back. Organized crime and gangland execution special agents weren't known for their optimism. Someone didn't expect the body count to stop at three. There was a jar of coffee, mugs and an electric urn on a white-topped table behind the spare whiteboards. A bank of printers sat on another white-topped table under the window that ran the length of the conference room. Supplies of paper, file covers and large manila envelopes plus packets of pens were spread across a bank of desks crammed into the far end of the room ,and dozens of new flat-pack cardboard file-boxes rested on the floor beside the desks, awaiting construction.

It's like the first day of school with the fresh smell of shiny new books and clean tables everywhere, reflected Booker, and, *Yep. That won't last. We'll be living in this room and dribbling toothpaste on our ties for the foreseeable future. By "we" I mean Kendrick and me. The women, they dress like women. And those two ex-Army Rangers and Cogliano turn up at the office dressed for a backyard bake out in Texas. Kendrick and I are the only ones who wear ties. We'll have to dribble for the team.*

He stood in front of the whiteboard dedicated to the first victim. It boasted Facebook screen grabs of the victim and crime scene shots along with satellite photographs of the Boneridge Quarry with relevant locations marked in yellow fluoro-pen. Booker couldn't get the word "uncanny" out of his head. Uncanny. These executions were staged. All of them. He finished another slice of pizza and called his team together. The special agents stood, sat or perched on the conference table around Booker.

"What have we got so far?" Booker queried.

Cogliano spoke first.

"Three shootings. Same MO. Victim is shot in the chest by, we suspect, but we're waiting for the ballistics, a short burst from an AK-47. The shooter then stabs the victim with the weapon and leaves it at the scene with a note. BAN THIS WEAPON. Each of the victims is a known gun fanatic. But here is the thing. Three different locations. So it looks like three different shooters." Booker turned and his eyes slowly scanned the intel displayed on the whiteboards behind him as Cogliano ID'd the victims.

"Hayden Brodski, 34, Boneridge Quarry, Pennsylvania.

"Desmond Colt, 55, Seminoe State Park, Wyoming.

"Carl Koober Jr, 28, Cesar's Head State Park, Sth Carolina."

"Three states. What's significant here?"

"Assault rifles aren't banned in those states?" suggested Skule.

"That flies. And timeline?" queried Booker.

"Times of death looks to be within 24 hours of each other. We can be more specific after the autopsy reports."

"Hmmph!" snorted Booker, "anything else?"

Mary Skule spoke up. A born bureaucrat, her plain grey suits matched her dull grey manner. Surprisingly, she was animated by this case.

"Symbolic gangland executions like this—well not exactly like this, but similar—are usually carried out to silence, to intimidate and/or shut down the opposition. The Black Muslims used targeted violence, murder mostly, although a few fingers were shot off, to grab control of all the black drug/racketeering/extortion and other trade in Philadelphia in the early seventies. It was very effective."

"Are you suggesting this could be another black gangland turf war?" Booker snorted.

"In this case, when I use the term black, I mean, like the cowboys in black hats." Bookers team didn't stick with rigid PC policy when it came to racial profiling, but each agent had to be alert to false assumptions.

"So we are talking black cowboys in black hats," harrumphed Booker. He always gave the profilers a hard time. Then again, he always heard them out. They might just find some piece of the jigsaw puzzle that helped the others fit.

O'Shea spoke next. Deadly and serious in the field—truly deadly—he was the comedian in the office. He'd worked undercover busting gunrunning cartels for several years and survived mainly due to an impressive hit count that made him a legend even among FBI special agents. Tough guy to the core. Now he was on something of a sabbatical. Taking it easy working as a special agent with the Organized Crime Unit.

"I will say, this is a gift from the gods. We usually get crims versus victims. Here we are dealing with dumb fucks with guns versus other dumb fucks with guns. What the fuck is not to like about that? It's got Hollywood blockbuster written all over it."

Then, placing one hand behind his ear and putting on his movie voiceover voice, O'Shea drawled, "*Who are the good guys? Who are the bad guys? And who is going to win when dumb asses with guns take on dumb asses with guns?*"

"Yeah. Real funny guy, you are," groaned Mary, "you'll have the ethics committee coming down on us like a ton of shit hitting the fan for unprofessional conduct."

She was half-serious. Then she threatened, "I'll profile you one day, O'Shea. That should terrify the rest of us."

Booker raised one eyebrow. The others looked a little surprised. They didn't know Mary Skule swore. She'd only been with the team for one month. Maybe she had the hots for O'Shea. She was single. Divorced. No kids. Taut and tanned. O'Shea had the riveting blue eyes of a Siberian Husky and a raw, undomesticated wildness to him. Despite his age, 45, and Irish-American heritage, he had the weathered looks of a young, blond, Aussie surfer. He was forever pushing his disheveled, collar length, sun-bleached locks back off his face. Apparently, and you may have to run your own straw poll to confirm the fact, girls swoon over this affectation. And in the charm department O'Shea nuked the competition. Not even a leprechaun could babble Irish bullshit like O'Shea.

O'Shea gave Mary a boyish grin, flicked a stray blond lock behind one ear, then drawled, with a hint of his childhood Belfast accent, "Okay! Fun's over. I'm looking at the rifles left at the scene. They're all AK-47s. US manufactured. 2014. Mikhail Kalashnikov would be turning in his grave if he knew American scum were manufacturing and selling his prized rifle now. Is there no end to the pain of Glasnost? We're following up sales of the rifles and ammo. Legal sales. Illegal sales, especially online, are another ball game. We can keep a watch on a few gun sales sites. We might pick up some vibe on the street, but it is difficult when the crime is spread across so many locations."

"Godbold?" Booker ordered, raising his hands in a what-have-you-got? gesture.

"I'm with O'Shea. I think we can get evidence from the weapons. They found 4 rounds in the dirt at the first crime scene. These rounds were completely shattered but forensics weighed the fragments. They're pretty sure there were 4 rounds. So the victim was killed by a short burst from the AK-47 that was left in his body. That's the current theory. And 2 of the rifles had old 6H3 bayonets attached. That might be useful."

Booker sat looking at the crime scene pictures for a moment then continued.

"These shootings aren't random. So communication has to be the key here. Volkman, track their phone records. Get in touch with the local cops and get your hands on their computer downloads. Did they text? Email? Or use gun chatrooms to set up each meet? Just one little slip up could lead us to the killers."

"Onto it, Chief," said Volkman.

"So the 'how' we know. We think," Booker summarized, "but the 'who' and the 'why?' we have no idea. We've got a whiteboard, so we're going to do some brainstorming, folks. Give me a name, any name, of any lunatic group you can think of that might get it into their collective heads to execute gun nutters."

Booker picked up a black marker pen and held it at the ready. As team members called out the usual suspects, he wrote them for all to see.

Drug gangs
Rival gunrunners
Terrorists
Animal liberationists
Black militants
Alt-right white Supremacists
Religious nutters
Mexican drug cartels
Psycho Park Rangers

Volkman interrupted the brainstorm.

"I've been looking for a connect between the three victims."

"Bad haircuts?" suggested Lucia Perez.

"Well, true," said Volkman seriously. Humor was not his strong suit. "The only significant link I've come up with so far is that they are all members of the NGSA, but that's almost meaningless. Many gun owners are. And who would take on the NGSA?"

"Wait," insisted O'Shea, "what did the CEO of the NGSA say after the Waco shootings? That 'the FBI was nothing but storm-trooper Nazis in black SS uniforms who send out death squads to kill ordinary citizens.' So maybe, just maybe, we should add the FBI to the list. I'm sure that what's-his-name, the current CEO of the NGSA, would put us on the list."

"DeKant. His name is Gig DeKant," said Volkman.

"Right, just wait for it. Mr. DeKant is bound to claim it's the FBI taking out blameless members of the NGSA," joked O'Shea.

"And raising the general IQ of the country," quipped Skule.

"Seriously," insisted Volkman, "who would attempt a cull of the NGSA? NGSA members could be packing a piece down the crotch of their briefs. Not gonna be easy targets."

"They've probably got room for three Glock G43s," joked O'Shea. The others laughed.

"Thanks, Volkman. I see your point," said Booker. "As for you, O'Shea, I'm not interested in NGSA dick size intel."

"I'm interested!" enthused Perez. Lucia Perez was a small curvaceous package of barely contained sexual heat. She would be interested. The team laughed again.

"Really, dick-size aside, you have to consider the possibility of an armed anti-gun activist group springing up from somewhere," insisted Perez. "My mom says someone should shoot those lunatic bastards in NGSA who want teachers to be armed to stop school shootings. They're all mad."

"Maybe we should add your mom to the list," joked O'Shea. Booker turned to the board and wrote:

Armed Anti-gun Activists

"That's a bit of an oxymoron, isn't it?" said Cogliano. "People against guns shooting people?"

"I will remind you," said Booker, "this is America, the greatest nation on earth ... so we have the greatest loonies, too."

More laughter. "If you hear anything, see anything, get the slightest whisper that one of these groups or any other group is involved ... follow it up," ordered Booker.

His cell rang. "I'll take this," he said, "but you lot keep brainstorming. I won't be a minute." Booker hated himself for grimacing when his phone rang. He thought it might be Charlotte. It wasn't. He withdrew to the window side of the room.

"Hello, Miss Le, what can I do for you?"

"You said I was to ring you if I came up with anything linking the killings. The three killings."

"Go on!" rumbled Booker.

"All the victims belong to the NGSA. I think there is some sort of AGB, Anti-Gun Brigade, going after members of the NGSA," Kee announced.

Booker sighed.

"You are being, if I might be frank, a little melodramatic, Miss Le. But we will definitely keep that possibility in mind along with all the others."

"And one of our reporters interviewed some of Brodski's pals, and it seems he did not own an AK-47. He was strictly a handgun man."

"Hmmm," Booker replied, thinking.

"And there's one more thing," Kee insisted. "Hayden Brodski's name came up in a number of women's chatrooms where they describe him as an "asshole" and a "creep". It sounded like that whole date rape thing. It could be relevant but no proof yet."

"How did you come by that information?"

"I just googled Hayden Brodski, Asshole, Creep."

"Now that, Miss Le, is smart work. You keep up that standard of inquiry, and you can have my job soon."

"Thanks, Mr. FBI, but I'd much rather be looking at pictures of cute cats all day than shot-up, ground-meat corpses, now that I've actually seen one."

"You may be right there," said Booker, "but good intel, Miss Le. Keep it coming." He pressed the end-call button.

"We have another possibility to add to the list," drawled Booker, returning to the front of the room. He wrote another phrase on the board:

Armed militant feminists

"Really?" gasped Mary Skule.

"I wonder why it has taken us so long!" enthused Perez. "If, in the seventies, instead of burning bras women had picked up AK-47s, men would have begun shopping and cooking, cleaning toilets and changing diapers a lot sooner."

The women laughed. The men looked unamused, which made the women laugh even more.

"Back in the real world—and this is not dismissing the possibility that there is a group of armed militant feminists terrorizing the male population of this great country of ours— the big question, as I see it," emphasized Booker walking away from the whiteboard to sit on the edge of the conference table, "is not only who, or why, but how? We know how they are killed. But *how* do they get their victims—unarmed members of the usually armed-to-the-teeth NGSA—into a quarry or a state park to get themselves shot, for goddamn sake? And I say that as a church-going man!"

Kerry Cue

This job, thought Booker, *would make a goddamned angel swear.* Blaspheming again. This was another bit of his soul gone to the devil. He really hoped he had a small remnant of soul left to occasionally do some good. He'd had a gut feeling about this case from the get-go. That's why he wanted to see the crime scene himself. He'd needed to be on the scene to get the feel of it. And he would goddamn get the pieces to fit somehow.

He checked the clock at the back of the incident room. 8:15 p.m.

"It's past 8. You've all got leads to follow up. But don't hammer this too late. We'll bring fresh eyes to this weird MM case in the morning." MM stood for mass murder.

Chapter 9

DeKant

Friday, the 15th of September

When the house phone rang at 8:25 p.m. on Friday night, Gig DeKant thought it would be his daughter, Emily, letting him know how his 6-year-old granddaughter, the cute-as-a-Peony-pixie Kelsey, was faring. She'd just had her tonsils out six days ago, and he was holding his breath and saying the odd prayer hoping she would come out of the ordeal all dimpled, rosy-cheeked and 100% recovered.

"Is that Gig DeKant?"

"Who is this?" demanded DeKant

"Hello, Mr. DeKant. My name is Kitchi Le, I'm a reporter with *The New England Gazette*," explained a female voice.

"How did you get this number? This is a private number?" he spat into the phone.

"I'm sorry," replied the voice, "but I have some news that you really need to hear."

Gig DeKant was not just the CEO of the NGSA, he was its brains trust, its mouthpiece, its Ring Master. DeKant was intractable. The media dance macabre after every mass shooting in America, be it in a school, a college, a nightclub or a shopping mall, always included a solo showpiece by Gig DeKant. He would fly in, head midtown in a cab, stand in front of the most prominent building in town, usually the law court, surrounded by a pre-briefed media scrum proclaiming into the microphones:

"No child in this great country of ours is safe while schools remain gun-free zones. Every psycho, every crackhead, every angry, tormented teen and every terrorist with a gun knows they can walk right in the school door unchallenged. This tragedy today is unforgivable. We cannot protect our children until schools have armed protection, locked and loaded."

DeKant was a media mega-star, a master of the punchy 10-second sound bite. Gig had also been at one time, though he remained silent on the subject, an angry, tormented teen. On paper and in media profiles, Gig had enjoyed an ideal childhood. He was born Heinrich DeKant Jr. in Sheridan, Wyoming, in 1945 while his father was, initially, away fighting a war, then guarding various American zones in parts of Europe. When Heinrich Sr. returned home, he used his old army contacts to build up a successful trucking business. So Gig grew up in a 1930s Sears Modern Home, a 2-story gracious bungalow with a stone-columned porch, gabled-roof and flag-flying flagpole out front.

But Gig's childhood was a long way from idyllic. Heinrich Sr. had been born in Prussia in the early 1900s. He and his young wife migrated to America in 1929; and, while registering at Staten Island, Heinrich, like many optimistic immigrants, Americanized his first name. Heinrich became Henry, a declaration encompassing all their hopes and dreams, but his wife still called Heinrich at home. When Heinrich Sr.'s only son was born, he too was named Henry, but also called Heinrich at home. Heinrich Sr., however, never lost the stiff-backed, authoritarian code of conduct of a Prussian Cavalry Lieutenant, beating his son unconscious at the age of 10 for stealing an orange from the family kitchen pantry.

Perhaps it was the war that twisted Heinrich Sr., instilling some sadistic drive, or perhaps his brutal nature was written into his genetic code. Heinrich Sr. dominated and terrified his wife. He ordered his son, in his Sunday best grey suit with the knee-length pants and long grey socks, to stand at attention for hours in the drawing room until the 6-year-old could recite pages of the Bible by heart. When Heinrich Jr., at the age of 17, came home intoxicated one night, his father beat the drunk and defenseless teen, threw him in their—recently installed—swimming pool, and fired shots at him with one of the Luger pistols Heinrich Sr. had brought back from the war. Heinrich Jr. was terrified. Later that night, after his father fell asleep in the study with an empty bottle of bourbon for company, Heinrich Jr. made three life-changing resolutions. First, he swore never to use his father's name again. He renamed himself "Gig" after the first film star's name that popped into his 17-year-old brain, Gig Young. Secondly, he decided that everyone over the age of 14 years should have the right to carry a gun to defend themselves when under fire, even if the shooter is in your own family. He would become intractable in this belief. Finally, he resolved to leave home the next day.

Gig packed his bags, kissed his sobbing mother and angry 15-year-old sister goodbye, and left home that morning with his sister Shirley's words trailing him out the front door and down the garden path.

"You are a coward, Heinrich!" she shouted, "I'll never forgive you for leaving me here with HIM!"

Gig never saw his father again. Six months after hoboing around the country, living by his wits, jumping trains and stealing milk, Gig was arrested as a vagrant in Texas. The judge gave him the option of staying in the jailhouse as a guest of the local sheriff or joining the army. This was a judgment outside the hard-line Republican judge's remit, but in the early sixties few had the will to protest; besides, Gig would have to face the draft sometime. He was already 18 years old. Gig enlisted in the Army. He won the Sharpshooter's Badge and the Expert Infantryman Badge, but left the corp after 18 months in 1965, wearied by the brainless routine and drills. Studying nights and working as an assistant to Republican Senator John Tower in Dallas, Texas, Gig eventually put himself through college, gaining a law degree from the University of Houston in 1968. This personal history is commonplace enough. But Gig's life experience added up to the perfect boot camp training for NGSA leadership. Firstly, he believed in gun ownership. Secondly, he believed in the unassailable rights of the individual to make their own decisions in their own life. And finally, he learned about the theatre of politics watching Senator Tower. Gig began working as a lawyer for the NGSA in 1970. He married his long-time girlfriend, Beverley Chapman, in 1973. They had four children: Amy, 36; Emily, 33; and the twins Brad and Logan, 27. Logan was born with cerebral palsy and was confined to a wheelchair. But Gig was a good father. He was a churchgoer and dedicated to his disabled adult son.

DeKant had headed up the NGSA legal team that flipped US gun laws on their head in 2008. It was such a simple case to carry so many gun-toting repercussions. Dick Heller was a 66-

year-old security guard at the Federal Judicial Center in Washington. He wanted to take his semi-automatic pistol home from work. t *The State of Columbia Vs Heller* case changed everything. Gig was forcefully adamant in the Supreme Court hearing that there was only one legal interpretation of the 2nd Amendment. He read out the Amendment with theatrical gravitas.

"A well regulated Militia, being necessary to the security of a free State, the right of the people to keep and bear Arms, shall not be infringed."

Completely ignoring the words "well-regulated" and "militia", Gig argued that this amendment gave the individual the inalienable right under the constitution to bear arms to defend home and hearth. And this right included their choice of firearm. The judges handed down a 5-4 ruling in favor of the plaintiff. The judges finding for the plaintiff did not agree that the "firearm of choice" applied under the 2nd Amendment. "Our founding fathers would not intend its citizens to arm themselves with tanks or stinger missiles," insisted renowned Republican Judge Scalia, "but handguns are the most popular weapon chosen by Americans for self-defense in the home, and a complete prohibition of their use in the home is invalid."

Heller won. The gun lobby won. And the citizens of Columbia won the right not only to own but also carry bottom-loading magazine-fed semi-automatic pistols in public. In an instant, handguns were legally back on the streets of America. A few more "2nd Amendment" cases and several years on, only a handful of states banned open carry; the majority allowed citizens to safely stroll, or arrogantly strut—it depends on which side of the gun control debate you sit—the streets of America openly displaying their "home and hearth", defending firearms in the majority of states without an open carry permit.

This was a coup d'état for the gun lobby and gun manufacturers. This significant court case win launched Gig DeKant into the NGSA stratosphere. In 2010, at the age of 65, he became the CEO of the NGSA. Gig announced his leadership style later that year when he sent out 50,000 Christmas cards to select friends and associates depicting his family: wife, children, their partners and the three grandchildren he had at the time, wearing red t-shirts, red Santa hats and all holding firearms, including the two Lugers he'd inherited from the dead father he hated.

When criticized for this gun-happy family portrait by various anti-gun lobby groups, Gig stood in front of the local courthouse in Fairfax, Virginia, holding a blown-up photograph of the family Christmas card and pointed to his disabled son, Logan, sitting in his wheelchair:

"See that boy?" he announced. "Look at him. Look at his face. Disabled from birth. But nothing gives more joy and more hope to a powerless disabled boy like my son Logan than to hold a Smith & Wesson .44 Magnum Revolver in his hand, knowing that he can be at home alone and defend himself. Look at his face. That is joy, my friends. Pure Joy."

Photographs of this meticulously staged stunt were plastered over every traditional and online media outlet worth its weight in Facebook "Likes". Not one member of the media had the presence of mind to ask at the time, "How can a severely disabled boy of 17 aim a .44 Magnum at an intruder, or at anything for that matter?" The media was gagged. Questioning the abilities of the disabled is a taboo topic. Gig was the Ring Master. He controlled members of the media (and more than one campaign-fund-hungry Republican senator) as if they were performing clowns, or hand-fed geese.

When Kee rang Gig DeKant on his home phone at 8:25 p.m. that Friday night with the news "he needed to hear," he was not impressed.

"What news?" he demanded.

"Three members of your organization were shot in execution-style murders yesterday."

DeKant took a deep breath thinking, "Just what I need! Another nutter."

"I am so sick to death of you fucked up prank callers."

"The news will be on CNN any minute, I'm sure. But if you go to *The New England Gazette* website, you'll get confirmation."

Gig did a quick search on his cell. He read the bold header on the *Gazette's* website: BAN THIS WEAPON.

"Jeeee-sus Christ almighty!" he yelped.

"Sorry to break the news to you, Mr. DeKant, but one of the victims was someone I knew. A real decent guy"—Kee was going for diplomatic overkill. She was up-skilling in the area of swaddled truth—"named Hayden Brodski. But there is more ...."

"Like what?"

"It looks like there is some sort of Anti-Gun Brigade, I'm calling them the AGB, targeting NGSA members for execution."

"Jeee-sus!"

"And you have to hear this. The shooter leaves an AK-47 sticking out of the body with a note attached. BAN THIS WEAPON. I'm wondering if you'd care to make a comment."

DeKant took a breath and launched himself into a gale-force "comment". His words exploded out of his mouth so fast it was difficult for a listener to make sense of anything he said.

"If those anti-gun motherfucker queers think they can intimidate the 5 million good and decent members of the NGSA who stand for and cherish the sacred values of America, they are completely out of their evil, godless, contemptible little minds. We're armed. We're ready. We have been expecting this. You tell those American-hating, mincing, pansy-boys who have not let go of their mothers' apron strings to *bring it on!*"

When DeKant took a quick breath, Kee instantly hit him with another question.

"We're using the acronym AGB for the present until we find out who is involved. Do you have any idea what group might decide to execute members of your organization?"

"I'll tell you. They'll belong to the godless elite, the Hollywood celebrities and media activists on the loony Left, the long-haired, tree-hugging, weed-smoking, vegetarian fringe group that doesn't want the good and decent citizens of this great nation, the ordinary average Americans who make up the heartland of this country, to be able to protect their families and their property with their legitimately bought guns. I tell you what, Missie," boomed DeKant, "this will give us the chance we have been waiting for. Now we can, we have the *right,* to defend ourselves. We will shoot every last one of those faggot loony Leftie motherfuckers. Every last one of them!"

"One last question, Mr. DeKant, because I realize this is very stressful for you," sympathized Kee. "Are you at all concerned for your own safety or that of your family?"

"That would be the day! We're the DeKant family. We are so well armed we might be the third largest armed force in the United States of America."

"Just one more thing," crooned Kee.

"Yes!"

Target 91

"Why do you think this Anti-Gun Brigade is targeting AK-47s made in America?"

"Because they want the AK-47 all to themselves. The global alliance of political power mongers, campus radicals, and media manipulators are pushing their Anti-America agenda. The godless Left doesn't want ordinary Americans to be armed. This self-appointed elite of political and media manipulators always join forces to insult, mock and disparage ordinary Americans going about their ordinary everyday lives. This elite, every one of those goddamn, pansy weed-heads of the morally depraved Left, want to rule this country by stealth. Well, they can't. We're armed. We're going after them!"

"Thank you, Mr. DeKant. I hope you and your family are safe," said Kee.

"What was your name again?" asked DeKant.

"Kitchi Le," replied Kee, "*New England Gazette.*"

"Hmmph!" grunted DeKant, and hung up.

Chapter 10

Kee

Saturday, the 16th of September

Kee had obviously caught DeKant on the back foot. His press releases were always rants, but well-worded rants. She had never, as far as she could remember, ever heard him cuss. But the write up of the DeKant interview would have to wait. It was well after midnight by the time she had typed the entire interview transcript into her laptop, and it had been a long day. Kee was so tired she really didn't feel that she had one little Tweet left in her. But she could not resist this sensational news. She Tweeted:

"NGSA Chief says gun down LOONY LEFTIES. See updates on *The New England Gazette* website" @KeeHasSpoken.

She drove home, pushed a complaining Harold off her pillow and dropped fully dressed onto her bed. Kee drifted into a crazed-dreamscape of guns, bodies and fluttering flags, thinking about the post she'd write for *The New England Gazette* website in the morning. *That would be, um, Saturday, she thought* drowsily, *but now I need some sleep, so - gunned down or not - the LOONY LEFTIES will have to wait.*

Kee woke up stiff, thirsty and seriously decaffeinated at 7:15 a.m. in the drearily dull morning light with Harold sitting on her head. Harold wasn't exactly on top of her head, but he was wedged between the top of her skull and the bed backboard.

"Seriously, Harold," she said, putting her hand over her head to push him to the other side of the double bed, "you have no respect for the rules of personal space." Harold was like a pillow of bread dough. Each time she pushed, his body flowed around her hand. Kee struggled to sit upright and swung her legs to the side of the bed.

"Ergh!" she grimaced, "my mouth tastes like fermented cat piss." Kee had no idea what fermented cat piss tasted like; but, she figured, whatever its taste it could not be more disgusting than her mouth right now. "What did I eat last night? Fried hot chili rat poison kebabs?" She couldn't remember.

"OMG! I've still got my clothes on." Her brain kicked into Warp Speed 8 again.

"OMG! I remember now. Yesterday was one hell of a Weird Shit Day."

She flicked through her Twitter feed. She had to peek at her number of followers.

"OMG! 63,804!" she gasped. *Note to self,* she thought, *I need a new acronym. How about OM-freaking-G!* It didn't stick. She looked at her private Twitter feed and screamed "OMG!" There was more news.

"Two more stiffs found" @PoliceBizz 5.00 Saturday, 16 Sept

"B. Randy Talbot, 49, Mark Twain National Park, Missouri." @PoliceBizz 5.13 Saturday, 16 Sept

"Lucky Dickson, 60, Mohave Desert, Nevada." @PoliceBizz 5.48 Saturday, 16 Sept

"Same MO. Sort of assuming that now." @PoliceBizz 5.02 Saturday, 16 Sept

"Did you check to see if these victims are in the NGSA? Save me some time." @KeeHasSpoken

"Yeah! Affirmative on that." @PoliceBizz

Whoa! My 35-year-old porn-addicted homeboy is turning pro, Kee mused.

"Copy that! Hey PoliceBizz, you going all heavy duty cop on me. Your real name Dirty Harry? Ha!" @KeeHasSpoken

"I wish." @PoliceBizz

"Spoke to Gig DeKant on the phone last night. He was not a happy little NGSA camper. Watch Gazette webpage for update." @KeeHasSpoken

It wasn't much in the you-scratch-my-back-and-I'll-scratch-yours department, but she had to give @PoliceBizz something for his troubles.

Kee picked up her cell, set it on Record again, and called Gig DeKant. "Oops! Ooops! I should have peed first. If he goes all ballistic again, I'll pee my pants!" she worried.

"Yes?"

She was amazed that he answered the phone.

"Mr. DeKant ... it's Kitchi Le again, from *The New England Gazette*. I have some more information you have to hear."

"Shoot," he snapped.

I don't believe he said that, Kee thought, then continued. "There have been two more victims of the Anti-Gun Brigade. Same MO. Would you like to comment?"

"Before I do ... and this is off the record ... I'm thankful to you, young lady. I can't say I slept last night ... but at least you've given me a chance to think about last night's statement. Could you remove all my little indiscretions ... I mean all the cussing. It's not a policy of the NGSA to cuss."

"Absolutely, Sir. Consider it done. I will be putting your comment online later this morning and I will make sure I edit out any extreme language. I want to give you a chance to put out your view, fair and square," replied Kee with honey-sweet diplomacy.

"I appreciate that. I can't say that I trust newspaper reporters. On the record. Off the record. It doesn't matter. They just want sensational headlines. Not the truth."

"I'm not like that, Sir. You represent a lot of people in this country and your views should be heard."

"Well, well. You're right on the money there. In fact, you may be the only newspaper reporter to understand where I'm coming from. I speak for five million citizens. Their views count. "

"Exactly," responded Kee.

"And since we understand each other," Kee continued boldly, "could I have your cell phone number just for news updates?"

"I'll tell you what. I'll give you my number, but at the first sign of screwing me around, you'll be blocked," snorted Gig.

"That's fine with me, Sir. I believe news stories should be balanced."

Gig gave her his cell number.

"Mr. DeKant, the body count for members of your association is up to five. Can you give me a comment?"

Kee heard Gig take a breath. He clearly had a few statements prepared in response to the current crisis. The Media Maestro turned into Preacher Man, eulogizing with heartfelt sorrow five dead members of his association whom he had never met.

"Today it is my very sad duty to announce that five of our brothers in arms, esteemed members of the NGSA, have been executed by some left-wing elitist, dope-smoking, racist gangsta wannabes simply because our boys believe in everything that is good and true about this great country of ours: justice, freedom, and self-reliance. These godless lefties are attacking our boys with a zealous, fanatical fervor designed to tear apart the very foundations of America, just like terrorists in other parts of the world. Today we mourn our brothers, sons, fathers, and friends who have given their lives because they believed in America. Tomorrow we will track down these depraved godless individuals, and we will annihilate them."

"Have you got that?" Gig asked.

"Yes. Thank you, Mr. DeKant. I recorded your statement. It will be on our website later this morning."

"That's that then."

Kee typed his statement into her laptop verbatim and sent out another click-bait Tweet:

"Our boys died protecting American Values says NGSA CHIEF. More tomorrow in Special Ed of *New England Gazette.*"#AntiGunBrigade @KeeHasSpoken

She looked at her phone. *OMG! It's only 7.55am. AM!* Kee texted her boss.

GOT 2 INTERVIEWS WITH GIG DEKANT. SOME KILLER HEADLINES FOR TOMOZ. TOTAL BLOCKBUSTERS. SEE MY TWITTER ACCT.

As an afterthought she sent a second text:

2 MORE BODIES. BODY COUNT STANDS AT 5.

She barely had time to pee when her cell rang. It was her boss. "What's the protocol here?" she wondered. "Like, is it okay to talk to your boss while you're perched on the loo or is that a bit sick?" Kee much preferred the British "loo" to the "can" or "john" of guy-speak. Perched on the loo and trying to pee quietly, she answered her phone.

"Good Morning, Mr. Bossy," she crooned.

"What's with this text thing? Just pick up the goddamn phone and talk to me. We've got stiffs coming out our ears and your wasting time tinky-winky texting!"

"Good morning to you too, Boss," she hummed.

"What are these killer headlines?" snorted Bradstreet.

"Oh. Ah. The first one is NGSA Chief says gun down loony lefties. Not bad, eh! But wait for this. Second banner: Our boys died protecting American values says NGSA Chief. You can almost hear the Star Spangled Banner sound track playing in the background."

"Hmmf!' grumped Bradstreet adding, "and where did you get that body count info?"

"Same source. My guy on Twitter. He's been 100% spot on the kill count so far."

"Okay, okay," grunted Bradstreet. "Get your fanny down here pronto, we're bringing out a special Sunday edition."

"Did you know that in Australia "fanny" means vagina?"

"Get all of your fannies down here pronto!" he ordered.

"Okey dokey! I'm on the way. Quick shower and I'm there."

Kee ended the call with a grin from ear to ear. Mr. Don't-Tinky-Winky-Text-Me had just ordered her to get her ass and vadge to the office. She laughed. "The boss and I are like sisters now. We'll start wearing each other's clothes soon. Ha!" Kee gloated, as she stood up and flushed the toilet.

"So here I am! It's Weird Shit Day 2. Maybe I should keep a diary."

Kee showered, hunted for a fresh work ensemble on the floor, protesting, "Harold, why do you have to curl up asleep on my black sweater? Look at it! It's covered in grey fur." She settled for a sloppy grey sweater ("You can't see Harold's hair on this one!"), some torn fake-designer jeans, and white canvas shoes. It was Saturday. Casual Dress Saturday.

Before she left for the office she typed DeKant's Brothers-in-Arms speech into her laptop. She posted both his loonie-lefties comment and his brothers-in-arms speech on her *Inside Out New England* blog. Kee was, however, good to her word. She was very discreet. She took all the cuss words out of the first statement, tidied up the text a little, and had it looking like a polished DeKant rant.

She slammed her laptop shut, calling, "Harold, mommy has to go to work today. Sorry, baby. I'll get back as soon as I can." She picked up her bag, threw it over her shoulder, grabbed her car keys and hurtled out the apartment door.

Chapter 11

Booker

Saturday, the 16th of September

Booker's day began early. He woke at 4 a.m. from an uneasy sleep. In that blurred state between reality and slumber, bloody scenes often flashed like a grotesque magic lantern in his dreams. This time he woke with an absurd tableau in his brain: an elderly neighbor staked with an AK-47 to his office wall. The moment he woke up, as always, he turned his head to look at Phillis. She was lying next to him, her back to him, body slightly curled, rhythmically breathing in her sleep. Her tight black curls were tinged with grey now. *That lick of grey makes her even more beautiful*, he thought. Phillis was the home, the hearth, the open fire and the open arms that kept him sane. She was the elevator counterweight to his blood-spattered work environment that stopped him hurtling to the ground at bone-shattering speed. Every day, he thanked the Lord that he woke up next to Phillis, and, even though she never saw it, every day he blew her a kiss before he climbed out of bed.

"Booker," he said to himself as he struggled to his feet, "62 is not old. Why is it you creak like the rusty hinges of an old barn door with every step?" He padded quietly to the bathroom opposite their bedroom in his bare feet, wearing his usual night outfit: boxers and a t-shirt. It was Phillis's dream to have an en-suite bathroom one day. But there was never enough money or enough room. This was a rent-controlled apartment in Washington Heights, New York. Tenants had a choice: live here until you die, or leave Manhattan and never return. "The likelihood of dying," mused Booker, "feels a lot closer today than it did yesterday." In the cloying darkness of a chilly morning, Booker could almost feel the Grim Reaper's cold breath on the back of his neck, a presence that manifested into a stronger reality when Booker had to wait for a good 2 to 3 seconds before the brain-dick-piss connect sprang into action. He put one hand on the back of his neck, an unconscious response.

"Something's not quite right," Booker murmured to himself. This case, this bizarre shooting spree that he had to solve, wasn't quite right. He was not seeing something. He had the details, but not the big picture—"the narrative" he called it—that made a murder story **THE** MURDER STORY that would some day be rewritten into a TV cop show. There was something not quite right.

"This could be the theme defining my life," Booker grumbled to himself as he quietly returned to the bedroom and rustled up his work clothes. At this rate he could be up, dressed, and on the road by 5 a.m. He would beat the traffic and, more importantly, have some quiet time in the office before the noise of phones, texts and team chatter built to a nerve-jarring cacophony.

Not quite right. His mother, Audrey, the nuclear core of the family who'd radiated energy into everything she did, who'd worked two bone-wearying jobs to pay for his and his brother's education, was not quite right. His eldest daughter Charlotte was not quite right. This last time when Charlotte had come home—from God only knows where—it had not been to dry out. She was quieter this time. No screaming. No kicking doors. She seemed sickly some days. She slept a lot. And Charlotte kept rearranging her room. Poor baby! Her behavior was definitely not quite right.

Booker's battered Jeep Patriot, parked out the front of his apartment block, was sprinkled in dew. Thankfully, he didn't have to chip ice off the windshield. He climbed into the Jeep with a spring in his step that surprised Booker himself. *It's amazing what the miraculous waters of a hot shower can do for an old, aching carcass*, thought Booker, adding out loud "Jesus loves me today," as he fired up the Jeep's engine.

Manny Garcia, Old Manny, on the front night desk at the office, welcomed Booker into the office at 5:30 a.m. as if he were making first contact with the only other survivor of a recent apocalypse. Old Manny wanted to talk. He really wanted to talk. He trailed behind Booker to the elevator door, talking. He pressed the up button for Booker, talking. He stepped into the elevator, talking. He walked Booker to the Incident Room on the 23rd floor, talking. The last thing Booker wanted was another voice rattling around inside his head. He had to give old Manny a task to send him on his way.

"Manny," sang Booker, "I need someone to do some intel on the illegal sale of AK-47s. Go into chat rooms, websites, gun range websites, gun magazines and get the feel for how it is done."

"Yes, Mr. Booker. I'll do that right away, Mr. Booker. I got three-and-a-half hours left on my shift. Should be able to turn up something."

"Good man," replied Booker. "At the end of your shift let me know what you've dug up."

Booker sat at the now cluttered conference table. tapping his pen on the tabletop and looking at the five whiteboards displaying almost duplicate images of each murder victim. There was so much intel involving maps, guns and crime scenes, the victims no longer scored their own whiteboard. Common intel flowed across the five whiteboards.

"Something is not quite right," he murmured to himself, shaking his head. "Where's the nitty-gritty small-detail evidence?" he wondered. "So far we have zilch. No shell casings. No witnesses. No CCTV. No DNA as yet. No useful specks of pollen, grains of dirt, threads of cloth, strands of hair, footprints, tire treads. Who are these shooters? Hairless ninjas?"

"Hold on," Booker gasped out loud. He quickly clicked open files on a nearby computer desktop. "Numbers do mean something," he muttered to himself. *Where are those AK-47 serial numbers? How many do we have? Five. First one. Serial Number S-F-3-6-3-6-7-5-1-4-9-5-N. 2nd one. Nope. 3rd. Yes! Same serial number. 4th. Yes! Again. 5th. Nope. So what we have here are illegally manufactured clone guns or parts. This means we're talking gunrunners and, maybe, a gun cartel or two.* "This is big," he announced to the empty Incident Room.

"And," continued Booker in thinking mode, "how do the shooters get their victims to the crime scene? Do they stalk them? Do they set them up? Or do they treat each shooting as some sort of game? Are the shooters hunting the victims?" Booker shuddered. It was an eerie thought, but he had to consider every possibility. After 50 minutes ruminating on the riddle of these strange murders, Booker had no new insights, no more case-cracking epiphanies to bring to the table.

The only breakthrough so far was identifying clone guns. Booker sighed. He went to his office to spend the next two hours shuffling through some necessary paperwork.

At 8:30 a.m. Volkman put his head in the door, saying, "Boss, you have to see this breaking news." Volkman and Booker walked the short distance down the hall to the Incident Room and stood watching the CNN News streaming on Volkman's laptop.

The cameras were turned onto Angel Lorca de la Vega, 26, the fiercest anti-gun lobbyist in the country. He was the president of PAAW, People Against Assault Weapons. His group set up offices in Dallas, Texas, because the illegal trade in assault weapons ran through Texas. Vega was speaking to the camera.

"Texas is not top of the list for gun fatalities. You export gun deaths by selling guns. Illegally. And we are here to stop illegal gun sales," roared De La Vega, another master of the media sound bite. PAAW's power lay in lobbying the racial groups who were mostly against guns. Blacks. Hispanics. Asians. And as he told more than one Republican standing for office, "These guys can vote. And we will make sure they turn up to vote."

Needless to say, Vega was the most hated man in Texas. "That fucking nigger-loving prick needs his brain's blown out!" was a typical chat room comment. De La Vega, with the fine-boned face, neat beard and ponytail, could have been a Spanish prince in a previous life. He was dressed simply in a white shirt and jeans, yet displayed all the fiery passion of the warrior duke who'd led the Spanish Armada. On this occasion, however, De La Vega was holding his head in frustration and disbelief.

As far as Booker and Volkman could work out from the TV footage, the Dallas office of PAAW had been raided by a number of different Dallas-based law enforcement agencies, who were removing file boxes and computers. De La Vega railed at the camera.

"This is a total infringement of our constitutional rights, of our human rights. We have nothing, I repeat, NOTHING to do with these tragic murders. We are an anti-gun organization, for God's sake. We DO NOT believe in guns. We do not own guns. We do not *use* guns."

De La Vega threw his hands in the air in disgust and walked away from the camera.

"Who are these cowboys?" inquired Booker. "They are screwing up our investigations. PAAW is not in our sights. These Dallas police bozos are not running the case; I am, and I want their balls on a plate."

"There's more," warned Volkman. "Give me a minute and I'll see if I can find a newsfeed. Got it."

This time officers had raided the headquarters of AFF, Animal Freedom Fighters, in Norfolk, Virginia. AFF was a different can of worms altogether. They broke into laboratories to free laboratory test animals. They were responsible, many believed, for the death of a farmer who ran a horrifically cruel caged-chicken egg farm, though no charges were ever laid. The AFF advocated the protection of animals, using violence if necessary. Their philosophy was, in a nutshell, let the animals live, humans be damned. AFF members wore t-shirts branded: MEAT IS MURDER, or SKIN HER WHO WEARS A FUR, or:

Countless creatures kept to die.
Electric shock. No reason why.
Tortured. Caged. Some sick quirk
'Cause your face cream doesn't work.

The AFF logo was a black-clad ninja glaring at the world through an oblong slot in a ski mask, holding up a clenched fist and cradling a baby fox. "There it was again," observed Booker, "the word ninja. Is that a key to this case or a red herring?"

The reaction of the AFF to these murders was curious. They didn't want to be associated with the killings, but they didn't sound as if they wanted them to stop, either. The AFF was rooting for the shooters. Their spokesperson faced the cameras, if faced is the right term, wearing a black balaclava.

"We at AFF do not condone these murders. The Freedom Fighters of the AFF have not been involved in these murders in any way. But it is interesting for us to watch humans facing what animals face every day—a cruel and painful death. That's all I have to say."

The AFF would be a real contender for these killings except for the fact that the AK-47 was not used to shoot animals, or, to be precise, not often. Sometimes they are used to get rid of feral dogs or wild hogs wrecking the ecosystem somewhere. Then again, there is always some idiot out there willing to provide evidence that evolution was moving backward, such as those drunken hunters in Tennessee who were trying to shoot wild hogs with assault rifles but ended up falling backwards in the pickup truck tray, shooting up the cabin and being hit by rounds that ricocheted off the roll bar.

Perez arrived clutching a bucket-sized coffee cup. She was followed a few minutes later by Mary Skule, who headed to the electric urn at the back of the room to brew a cup of tea. She seemed to have quaint, old-fashioned ways for a top criminal profiler. Booker imagined she wore fifties-style white bloomers. Then he crushed that thought. *Be professional*, he reprimanded himself. Cogliano and Godbold were the last agents in the door.

Booker addressed the team. "We have just become part of a Reality TV show called Watch the FBI Screw Up This One. Everyone will jump on us hard with every move we make. Politicians. Mayors. Lobby groups. Academics. Victims' families. No stone will be left unturned; every one of them will be picked up and thrown at us. I've discovered one small piece of the jigsaw. Three of the guns are cartel clones. They share the same serial number. Two of the assault rifles were bought legally, then sold hand-to-hand illegally. Immediate questions: How did they lure the victims to the remote sites? How did they kill them? How did they leave so little evidence behind? Now, what else have we got on the murders?" demanded Booker.

"We've got the ballistics back. That was easy. All the victims were shot with a four-round burst from the AK-47 left in their body. No prints. No DNA. The victims were lying down when shot so all the round fragments were recovered from the soil under the body," explained Godbold. "Do we assume the shooter owned the gun, or was the victim shot with his own gun?"

"Intel suggests the first victim, Brodski, didn't own an AK-47. His autopsy results are back. Alcohol. No drugs. But *why*," said Booker, "would a victim lie down to be shot? Did the shooter/ shooters order the victim to lie down? And if so, why would they comply?"

Mary Skule interjected. "I think the victims owned the guns. Why would you turn up to a remote location to buy a gun? You would have to feel vulnerable. But if you were selling an assault rifle, man, I'm armed, no one can touch me."

"Makes sense," commented Booker.

"But why turn up at a remote location to sell the thing?" asked Cogliano. "And how did they end up being shot by their own gun?"

"Cash is the motivator," suggested Volkman. "The seller gets an over the market price offer for a cash sale. Sounds good. Worth a trip to some remote location."

"That works," said Skule.

There was a flurry of footsteps into the Incident Room.

"Mr. Booker, Mr. Booker!" cried Old Manny, shuffling into the room. "I think I've found something. Anyway, it might help. I went through all those gun chat rooms like you said, and the talk is that when you buy an illegal AK-47 you can't go to the local firing range because they want the guns on their premises to be all kosher like, registered and all that. When you buy a gun on the side you have to wonder, like, is this illegal AK the full package? So the seller volunteers to give you a demonstration out along some deserted back road somewhere. So we're talking AK-47 demonstrations, like, in the middle of nowhere."

"Thanks, Manny," said Booker, "you have just found one very important piece of the puzzle. The victims—keep open minds just the same—may have been selling illegal guns, but they had to meet the buyer in some remote spot. They're not worried. They're armed with an AK-47. Thanks, Manny. If I have some more research along those lines, you're the man."

Old Manny nodded and left. His shift was done. He was heading home. But he sure did appreciate the praise. The night shift got so little of it.

"I like this," said Cogliano, "it fits the MO. Pose as buyer. Lure victim. When the gun's in your hands, shoot him. Leave the rifle."

"But why would they lie down?" insisted Booker again.

Cogliano looked puzzled. He went to speak, but shook his head.

Booker's phone buzzed. He had it on silent. This one he couldn't ignore. It was Phillis.

"I'll just take this," he said. "Have a look at timing next, would you?"

Booker walked over to the conference room window.

"Hello, babe, how did the appointment go?" he asked. Phillis had talked Charlotte into seeing a doctor at the local Community Healthcare Network in Washington Heights, taking Charlotte by taxi to the clinic to make sure she went to the appointment. Phillis also thought some mother-daughter bonding over lunch might nudge family harmony in the right direction.

"Get ready for this," Phillis announced very matter-of-factly, "she's pregnant. She is nearly full term, but there is a hitch. She will not, she totally refuses, to accept she is pregnant."

"Mmm," replied Booker, not wanting to sound alarmed.

"She just said 'No way' to the doctor and stormed out. I cannot believe I didn't notice. But she has been wearing bulky, loose-fitting sweaters of late. The doctor came out of the surgery and asked to have a few quiet words with me."

"Mmm," repeated Booker.

"He said that privacy issues were a problem, except in the case of mental illness when harm could come to the patient and/or the baby. I have to tell you, Quince, I nearly fainted right there in the surgery."

"Mmm."

"He says she needs a therapist. She has to accept that she is pregnant before she goes into labor. How we are going to do that? I drove her home. She's upstairs having a nap now."

"Thanks, babe. I'll ask around. Some of the psychologists here might have a few ideas and give us some advice."

"That'd be a start. We need some serious help here. Thanks. Love you."

"Lovin' ya back."

Booker ended the call and returned to the front of the Incident Room.

"What was the timeline for the 6 shootings? Cogliano?"

"It looks like 24 hours. We want confirmation on two of them, but the timing appears synchronized," replied Cogliano.

"Okay, listen up, folks. We know there's more than one shooter. They're organized. Synchronized! I'm going to send each of you out to a different crime scene. Godbold, you go to Wyoming. Cogliano, you go to South Carolina. Volkman, can you do New Mexico? Skule, I think as a profiler you should see the lay of the land. Ae you up for Missouri? Perez, I want you to stay back with me in the office, and we'll start working through the piles of data. It's 9.55 a.m. I want all of you at the crime scenes before nightfall. Then back ASAP. Take a redeye flight overnight if you have to. Back here, say, mid-afternoon tomorrow."

The front desk rang. "There are a number of TV crews massing outside the office, Mr. Booker. What do you want me to do with them?"

"Damn. Damn. I thought I'd get a few more hours' peace before the vultures landed," complained Booker. "Tell them I'll come down to give them a statement at 1 p.m. They can live with that."

Booker spent what little time he had before the press conference giving final instructions to his team. Then he turned his attention to blasting through the belligerent defiance of the Texas Police Agencies—all of them—until they, between gritted teeth, admitted that these cross-state-line murders were an FBI case, and that all deployments of police resources must be determined by the FBI team responsible for this investigation.

Or, to put it more bluntly—this was Texas after all—"If you screw up this investigation by going off half-assed and doing some rogue cowboy investigation without going through proper channels, I will come down there to Dallas and personally shove an AK-47 up your ass." And that was to the Dallas Chief of Police. This was another fine example of cooperation between law enforcement agencies.

Perez gave Booker her reproachful school marm look.

"I know, I know, threatening to shove a firearm up the rear end of a fellow officer is not a part of Leadership Training 101, but sometimes ya gotta hit 'em on the head with a 2x4 plank to get the message through," explained Booker. He didn't bother explaining that the message was, in fact, "I'm the man with the hairy balls. Don't fuck with me." He decided to leave his passive-aggressive instructions to the police agencies in Virginia for later that afternoon.

Booker had one more item on his agenda that he needed to tick off before he faced the cameras. He called Mary Skule into his office down the hall and explained the extraordinary situation with his daughter Charlotte.

"How old is she?" asked Skule.

"22."

"And she won't admit she's pregnant. Not at all."

"That's right," confirmed Booker.

"I have heard of such cases, especially in relation to date rape drugs. Without actually talking to your daughter, I can't give you specific advice. It sounds like Post Traumatic Amnesia. The condition is common after head injuries in car accidents or barroom brawls. Sometimes rape victims and drug users cannot remember a traumatic event. I know that if a girl will not or cannot admit she is pregnant despite the, um, growing evidence, families are advised to stop telling the girl she is pregnant. It won't help. The best approach, as I understand it, is for the family to start getting all enthusiastic about babies. Buy fluffy toys. A cot. Some little clothes. Do you have other daughters?"

"My eldest, Nikki, is 25. She just got married."

"Perfect. Just pretend that you hope Nikki might get pregnant one day. And you are getting ready for that day. But you better explain this strategy to your eldest daughter, or she really will think you're seriously off the planet."

"That helps a lot," replied Booker. "At least that's something we can do."

He rang Phillis and told her; straight away she was onto it.

"Don't worry, Quince. I do actually like babies. Love you."

Booker hung up the phone. Took a deep breath and headed down in the lift to face the cameras. Where had the time gone? The clock in the FBI lobby showed 13.00 hours.

The tsunami was in full swirling, churning, disorienting motion.

Chapter 12

Kee

Saturday, the 16th of September

Kee parked the Silver Beast in the vacant lot in Bailey Ave and headed toward the office, moaning zombie-style, "Caffeine. Got to get caffeine. Get caffeine or kill. Must kill. Eat human flesh." Strong words for a vegetarian, part-time vegan. She walked briskly past the *Gazette*'s office with her right-hand raised shielding her face. "Beware of Mr. Bossy," she muttered. "If he sees me avoiding the office, he might run out and Taser me." She shook her head.

"You are going crazy. Soon you will start to believe the CIA is listening to your thoughts through the overhead satellites. Hello. Testing 1,2,3 .... CIA are you listening? Maybe they can even control my mind. Yeah! Just try it, Mr, my crazy thoughts will easily break YOUR super surveillance system. Ha! HA! (*Evil laugh*)."

Kee arrived at the nearest café , called (*OMG! This is weird!*) Tazza, walked in the door so desperate for caffeine that she gasped, then pointed wordlessly to the most massive coffee cup on display and then her mouth.

"Got it, Kee. Grande Latte. Extra quick," snapped Jerome the barista. "Hey, the news about the Anti-Gun Brigade is pretty awesome. Like, some anti-gun dudes are gunning down pro-gun dudes."

Kee took a breath. "Yeah. It is amazing."

"And you saw the corpse. Like, yeah!" enthused Jerome.

"Yeah."

"Was it really gruesome? Like, you know, in the movies ... blood splattered everywhere and stuff?" persisted Jerome.

"Ahhhh," Kee groped for reporter-words through her caffeine-deprived fog, "it's not like in the movies ... it's more like, um, in a hospital when they're operating on a real person pulling out guts and that."

"Cool!" replied Jerome, handing over the latte.

Kee noticed that the handful of early morning customers sitting inside the café , or even outside braving the extra-crisp Autumn air, were reading the *Gazette*, not *The New York Times* or *The Washington Post*, but the little old *Gazette*. "We've hit the big time," murmured Kee.

As she stepped out the front door with the jarring ding-linging of the tiny brass doorbell echoing in her ear, she was collared by an old guy in a flat cap and plain brown Lands End coat out walking his Shih Tzu.

"Miss Le, I have read your article this morning about this terrible, terrible business. Young men being killed like this. Do you think it might be an Islamic terrorist cell? You know what they're like," he confided.

Kee's brain refused to provide a response. She stood there, clutching her latte.

"Or, it could be, I was thinking, North Korea. They want to take our God-given freedom."

"I'll let the CIA know," Kee replied, inching around the old guy and stepping over his dog. "I'm sure they want to keep all options on the table at this time."

"Yes! Yes! Quite right!" agreed the old guy to Kee's back.

That CIA plan to control minds seems to be working, she mused. "We're off to see the Wizard, the wonderful wizard of Oz!" sang Kee to herself. "I'm Kitchi Le, the world famous reporter from *The New England Gazette*. Byline. Byline photo. And now I have a fan!"

Hollis was sitting at her desk hammering on her keyboard when Kee rocked in the door. She noticed a stack of *Gazettes* on the front counter. She had to pick one up and admire the glorious front page of the Saturday 16th September Special Edition with the headline screaming its news to the world in bold font: BAN THIS WEAPON above a full-page picture of an AK-47 sporting a small stars and stripes flag. The smaller header under the photo, with Kee's name in the byline, read: IS THE NGSA BEING TARGETED BY THE AGB ANTI GUN BRIGADE?

"They're selling like hotcakes!" proclaimed Hollis. "I'm trying to drum up some advertising for tomorrow's bumper edition. Getting there. We've got Ed's Everglide Garage Doors and Milane's Native Plant Nursery on board. Maybe I should try some gun shops. A few random executions in the news must be good for business." The advent of random executions had also rebooted Hollis's outlook on life. Her gloomy cynicism had somehow lifted. Her face was as vibrant as the primary color chaos of her clothes.

"Hollis! I like your attitude, girl. Our plan to take over the world seems to be working. You can be Catgirl, and I'll be Viper."

"Not too sure that Catgirl suit thing would work for me," remarked Hollis, "not unless it comes in jumbo kitty size and candy pink with blue spots."

Kee laughed as she pulled her laptop out of her battered brown leather shoulder bag *cum* personal junk storage facility, slid her laptop onto her desk, took her cell out and began checking her Twitter feed. 65,034 followers.

Graeme Bradstreet strode in the door, clapping his hands.

"Come on, people. Have we got news copy happening? Do we have advertising copy ready? I've been out delivering bundles of papers around the district from 5-God-help-us-A.M. this morning to keep those bumper sales up. Our distributors are complaining about this extra print run. But they can shut the hell up because we're paying them. So what's happening at the main office of this great news emporium today?"

Bradstreet was joking. There were only two overworked journalists in the office multi-tasking everything from answering phones to checking ad copy to breaking national news to running out and buying more ink for the printers. Chivonn's mom couldn't do the babysitting at such short notice, as she'd had a quiet and complete mental meltdown after doing a day with three under 3s, and Aron was driving in ever decreasing circles around the district delivering *Gazette* bundles in his heavy-duty grunt Ford F-Series truck. That truck vacuumed up all his money, plus some. Aron's mom and dad had the good fortune of having one growing son and one hungry F-series pickup to feed. Lucky them!

"Got you some good ads for tomorrow, Boss," sang Hollis. "If they don't get their new copy in by 6 I'll cut and paste their old copy."

"Good work," noted Bradstreet. This was effusive praise from the generally disgruntled Mr. Bossy.

"We're totally onto it, Boss. You go off and be a delivery boy. It's all in good hands here," insisted Kee. Bradstreet clapped his hands again, saying "Right! 'Into the jaws of death rode the Six Hundred!'" and, without further ceremony, left the office.

"Ooo-eee!" Kee called out to Hollis. "That was weird, being visited by Happy Clappy Man. I officially call this day WSD 2. Weird Shit Day 2."

"My goodness, Miss Le. I do believe your observations on the strangeness of these past two days is 100% correct. WSD 2 it is."

Hollis returned to her ad-hustling on the phone, and Kee set about getting her blog, Facebook and *Gazette* website up to speed under the "LOONY LEFTIES" and "NGSA CHIEF SAYS" headlines.

She had scooped the media scrum once more, because she had all her copy sorted and posted by 8.45 a.m. Later that morning, at 9.00 a.m. precisely, Gig DeKant stood in front of the NGSA headquarters in Fairfax, Virginia, beside the flagpole with the American flag set at half-mast, and solemnly read out his Brothers-in-Arms speech word for word.

Kee typed a private Tweet to @PoliceBizz asking if he had heard of any more stiffs popping up in unexpected places. Just as she hit Send, all hell broke loose at the *Gazette* front counter. This particular hell—as Kee explained later—had a lot to do with a woman brutally scorned. And she was on the path of righteous vengeance.

A ferret-faced woman in a light blue faux-fur-trimmed puffy coat, who appeared to have been slapped around by life a few times, stormed in, yelling accusations, sobbing, wiping her nose and banging on the front counter bell for attention. She was in her thirties with two ferret-faced kids in tow, a grimy-faced 7-year-old boy and an even more grimy-faced 8-year-old girl.

"That fucking asshole! That shithead got what he deserved! That asshole!" she shouted, pounding her hand on the front counter bell.

"Stop sniveling, Sheree," she ordered the girl. The woman really didn't have to ring that bell. Her presence didn't go unnoticed.

"May I help you?" Hollis purred, gliding over to the front counter.

"Now that the asshole is dead, I want the world to know what a complete shithead he was. Shooting people like him is only doing us all one big fucking favor."

"To whom are you referring?" Hollis asked, smiling at the sniveling little Sheree, who was wiping snot off her runny nose onto her sleeve.

"That shithead Hayden Brodski!" the woman screamed at Hollis.

Kee's eyes lit up. She whisked herself over to the front counter saying, "Don't we have some lollipops for the lovely little children?" while flicking her eyes sideways in a get-them-outa-the-road signal to Hollis.

"Lordy, Lordy, I do believe we have some candy here!" Hollis plucked two sweets out of a Dog Rescue Charity Fundraiser box on the front counter and handed one to each child, while Kee sidled over to the woman.

"Come in and sit down, Miss ... ?"

"Shaw. Sydnee Shaw."

"My name is Kitchi Le. Would you like a cup of coffee, Miss Shaw?" Kee asked.

"Y-yeah," sniffed Sydnee, cooling down a little, "that'd be nice."

Kee rustled up instant coffee in a dirty staff coffee mug. *Once it's full of coffee, she can't see the Keep Calm and Take Prozac mug is cracked and caked with 10 years of coffee stains on the inside*, Kee thought, as she returned to her desk and the outraged woman. The story was horrific. Sydnee Shaw explained between sniffs, cusses and sobs that 3 weeks ago she had hooked up with Hayden Brodski on Tinder.

"I was," Sydnee sniveled between sips of coffee from the Prozac mug, "just looking for some company like. You know. A drink. A bit of a laugh. With these kids you'd go screaming-your-head-off crazy if you didn't get out sometimes. Their lazy good-for-nothing shit of a father, who gives me nothing but grief, had them for the weekend. I don't like it, but he's gone all legal on me.

"So I meet this guy at this bar, near Ridgefield but way outa town. For one drink," she explained. "I wasn't going to do anything more until I'd checked him out. 'Hi. My name is Hayden,' he says, real polite like. There are these tattooed dudes at the bar that know him. One then another come up and crap on about guy stuff. You know, pickup trucks, engine grunt, stuff like that. It's all, you know, sort of, normal, like. Then he says he lives in a trailer nearby, and he had a special 20-year-old bourbon, so we should go there for another drink. He was being all sweet and romantic, so I say 'Alright.' And one thing leads to another. We're on the bed, still dressed, mind; then he's on top of me, straddling me, pulling his leather belt with the colt revolver buckle out of his jeans. I didn't like it one bit. I say, 'I'm not up for this.' Next thing he pulls out a gun. Holds it under my chin and says, 'You'll do what I fucking tell you to do, bitch.' He was half-choking me for … it seemed like hours. I end up with bruises around my throat and a black eye. And then that shithead flips me over and rapes me' (she leaned in and whispered) 'in the ass. I got out of that van as fast as I could. And I swore I'd never go anywhere near this shit hole of a town ever again. Then I saw his face on the news this morning. I knew it was him."

"Did you go to the police?" asked Kee.

"I've had enough custody problems with my kids to go off making my life more of a shitty hellhole than it is already."

"What would you like me to do with this information?" Kee asked. "You don't want your name in the paper, I'd imagine."

"Fuck no!" she retorted.

"So what would you like to happen?"

"Um … just tell everyone he was an asshole, will ya? That would sorta make me feel a bit better about it," explained Sydnee.

"Miss Shaw, I will absolutely make sure that your story is heard. If he has raped you there will be others. So thank you for coming in, and get yourself a copy of the *Gazette* tomorrow. One more thing, while you're here. You saw inside his trailer. Did he own any assault rifles? Like this one?"

Kee pulled up a picture of an AK-47 on her computer screen.

"Yeah! Like. Yeah! He had one-a those. I saw it inside the closet. The door was open, like. That's what scared me shitless.

This, like, total maniac with all those fucking guns ... and his itchy finger on the trigger."

Hollis ushered the children to the front of the office, gave them the last two candies from the charity box, and fell backward against the glass window of the door as soon as Sydnee and her mini-gang left.

"I was playing I-spy with those kids. I say, 'I spy with my little eye something beginning with P.' I'm thinking paper, but the boy shouts, 'I wanna pee!' and the girl yells, 'I don't wanna pee!' Mercy! Mercy! It was a setup. I had to get Pee Boy into the staff toilet without taking my eyes off Kleptomaniac Girl. She was eyeing off my cell. Pee Boy comes out, his coat padded out with toilet rolls. I thought we could sacrifice them for the cause, but I sooooo wanted to pat Kleptomaniac Girl down before she left. Arrrgh!" huffed Hollis.

"That's just normal for this weirded-out workday. But do you realize we have something solid on Brodski? I didn't think he was a sleazer, you know, one of those creepy guys that run their eyeballs all over you and undresses you while they're talking to you. Errrck! But he was. A total creep/asshole, and I'm going after him."

"'Book him, Danno,'" said Hollis.

"What?" asked Kee, perplexed.

"Don't worry. It's what they call a 'cultural reference' these days. It's from a seventies TV show called *Hawaii Five-O*. Doesn't matter," explained Hollis.

"No, no, I remember it. They remade the series in 2010-something," replied Kee.

"What's wrong with the world? Don't people get original ideas anymore? Sheesh!" lamented Hollis.

Kee was onto the case. First, she sent a Tweet to @PoliceBizz

"Confirmed. Brodski an asshole/creep. A woman says he raped her with GUN at her head!!!" @KeeHasSpoken.

Then she rang Booker.

"Booker here."

"Hello, Mr. FBI. I've got something for you."

"Shoot."

Not another one, thought Kee, amused. *Is it Freudian? You see a bullet hole in a corpse, and you can't stop saying "Shoot".*

"Wait, wait," said Kee, putting her back-scratching theory into practice. "Do you have anything for me?"

"Nothing to report yet," said Booker.

"You mean all those autopsy results, DNA tests, fingerprint analyses and profiling have not turned up a thing?"

"Sweet FA so far. But it's early days. This is not a TV cop show, Miss Le, where the DNA is tested and matched during the ad break for back pain pills," said Booker.

"Sweet FA!" Awesome. I'm on friendly cuss terms with the freaking FBI now, thought Kee.

"What have you got for me?" asked Booker.

"I have confirmation. Brodski was a card-carrying creep/asshole. A woman came into the office explaining how he had raped her while ... wait for it ... holding a handgun to her head!"

"Any more?" queried Booker.

"That's not bad!" grumbled Kee.

"It might be time, Miss Le, to do a creep/asshole search on all the victims."

"OMG! Yes! And there is one more thing. He did own an AK-47. I showed her a photograph, and she confirmed that too."

"Anything else?"

"No," replied Kee.

Booker hung up.

An hour later Kee had another piece for Sunday's bumper edition under the bold banner heading:

AGB GUNNING FOR CREEPS

Across the room Hollis yelped. "That little kleptomaniac stole my can of soda, two cans. Miss Sydnee's little darlin's might be a handful this afternoon," she complained. "They were cans of ready mix Vodka and orange!" Kee laughed so hard she started to snort.

"See what you have done, Miss Hollis. You've turned me into a ... freaking pig!"

Bradstreet returned to the office carrying some pastrami Grinders in a white paper carry bag.

"Lunch, my little wage-slaves. Don't tell me I'm a tight-ass who never buys you any goddamn thing!"

Bradstreet tossed a Grinder at each "slave". Kee grabbed her package, ripped it open and inspected the filling. Freaking hell. Bacon. *It is so hard to be a moral vegetarian when it's raining pig-butt sandwiches*, she mused, extracting with some difficulty rashers covered in stringy cheese-melt from her Grinder.

"Don't waste that be-au-tiful bacon," called Hollis, marching over to Kee's desk. Hollis picked up the bacon with her fingers and dropped it into her mouth, saying, "Mmmm, mm!"

That was the main conversation of the moment. "Mmm! Mmmm!" murmured Kee, adding, "Ish good," as she chomped down the Grinder in 10 seconds flat.

"It's like feeding time at the zoo," observed Hollis.

"Any updates? And where is Shidfa?" asked Bradstreet.

"'Did he ever return? No, he never returned and his fate is still unknown. He may ride forever 'neath the streets of Boston. He's the man who never returned!'" sang Hollis through a mouth full of Grinder. "Mm-Mmm! Another cultural reference, Miss Le. The Kingston Trio. Folk music gods, back in the day."

Aron turned up at the office a few minutes later. It was 1:30 p.m.

"Where the hell have you been?" demanded Bradstreet, "we're working our asses off here."

"You said to deliver the *Gazettes*," said Shidfa. "I delivered them."

"And ...?"

"The man at the last depot where I had to drop off 6 bundles gave me all the addresses. It took forever," sighed Aron.

"You *home delivered* them?" Bradstreet roared.

"Yes, sir."

"You idiot. That's *their* job. I pay them to deliver those papers," the boss grumbled. 'Now sit your butt down and write up all the school football results for today."

"Right, Boss," replied Aron, returning his earbuds to his ears to set his brain beating to his favorite doof-doof electric dance music.

"Oh! Mr. Bossy," said Kee, wiping the side of her mouth, "I forgot to tell you about our creep/asshole update." She did so.

"Beautiful," proclaimed Bradstreet, holding his hands up in the air like an evangelical preacher. "The God of All Fuck-ups just keeps raining down his blessings upon us. Let's get those printing presses rolling!"

None of them realized that breaking news was roaring towards them like an unstoppable tsunami and very soon they'd all be swept along, tossed and turned, and become a part of it.

Chapter 13

Kee

A Terrifying Text

Kee was still hammering copy into her computer when the 6 o'clock deadline clicked over.

"Nearly there!" she shouted at Bradstreet. "Nearly, nearly ... " She was just finishing the piece under the banner heading: WAS SLAIN LOCAL A TOTAL CREEP?

"Done!" she said proudly. "You got it, Mr. Bossy?"

"Ye-rrr! Yes! It's here. But I'm dropping it in on page 3. Front page is still NGSA CHIEF SAYS GUN DOWN LOONY LEFTIES.

"Mr. Bossy, it's 6 o'clock already. I have to go and feed Harold. And I've got to buy some food first."

"We're done here," announced Bradstreet, "you can go. Don't come back. Take the night off. Not that you have ever worked a night in the office."

"Boss, we've declared it Weird Shit Day 2," Hollis called out from the front door as she pulled on her coat.

"That's it. You've nailed that one," agreed Bradstreet. Bradstreet strode over to Aron, tapped him on the shoulder and mimed "Take out your earbuds." Aron was playing Super Mario Bros on his computer.

"You can go home now, son. It's a wrap. Tomorrow's special edition is in the can. But I'll need you and your pickup at sparrow's fart in the morning—that's 5 zero zero a.m. cell phone time to you—for more bundle drops. Just bundle *drops*. Right?"

"Yeah! Yeah! Got it, Boss!" replied Aron, his head turned towards Bradstreet but his eyes still glued to the game.

"Go home," mouthed Bradstreet. Aron tried to do his job, which had been watered down and down until it consisted of sports results for the Tuesday and Thursday editions. Bradstreet had to keep Aron away from house auction results, as he seemed blind to counting zeros and reported houses selling for $14m instead of $1.4m. Real estate agents get mighty fussy about those details, and they are the mainstay of a paper's advertising income. Aron seemed to bounce through life totally oblivious to his shortcomings or his surroundings. This is the province of fools. Bradstreet grabbed the back of Aron's office chair and pulled it away from the desk. Thankfully, Aron took the hint.

"Okay. Bye, Boss. See you tomorrow. Real early like."

Kee was still sorting notes on her desk and shoving them into her shoulder bag when Aron loped out the front door. Bradstreet looked skyward, saying, "Lord, give me strength ... I just want to beat some sense into the pea-sized brain of that moron."

"Boss," she asked Bradstreet, "you're pretty smart. You know about newsroom stuff and that. How is it you hired Aron? He's a nice enough kid, but ...."

"What idiot hired him, you mean?" Bradstreet complained, adding, "That would be ... me! But I was impressed by those few words on his CV. Granddad owns the paper."

Finally, Bradstreet could flick off the office lights and drag his own weary ass home to his wife Zelda and their gloriously peaceful, childfree home. Just the previous week he'd told Kee, "Zelda and I are popping the champagne tonight. The last of our three kids have finally, and please God let it be permanently, left home. He is 33 years old. If they told us when we were carrying that little bundle home from the hospital that we'd have him for the next 33 long years, we might have had second thoughts!"

Kee collected some vitals from Milillo Farms grocery, drove home and danced quickly up the stairs, calling, "Harold! Baby! Mommy's home. I wouldn't let you starve, baby."

OMG! she thought, I *said "mommy". I'm a cat "mommy" now. I'm turning into one of those scary cat ladies who dies alone in her apartment and gets eaten by her 37 cats.*

As soon as the key rattled in the door, Harold appeared out of the gloom, stretching and mewing and reaching his claws up to her sloppy grey sweater. Kee picked Harold up, saying, "Baby, so sorry. My big fat fuzzy baby. Come on, we'll get you din dins."

As soon as Harold was fed, including some bonus spoonfuls of pinkish-grey "real fish" muck out of a foil packet (this was to ease her conscience for being an absent "mommy"), Kee kicked off her shoes and sat on her lumpy charity-shop couch with her feet on the cluttered coffee table scrolling through her Twitter feed.

"Good work. Like the creep angle on shootings. You think this is the motive?" @PoliceBizz

"Not sure. But there are links. NGSA or Assholes. Or both. Like Alice said, 'Curiouser and Curiouser'@KeeHasSpoken

She forced herself to get off her ass and shuffle to the kitchenette at the back of her apartment to rustle up dinner. This was a fairly quick rustle. She simply pulled a frozen Louis's

Low-Fat Vegetarian Cuisine packet out of the supermarket bag, saying, "Yumbo! Scrumbo! Sweet and Spicy Tofu Supreme. Remove wrap. Cook on High for 4 mins. Done. I don't know, Harold. It's a tough choice. Your gourmet "real fish" for discerning cats or my Tofu Supreme."

She was watching the microwave base plate turn when she heard her cell sound. It was a Foghorn blast signaling a text message.

"Hungry. Hungry. I'm so hungry. Alright then, what's new?" she asked her cell as she picked it up to read the text.

The text was written entirely in Upper Case. *What's happening, peeps? You're all shouting in texts these days!* She thought the text might be from Joe Lyman at the Mayor's Office. It wasn't.

"THIS IS THE AGB. WE HAVE A MESSAGE FOR KEE LE. REPLY."

"Great. Now I've got my very own nutter phone stalker." She ignored the text. She was about to put a block on the number when a second text arrived.

"THIS IS THE AGB. WE HAVE AN IMPORTANT MESSAGE FOR THE NGSA."

Kee texted back. "HOW DO I KNOW YOU ARE NOT A NUTTER?" She nearly added a smiley face emoji.

"BECAUSE I HAVE PROOF."

"YEAH? WHAT?"

"I WILL GIVE YOU THE SERIAL NUMBER OF THE AK-47 USED TO SHOOT THE FIRST VICTIM."

She nearly texted, "OK SHOOT." *This subliminal crap,* she thought. *Really, I'm talking gun talk now.*

She settled for "WHAT IS IT?"

"SF3636751495N THIS WILL BE OUR ID FOR FUTURE COMMUNICATIONS."

"WHAT'S THE MSG?"

"WE OF THE AGB—NICE TOUCH, MISS LE. WE RATHER LIKE THAT TAG—WILL DESTROY THE NGSA ONE MEMBER @ A TIME. WE WILL STRIKE AT RANDOM. ANY STATE. ANYWHERE. ANY TIME. THE KILL COUNT WILL REACH 91 MEMBERS OF THE NGSA. OUR CODE NAME FOR THIS MISSION IS TARGET 91. THAT LAST ONE IS FOR GIG DEKANT, CEO OF THE NGSA. HE IS TARGET 91."

Kee texted a brief reply:

"GOT IT. WILL PASS ON MESSAGE."

Kee's knees began to shake. "What if they're for real?" she kept saying to herself over and over. "Really! What if they're for real and they know where I live?" She was hyperventilating with fear-laced, eye-popping excitement. *Whoa! This is some badass news story*, she thought. Louis's Low-Fat Vegetarian Cuisine sat in her microwave going cold and gluggy as she made several urgent phone calls. First off she rang Booker.

"Miss Le?" queried Booker.

"Sorry. Sorry for ringing on a Saturday night. But something weird has just happened."

"What's that?"

"Someone texted me saying they were from the AGB. The Anti-Gun Brigade."

"It'll be some crank. I'm afraid you'll meet a few of them in your time as a crime scene reporter."

"Could be," agreed Kee, "but how did they get my number?"

"You've probably given it to someone on your card, not realizing they were a crank."

"Ergh! I suppose that could happen, but get this. They gave me the serial number of the AK-47 left sticking out of Brodski."

"They *what*? That's a little different. This could be a game changer, Miss Le."

"Do you want the serial number?"

"Shoot," said Booker.

"Do you realize, Mr. FBI, that you are saying 'shoot' all the time? This can't be a good thing in your line of work. And now I'm saying it."

Booker laughed. "Come on. Read out the serial number."

"S-F-3-6-3-6-7-5-1-4-9-5-N"

"Got it. Now you stay right there, Miss Le, I'll just open my computer ... now ... and look up this number in my files ... SF363675149N ...."

"Sweet Jesus, that's it!" shouted Booker.

"Awwww, nooooo!" groaned Kee in a fear-choked voice. "Do they want to shoot me?" She thought she might vomit.

"No. Calm down. This organization is running news through you. They need you. Did they give you a message to pass on?"

"Awwww," she groaned again, "this is really scary ... REALLY ... they said they're going to kill 91 members of the NGSA. Their Code Name for this operation is Target 91."

"Got it," said Booker.

"The 1 is for Gig DeKant. *He* is Target 91"

"Sweet Jesus."

"I'll send you the text messages."

"Do that. Now, Miss Le, I don't think you will be a target yourself, but we cannot take any chances."

"Ah, would I be a target for a bunch of anti-gun crazies with guns? Or would I be target for one of the pro-gun crazies with guns who now think I'm with the anti-gun crazies? Awwwww!" She gave a deep groan. "I don't like this!"

"Now, Miss Le. Kee. First I'll talk to you like a special FBI agent. Then I'll talk to you like a father. I have daughters around your age."

"Okay!"

"First of all, you have to realize that you have now become the news story. Everyone will want to interview you. As soon as this news gets out, you will be hounded by TV, radio, and print media teams day and night. Ridgefield will be swarming with jerks shoving microphones into people's faces. And there is a possibility that some copycat psycho might get ideas in his head. It's been known to happen."

"Awwwwww!" Kee gave a deep, troubled groan. "I don't like this. I think I am going to throw up."

"I will send you one of the best guys on my team, a sharpshooter, to advise and guard you. His name is Denney O'Shea. He'll arrive at your place in an hour or two. He'll ring you first, so you know to let him in."

"You don't know where I live," Kee objected.

"Miss Le. We're the FBI. We can find out what side of the bed you sleep on."

"That sounds like something, I guess."

"Try and take his advice. He's had experience in these sorts of things. He will be advising you to keep away from all news reporters. We want to keep the channels open for the shooters, the AGB."

"Yeah! Do I have to keep away from windows and watch for cars parked outside my apartment and all that stuff?"

"Use your common sense," Booker replied.

"Now I'm telling you as a father that you will be under a lot of stress over the next few days. Stick close to the people you trust. DO NOT, I repeat, DO NOT answer calls from anyone you do not know, except O'Shea. I'll text you his number. I'm telling you this because you will have all sorts of crazies coming out of the woodwork wanting to get in on this circus. Close up all your social media."

"But that's my job," she pleaded.

"It isn't now. Your job is to stop innocent people from being killed. You are to keep away from all media that allows open comments. Twitter. Facebook. Your blog. You can write for the paper's website or the print edition, but give the others a rest."

"I don't know if I can do that. You're asking me to take a vow of silence. That's professional suicide."

"I am, but for your own good."

"Before I pull the plug on the social media I want to post a couple of Tweets and, um, call my boss and give Gig DeKant a heads up. I have to pass on that message."

"And that's it. Do not even look at your social media accounts. You do not want to see how that can explode. Some hacker will get in and post pictures of porn, or beheaded bodies. Or some misogynists will start calling you a nazi feminist bitch and announce they're going to do all sorts of terrible things to you. Keep away from social media. Do you hear me?"

"Yes, sir!" Kee snapped.

"You will thank me, Miss Le. There is a shit storm a-comin' and you will be at the center of it."

"Now you are scaring me again." She winced.

"You can take steps to protect yourself. That's what I am telling you. Take precautions. Get a new email address and send it to me. Quincey—with an E—BookerWashington@fbi.gov. I'll text it to you. And keep me up to date."

"Mr. Booker, I don't want to hang up. I feel safe talking to you."

"You'll be fine. You are our big break in this case. We have to look out for you."

"Soooo, goodbye then."

"Goodbye, Miss Le," said Booker, and hung up. Her fog horn text ID sounded.

Freak. Freak. Freaking hell, Kee thought. *He said goodbye. He never does that.*

Kee rang her boss, who answered his cell with the encouraging words, "What the fuck now?"

After she explained the 91 kill count, all he could say was "What the bejeezus? This is unbelievable ...." He took a breath. "Office. Tomorrow. We're going to milk this until it's dead. Special edition, Monday."

"Or I'm dead," Kee moaned, adding "it's all right for you. You're not in the crosshairs. I might be the target of some loony pro-gun or some loony anti-gun group. I'm getting my own FBI agent, you know. They're sending him now."

"Bring him to the office. The more the merrier in this crazy clusterfuck. If you do get scared out of your mind tonight, get in your car and come over to our place. We've already gotten rid of the extra bed, but there is a couch. You're our star reporter. We can't lose you!"

"What about Harold?"

"Who the hell is Harold?"

"My cat."

"God help us. Yes! Bring Harold too, if you must."

"I think I'll be okay. But if you hear the screech of tires in the night, it'll be me and Harold."

"Take care," said Bradstreet. "Don't worry, we won't let the crazy screw-ups win."

"That's a little tricky if you don't know who the, um, crazy screw-ups are," she responded in Star Reporter mode.

"True. But it sounded triumphantly patriotic, don't you think?"

Her Fog Horn text ID sounded again. Now she had Denney O'Shea's cell number. She put him in her contact list, then she rang Gig DeKant. Being a star reporter on the frontline was a buzz, but she felt a bit buzzed out. She'd had enough sensational news headlines for one day.

AGB SAYS WE WILL KILL 91 IN NGSA. That was hard to beat. Still, she had investigative journo's blood throbbing in her veins. She wanted to be the first one to break the news to the NGSA chief and check out his response. What time was it? 9:15 p.m. She could make the call.

"Hello, Mr. DeKant? This is Kitchi Le."

"I know who you are. What do you want now?" growled DeKant.

I just received a message from the Anti-Gun Brigade. They gave me the serial number of the first AK-47 used in the shootings. And this was confirmed by the FBI. Now I'm delivering a message they asked me to pass on to you."

Please don't say "Shoot," she was thinking. She was worried that she might laugh inappropriately because she could feel herself churning inside. She was verging on hysterical.

"Go on," he said.

"I have to tell you the message is very, um, upsetting."

"I think I can handle it."

She took a deep breath. "The AGB texted me that they intend to keep shooting members of the NGSA. At random. At any time. In any state. Their target is 91 members. They have a Code name for their mission. TARGET 91. I'm very sorry to say this, Mr. DeKant, but they said that last 1 is for you. You are Target 91."

DeKant went ballistic. "Jeee-sus wept!" he screamed three different ways. "Those sickos have gone too far! We will gun them down like prairie buffalo. This is Armageddon. This is the Third World War."

"Can I ask you for a comment?" Kee persisted.

DeKant took a breath and composed himself. He was good. He slipped right back into Media Circus Ring Master role.

"A grave threat has just been leveled at our brotherhood in arms," he solemnly pronounced. "I am calling on all members, honest and true, of the NGSA, who keep this great country of ours safe from the depraved, the godless, the racists, and the Loony Left. We must prepare for war. The power-hungry pinkos, the homosexual degenerates, the mafia drug cartels, the Mexican invaders, the bloodthirsty jihadists, the rapists and the beheaders of the Anti-Gun Brigade have declared themselves. They want to kill us off one by one so that they can take over the running of this country. This is not going to happen. Prepare yourself. Arm yourself. Protect your families. Protect your children. Protect your property. Mark my words. We will track down these twisted perverts and tear their livers out. And we will not rest until every last one of these sick deviants is 6 feet under ground."

"Thank you, Mr. DeKant. I hope you'll be all right."

"Don't worry about me, young lady. They don't intimidate me one little bit. Good night."

Target 91

Of course they don't, thought Kee, *but I bet you are opening up your gun locker and taking out your full arsenal tonight.* She had recorded DeKant's statements and was typing them into her laptop verbatim.

Her last chore was to add two comments to her Twitter account:

"FBI confirms AGB threat. AGB claim 'We will kill 91 members of the NGSA'. More @ *The New England Gazette* website" #Target91 @KeeHasSpoken

"Listen up, peeps! I'm getting my very own FBI minder. Cool! Read more in *The New England Gazette*" #Target91 @KeeHasSpoken

Kee posted two brief articles on her *Inside Out New England* blog. The first heading was:

AGB THREATEN TO KILL 91 MEMBERS OF NGSA

The second heading read:

WE WILL TEAR OUT THEIR LIVERS SAYS NGSA CHIEF

Finally, she sent a private Tweet to PoliceBizz.

"Big, big happenings here. May have to go off the radar soon. AGB plan to kill 91 in NGSA. I get my own FBI agent. Cool." @KeeHasSpoken

"You've hit the big time. Still want intel?" @PoliceBizz

"Yeah! But I may not be able to reply." @KeeHasSpoken

It wasn't until well past midnight when Kee finally got to eat her Louis's Low-Fat Vegetarian Cuisine meal, cold and straight out of the plastic tray. "It tastes like Sweet and Spicy hair gel," she complained to her cat. Then she threw off her clothes, pulled on a grey hoody and lay on her bed with her heart thudding in her chest and her brain too clogged with traffic to let her think. She fell asleep with Harold sitting, more or less, on her head.

Then her foghorn text ID sounded. It was so loud in the dead of night she briefly imagined that a container ship was about to crash through her bedroom wall.

Chapter 14

O'Shea

Saturday, the 16th of September

O'Shea was at the FBI rifle range at Fort Dix, New Jersey, when Booker called at 8:30 p.m. It was Saturday, so he'd left the office early and ridden his Yamaha YZF 1000 motorbike to the range to get in some shooting practice. All agents had to keep their pistol accreditation up to date, but O'Shea had moved his certification up several notches. He'd completed anti-terrorism training. His anti-terrorist certification meant he could back up an FBI SWAT team in a house/shop/factory bust; he had done so on more than one occasion.

This was a speed drill requiring the simultaneous use of a standard FBI issue handgun, such as a Smith and Wesson .40—he preferred the slim line Glock 26—and a 9mm Heckler & Koch semi-automatic carbine. The shooter had to holster the pistol and shoulder the rifle, rapidly changing from one weapon to the other in a fixed and moving target scenario. Certification depended on a point score combining timing with accuracy. As always, O'Shea ran into trouble with the standard issue weapons. He was a southpaw; he had to have a left-handed rifle. The hot, spent brass from the fired cartridge of self-loading rifles needs to exit away from the shooter's face. Obviously. A southpaw can be hit in the eye with a rapidly exiting shell ejected from some right-handed rifles. The US Armed Forces solved the problem by adding a small metal deflector behind the ejection port of the M-16, which can be set to deflect shells in either direction. They couldn't have a soldier picking up a discarded weapon in battle and taking out his own eye.

Non-military sniper rifles, however, are a different matter. Some, such as the Stag 3TL-M, O'Shea's preferred sniper rifle, can be reassembled with a mirror image exit port. It should be noted that the Ancient Romans believed there was something innately sinister about left-handers. *Sinister manus* in Latin means the left hand. The Stag 3TL-M looked positively sinister on every level but very useful. O'Shea could disassemble it for easy carriage.

O'Shea was the only shooter at the pistol range when he felt his phone vibrate in his pocket. He looked at the caller ID. It was Booker. He pulled off his gun range earmuffs and answered the call.

"Yes, Chief. What's up?"

Booker told O'Shea about the text sent to Kee.

"These deadshits in the AGB are certainly ramping up the pressure on DeKant. So what's the plan, Chief?"

Booker explained that he was sending O'Shea to shadow and protect Miss Le, that O'Shea should text her on arrival and enter via the back stairs, that he would text through her address and phone number after the call.

"How long will it take you to get to her place in Ridgefield?" Booker asked.

"Christ, Chief. Let me see. I've got my kit with me, so maybe 2 hours-plus."

"I'll let Miss Le know," announced Booker. He ended the call.

O'Shea was Booker's secret weapon. With no strings and no commitments, O'Shea was Booker's one-man SWAT team that he could drop into the field on short notice. This suited Booker. It suited O'Shea too. He was sick of working undercover. The real danger of that job, apart from getting a bullet in the back of your head in some desolate, trashed and graffitied lot under a busy city freeway, was becoming one of them. An agent working undercover had to con the con men, rip off the rip off merchants, out-talk the big noters, out-heavy the two-bit thugs and brainless enforcers, and generally out-asshole the assholes. But the current job had its costs. The Organized Crime Unit mostly worked crime scenes after the fact. O'Shea missed the hot-wired action of busting crims in situ. So he was happy to take up any instant assignment Booker threw his way. It kept his armed operative skills in play and his adrenaline pumping. O'Shea knew exactly what price he'd paid for his covert ops. He'd held his emotions in lockdown for so long working undercover, sometimes he felt no emotions at all. Like the actor who has played the same role 1,000 times, he could put on the mask and act out the part, but he felt nothing. He had his favorite roles. Cool, menacing, tough guy was his undercover persona. Funny guy was his default schtick. He could slip into these roles in an instant, but still, most days he felt nothing. Adrenaline had become his drug of choice. He was Dr. Frankenstein's monster, and adrenaline was the bolt of electricity jolting him to life.

O'Shea arrived outside his destination at 11 p.m. He sat in a side street for a good hour assessing movement in the area.

None. He opened the side gate, cased the area behind the Pampered Pooch Snip 'n Clip, then pushed his bike into the yard. O'Shea did not understand the whole dog coiffure thing, especially tying little pink bows in fluffy dogs' hair. It made about as much sense to him as putting makeup on a rat. Why did people do it?

He stood outside his assignment's apartment door in his black biker-leathers with his helmet and emergency evacuation kit at his feet, texting the message:

"I'M OUTSIDE."

He could hear a foghorn text tone sound through the door. Nothing happened. He resent the message. He heard the foghorn text tone again. Nothing. He waited. A light came on in the apartment.

"OUTSIDE WHAT?" Came the text reply.

"YOUR DOOR" replied O'Shea.

O'Shea could hear slight footfalls approaching the door.

"ARE YOU SURE?"

"OPEN THE DOOR. THEY CAN HEAR YOUR FOG HORN TEXT ID IN BOSTON."

The main light flicked on, the door edged open to reveal a young woman, late twenties, early thirties, with puffy eyes and bedraggled hair hanging around her face, holding a cat. O'Shea thought he was a hotshot at nailing women's ages, but she was baffling. She could pass as a 15-year-old in the right outfit, but apart from the fact she was old enough to be a journalist, the look on her face was as confrontational as war paint.

"Oh! Great!" grumbled catgirl, "I've got crazies after me, and they send Mid-Life-Crisis Guy to protect me."

Denney grinned. He wasn't about to be pussy-whipped in the first two seconds of meeting his charge. *She has some serious issues with men*, he thought.

"May I come in?" asked O'Shea. "You may have to help me, seeing as I'm limping through a tragic mid-life crisis."

"Yeah! Funny guy too. Come in," she grumbled.

O'Shea walked in the door, unzipping his leather jacket. He couldn't find anywhere to throw it. The place was a disaster. It was way beyond "sooo sorry about the mess." This apartment could feature in a reality TV show titled *You're Trapped Inside a Dumpster and You'reGonna Die*. This was a nightmare scenario for an operative. The shooting range did not have clothes, sneakers, empty takeout boxes and magazines dumped all over the floor. Under fire, an operative moving quickly to a defensive position on the wall next to the window say, might slip and accidentally discharge a round into the individual he was meant to be protecting. Or his own foot. O'Shea scanned the room in disgust, but his face remained blank. He was operating in his undercover mode. Alert. Observant. Expressionless.

"Can I put my jacket somewhere?" he asked.

Catgirl kicked some random dirty clothes under the couch and scooped mounds of other dirty laundry off the floor and dumped them on her bed.

"You forgot these," grinned O'Shea, holding up a pair of black lacy bikini panties. "Used lady's panties. I could sell them online for a fortune, you know. There are some weird fetish creeps out there."

Catgirl looked scornfully at O'Shea.

"Keep them," she scoffed. "I wouldn't want to deprive you and your weird little fetish friends."

And fuck you too, thought O'Shea, *you humorless bitch.*

"You can put your stuff on the couch," ordered catgirl matter-of-factly. "And, um ...."

She raced to her kitchenette, grabbed an empty cardboard box and swept all the coffee table debris into it: takeout food packets, dirty coffee mugs, plates, cutlery, the lot.

"I wasn't expecting company," she huffed.

"That's a good thing. Someone might catch typhoid in here," he retorted, blank-faced.

Catgirl was not amused. "So the FBI runs housekeeping inspections now, do they?" she grumbled, as she bent over to sort the clutter of shoes by the coffee table.

Full of lip, that one. Bit of a firecracker, thought O'Shea. *Nice ass, though. As if! You do not go anywhere near crazy, clingy catgirls. I've been down that road before. No way. No how. Never again.* It was just a passing flicker of a thought. He was here on an assignment, and he took fieldwork seriously. Very seriously. That is how he'd survived working undercover for so long. He never indulged distractions. O'Shea threw his leather jacket, black backpack and black emergency-evacuation duffle bag on the lumpy, seventies-green-velvet couch and looked around the apartment.

"Why am I mid-life crisis guy?" he asked.

"You're sort of a cliché, aren't you?" humorless catgirl retorted, "Old. Bleached hair. Motorbike. Isn't that the mid-life crisis package?"

"How old do you think I am?" asked O'Shea, annoyed.

"Aw, 40-something."

"I'm 45," he snapped.

"There you go," said catgirl. "Live to 90 if you're lucky. 45 is mid-life. Motorbike. Blond hair. That all screams crisis. You probably have a late-life tattoo too."

She's really getting annoying now, thought O'Shea. *I'm meant to protect this motor-mouth princess? If some lunatic came to take her out ... I'd be tempted to say, "Be my guest!"*

O'Shea stood, noting exits—there was, unfortunately, only one back door—and generally summing up security when catgirl bounded over to stand beside him. The next instant, her cell flashed.

"What do you think you're doing?" he yelped.

"Taking a selfie with my FBI guy for my Twitter Feed," replied catgirl, who was wearing a grey hoodie over underpants and still holding her cat.

"What are you, 12 years old?" he snapped, grabbing her phone and deleting the picture. "First of all, this is not a game. Secondly, I'm here *undercover* to protect you ... Jesus wept ... in what's turning out to be a major pain-in-the-ass assignment, and I've only been here 3 minutes. Finally, I'm here to collect intel about the AGB that's coming through you, NOT get my ID blown by being seen as a poster boy prop for your professional ego!" He chastised her as if she really were 12 years old.

"I'm 32 for your information," snorted catgirl.

"Act your age."

"Act your age," mimicked catgirl.

O'Shea glared at her. *How can a 30-something woman, who looks about 15 years old—a man could be arrested as a pedophile just standing with her in a hotel lobby—make an ex-marine Ranger who can sit for 3 days without moving, want to go postal within 3 minutes of meeting her?* O'Shea checked himself. *Angry? You don't get angry. Are you fucking mad?* O'Shea berated himself and resumed his blank expression. *Back off. Focus. Do your job. And keep away from crazy catgirls.*

He walked over to his backpack, unzipped a side pocket, took out a computer-chip sized device and fitted it to catgirl's phone.

"What are you doing?" she asked.

"I'm connecting a call-tracker to your cell phone. It tethers your cell to mine so I can monitor all your calls and texts."

"So the FBI is spying on me now. Cool! I thought it was just the CIA listening to me through their satellites," catgirl joked.

O'Shea handed back her cell. "Thanks, I guess," said catgirl. "Look. Things have been pretty weird for me the last couple of days. You're the first easy target. I'm just dumping a whole lot of saved up emotional crap on you. So I'm going to back up and start again. Hello, my name is Kitchi Le, my friends call me Kee." She held out her hand.

"I'll read that as a truce," said O'Shea warily, "Hello, I'm Denney O'Shea. FBI."

"So where's your suit, dark sunglasses, and the squiggly hearing thing sticking out your ear?"

"That's the Secret Service."

"It's not much of a secret. You see them all the time on the news with the president."

"They won't see me on the news, or your AGB guy might stop contacting you."

"Aw. I tweeted that I was getting my own FBI guy."

"Get rid of it. Now!" barked O'Shea.

"You turned all Drill Sergeant in a hurry. Next thing you'll be yelling at me to drop to the floor and give you 10."

I'd be tempted to give her ten across that pert ass of hers, flitted across O'Shea's brain, but he said nothing. He was quietly fuming. He was in charge now. She followed his orders. But crazy catgirl didn't get it.

Catgirl's thumbs appeared as a blur as she moved them across her cell. "There, Sgt. Done. Tweet delete, Sir! Happy now? So what do I call you? My FBI guy?"

"Why not call me Denney? I do prefer that to Fuck Off, and we're going to be living in pretty close quarters over the next few days. Weeks. However long it takes. So we might as well be on first name terms."

"I was really hoping I got to call you Agent 85 or something," she complained.

"Denney will do."

They shook hands. It was a temporary truce.

Denny's cell rang or, to be accurate, vibrated. He turned his back on the crazy catgirl and answered.

"Yep, I'm here. The package is not exactly easy to handle."

"Hello, Booker," called catgirl, "we've already had five lovers' tiffs and we've only just met." O'Shea looked at her, baffled. *What is wrong with her?* he wondered. *This is no joking matter.*

"He wants to talk to you," announced O'Shea, turning the cell onto speaker mode. She put the cat on the bed and held the cell in her lap.

"You clairvoyant now, Miss Le?" asked Booker.

"Gotta keep the old brain buzzing. Otherwise, it thinks up all sorts of crazy thoughts," she replied.

Standing behind her, O'Shea smirked a little. *Got that right,* he silently agreed.

"Now Miss Le, try and take O'Shea's advice. He is there to protect you, and he is, of course, armed. So if he gives you directions don't stand there arguing," urged Booker.

"What is he going to do? Shoot me?"

I'll keep that option open, mused O'Shea.

"It may have crossed his mind, but NO. You'll be all right if you listen to his advice."

"Right, Dad," retorted Kee, like a sulking child.

"I do have daughters about your age, and they tend to argue about ... everything."

"Don't worry, Mr. FBI, I get it. I do."

She handed the phone back to O'Shea.

"Yep! Right. Same MO. So not exactly hollow threats then!"

O'Shea turned to the crazy catgirl and announced, "There's been another body found. New Mexico. Same MO."

"Awwww," moaned Kee, "the AGB really do mean business."

"I'll copy you in on the case intel. You have to be up to speed to communicate with them."

"I have my own intel guy," insisted catgirl.

"@PoliceBizz," said O'Shea.

"Freaking freak hell! How did you know that?"

"I'm reading your Twitter feed," replied O'Shea.

She started typing the latest intel into her Twitter account.

"What are you doing?" demanded O'Shea, grabbing for her phone. She was ready for him this time, so there was a little bit of argy-bargy until he used his "FBI secret powers", as she called them, to wrench the cell out of her hand.

"I was just tweeting an update on the body count," explained Kee.

"I will say this slowly. Run ANY little thought that comes into your head past me first."

"Can I go pee, sir?" mocked catgirl.

"You might think it's a joke, but there may be a time you can't go pee," O'Shea retorted, adding, "Booker wants you off all social media."

"Booker is not my boss. I thought about it. I really did. This is my one big break. If I don't use it, I'd be an idiot. I've got 102,658 followers on Twitter now. So I will post FBI approved Tweets. I just have to keep feeding the mob snippets to keep them happy, but I won't read the loony responses. I did once. I can't now. Too crazy. Too many."

"Booker said you'd be a handful," O'Shea sighed. "You are a minder's total mindfuck."

"I'll take that as a compliment. So here's the Tweet."

She showed O'Shea her cell.

"Actually, I've got it here."

"That's creepy. Are you grooming me as a covert mouthpiece for the FBI?"

"I'm not grooming you. That Tweet is fine. Just keep up the intel as you have in the past. Make it all seem normal."

"Freaking freak hell. I'm being groomed."

"You are not being groomed," spat O'Shea, frustrated. "You are being protected. And this is how we do it. You give me anything you hear, see or think."

"I'm thinking you're a pedophile and I'm being groomed," retorted crazy catgirl.

O'Shea looked at her puzzled. This conversation was way outside the boundaries of standard logic. He felt as if his brain would implode. He spoke slowly, as if she really were out-of-her-crazy-tree.

"You are 32 years old, way too old to interest a pedophile. Regarding this bizarre conversation, you are safe."

"Okay," replied catgirl nonchalantly, her fingers already flying.

She tweeted: "Another body found in New Mexico in the AGB cult killings of NGSA. Read more in tomorrow's *New England Gazette*." #Target91 @KeeHasSpoken

O'Shea shrugged off the bizarre conversation to concentrate on securing the joint. He picked trash off the floor, clearing a corridor to each window and the back door.

"I know this looks like I'm working on my FBI homemakers badge, but I need quick access to each window and the back door. I hope that makes sense to you."

Catgirl just shrugged in a "Whatever!" way.

He dumped some of the clutter in a pile beside the couch and walked to the kitchenette, asking, "Is there anything to eat?" and peered in the fridge.

He stared dumbstruck at the 3 limp sticks of celery, a dubious tub of mixed berry yogurt, one open can of cat food and 3 cartons of milk.

"Louis's Low Fat Vegetarian Cuisine?" suggested catgirl.

"Christ," he muttered, "don't you even have the basics, like eggs?"

"I didn't know I'd be feeding the FBI's hungriest agent, did I?" she huffed. "There's some Trail Pack Fruit and Nut Mix," she suggested.

"That'll do," he replied, rattling a few canisters. "And I'm really going out on a limb here, but do you have any coffee?"

"Black?"

"Yep, black is fine."

"Good. The milk's off."

O'Shea picked up one carton and smelled the rip-your-nostrils-off-your-face contents.

"Argh!" he gasped. "You have three cartons of milk here in various stages of putrefaction. Don't you ever throw anything out?"

"Don't you ever keep your nose out of other people's business?" she snapped.

"Fair call," replied O'Shea, "under the UN Convention on the Domestic Truce, sarcasm is banned. So let's have our," he checked his watch, "one a.m. feast. Coffee and tantalizing Trail Mix."

"You said sarcasm was banned."

"I actually like Trail Mix. I've lived on the stuff for days," replied O'Shea.

Catgirl and O'Shea sat at the wobbly table that she'd pulled from a dumpster in Peachable St—it was a posh dumpster—on two foldout Ikea chairs, struggling with a very awkward conversation.

The cat began curling around his owner's legs, complaining. O'Shea rolled his eyes. Dealing with a catgirl was bad enough; the other problem was, they always came with a cat.

"What is the time?" Asked Kee. "1:30-freaking-a.m.? I suppose you can have a special treat."

Kee pattered into the kitchenette and pulled a bag of dry cat food from the cupboard under the sink.

"Here you are, Mr Harold. Just a little snack," she cooed, as she dropped the pellets into the cat's food bowl.

"You can have a special treat too," she suggested to O'Shea, "rich in Vitamin B."

"No, thanks. I'll stick with the Trail Mix. Look, we better get some sleep. I'll take the couch," yawned O'Shea.

"It's pretty pathetic. A lumpy break-ass couch."

"I'll take the lumpy break-ass couch. What time are you in the office?" he asked.

"It's Sunday. Then again, the fact that the AGB plans to kill 91 NGSA members is some news story to get out. So up at 8. NO! Make it 9. Then it's, 'Hello, Weird Shit Day 3.'"

The crazy catgirl curled up on her bed, pulled the duvet over her bare legs, and then, as O'Shea watched in astonishment, the cat curled up on her head. He was right. She really was a Crazy Catlady in the making. He unzipped the left-hand pocket in his leather pants, took out his Glock 26 and placed it on the stepladder beside his couch-bed, stripped down to his T and boxers and dropped onto the break-ass couch. It felt as comfortable as a sack full of spongy potatoes. O'Shea adjusted the couch cushion-pillow under his head and fell asleep.

Both of them utterly failed to anticipate just how weird Weird Shit Day 3 would be.

Chapter 15

O'Shea

Sunday, the 17th of September

O'Shea woke early. He'd set his cell alarm to buzz him awake at 7am. Showered and dressed, he slipped quickly and quietly out the back door and, taking the key, left on his bike to buy up some supplies. He found the local Stop 'n Shop supermarket and returned with a breakfast feast in a bag.

Catgirl yawned and sat up in bed, rubbing her eyes.

"Eggs. Bacon. I can smell eggs and bacon. Fresh coffee!" she gasped, turning towards O'Shea, who was in the kitchenette cooking up a storm.

"I'm a vegetarian," she objected, shuffling over to the kitchenette draped in the duvet cover.

"Why am I not surprised," sighed O'Shea, flipping an omelet.

He turned towards catgirl and gave a mock scream.

"Argghhhh! It's a Wookie! No, it's Miss Le. You, madam, are suffering from a near terminal case of bedhead hair."

"Don't talk to me. Don't even open your mouth until I've had caffeine. Give. Caffeine. Nowwwwww," she ordered, pushing malignant product gummed bedhead hair off her nose. It fell back in place. She grabbed the proffered mug of freshly brewed coffee and clung to it, sitting on the barstool *cum* stepladder by the kitchenette counter.

"Milk? Putrefied or fresh?"

She sneered.

"Fresh it is!" said O'Shea.

Both their cell call tones sounded.

It was a voicemail from Bradstreet. Catgirl pressed Replay.

"Get your ass into the office, pronto. Shit is happening here. It's 8:30. Be here by 9."

"Shit is happening here too, buddy," she complained to the unresponsive cell. "Coffee. Mmmmmm."

"Orange juice, omelet, and a blueberry muffin!" O'Shea announced, as he put a plate of muffins in front of her.

"You get your junior cooking badge with the FBI, did you?" she mumbled through a mouthful of muffin.

"Ah! It speaks," said O'Shea. "Now seriously, you've got to eat. This is only the beginning of Weird Shit Day 3, remember."

"Yeah! And it's weirding me out already. Me and my FBI homeboy ... freaking weird."

O'Shea placed the omelet and accouterments on the table, saying, "Madam Catlady. Enjoy." He immediately wished he'd shut the fuck up. He shouldn't insult his charge. Lowers cooperation.

"Yeah! I'm a crazy catlady, and you're just a prick," catgirl snapped.

"I cooked you breakfast," he pleaded.

"Yeah. You did. You are a little prick." She laughed at her own joke.

Kee's foghorn text ID sounded. It was Bradstreet.

TURN ON TV. DEKANT TEAR OUT LIVER TALK ON NOW. WE SCOOPED THE BASTARDS.

Kee picked up the remote and flicked on the telly. DeKant's tear-out-their-livers speech was being broadcast by all news channels live to air.

"I know that speech. I got it when I interviewed DeKant on the phone last night."

"You've got DeKant's cell number?" O'Shea asked, incredulous.

"Yes, sir! Me and DeKant, we're like that," she said, holding up crossed fingers, "best buds."

"Seriously?" asked O'Shea.

"I put his side of the story fair and square. He trusts me. And yeah, I've got his cell number."

O'Shea looked at the crazy catgirl in a new light. Not so crazy, then.

DeKant added a coda to his well-prepared speech.

"As all members of the NGSA know, and the public fails to appreciate, your government cannot protect you. They cannot protect you in a hurricane. They cannot protect you in a flood. They cannot protect you from crazy lowlife criminals who want to break into your home, rape your women and steal your possessions. I am fortunate. I have my four lieutenants here to protect me."

The TV camera focus zoomed out to show DeKant surrounded by his four "lieutenants". It was difficult to tell whether Gig's armed guards were pulled from the ranks of regular NGSA membership or consisted entirely of hired-mercenaries. Each lieutenant was in his early forties, had cropped military style hair, sported a camouflage flak-vest, a Secret Service style communication earpiece, and wrap-around sunglasses. Each was armed with an assault rifle, side-arm, and a night-stick.

"You people at home watching this broadcast may not be so lucky. It is time to act. Protect yourself. Arm yourself. This is war."

"What a jerk!" said O'Shea. "The FBI offered him protection. He knocked it back. He knows how to work the media circus. Plus some."

"Do you think the AGB will get him?" she asked.

"Maybe. These guys are pros. They aren't dumbfucks who just wandered into Walmart or a gun show and thought, 'Yo! A gun. A *big* motherfucker. Yo! I want one-a them.' They go home, shove the pistol in their jeans belt, admire themselves in the bedroom mirror and blow off one of their balls before the week's out. These guys in the AGB, they're smart. They'll get at DeKant, but they will want him sweating it out and doing a little media dance first. This time he is playing into their hands."

"I feel sorry for him," she said.

"Don't. He shot a kid, you know. A 15-year-old Latino boy, who DeKant claimed was stalking him. Shot him dead. The kid didn't have a gun. He was taking a message to one of DeKant's gardeners. But the kid was carrying a multi-tool pocket knife in a leather holster attached to his belt. That was 2007. So the kid gets shot for carrying a fancy screw driver. Besides, you know how much DeKant's paid to run this NGSA sideshow?"

"How much?"

"$900,000 a year."

She nearly choked on her blueberry muffin. "I'm in the wrong business," she spluttered.

"So now I will brief you on today's procedure. Are you listening?"

"Yeah, yeah. Nine hundred grand," she said, carefully pronouncing each word, "Nine! Hundred! Grand! More than the President of the United States."

"Double the President's salary," O'Shea replied.

"This is a Weird-as-Hell World."

"Copy that," said O'Shea, "Now listen up, Le."

"There's only one of me, O'Shea," complained catgirl, "you don't have to do that whole Mission Ops speech thing."

She can be so fucking irritating, thought O'Shea, *if she were in my team she'd be out on that cute ass of hers in no time.* He took a deep breath. Not fighting with the amateurs was Step 1 in How to Build Trust from the FBI siege negotiator's handbook.

"Kill that smart-ass attitude, Le. Your life might depend on you listening to advice for a change."

"All right, all right. Shoot!" O'Shea didn't seem to catch the gun pun.

"Today you go to work. I follow you on my motorbike and casually hang around outside the office watching for any strange characters. If anyone you do not know comes into the office for any purpose, call me. If anyone approaches you that you do not know, call me. I'll be ten seconds away. Text 85. That's enough. We want the AGB to keep in contact with you, so I'm keeping in the background. We don't expect anyone to target you. But keep your eyes and ears open. Got that? I've already spoken to Bradstreet. There are ten TV/radio crews outside the office waiting to interview you. Don't draw attention to yourself. Don't talk to them. Bradstreet says park away from the Bailey Ave. Walk through the shopping mall behind the office, and he'll open the back gate."

"Mmm! Mmm!" agreed Kee, shoving a last piece of sticky blueberry muffin into her blueberry-smeared mouth.

"TEN FILM CREWS! DID YOU HEAR THAT, LE?" O'Shea shouted.

"I heard," she retorted, offended. "You said not to talk to them." She made a zipping gesture across her mouth.

"You keeping your mouth shut, that's hard to believe. Go and do your girl-emerges-from-a-Wookie thing and we'll get going. Backstreets all the way. Okay?"

Le nodded as she licked her fingers and gulped down her second mug of coffee. She shuffled over to her bed and started picking up clothes and smelling them to locate a minimalist *odeur-de*-pong ensemble. She had to throw Harold off the pile of laundry first. Harold complained.

O'Shea started laughing. "Do you need any help there? Underwear Sniffing 101 is just one of the FBI training courses. I have my certificate."

"Yeah, real funny guy. You wait," she snarled. "You'll run out of clean clothes soon enough, Mr. Anal Retentive Neat 'n Tidy Man. No washing machine here."

Le approached her clothes rack and, forgetting she had company, started muttering out loud, "I'll go in my professional navy suit today. Mid-heels. Business-style ponytail. Cleanish cream-shirt with see-through lace bodice."

"I do fashion advice too," chimed in O'Shea, as Le shuffled into the bathroom. O'Shea's washed tee and boxers hung on the shower curtain rod.

"Anal retentive freaking retard!" she called through the bathroom door.

"I heard that, Le!" yelled O'Shea.

Dressed and office-bound, Kee asked PoliceBizz for the latest intel.

"Any news?" @KeeHasSpoken

"Identity of latest AGB victim in NGSA killings confirmed. Jesus Escobar, 63, Chihuahuan Desert, New Mexico." @PoliceBizz

"Booker wants you off all social media," O'Shea called out from the kitchenette.

"I forgot, you're my online stalker now. How does that work?"

O'Shea sighed. "Two phones. Two numbers on each phone. Save any questions for later. I'm living here, remember."

"Boxer shorts in the bathroom. How can I forget?"

"One of us has to support a body odor-free environment," O'Shea deadpanned.

"Touché, O'Shea," retorted Le, adding, "Can I tweet that update, Sir?"

"Y-yeah, if you must," replied O'Shea, watching his cell and washing the last of the dishes.

"I must," she said.

As Le's thumbs worked her phone, she asked, "But why me? Why did the AGB pick me to be their messenger? I don't get it."

"You hit the headlines big time. You broke this story," explained O'Shea.

"Yes, I guess. But I write for *The New England* Goddamn *Gazette*. It's not exactly *The New York Times*, is it?"

"Doesn't matter. Everything is online now. The AGB think they have you in their pocket."

She was actually struck speechless by this. *Miracles do happen*, mused O'Shea. "Ready?" he asked.

Le sighed.

"Harold, mummy's going out now. Be a good cat. No dragging in dead rats. And I'll be back to feed you as soon as I can," she cooed to her cat. O'Shea rolled his eyes and Kee looked daggers at him.

"I didn't say a thing," intoned O'Shea.

"Hmph!" she snorted.

Chapter 16

Kee

Sunday, the 17th of September

Kee creaked down the stairs into the dull Sunday morning light. The weather bureau promised a perfect day once the sun had burned off the lingering haze. A black Yamaha YZF 1000 R1 was parked in the backyard. O'Shea had the key in the lock and was shifting the bike off its stand. There was not one jarring element to the aerodynamic design. O'Shea's motorbike was a sleek, rumbling, pure speed machine.

Kee dragged the side gate open so that O'Shea could wheel his bike into the street. She dragged the gate shut again, grumbling, "Thank you, Miss Le," and walked over to the Silver Beast. O'Shea swung one leg over the bike's futuristic exoskeleton and throttled up the engine. It hummed with the raw energy of total torque. With his all-black leathers, black helmet and black bike, O'Shea looked like a menacing alien ant from an evil planet, or so it seemed to Kee as he held up one gloved hand and waved at her to get moving.

When Kee parked the Silver Beast, as instructed, away from the office, O'Shea vanished. She found her way through the back gate, past the office dumpster and through the back door with little trouble. It was 9:25 a.m. She was late. "But come on," Kee argued to herself, "it is Sunday, after all. The day of rest."

"Where the hell have you been!" shouted Bradstreet as soon as he saw Kee. "The phones have been ringing non-stop. I've had to take them off the hook. *The Washington Post* wants to give you a job. Don't trust them. Everyone wants to interview you. CBS. FOX News. The Morning shows. *60 Minutes*. The BBC. The fucking Queen of England will want to interview you next. And outside our front door is camped a full-on media circus consisting of, at last count, fifty bozos waving microphones."

"Hello, Miss Le. Welcome to Weird Shit Day 3!" called Hollis from her desk. She was holding a phone in each hand. Chivonn, who had sweet-talked her terrified partner—he'd already rung her 4 times that morning—into solo baby-watch duty, was talking into another phone. She waved to Kee.

Aron didn't have earbuds in his ears this time. "What did you do, Kee?" he asked. "Assassinate someone who is, like, real famous, like, Nelson Mandela?"

"He's already dead," replied Kee.

"Whoa! Who killed him?" Aron demanded.

"We are in Chaos Control mode here," urged Bradstreet. "Look out the front window."

Kee was dumbstruck. There was a wall of TV cameras, microphones and an elbowing scrum of journalists, TV reporters, and God knows what all. TV news vans cluttered the street. NBC NEWS. ABC NEWS. CBS NEWS. TV reporters were giving on the spot reports live to assorted TV cameras, using the *Gazette* office as the backdrop to their story.

"Everyman, his idiot assistant, and his dog are here," complained Bradstreet.

Everyone, including albino monk assassins. No, wait, that was The Da Vinci Code, thought Kee.

Cameras started flashing as soon as Kee appeared at the window. She scurried to the back of the office.

"Sorry, Mr. Bossy. I don't know how all of this happened," she apologized.

"Sorry? Don't be sorry. There is nothing like the smell of ball-breaking news in the morning. We'll get another special edition out of this. But you'll have to do something. Feed the baying hounds a scrap or two or they'll break the windows."

"The FBI told me not to say anything to the reporters," Kee objected. "What can I do?"

"The FB-fucking-I!" complained Bradstreet. Kee could see a Praise-the-Lord-and-Pass-the-Ammunition revival in her boss. Two days ago, the blood pumping in his veins barely supported his grumbling bitter-boss demeanor. Now Jupiter had aligned with fucked-up Mars. He was a hard-edge journo again, a hotshot editor under siege. And he was reveling in his one last shot at breaking a big-time news story.

"The FB-fucking-I don't have to put up with these news-hungry idiots," continued Bradstreet. "We can't get in or out the door. I've had to throw three of them out onto the street. Physically. If I had an AK-47 .... If!"

"What should I say?"

"It's not that hard," insisted Bradstreet. "Go out there and read them a statement. You don't have to answer questions. Just get 'em off our backs, will you? Come into my office. Bring your laptop. We'll write an editorial piece. You can use it tomorrow in a column. And they might just go away."

Twenty minutes later Kee stood, knees knocking, on the front step of the *New England Gazette* office building beside Bradstreet, clutching her statement in sweating hands.

A voice called out, "Guns don't kill people. People do!" It was a long-haired, lean, leather-faced cowboy, a pro-gun protester. He was probably an unofficial representative of the NGSA. The t-shirt he wore under his light-blue denim jacket read: THE BULLSHIT STOPS WHEN THE HAMMER DROPS.

A sound-recordist yelled, "Shut up, fuck-face, let her speak."

Bradstreet introduced Kee and insisted that no questions would be answered.

"My name is Kitchi Le. I am a staff reporter for *The New England Gazette.* I started my investigation into the NGSA slayings 2 days ago when it was reported that the body of a Ridgefield man had been found in the Boneridge Quarry near Hawley, Pennsylvania. I visited the crime scene and found that I knew the victim. His name was Hayden Brodski. Mr. Brodski had always been decent to me, but some very disturbing stories have since emerged about Brodski from witnesses. You will find details of these reports in our special edition.

"I pass on my sympathy to the family and friends of Mr. Brodski.

"For some reason, the AGB has singled me out to be the mouthpiece for their messages to the NGSA. The FBI confirmed the ID of these messages. The AGB sent me the serial number of the gun found in the body of Mr. Brodski. I regret that I next have to pass on a terrifying message to the NGSA. But I feel it is my duty.

"The Anti-Gun Brigade plans to kill 91 members of the NGSA. The 1, I was told, stands for the CEO of the NGSA, Gig DeKant. He is Target 91.

"Thank you for your attention. No questions. You can read *The New England Gazette* website for updates."

Kee was blinded by flashing cameras, and she had to duck twice when she was almost hit on the head by a TV audio-sound crane known as "the hamster-on-a-stick". Kee and Bradstreet were still facing down a barrage of questions from the media throng when a well-groomed corporate Suit walked center stage, stood directly in front of them, and addressed the cameras.

"Un-goddamn-believable," Bradstreet whispered under his breath. "Guess who can smell a few votes in the air."

The Suit was none other than Frank Rubino, the Mayor.

"Let me introduce myself. I am Frank Rubino, the First Selectman of this town. I want you to know that Ridgefield is a decent, law abiding town. I can tell you the citizens of Ridgefield are all decent, hard working folk. I can guarantee that no crime has been committed here."

"How many goddamn I's can one egomaniac fit into one press statement?" Bradstreet whispered to Kee.

"Now I will hand you over to my Police Chief, John Griswold, and he'll be happy to answer any of your questions."

The uniformed police chief walked up with a huddle of four local officers and stood facing the crowd and the cameras, one hand resting on the polished-walnut stock of his Colt New Frontier 44 revolver, to address the crowd in his Texan drawl. Not all Texans have a drawl, a six-shooter, and a horse, but the police chief felt it was his duty to bring a little of the Wild West Sheriff to Ridgefield to honor his commitment to enforcing some of those "Goddam" trash can laws.

"We will do everything in our power to bring these violent criminals to justice. This outrageous unprovoked crime of killing innocent—"

He didn't get to finish his sentence. Some jerk slammed a tire lever into a street trashcan. It sounded like a gun retort. Instantly, all the police officers drew their guns. The camera crews panicked. They were looking down the barrels of five handguns and facing the horrifying scenario that they might be caught in the crossfire between the local cops and a revenge-bent, pro-gun street gang. They scattered. It was amazing how fast some of those Morning Talk Show ladies could run in high heels. Some of the jeans-and-sneaker brigade, including three overweight cameramen shouldering large TV cameras, proved to be remarkably light on their feet, too. They outflanked the sound-recordists by car lengths.

Bradstreet pushed Kee back in the office door, but he rather suspected the whole "gunshot" incident was a setup. He was right. Within 15 minutes, amateur footage of the camera crews running for cover was posted on You Tube under the heading, CAMERA CREWS LOSE THEIR COOL AT THE OK CORRAL. The clip already had 1,000 hits! Kee noticed that the alias for the post was PoliceBizz. *So I was standing looking at you, PoliceBizz. I wonder who you are? Nice pun on my name.*

Back in the office, Kee felt a little shell-shocked. She looked at her cell phone.

WARNING BB. MAYOR ON WARPATH. WILL TRY AND STEAL YOUR LIMELIGHT. JO

It was Joe Lyman from the Mayor's office.

TOO LATE IRONMAN. TOTAL FIASCO DOWN HERE. YOU MISSED A GOOD SHOW. BB

"You wanna nip of bourbon?" asked Hollis quietly. "You do look a bit pale, girl."

"Thanks, Hollis," sighed Kee, "not now. But I'll take a rain check on that. Might need it before the day is out." Hollis took a swig herself, muttering, "Mmm-mm!"

Aron was streaming CBS news on his computer. It was running the footage of Kee's announcement.

"Hey, Kee, you're a TV star now!" he cheered. "You can go on *Dancing with the Stars*."

"Oh, no!" gasped Kee looking at her image on the screen. "I'm looking down too much. And I've rounded my back. I really hate my outfit on TV."

Her litany of self-criticism was cut short by Bradstreet, who was back on mission.

"Quick, Aron, get a screenshot of the interview. We'll use the picture to go with Kee's column. Make sure you get my good side," he joked.

Bradstreet walked around the office, clapping his hands.

"Looks like Happy Clappy Man is back," grinned Hollis.

"I think we'll have no more trouble from those media scumbags. So come on, my little wage slaves. There is a paper to get out!"

Chapter 17

DeKant

Sunday, the 17th of September

Gig DeKant lived on an 80-acre wooded estate, located 40 minutes outside Fairfax, with his wife, Beverley, and their 27-year-old disabled son, Logan. The estate bore all the symbols of wealth and prestige associated with a corporate mercenary who had stomped on enough fingers and heads on the way up the corporate ladder to achieve the highest echelons of corporate life. Grey stone columns with towering, white-painted, cast-iron gates stood as sentinels to the estate, which was surrounded by a white post and rail fence. The long, Claret Ash-lined drive ran up to the front door and ended in a circular turnaround surrounding an ornamental garden bed with a three-tiered bowl-shaped fountain in the center. The splash of fall leaf show along each side of the Claret Ash avenue was so deep and so robust, it would make a wine enthusiast thirsty just looking at it.

Inside, the DeKant home was a monument to Gig's lifelong dedication to guns. Mounted in the living room of the luxurious single level ranch style home, beneath the cathedral ceiling with exposed beams, on the vast exposed-brick chimney above the fireplace, three Civil War vintage rifles were on display, surrounded by DeKant's hunting trophies: the heads of a red wildebeest, a bezoar ibex, and DeKant's much prized bull bison. This was not a bison that had been bred in captivity; this had been a wild bison, and hunting for such a trophy costs over $50,000 a head. (A human head, that is. The humans in the hunting party were left to argue over who got the bison head.)

Gig woke at 6:30 a.m. as usual, showered and shaved, put on a crisply-ironed light blue and white check shirt, navy suit, and NGSA emblem tie. It was a Sunday, but in view of the recent threats to NGSA members, he was going into the office.

Gig looked the part, but he wasn't feeling his normal revved-up-and-ready-for-action self. He had slept in fits and starts, stayed awake for what seemed like hours listening to the ghostly shriek of some local red foxes prowling the property, and gone to the john four times, possibly because of the bourbon nightcap in which he had indulged. He did not believe in pills. His sleeping draught was Kentucky Vintage Bourbon. He'd had one or two, possibly four, before bed. He tried to keep track of his intake. He didn't want to end up like his father, shit-faced and brain-dead, drinking a bottle of bourbon each night, but needs must. He'd actually run out of the vintage and had had to open the no name brand given to him by Beverley's brothers for his 70th birthday, the miserable tightwad bastards. They'd been drinking his vintage for over 40 years, and in all that time they'd given him one bottle that cost them 20 bucks, tops, at the drugstore. He'd had to resort to a slug of that donkey's piss. Bourbon usually did the trick for Gig. But last night, it seemed to have lost its magic. Normally, Gig looked very well preserved for a 72-year-old. He had height, square shoulders and a full head of grey hair. But today his age showed in the bags under his eyes and the deep folds that slashed his face either side of his nose.

He walked through the house to the kitchen where his son Logan sat in his wheelchair at the table, eating breakfast. *Cerebral palsy was a goddamn life-sentence of a torment. It could make a man lose faith in the almighty*, thought Gig, and not for the first time. Logan had dribbled some crumbs and egg down his shirtfront. Gig ruffled his son's hair and asked, "How are you today, boy?" as he wiped Logan's shirtfront. Logan choked out an answer, which was not exactly in the form of a word, it was more a guttural cough. Gig turned, walked the length of the extra long, black granite-topped kitchen counter, and put one arm around Beverly at the stove, asking, "What's for breakfast?"

"With all these crazy threats and shootings, what you need, Gig, is a good and hearty breakfast," replied Beverley, turning some mushrooms in the pan. "You're having poached eggs over warm corned beef on top of wholemeal toast, covered with a bacon hollandaise sauce and served with a side of mushrooms and homemade hash browns, brewed coffee. Also waffles and maple if you want them."

Those TV cooking shows certainly improve the husband's lot, thought Gig. He bought any cookbook she fancied from any show Beverley watched, and these gifts paid off in full. Though he did not like her excessive enthusiasm for that vegetable. What was it? Fennel. Ergh! It smelled like fermented donkey's piss. Maybe they add it to the cheap Bourbon.

Gig sat at the white-painted cottage style table, eating his breakfast and flipping through the 3 newspapers he had home delivered.

"I'm on the front cover of *The New York Times* again," he noted, reading out, "'Gig DeKant, CEO of the NGSA, said yesterday that, and I quote, "Today it is my very sad duty to announce that five of our brothers in arms,"' et cetera, et cetera .... "'Today we mourn our brothers, sons, fathers, and friends .... Tomorrow we will track down these depraved, godless individuals and we will annihilate them."' Good. They got it right. They included the entire speech too. Very Good."

"You be careful, Gig. I don't like these anti-gun crazies naming you. I worry about you all the time now," pleaded Beverley.

"Bev, you know me. I've been around for a very long time. I've spoken with the board. They're behind me all the way. And I'm going to hire some hotshot security guards. You'll see."

Gig was, in fact, enjoying being center stage of the media kerfuffle. That's how he saw it. He was playing a chess game with some gun-obsessed psychos. It was entertaining. And he was safe. It was as if his whole life had been a training camp for this moment. He understood guns. He was an advocate for guns. He had argued before the Supreme Court to extend the interpretation of the 2nd amendment, and he'd won. These gun-obsessed psychos could not touch him. No way.

His cell buzzed and he saw the sender's name. "Christ," he spat through clenched teeth. Then he took a deep breath and answered the call with great warmth.

"Senator Cotton, what can I do for you today? ... Yes! ... I know assault rifles will be back on the political agenda ... Hmmm ... Hmmm ... Yes! The Democrats are making a lot of noise but that particular issue is up to individual states. You only have to worry about your own state. And I can't see Alaska changing its stripes any time soon. Yes! ... Yes-sss! I'll take it up with our CFO. How much did you say? ... Right. Bye." Adding, under his breath so Beverley would not hear, "Greedy asshole."

He finished his coffee, straightened his tie and kissed Beverly on the cheek, saying, "I'm off, now."

"Have a good day," she replied.

"I will," Gig said confidently. He picked up his cell and put it in his briefcase, folded *The New York Times* and put it under his arm, and headed for the front door. His driver was out front, waiting for him in the black BMW SUV with the dark tinted windows that pushed the darkest boundaries of Virginia's car window tint laws.

He arrived at the office, greeted the few staff members who had come in on their day off, and headed towards the lift to his office on the 8th floor.

"Mr DeKant," called one of the girls from the Media department. What was her name? Lea? Lara? Lana? They all sounded the same to him. Those young girls with long straight hair, city suits and white blouses all looked the same, too. He snapped out of his cheerful reverie.

"My Dad says you give the best speeches ever, better than our Founding Fathers," said Lea-Lara-Lana.

"Does he, now? Well, you tell your daddy there will be more rousing speeches before this AGB business is done and dusted and thrown in the trash can."

"I will tell him that. He'll be pleased," enthused Lea-Lara-Lana.

Waiting in his office were 4 flak jacket-clad, armed security personnel, wearing military fatigues, with wrap around sunglasses perched on their heads. Multiple aluminum carry cases and padded canvas firearm carry bags were stacked on the office floor. Gig was impressed. These tanned, taut, tough guys looked the business. Gig had organized the security detail the night before. He'd rung Commando Personal Security Inc. Gig had been given the number by one of his friends in the unofficial pro-gun network that met about once a month. This friend was on the Forbes rich list. He was described in the casual media as "loaded", which Gig thought funny, as he was in fact an arms manufacturer. About 10 years ago, the friend's daughter had been kidnapped in Slovenia or Slovakia, one of those Russian satellite states, Gig couldn't remember which one. The family had quietly paid out a fortune for her release. After that little escapade, the family had ramped up their personal security measures. They'd been using this security company for years.

"Hello, Sir, my name is Dan," said one of the security guards, standing almost at attention. Definitely ex-military. It showed. Introducing the boys, he said, "This is Mike, and Mac, and Mark." At least, those were the names DeKant thought he heard. "We're your Security Team 24/7 for however long it takes."

God help us, thought Gig, *I've hired a pack of M&Ms*. Addressing Mike, Mac, Mark, and the other one, whatever his name was, Gig said, "It's good to see you, boys. I hope nothing will happen. But you are here to make sure nothing happens. I think we can all agree on that."

"Yes, sir," replied Dan, handing Gig an envelope. "And here is the contract. If you would read it and sign two copies, we'll get down to business." Gig quickly skimmed through and signed on the dotted line. He'd already reviewed the contract emailed to him the night before.

At 9.00 a.m. precisely, Gig returned to the lift, flanked by his security guards, and descended to the ground floor. Being surrounded by a security retinue made Gig feel like a rich Middle Eastern Oil Sheik with a price on his head. He strode out the front door to the portable lectern outside the NGSA office and, before a full media contingent, delivered his "tear out their livers" speech. He savored his moment in the bright light of day and camera lighting glare. Newsprint. TV. Radio. Microphones thrust in his face. His speech was delivered with steady, measured menace. He particularly liked the line about tearing out their livers and delivered it with relish. The speech went to plan like clockwork. He gave a barely discernible smile, refused to answer questions, and returned to his office. Gig could relax for now, but he had a more spectacular media event lined up for later in the day. Gig was looking forward to his next announcement; he had a real dog and pony show planned for the cameras.

At 4.00 p.m. precisely, Gig stood at the lectern in front of the NGSA office to make another public announcement. A group of about 20 anti-gun protesters had gathered outside the NGSA office mid-morning and had, according to Gig, who'd watched them from his office window, "carried on like a pack of B-grade kindergarten fairies." They were each dressed in black clothes and wore face masks. Some sported the white Guy-Fawkes face-mask with the black pencil mustache, slimline goatee, and sneering grin. Others wore the altogether more menacing Joker mask with the slashed mouth smudged in a red across the face. Some performers wore black capes. Each carried a metal cooking pan and a metal spoon. The protesters were chanting, "Bang. Bang. Shoot him. Shoot him. Shoot him dead. Bang. Bang. Right in. Right in. Right in the head. Bang Bang. The Good Guys shot him dead."

The Anti-gun protesters had refined their street performance into a synchronized art form. They banged their saucepans and fry pans—a nod to the YouTube clip from Ridgefield posted earlier in the day—to simulate the sound of a gun firing. After each rendition of the chorus, one member of the protest group dropped to the ground dead and held up a toy AK-47 to simulate the murder scene. Another anonymous performer would then draw a chalk outline of the victim. The protesters continued until 6 victims were lying dead on the ground. Then they moved their performance to another location in front of the NGSA building. Their chanting was audible behind the media throng.

Gig DeKant was irritated by this parasitic, lunatic fringe of the left disrupting his scheduled media announcement. He had already called the Fairfax Police to clear the faggot scumbags away from the NGSA precinct. He knew the police chief—the man was a member of the NGSA. The chief had informed him, regretfully and apologetically, "My hands are tied on this one, Gig. A lawyer—let me make this quite clear, a transgendered lawyer—for the group has submitted all the appropriate paperwork for a public demonstration at that location on this date. Christ, Gig, we can't go anywhere near them. If one of my officers as much as sneezed on an LBGQ Transweirdo or—God help us!—some dreadlocked crazy waving a rainbow flag, the department would be up for all sorts of Human Rights violations. They've already threatened to sue the bejeezus out of the Department if the police interfere."

Gig stood stern-faced at the temporary lectern emblazoned with the NGSA logo, fighting the rising bitter bile of aggravation in his gut. He tried to be patient, but the noise from the street performance was getting louder and louder, at least in his mind. And he was suffering from a second night of serious sleep deprivation. His brain could not hold onto an idea for long, as if his thoughts had gone on vacation to a distant fishing village where the cell phone coverage erratically came and went. He smiled at the media. He coughed several times. He blinked rapidly to try and focus his thoughts. This made him look slightly unhinged. DeKant began to read his statement to the cameras, even though the "Bang ... Bang" chanting could be clearly heard in the background.

"It is the constitutional right of NGSA members to carry guns. It is the right of every good and decent citizen of these United States of America to carry a gun to protect themselves and their families. That our brothers-in-arms could be executed for owning a gun is abhorrent and stands against everything this great country stands for."

A reporter from CBS news interjected.

"But Mr. DeKant, if the victims were armed, how could they be executed? They had guns. Surely they could protect themselves."

DeKant went ballistic. Froth formed at the side of his mouth as he launched into a major rant, with "Bang ... Bang" echoing in the background.

"The reason we have guns is to defend ourselves! This is our right! It is written into the constitution. But an evil force is among us today. We do not know who it is. We do not know why they are attacking our members. Look to the guy to the left of you and the guy to the right of you and ask yourself, "Is *he* a murderer? Is that Loony Leftie politician the murderer? Is that Black street gang member the murderer? Is that Hispanic drug dealer the murderer? Is that homosexual deviant the murderer? Is that communist sicko the murderer? Is that doped-out junkie the murderer? Is that babbling Muslim imam the murderer? Is that Anti-Gun Protester—who, like the protesters here today, are such yellow-bellied pussies they do not even have the guts to show their faces in public—are they the murderers?

Never give street artists a second chance at the last word. In an instant, the protest troop changed their chant to "Murderer. Murderer. Murderer..." as they moved slowly towards DeKant. His lieutenants were jumpy. They were army trained but had no understanding of, or timing for, theatricals. One pointed his AK-47 at the protesters, screaming, "Get back! Get back!"

The protesters kept chanting and moving toward DeKant. Some "joker" threw a lit firecracker from under his black cape. The noise was deafening. DeKant hit the ground while his lieutenants converged around him protectively, gun barrels bristling in all directions like a metallic hedgehog. The reporters who had seen the firecracker toss ignored it and kept firing questions at DeKant:

"Do you believe the murders are racially motivated?"

"Are they targeting White gun owners?"

"Do you think Gays are responsible?"

"Are Islamic terrorists targeting your organization to destabilize America?"

"Do you think Democrats are trying to kill off Republicans?"

Two of the security goons grabbed the prostrate DeKant under the armpits and dragged him back towards the NGSA head office. This operation was made particularly difficult by the fact that DeKant was trying to fight them off. The other two goons aimed their guns at the assembled media. One backward-walking goon tripped and fell on the struggling DeKant. The lead goons dropped him, swore, and shouldered their rifles. DeKant tried to get up but the goon squad quickly regrouped, contained DeKant's struggling horizontal form, got him in a firm grip and carried him, like an uncooperative corpse, in fits and starts back through the front door.

Inside the building, DeKant finally managed to free himself from his "protectors".

"You mother-fucking clowns!" he roared, as two of the goons tried to help him to his feet. "Just back off. I can't even bear to look at you!" he snapped, straightening his disheveled suit and tie. With those words of appreciation, DeKant stormed over to the lift and made his way back into his office, where he slammed the door shut.

Outside, moments after DeKant's undignified exit, one TV cameraman stopped videoing and turned to look at the station news reporter, a young woman in her late twenties, and they both burst out laughing. It took the young reporter 10 minutes to wipe tears from her eyes, straighten her skirt and compose herself, to do the serious, on location report to the camera.

Chapter 18

Kee

Sunday, the 17th of September

Just after midday, Bradstreet stepped out of his office again to check on the progress of Monday's bumper edition of *The New England Gazette.*

"How are all my little foot soldiers doing on the news front? Any trouble in the trenches?" he asked no one in particular.

"All good, Boss," Hollis chortled, without taking her eyes off her computer screen.

"And our star reporter?" queried Bradstreet.

"Getting there," Kee replied, hammering out copy with a pen shoved behind one ear, classic old-school-reporter style.

"How is our other star reporter doing?" asked the boss.

Everyone looked up puzzled.

"That would be none other than Mr. Aron 'Brain-Trust' Whittle the Third!" announced Bradstreet.

They all turned and looked at Aron, who was leaning back precariously on his office chair, staring at his cell phone and chewing gum.

Bradstreet had sent Shidfa out the previous day to ask the "decent, law-abiding citizens" of the district what they thought of the NGSA. Their responses where pure gold.

"Come on, Mr. Whittle, Star Reporter, for our edification read out some of your quotes."

"Who's Ed Focation?" asked Aron. It was his consistent and complete obliviousness to the conversation going on around him or even, sometimes, the one he was in, that had earned Aron the nickname Shidfa. If there was a Dumb Comment Hall of Fame, Aron would be their star inductee.

"Just read the quotes," sighed Bradstreet.

Aron scrolled through his phone. His high-speed dual thumb action meant he could type all of his interviews in situ into Notes on his cell. *Perhaps,* mused Bradstreet, *this is the big skill for the new tech-driven era. But I have to correct Shidfa's spelling. He could throw a can of alphabet soup on the page and get the same result.*

Aron began to read slowly, as Kee, Hollis, and Chivonn gathered to listen.

"Um, Edinson Diekmann, 84, of Wilton says, 'My daddy took me out shootin' when I was a boy. I shot my first white-tail deer when I was just 8 years old. I think the NGSA has done a mighty fine job protecting our right to carry guns. Every little kiddie should have the right to go shoot a deer with their daddy.'"

"Every kiddie should shoot a deer. Hear that, folks? There are about 60 million little kiddies in this country. We have enough guns. That would wipe out the White-Tail deer population overnight," said Bradstreet. "Then again, maybe old Eddie has a point. Perhaps he is an eco-warrior at heart. A Bambi cull would stop those pesky marauders trampling all over our endangered forest greenery."

"I don't think giving 60 million kids guns is good idea, Boss," objected Chivonn. 'That would take sibling rivalry to a whole new level. I wouldn't even let my kids near wooden spoons. Soft toys, that's all you can trust them with."

Bradstreet laughed, and when he explained, "Imagine arming our esteemed Ridgefield Police force with soft toys," the others laughed too.

"Aron," continued Bradstreet, "tell us about Patty."

Aron scrolled through his notes.

"Here it is. Patty O'Donnell, 48, Redding. She said, 'More babies—God bless their little souls—are murdered by abortionists than is shot by guns. I think the NGSA should do something about them, abortionists.'"

"Hallelujah, sister. She wants to arm fetuses now. Wouldn't the NGSA love that! Born with a Silver Smith & Wesson in his hand. Not in his mouth. It's a bit early for suicide, isn't? At birth?" huffed Bradstreet.

The front door whooshed open. Once the media pack had split up at 9:45 a.m. and scattered along the street, locals could go about their local business, which included dropping into the office to buy the latest copy of *The New England Gazette*. Locals were dropping in to eyeball their crack team of reporters.

Chivonn was very good at ushering them out the door again without offense.

"There are some new developments," she'd whisper to the latest inquisitive local. "Can't tell you now. But—OMG—this case is huge."

This time she spied old Mrs. Ryan, who looked every day of her 90-year milestone. She had been pictured in the *Gazette* on her 90th birthday blowing out the candles on her enormous white and pink piped cream birthday cake. It was a wonder the effort hadn't finished her off. Old Mrs. Ryan was struggling to push her walking frame in the door. Local Police Officer Jack Logan, who the Police Chief had stationed at the front door, was holding the door open for her.

"Thank you, young man," piped old Mrs. Ryan, wobbling in on her walking frame.

"Mrs. Ryan, lovely to see you again,' said Chivonn, oozing so much charm it could have trickled down her legs.

"Hello, Dear. I've got something for that young girl who is having all that trouble with those horrible gun people. I've made her a cake. Upside down New England apple cake." Old Mrs. Ryan opened the seat of her walker and pulled out a boxed cake.

"Oh, thank you sooo much, Mrs. Ryan. We can't stop now, but I'll make sure she gets it."

Mrs. Ryan nodded and wobbled out of the office.

"Aron, read out the holocaust one," Bradstreet ordered.

Aron scrolled through his phone again.

"Wade Suggs, 43, said, "If them Jews had their own guns when Hitler was comin' for them, there wouldn'a been no goddamned Holocaust, that's f'r sure! The NGSA is right. Yuh gotta be ready to defend y'rself against anyone. Includin' yer own Government."

"Get ready for the Civil War Remix!" laughed Bradstreet. "Or it could be all of us against Alaska."

"I dug out that quote of Roy Cotton, Republican senator for Alaska," chimed in Hollis. "Where is it ... here! 'We in Alaska have to stand our ground and stand up for our rights. If that means taking up guns to defend ourselves from the Government ... then that's what we will do.'"

"The senator wants to take up arms against himself!" snorted Bradstreet.

They all laughed. Hollis shook her head.

"Weird Shit Day 3 just keeps on giving," she said to Kee.

Next in the door was Bob McNeice, a retired orthodontist. He often dropped into the *Gazette* office for a long, long, long chat. He, obviously missed his audience of long-suffering patients: sedated, trapped in a dentist's chair and unable to answer back. Chivonn always did her best to politely nudge him out the door, but McNeice hung around like an infestation of fleas. He was that irritating.

"Oh, no!" gasped Chivonn. She turned and stage-whispered to Hollis, "It's Babble-on-Bob." She quickly swung around again and forced her mouth into a cheesy grin.

"Hello, Mr. McNeice," crooned Chivonn. "What can we do for you today?"

"Isn't this the most amazing situation? To think Ridgefield is caught in the middle of a national crime wave. Unthinkable. When I was doing my national service in the sixties—"

"Things are a little hectic here today, Mr. McNeice. Can I help you with something in particular?"

"Quite so, quite so," replied Babble-on-Bob. "I just dropped in to ask if the young lady reporter who was on the television today ... I wanted to ask her if she would give a talk about her experiences at our next Rotary Club Meeting."

"Lovely. I'm sure she'd be delighted," said Chivonn. "She's just popped out for a minute." In fact, Kee was hunkered down behind the front counter, looking at Aron's computer screen. When she heard the words "Rotary Club" and "delighted" she turned to Chivonn and gave her an "I'll wring your neck" sign with her hands.

Chivonn smiled ever so sweetly. "Would you like to write her a formal invitation? Her name is Ms. Le. You will find her byline in today's paper," suggested Chivonn, walking around the front counter.

"I'll do that. Yes. I will," said Babble-on-Bob, as Chivonn placed one hand on his shoulder and gently pushed him out the door.

Outside the office, Bailey Avenue was a long way from its usual sleepy self. Ten-year-olds on bicycles rode up to the window of the office and acted out the youtube clip by forming their fingers into handguns and shooting one another as they yelled, "Bang. Bang." They thought this hilariously funny. An-out of town busker in a WWII army coat defied the local anti-busking ordinance by standing at the corner of Bailey and Main Street, strumming a guitar and singing, "All we are saying is give peace a chance." A Jesus freak appeared on a soapbox opposite the *Gazette* office. He had ridden on a Greyhound bus for two days to reach Ridgefield from New Orleans. Wearing a natty tie, houndstooth suit and cloth cap, he berated passing pedestrians, who appeared unconcerned about their imminent damnation. "Truly, I say unto you, it will be more bearable on the day of judgment for the fornicators and sodomites from the land of Sodom and Gomorrah than the wretched sinners of THIS town."

Kee's foghorn Text ID kept sounding.

"Shut that thing up!" yelled Bradstreet from his office.

"*60 Minutes* wants to interview me. *The New York Times* wants me to do an OP Ed piece. They'll pay me $1,000. Did you hear that, Mr. Bossy? $1,000!!!"

"I'll pay you $100 to shut up!" he roared.

There was a text from O'Shea: LAST TWO VICTIMS REAL SCUMBAGS. COYOTES RUNNING MIGRANTS OVER BORDER. RUN STASH HOUSES. HAVE SHOT KIDS."

Kee knew the back story. Mexican illegals who had left their kids with their grandparents while they established themselves in the states would pay "Coyotes" to bring their kids illegally into the country. The going rate was $7,000. But some scumbags held the kids for ransom in stash houses. If the parents didn't pay more money, the kids were shot. Being illegals, the parents couldn't go to the police. *I'd shoot the scumbags myself*, Kee thought.

She sent a text to O'Shea.

CAN I TWEET THIS UPDATE?

YEP! was his reply.

"Latest victims of AGB criminals with form. Kidnap kids of illegals. Hold in Stash House for ransom. Kids young as 4 yrs have been shot." #Target91 @KeeHasSpoken

She noticed another Tweet from PoliceBizz.

"Weird. FBI stumped by AGB. NO buzz. NO chatter. Means NO clue." @PoliceBizz

"Hey PoliceBizz, nice work with You Tube clip. You should have said "hello." @KeeHasSpoken

"Soon, maybe!" @PoliceBizz

Kee's phone rang. She looked at the ID. It was her father.

"Hello, Pops."

"I just see you on television set. You come home now, Little Moon." Little Moon was her father's pet name for her.

Kee inhaled a big breath. She adored her father. But she found him so frustrating these days. When she was growing up her parents had little time for the old traditions of the old country. The truth was, working in the bakery they'd had no time at all. They wanted their two children to be successful Americans. This they had achieved. But their children knew very little about Vietnam. They could barely speak the language. They couldn't read Vietnamese other than in menus. Their knowledge of their inherited culture came from random outbursts of parental enthusiasm. One time in Grade 3, for instance, Kee's mother dressed her as the Moon Goddess—traditional silk tunic with a full-gold-halo headdress—for Halloween celebrations at school. Kee found herself surrounded by witches and zombies, so she told the other kids that she was a wizard. Later, at Columbia, she had to write an essay on her roots. She did some digging around and was astounded, truly astounded, by the complexity and antiquity of Vietnamese myths and traditions. Suddenly, Western Culture looked like popcorn in contrast. She had, for instance, adored the Spice Girls in Middle School. This fabricated group was classic cultural popcorn, easy to consume but quickly forgotten. Nothing like the Vietnamese folk music she'd discovered. She had bookmarked her brain with a do-more-research-when-I have-time tag; but, she wondered, when would that be?

When Kee's mother had died five years ago, her father had struggled. Part of Vinh's problem was that his wife had been the brains of the family. Kee's father was the gentlest of men, a real softy. His only vice was smoking, which, in a role reversal scenario, he tried to hide from Kee. He'd worked hard all his life but, basically, only doing what he was told. Her mother had run their business, run their finances. She'd organized their investments. She'd paid the bills. She'd organized their social life. She'd even bought his clothes. He was in a muddle without her. Kee had set up his accounts so that most bills were covered by auto pay and regular deposits were paid into his cash account, but every time he rang she panicked.

The trouble began when Vihn rekindled his interest in the old country. He read Vietnamese newspapers, watched

Vietnamese news on TV and went to social events at the Vietnamese Heritage Community Centre. Sadly, he only knew Vietnam before the war. He was, Kee realized, pining for a country that no longer existed. Vinh met the 2 witches—Kee's name for them—at the Community Center. Ba and Pham. The word had gone out in the community that Vinh Le was loaded. He'd sold the bakery business when Kee's mom died, but he kept the premises. He also owned the apartment in Tribeca. Now he was being stalked, targeted, hunted—Kee wasn't quite sure what the right word was to describe these circumstances—by these 2 conniving, competing, weathered old witches. Kee believed they looked at him with $ signs in their eyes. Each one claimed she was his girlfriend, and Kee's father did nothing to discourage their attention. Why would he? They cooked special meals for him. Fussed over him. Brought him little gifts. One witch, Pham, who was 75 years old, had given him a Home Chicken Rotisserie as a gift. Who in their right mind wants a Chicken Rotisserie cluttering up the kitchen?

It's funny, thought Kee, *how strong his accent sounds on the phone.*

"You come home. Very important," he repeated, "you to talk to bank manager."

"Why, Pops?"

"Not over phone," he whispered.

"What's going on now?" she demanded.

"You come see, Little Moon. Very important. She want 2 thousand dollar."

Oh, God! What's happened? thought Kee. "I'll come home soon, Pops. Love you." She pushed the red end-call button and sighed. She hoped he wasn't about to do something loopy, like marry one of the witches. But which witch? Ba or Pham? Argh!

Bradstreet—Bless his ironclad heart—had sent Aron out to buy some Sliders and fries for his wage slaves. *Mr. Don'a-Spenda-Mya-Money has bought us lunch two days in a row. It's a miracle. I should write to the Pope and let him know,* thought Kee.

Aron walked around the office, calling out Slider contents as he pulled them from a carry bag.

"Pulled Pork."

"Me! Me!" called Hollis. Aron threw the wrapped slider onto her desk.

"BLT."

"Mine!" yelled Bradstreet from his office.

"Vegetarian crap."

"I guess that's mine," responded Kee.

Kee ate with one hand and typed with the other. She had copy to write for Monday's special edition. The front-page headline was terrifying enough:

AGB SAYS WE WILL KILL 91 IN NGSA

But more terrifying for Kee was the fact that she had now become a focal point of the news story.

Kee was finishing off some copy for Monday's special edition when Aron excitedly called her over to his desk. He had appointed himself electronic news media monitor, a job he was born to do. He would yell, "Come and have a look at this one!" every two minutes. The news, Kee had to admit, was fascinating and highly addictive. You only had to watch one news item and you were drawn into the ongoing domino effect triggered by the AK-47 murders. This time Booker was fronting the cameras outside the New York office of the FBI.

"My name is special Agent Quincey Booker."

"I know him!" crowed Kee, "I've got his cell number."

"… I'm coordinating the investigation into XC1 murders."

"The XC what?" asked Kee of no one in particular. "Gotta check that out."

"We are making progress. We have officers at each crime scene collecting vital evidence. The only connection between victims so far appears to be the fact that they are members of the NGSA and are known to police. If any member of the public has any information at all, please pass it on to your local police or ring the FBI here in New York."

"Why won't you offer protection to Gig DeKant?" demanded a reporter from WINS news radio.

"We have offered Mr. DeKant full protection, but he has declined our offer," intoned Booker.

"Why has the AGB sent their messages through that *New England Gazette* reporter?" asked another news hound, this time from WCBS news radio.

"We do not know why Miss Le has been singled out. But I can tell you that Miss Le is cooperating fully with the FBI, and she will have all possible assistance from our agency if and when she needs it. Thank you. That's all."

"You're famous, Kee. Reporters are, like, asking questions about you. I should get your autograph," said Aron.

Kee shot him him her mama's-not-happy look, which could terrify stray dogs and young children, and returned to her desk. Aron excitedly called out again.

"Not now, Aron," objected Kee. "I have to get some work done. Call me if anything, like, REALLY amaaaazing happens."

The afternoon passed for Kee in a dreamy chaos of disjointed confusion, broken by bizarre TV news reports and locals dropping in just to say hi. She managed to put several pieces together for the Special Edition, including her televised statement. She wrote a "Can the AGB live up to their threat?" piece. She had inside intel. Although she couldn't quote O'Shea, she did mention FBI sources. She wrote up Gig DeKant's response, updated *The New England Gazette* website, and fed the Twitter chatterati a snippet or two.

Just on 4 p.m., something "REALLY amaaaazing" happened.

"Holy Crap! Come and have a look. Quick. Quick! Come and have a look at this one!" Aron yelled.

Kee dragged herself over to Aron's desk. This time it was the ABC news. Gig DeKant was talking to camera outside the NGSA headquarters in Virginia once again, but matters had turned decidedly bizarre.

Kee and Aron, joined by Chivonn and Bradstreet, stared at the screen, mesmerized. The whole broadcast shifted in a 4-minute segment from drama to tragedy to farce to a comedy sketch from *Saturday Night Live* starring Chris Rock and Woody Harrelson. Gig DeKant—the Woody on this occasion—started to make a speech, but there was a loud bang and Gig and his men hit the turf. Had DeKant been shot? Apparently not, because the corpse refused to die and was struggling with his sidekicks as they tried to carry him back to safety in the NGSA office. Meanwhile some cloaked and masked street performers took centre stage and re-enacted the non-dead DeKant corpse fighting off his protectors. The fighting corpse performer could have taken out the Chris Rock Award for a cameo comedy sketch. He freed himself from his oppressors and pirouetted around the podium, throwing kisses to the audience. Then the other performers sang a chorus or two of "Bye Bye, Baby, Goodbye", which was the cue for the reenactment to reboot for the next take. The cameras kept rolling the whole time. None of them in the *Gazette* office could work out what had happened exactly, as there was too much background noise and shouting, but whatever had happened, it was hilarious.

"Like I said before, this news story is a gift from the God of all Fuck-ups. It's sixteen-hundred hours, people. We're looking at two hours to put this baby to bed!" Bradstreet announced.

A few minutes later, the front door whooshed open once again.

"Hello, Tucker, what can I do for you today?" asked Hollis. Tucker Wood worked in a lumber yard. Or he had worked in a lumber yard until the accident. He'd lost 3 fingers off one hand and had been living off the payout for the last 2 years. Tattooed in the old style with blurred blue ink images, Tucker was a three hundred pounder with triple chins, a broken front tooth, and a shiny shaved head. He wore a checked lumberjack shirt, a faded navy blue tank top, and grimy jeans, and held a blue double-handled duffle bag in his good hand. Tucker was known around Ridgefield for doing odd garden jobs and furniture removal. He had already greeted Officer Jack Logan out front as he opened the *Gazette* office door.

Tucker walked into the office, dropped his bag on the ground, pulled out a sawn-off shotgun and shouted, "Where's that fucking bitch who says Hayden Brodski was a psycho?"

The gun wasn't loaded. It was a vintage piece and had been decommissioned years ago. The *Gazette* staff, however, were unaware of this significant fact. Hollis froze. At that moment, Chivonn came wandering into the office from the toilet. Her greeting morphed to a cry of terror. "Howdy, Tuck ... Tuck ... AHHH!"

She said later that it was a good thing she'd just been to the bathroom or she would have wet herself on the spot. Chivonn slowly backed her way out of the front office.

Bradstreet took charge. During the Chivonn distraction, he pushed Kee out of sight under her desk and walked over to the front counter.

"Is there a problem, Tucker?" he asked.

"That bitch ... it's all bullshit. She says my buddy Hayden Brodski was a ... what did she say?" barked Tucker.

"She said there were disturbing stories," explained Bradstreet. He was well aware of Kee's statement, as he'd sub-edited the piece.

"Y-y-yeah. 'Disturbed.' Hayden was no wacko," grunted Tucker.

"I'm glad you've come in, Tucker, because we need to hear your side of the story. Maybe if you can put that gun down ...."

But Tucker wasn't buying the siege-negotiator's spiel. He aimed the gun at Bradstreets' head.

Meanwhile, Kee sat cross-legged, crammed into the space under her desk, Tweeting frantically.

"There's a madman in the office with a gun. Now. Help." @KeeHasSpoken.

"Someone tell the officer out front to turn around." @KeeHasSpoken.

"Someone call the police. I'm stuck under my desk. Can't make a noise." @KeeHasSpoken.

Then Kee sent O'Shea a two-character text. "85."

But he'd already read her Tweets.

A young pedestrian, 18, skinny jeans, straight blonde hair and a puffy jacket, was walking down Bailey Ave., reading her cell phone and listening to music through her phone earbuds. She was one of Kee's 125,000-plus followers on Twitter. She looked at Officer Logan, had a little peek in the *Gazette* office door, tapped the officer on the shoulder and pointed at Tucker.

The officer turned around and nearly had a seizure. He drew his gun and pushed open the door.

"What the fuck, Tucker?" he shouted, aiming his gun at Tucker's head. Bradstreet rolled his eyes and waved his arms at Logan in a "Get him to put down the gun!" gesture.

Tucker froze. He was obviously trying to think, despite the fact that he'd had very little experience in that department.

Finally, Logan spoke in a low, I-really-mean-this voice. "Put down the gun, Tucker, or this is not going to end well."

Tucker complied. Meanwhile, other Twitter followers had called the police. A convoy of 5 police cars with sirens blaring descended on *The New England Gazette's* newspaper office. Bradstreet dashed over to Aron's desk and nearly dislocated his shoulder by pulling him off his chair while yelling, "Get some photographs! Now!"

Once Tucker was on the ground, trussed up like the Thanksgiving turkey with his hands cuffed behind his back, the young Twitter reader flounced into the office of *The New England Gazette* and announced, "I saved your butts, people, I told the officer to turn around."

"Hollis, another story. Aron, photos!" snapped Bradstreet. He went to help Kee from under her desk, but she was gone.

Chapter 19

Booker

Sunday, the 17th of September

Booker sat at his desk tapping his pen on the wooden desktop. It was 7:45 a.m., Day 3 in the XC1 Murder investigation. Coming up with a code name for this mass shooting had taken Booker's team an unusually long time. The Zodiac Killer in the sixties in California was easy to name. That psycho had included ciphers in the taunting letters he sent to newspapers at the time. Booker's team needed an equally succinct name, but The AK-47 Murders sounded too terrifying. The NGSA Killings was too targeted. The NGSA Cull Killings, suggested by Perez, wasn't going to happen. And the Anti-Gun Gun Murders was too farcical.

"It's almost like a treasure hunt. Why not the X-Marks-the-Spot Murders?" joked Godbold. That's when Volkman came up with the XC1 tag. Booker's team figured most Americans could only count up to 12 in Roman Numerals. So the XC1 Murders it was.

But now the pressure was on from every which way. These murders had grabbed so much media attention that some channels were scrolling body counts under regular, scheduled programs. The case was too big to hang a "Gone fishing" sign on the Organized Crime Unit door. The team was working through the weekend. Booker and Perez were pushing paper in the office. O'Shea was shadowing Miss Le. Booker smiled. "Like herding a psycho-cat," was O'Shea's description of his assignment, along with a spray of colorful expletives. Booker had rounded up 4 FBI rookies to man the phones in the incident room, at least from 9 to 5. The public were vociferous with their suggestions of suspects: UFOs, the anti-Christ, terrorist cells, Russian Agents, the CIA, Mel Gibson (or to be accurate, a clone that had replaced the real Mel Gibson) and Napoleon.

Meanwhile, the team had collected reams of data. Cell phone data. The text messages to Miss Le came from prepaid cards using virtual numbers out of Belgium. Dead end. The text message origins could be traced back to the cellphone towers. But these text messages pinged off towers in 3 different states, which was equally useless. CCTV footage—mostly, miles from the crime and useless. Credit card details. Victim location timelines. Social security data. Ballistics. Autopsy reports. No consistent drug found. Friends and family interviews. Despite criminal records, domestic violence convictions and no-contact court orders, they were all really "great guys". Gun licenses. Gun serial numbers. Sales histories. Only two of the AK-47s had any traceable history. One came from a Texas gun shop, sold via Craig's List out of a car trunk in a supermarket car lot in Orlando, Florida at 10:15 p.m. one night to a legitimate member of the Franklin Patriots Rifle and Pistol Club, Athens, Georgia. The gun safes at the club had later been "rifled" and the gun sold on the black market. One other rifle had traveled via a Gun and Knife Show in North Carolina when an exhibitor's van was stolen while he was setting up his stall. Yet, despite all this data, there were no firm leads.

"And what is the significance of the number 91? It means something to someone!" Booker said out loud. Booker and Perez were office-bound, working through some of this intel. Booker's desktop phone rang. It was the Pennsylvania state police.

"Right.... Where? Text me the location," urged Booker. He gave the trooper his cell number.

"Perez!" Booker shouted into the next office, "there's been another one."

Perez appeared at his office door clutching a folder.

"You're joking. Where, Chief?" she asked.

"Lackawanna State Park, Pennsylvania."

"You know, Chief, I've been thinking. Apart from that first crime scene, the shooters have used state parks and locations where hunting is permitted. A few gunshots in a hunting ground would hardly draw attention. Hunters bang away from dawn 'til dusk and into the night."

"Hall-e-lu-jah," caroled Booker. "I was thinking remote location. But the opposite MO makes more sense. Hang out where shooters hang out. Perez, you and I are going to the latest crime scene. I've Googled it. 2 to 3 hours by car, if you're lucky, so I'm booking a chopper. Our budget can take the hit. We need to move fast. Grab your gear. We've got 20 minutes to get to the Hudson River Helipad."

They were airborne in a black Mcdonnell Douglas 530 Little Bird by 8:35 a.m. Booker and Perez were kitted out with Madonna-style headsets, yet he could clearly hear the rhythmic thud of the blades butchering the air with each sweep. The entire cabin vibrated in time to the blade beat.

It was a shame, thought Booker, that he had to balance the books, because chopper was the only way to travel. He looked down on the man-made canyons of New York City as the autumn sun edged its way above various high rises, and he was amazed, yet again, by the beauty of this geometric grid filled with towering, twinkling glass oblongs and shards. The wonder of this panoramic view never left him, the running boy from Kansas. He felt he was looking down on a futuristic civilization that led the way for the world. It was a shame that, on street level, the futuristic civilization was tarnished by so many crims and crazies.

The chopper landed on the lake's edge a mile and a half from the crime scene. The local trooper had given Booker instructions to walk along a little used track and turn up a creek bed. This was, Booker reflected, the first time he'd been given official instructions to take himself up Shit Creek without a paddle. But, then again, this case ....

Booker and Perez climbed out of the chopper and bent over as they ran under the blades towards the track. It wasn't really that much of an emergency. But if you arrive anywhere by chopper, you feel obliged to look as if you have urgent business at hand. The chopper blades geared down. This was their air taxi. It would wait for them.

Booker looked at the park map on his phone and pointed in the direction. He and Perez headed away from the lake, up a nearby slope. It was a half hour hike up and then down minor mountain paths to the crime scene.

At first, Booker was enchanted by the sound of the dried leaves and gravel crunching underfoot, the crazed pattern of soft leafy light rippling across the path, and the smell of the sweet, menthol-fresh forest air, but not for long. Puffing and sweating soon ruined any euphoric high from communing with nature. "Quincey," he said to himself as he puffed uphill, "62 ain't old." This was something of a mantra for Booker. He was continually telling himself he wasn't old, as if the statement conjured up an invisible shield to fend off time.

After they'd been walking uphill for 15 minutes, they stumbled on a viewing point through the forest. Booker climbed up on a bolder and took in the vista. It was late Sunday morning. Early Fall. Postcard perfect. Lackawanna State Park at its best. Soft sunlight dusted the lake surface below. The vivid rust red, antique gold and majestic green of the fall forest trees were vividly reflected in the glass-smooth surface of the lake, as if God had deliberately created a giant tricolored Rorschach inkblot test. Perez snapped a picture on her cell.

"I may never return here," she said. "I want to remind myself there are some amazingly beautiful places in this country. Otherwise, all my souvenir photos come from the Corpse Tour of America."

Booker—puff-grumbled his agreement. After five more minutes of hiking and puffing, they reached the road that ran through the hunting reserve. Several State Trooper cars were parked on the edge of this road, so they were in the right spot. Finally, following the little-used track downhill—*At last, thank you Lord*, thought Booker—they reached crime scene tape, tied to two tree trunks and strung across a minor creek bed leading away from the track.

Booker and Perez stumbled along the rocky and damp creek bed to a small clearing. The first thing Booker registered before he even saw the body was the smell. Crisp, earthy with a touch of leaf rot, and a strong note of full-bodied, overripe corpse. The MO was the same as the others. There was the body. The AK-47 stuck barrel down. The US flag. The BAN THIS WEAPON sign. *Same font. Arial bold*, noted Booker. A small but vital detail.

He introduced himself and Perez to the local police lieutenant.

"Who found the body?" he asked Lieutenant Ed Selfridge.

"Some early morning hunters, Jack Moore and his son, Hank. They were out looking for ruffled grouse. Called us about 4:45 a.m. They were setting themselves up in a makeshift hide when they noticed the flag," explained the officer. "Looks to me like a scene from one of them Zombie movies." The lieutenant shook his head, "it's hard to believe it's real."

"Copy that," replied Booker, adding, "I want to scout around. Does your forensics team have a time frame?"

"Death probably over 24 hours ago. Maybe ... two days," the officer read from his notes.

"So this is the seventh shooting within, possibly, a twenty-four hour period," said Booker, thinking out loud.

"Perez, I want you to walk around the scene and try and think like the shooter."

"Okay, Boss. But there is some real sicko behavior going on here," protested Perez.

"You said it, Ma'am," said Lieutenant Selfridge, adding, "I'm very glad to hand this one over to you Feds. God knows we have our psychos, but this one, this one is a pro ... a pro psycho, if there is such a thing."

It was the mention of the word "hide" that got Booker thinking. "What if," he muttered, "what if the victim *wasn't* killed with his own rifle, but was taken out by a hidden shooter, a sniper?" Booker called Perez over and explained his theory. Together they worked out trajectories and possible "hides" for a shooter.

Concealment, mused Booker, *involves a totally different game plan from cover.* A shooter took cover behind a rock, say; or, in the city, it might be a dumpster. The FBI manual stated that cover should block a round fired from a gun with a caliber similar to your own. Booker used a Glock 22; a dumpster could stop a .40 caliber round. Cover was short term, immediate. But snipers used concealment. They could sit for days waiting in their ghillie suits.

That suit, thought Booker, *is like Harry Potter's invisibility cape.* He remembered a joint training exercise with the FBI and an Army Rangers unit. *We were flown out to Tacoma, Washington, bussed to the Joint Base Lewis McChord and taken out to the firing range. Then a Combat Marksmanship Training Sergeant, in full camouflage BDUs invites us to spot one of his men hiding in some bushes on the range. We all looked back at him blank faced. The sergeant yells "Junior stand up" and this 250 pound, six-foot-six-inch mountain of a man pops up from all of 50 yards away pointing an M-16 sniper rifle straight at us. He was wearing the rag-torn camouflage outfit called the Ghillie Suit.*

"Is that rifle loaded, Junior?" yells the Sergeant at top drill sergeant volume.

"No, sir!" yells the largest sized Junior on earth in reply.

"Junior, tell me this. Could you have shot any of our good friends in the FBI?" demands the Sergeant.

"Yes, sir. All of them, sir," snaps Junior in reply. There were 30 of us from the FBI.

"That's all, Junior," says the sergeant, and with that, Junior pops down into the bushes and completely vanishes again.

He and Perez started looking for a hide. Booker co-opted all the young officers at the scene for his search—there were six—

and sent them radiating out in a hemisphere up the hill from the crime scene.

"What you are looking for is any indentations in the undergrowth, broken branches, or disturbed ground litter that might suggest a sniper was waiting for his victim," explained Booker. After 20 minutes combing the area, Booker was losing faith in his theory, when a young officer, a small compact girl with a blonde ponytail, called him over. She was a good 250 yards from the victim but in a direct line of sight.

"What have you got?" asked Booker, puffing up the hill. "Hill? Slight incline," he grumbled to himself.

"Sir, I think this looks like a ... like you said, a sniper's nest," explained the officer.

"Bingo," said Booker. "This is it. It does look like a nest. Someone has spent a few hours here, waiting for their victim. But you'll notice there is no trash. This sniper has smarts. We won't find a spent shell. Come here, Perez. Have a look at this. Get a photo."

The FBI officer joined Booker at the sniper hide.

"So here is what I'm thinking. The shooter contacts the target, who is selling an AK-47. Says he will buy one, but he wants to see the gun in action to make sure it's the real deal. Or, maybe, he claims he knows nothing about guns. He's willing to pay big bucks, but needs a lesson or two. Then the sniper settles into place and waits for the victim to arrive. The victim is pretty cocky. 'I've got an AK-47, clip in place.' The victim is taken out by one shot through the heart. Our sniper is good. Total hotshot. Then he walks over. Puts a four-round burst from the AK-47 through the sniper bullet path. Plants the assault rifle. Sticks on the flag and vanishes."

"So now we know what we are looking for," announced Booker, "a sniper. Or several snipers."

"Perez, you contact the rest of the team. They should be at their appointed crime scenes by now. Text them the photo. Tell each of them to look for signs of a sniper hide. If they have left the scene, tell them to go back. We need this intel." He looked at his watch. "Back in the office at fifteen hundred hours if at all possible."

"Right, Boss," Perez replied.

"We're done here," Booker told Lieutenant Selfridge, "but thank your officers. This is a breakthrough. We'll never find the spent round. It could be anywhere. But we have a clear picture now of the MO. And get forensics to look at the sniper nest. He may have slipped up. Spat on the ground. Left a hair. Anything."

Later, during the chopper ride back to Manhattan, Booker scribbled on a piece of paper and passed it over to Perez.

"MO. Sniper shoots victim through the heart. Then puts a 4 round burst from AK-47 into the body. The shooter didn't have to make the victim lie down. They were already dead."

Booker was feeling triumphant, as he always did after a breakthrough. There was a mountain of paperwork to be done, but he had his narrative. Almost. The "why?" was missing. But he'd nailed the "how". His phone buzzed in his pocket. He read the text.

"Oh, no!" he gasped, but his words were lost to the rhythmic chop of the MD 530 Little Bird rotor blades.

Chapter 20

Booker

Death of an Angel

"Angel Lorca de La Vega. Dead." Booker couldn't shake the heavy weight of sadness out of his heart.

It had been a drive-by shooting. The young activist had been DOA when an ambulance rushed him to the hospital.

Booker looked at his watch. 2:15 p.m. Sunday. Day 3 of the XC1 murder investigation. Only Day 3. He decided to give the media mob outside the FBI headquarters an update and scratch that duty off his to-do list before he tackled the latest XC1 murder intel. But on the drive from the heliport to the office, parking the car, getting out of the car, walking to the elevator, his thoughts were about Angel's death. It was still in his brain when he fronted the news cameras outside the FBI headquarters. All those execution-style murders in the XC1 case had hardly registered on his emotional radar. But this killing did. This was the death of a young man trying to change the world for the better. Angel's death was truly a loss for a society that couldn't afford to lose young men like him. Booker took a deep breath and focused on the duty at hand.

He announced, "A seventh victim has been found in the XC1 murders. The body was located in the Lackawanna State Park, Pennsylvania. We cannot release the name of the victim until relatives have been notified."

A CBS news reporter called out, "Was the body found with an AK-47 and the Ban this Weapon sign like all the others?"

The FBI had not, as yet, released this information to the press, but as Ms. Le had said, the authorities cannot stop social media. This story was blazing a trail through the blogosphere.

"I can confirm that the victims have each been shot by an AK-47, that the rifle has then been left barrel down in the body, and that a small note with an American flag on one side and the words "Ban this Weapon" on the other has been found attached to the rifle stock."

"Who are the AGB?" demanded a CNN reporter.

"We do not yet know where or how the Anti-Gun Brigade formed, whether they are affiliated with local or foreign agencies, or if they really do intend to follow through on their threat to kill 91 members of the NGSA," replied Booker.

Questions were shot at Booker as if fired from a standard issue army M16.

"No more questions," he announced. He turned and walked with a determined step through the office front door and on to his office.

He spent some time sorting paper work, then headed towards the Incident Room. Booker called out to the young recruits manning the phones at the back of the room to take a break. He was always up for mentoring and showing young officers the ropes, but it took time and patience, and he'd run out of both.

"Give us about an hour," he told the recruits. There were three males and one female recruit, all in their twenties, who looked so shiny-young and fresh-faced they could have sung for the local Baptist Youth Choir. The phones kept ringing. "And pull the plug on those goddam phones before you leave," he snapped. Definitely out of patience.

Booker taped another crime scene picture to one very crowded information board and turned to address his team.

"3:15 p.m. Day 3 of XC1 Murder investigation. Carter McColl, 48, Lackawanna State Park, Pennsylvania. Same MO." Booker stopped as he took in the expressions of his team. "My oh my," he rumbled, "you lot look like the sad leftovers of last night's rave party."

"I feel as if some jerk with an adjustable wrench tightened all my joints," complained Volkman, groaning as he stretched out one lanky leg and then the other. "Traveling for four ass-numbing hours cattle class from New York to Albuquerque should be a violation of the UN Human Rights agreement. And then there was the four-hour return."

"You can't complain, Volkman," insisted Godbold. "Cogliano hasn't even showed. He might be still wandering around lost in the backwoods of South Carolina, poor bastard."

"Sob story time is over. I want crime scene intel," demanded Booker. "You first, Godbold."

"I've come back with a maybe. The crime scene in Seminoe State Park, Wyoming, was rocky with grass patches and low shrubs. Working on the line of sight, I found one possibility of a sniper nest. Here's the pic." He texted them all the photograph.

"Mmmm," said Booker. "How about you, Volkman?"

"A definite positive," he replied. "You'd think the desert would be indecipherable, but some of that low saltbush had been dislodged in a definite nesting pattern." He texted the photographs.

"Skule?"

"Establishing the line of sight was difficult in a forest in Missouri, especially as the Mark Twain National Park is full of sightseers, but there was this leaf pattern that ... here." She texted her photo.

"So what do you all think about the sniper theory?" asked Booker. They all started talking at once, but there was general agreement. This theory flew.

"If we are looking for a sniper, or a number of snipers, what is it that makes a sniper tick? Godbold, you were in Iraq. Did you do a stint as a sniper?" asked Booker.

"Fuck, no," said Godbold. "My job was to collect intel from local thieving, lying bastards. All I had to do was work out which thieving, lying bastards were on our side and which weren't. Piece of cake that job, compared to snipers. Those guys are total fucking lunatics. In Iraq, they'd take an overwatch position, lie on some god-forsaken rooftop with the sun hammering down on them, trying to decide if the thieving, lying bastard they can see in their scope 500 yards away is on our side or about to blow our ground squad's asses to kingdom come. They've got 3 seconds to decide. Sometimes they sit for days, piss their pants, eat their right arm rather than lose their target. Total fucking lunatics. "

"What about you, Skule? Do you have a sniper profile in your file?" continued Booker.

"There's one thing that stands out. Snipers watch their victims for hours, for days sometimes, through their scopes. They watch them eat, laugh, pee, waiting for a clean shot. They know their victims. So their kill is a cold-hearted kill. It's not like shooting someone in the heat of battle. Or pressing a missile button from some remote location. Their MO is cold and precise. One shot. That's all they get. Often they don't even bother to use a clip. All they have is that one bullet in the chamber. So precision and discipline are paramount," replied Skule.

"So you all agree with this scenario … and the discipline angle fits, too. I'll tell you why it fits. This group, the AGB, have no manifesto, no rant, no ego, no frills. Everything they do is simple and precise. They're like the German Army in World War One. Before they even marched into Belgium, the Germans had calculated the number of locals they had to shoot in each village to control that village. Cold-hearted. Precise. Very effective!"

"So who trains snipers?" asked Booker.

There was a long list. Army. Rangers. Police. SWAT teams. FBI. Special Ops. Marines. Airforce. Navy Seals.

"Police snipers are totally screwed over," remarked Godbold. "Truly. They take an overwatch position at some hostage situation and are told to take out the shooter if any member of the public or their team is in danger. But if a police sniper takes out the shooter, they're charged with murder!!! Un-fucking-believable. These guys get totally screwed in the head. Instead of getting a medal, they get a Grand Jury. It can take months. What, for fuck's sake, do the guys with the badges and the strut think a sniper should do in a hostage situation? Sorry, Chief, I get pissed every time I think of it. What I'm saying is … police snipers are screwed up enough in the head to be up for this. And there have been snipers taking out police of late. There's Dallas for starters. What was it? Five Dead. Nine wounded and fucked-over for life. Maybe, in their screwed up brains, these ex-police snipers think the public shouldn't have access to sniper rifles. Maybe they think it puts police in the crosshairs too often. And they've taken on a campaign to take assault rifles out of the public's hands. In their eyes, they're heroes. Lone Rangers."

"That works. But don't discount other possibilities. For now, we'll work with the sniper theory. We want names of snipers across the board who have a criminal record—unauthorized shooting, violence, or any other form. Perez, this is one for you. See if you can sweet-talk the names of snipers and former snipers from the various services. That intel won't be on a charge sheet. We'll have to cross-match snipers with misdemeanors. I'm assuming felons will be behind bars. It's 3:45. Where does the day go? Let's get moving."

"Can I have a quiet word, Boss?" asked Skule. She walked with Booker to the side of the Incident Room away from the others. "I've done some more digging regarding the situation with your daughter. It seems critical that she go through a natural birth if she is to bond with the baby. It makes sense. If they put her under and give her a caesarian, she won't recognize the baby as her own. In cases like hers, the mother will own the baby if she has to work for it. And there have been many positive outcomes, too, I'm glad to say."

"Thanks, Skule. My wife tells me that the whole family has been working on the baby-friendly theme. But so far it doesn't sound like we've made any progress, other than convincing Charlotte that her family are all barking mad."

"Do you blame her?" joked Skule.

"Not one bit," replied Booker.

"Chief, you might want to see this," Volkman called from the far end of the Incident Room. He was flicking through news feeds on a desktop computer.

Booker strolled over to see what was getting Volkman all excited. Volkman was not the excitable type. Booker could tell something interesting was afoot because Volkman was getting all worked up—Volkman style. He had slightly loosened his tie.

"What's up?" asked Booker.

"Look, Chief," urged the almost-excited Volkman with the slightly loosened tie, "there's that *New England Gazette* reporter. She's on every channel. This is a *Fox News* break."

"She may not realize it," said Booker, looking over Volkman's shoulder to Kee reading her statement to the collected media throng, "but on the Zero to Ten scale of newsworthiness, that young lady now rates a Fifteen-plus."

And here it comes, Booker thought to himself. At the first crime scene, he'd felt like the vacationer looking baffled at the long stretch of the seabed as the ocean inexplicably withdrew. Now he knew the tsunami was about to hit.

Chapter 21

O'Shea

Sunday 17th September

When O'Shea read the first Tweet, he moved. Fast. He arrived within seconds at the back gate leading to the office. After a quick security check—the exit route was clear—he slipped in through the back door of the *New England Gazette* office. He crawled military style to Le's desk while Officer Logan held a gun at Tucker's head. O'Shea grabbed Kee by the wrist. She balked at first, but relaxed when she saw it was O'Shea. He held up his hand, signaling her to wait. When Officer Logan had Tucker contained on the floor, O'Shea signaled to the girl to leave, quietly. No one in the office noticed them go.

The ashen-faced girl looked straight ahead and walked with a robotic gait. She said nothing. Totally unresponsive to her surroundings, she could have been a zombie. O'Shea took charge. "I'm going to drive you home in your car, Le. Make sure your apartment is secure. Then I'll park the car away from your apartment. It's like a neon sign announcing that you're home. I won't be long. Then I'll come back and cook a meal." The girl didn't respond.

Target 91

O'Shea parked Kee's car outside her apartment and walked her to the foot of the staircase leading to her door. He leaped up the steps two at a time and let himself in. *Fucking disaster zone,* he thought, then corrected himself. *The FBI doesn't do home inspections. Remember, don't be an asshole.* The area was secure. O'Shea walked the girl up the back stairs and into her apartment. She was still in a daze. Harold greeted her—curling his warm, fluffy body around her legs. She picked him up, walked over to her bed, sat down, buried her face in the fur of her big fuzz-ball of a cat, and started sobbing.

O'Shea knew she was in shock. He recognized the symptoms. He'd seen it enough in rookies after their first engagement in Iraq. They couldn't process all the information coming their way. Too much. Too fast. O'Shea did what he would do for any young kid in shock in his squad. He pulled a chair over to the bed facing the girl and started talking. He knew if he could get them talking about things they knew away from the battlefield, sometimes the conversation slowly brought them back to life. He talked about anything that came into his head. The weather. Baseball. But his words kept bouncing off her.

The problem was, he couldn't think of one damn thing he might have in common with the girl. Running out of things to say, he started talking about his childhood. Sometimes that worked.

"I grew up in Belfast during the troubles. What a fucked-up childhood that turned out to be. Jesus, Mary, and Joseph. I don't know that I had a childhood. As a kid, I was living in a war zone. You could hear gunfire. Explosions in the background. A two bomb day was not so bad as long as you and your home were still standing after the explosion. There were cyclone wire fences and razor wire coils everywhere. You couldn't go into some parts of the city. The No-Go zones were patrolled by members of the IRA wearing balaclavas and carrying rifles. No one spoke while traveling on the buses. Someone might hear you or think they heard what you were saying. And the IRA was in the habit of dragging people off in the middle of the night and shooting them for speaking out against the cause or allegedly collaborating with the enemy. Nightmare stuff. There were police checkpoints, Army checkpoints, guns pointed at you from rooftops. Even as a kid you had to empty everything out of your bag before you could go into a shop. British troops patrolled the streets in massive armored vehicles. They had sandbagged guard posts. My dad was Irish, Protestant, and my mom was American, Catholic. So I'm screwed up, basically."

Slowly, very slowly, the girl asked, "Were you scared?"

That's it. That's what he was looking for. A response.

"Ah, scared? Sometimes. But mostly you got used to it. I remember being in Woolworth's one time with my mom and a bomb went off just across the alley. For a split second the girl counting out the change was blinded by the flash, then she continued counting. Everyone carried on as if nothing had happened."

"But how did you end up here ... I mean, in America?"

"When my parents split, mom brought me and my brother back home to Philly. I was nine years old. We lived in this endless stream of Hippie communes ending up in New Hope, Pennsylvania. I can't stand the hippie culture. All drum circles and chanting. All idyllic stuff, but hippies don't build roads or build cars or even manufacture their own vegan food. They expect others to do that. They are self-righteous, walk-gently-on-the-earth hypocrites. I'd always looked up to those young British soldiers in Belfast. And street life for a kid during the troubles was exciting. We collected gun shells and army stuff. My friend Matt found a bayonet. That was so cool. The British soldiers would give me PK chewing gum and joke with me. So as soon as I could, I got my hippie-hair cut off and joined the Marines."

"What did your mother say?" asked the girl.

"My mom. Ha! She thought I'd sold out. Joined the enemy. She would hardly talk to me for weeks. But she came to my boot camp graduation. Cried all the way through. Other parents thought she was proud of me. If she'd opened her mouth, she would have said something like, 'You're all brainless pawns of the industrial military money-machine, marching off to be gun fodder in some pointless war. America, O yeah! Land of the dumb and home of the fucked!'"

The girl snickered. This was a good sign.

"What about your mom?" asked O'Shea.

"My mom? Ah! She was amazing. Smart. Feisty. But she died."

"Come on. Tell me about your mom."

The girl fell silent for a moment, lost in thought. She was looking up, but straight through O'Shea. Then she smiled. Really smiled. She continued, more animated this time.

"I can remember when this big tattooed biker stormed into my parents' bakery, cussing and threatening. I was sitting cross-legged beside some bread racks, coloring in a coloring book. So I was quite young. I sat there gazing up at this hot and hairy Neanderthal. To me, he looked all jagged teeth and flaring nostrils, like the angry beast from *Beauty and the Beast*, but wearing a Ghostbusters t-shirt. Funny, I remember that. My mom picked up a rolling pin and brandished it, shouting, "You go now! You not say these things in my shop." Kee didn't know what the customer had said, but she knew her mother would have used the rolling pin, even if she could only manage to take out one of the Beast's kneecaps. The Beast retreated, breadless. "Then Má turned to me and said, 'Your Má is Ghost Buster, Agatha.' We both laughed."

"Agatha?" asked O'Shea, puzzled.

"Aw! That's my first name. You must never, ever use that name or will I put a picture of you, FBI Guy, asleep and drooling all over Twitter."

"I'm sworn to secrecy," O'Shea promised.

Dual ring tones sounded, first on her cell, then on O'Shea's. It was a text from Bradstreet.

WHERE THE HELL ARE U?

The girl looked at her cell and replied: AM OK. FBI GUY SAID LEAVE. ESCORTED ME HOME.

Bradstreet: U FRIGHTENED THE B-JESUS OUT ME.

Kee: SORRY BOSS. IT'S A WEIRD SHIT DAY.

Bradstreet: YOU GOT THAT RIGHT. SEE U TOMOZ.

Kee: WILL DO!

"Look. You need to freshen up, Le. I suggest you have a hot shower and put on some new gear," O'Shea advised, "and I'll go and shift your car."

"Really? You're my mother now?" quipped Kee.

"Didn't I tell you? I have my FBI Mothering Badge."

This was becoming their running joke.

The girl laughed. She was, figured O'Shea, being recalled to life. She'd be okay.

"Back in a minute," he said, picking up the car keys. "You'll be fine on your own for a bit."

Walking to the car, O'Shea checked in with the local police. They gave him a heads up on the Tucker incident. The shotgun, harmless. Decommissioned years ago. O'Shea briefed Booker, and Perez gave him an update on the XC1 murders. He was very efficient at parking the car, retrieving his motorbike and rounding up some supplies. O'Shea rode his motorbike back to the girl's apartment building, pushed it down the path beside the Pampered Pooch Snip 'n Clip, kicked out the stand and bounded up the steps two-at-a-time, whistling, with the supermarket bag of supplies in his backpack. He had already sent a text to the girl: I'M ON MY WAY.

When he arrived outside the apartment door, he knocked quietly, saying, "It's me."

"Why," the girl asked, as she cautiously opened the door for O'Shea, "do we ring a friend or knock on a door and say, 'It's me'? It's crazy. All a psycho murderer has to do is sneak up to someone's apartment, knock and quietly say 'It's me' and the victim will cheerfully let them in."

"Would you prefer I said, 'Hello, it's your friendly neighborhood ax murderer here'?" retorted O'Shea, "with beer, a baguette and the ingredients to make a Sea Food Marinara that will make you weak at the knees."

"Difficult, but you forgot I'm a vegetarian," Kee complained, apologetically.

O'Shea put his hand into the supplies bag and held up a packet of Tofu.

"I'm a very thoughtful Ax Murderer," he quipped.

"What about the ax?" she asked.

"We ax murderers are very cunning," explained O'Shea, as he unpacked the supermarket supplies and uncapped two Budweisers, handing one to Kee.

"Cheers," he said as they clinked bottles. "We get the victim drunk first, and then ... BANG! (He slammed the breadboard on the bench) Out comes the ax."

The girl jumped.

"I've had enough excitement for one day, thank you very much."

O'Shea threw off his black leather jacket and worked in the kitchen in a t-shirt and leather biker trousers, preparing twin Marinara dishes: the Spaghetti Tofu Faux-Marinara and a Marinara Sea Food Classic. He was thinking, *Christ Almighty! The caveman had it good. No vegan-friendly faux Mammoth or diet sodas to worry about. You just speared your Mammoth, dragged it back to camp, and you were a hero. The tribe was so grateful they painted a picture of you slaying the mammoth on the cave wall.* He had a pot of water on the boil; garlic, onion, and tomato chopped. The girl sat on the stepladder by the kitchenette bench in a grey sweatsuit, brushing her wet hair, drinking her beer and watching with apparent amusement as her FBI Homeboy swung into action.

"That smells good," Kee enthused. O'Shea had sautéed the garlic and onions and set the pan aside on the stovetop. She gave a little laugh.

"What?" asked O'Shea.

"I just can't get used to the full FBI home treatment. I doubt the public is aware of all the services provided." She laughed again. "By the way, I've turned on the heating, if you can call two gurgling, hissing wall radiators heating." Changing to a mommy tone, she turned towards the cat curled up on her bed, saying, "You thought it was a bit nippy, didn't you Mr. Harold?" She looked up accusingly at O'Shea.

He held up his hands in the air. "I said nothing. If Mr. Harold thinks it's nippy, then ...." His words trailed off and he shrugged.

"Oh! Mommy nearly forgot to feed you, Mr. Harold!" she said, aghast.

Kee filled the cat's bowl with dried food Fish Delights and some gourmet packaged Lamb Cuisine, then flicked on the TV. Pixie Peters of Fox News was sharing her view on the XC1 murders. The body count was highlighted by the scrolling news update: 6 DEAD. 85 FURTHER DEATHS EXPECTED IN XC1 MURDERS.

"We, as a nation, are in lockdown this evening," Pixie declared. "There are crazy people out there with guns roaming the streets looking for you. If you have any sense at all, you will stay inside with the doors locked and your guns loaded. This is war. It is a war on liberty. It is a war on the Constitution. It is a war on guns. Some self-appointed terrorists have decided that they will challenge your constitutional right to own a gun. And they are prepared to kill anyone who stands in their way. There have been six tragic deaths, and the body count is expected to rise to ninety-one."

Pixie did not mention the criminal records of any of the victims.

"Make yourself useful, Le," O'Shea called out. "Come and shell some of these shrimp."

"Great," she moaned, "now I'm shacked up with the Kitchen Nazi. Yes, sir! Aye aye, Captain, sir."

The girl climbed off the stepladder, hauled off her sweat top and threw it on the bed. Harold immediately relocated himself on the sweat top with a happy mew. Kee was wearing a thin and slinky silver camisole top—and no bra.

Jesus, Mary, and Joseph! Don't do that, O'Shea thought, pleading to himself as much as to the heavens. He regretted asking her for help. *She's half dressed, and this domestic role-playing in close quarters stunt is fucking awkward.*

Kee and O'Shea stood side by side in the cramped kitchenette, stumbling uncomfortably through small talk. Normally, both were masters of the smart-ass quip, yet they were both tripping over their own words as if some electrical interference had disrupted the broadcast from their brains.

"I ... where's the ..." muttered O'Shea.

"What? Do, um, do you wash the shrimp first? Mr. Kitchen Nazi," asked Kee.

"Yes, wash them," replied O'Shea. "Didn't your mother teach you to cook, Le?"

"Too busy. Remember, I grew up in a bakery. My mother cooked for all of New York."

The girl threw the shrimp into a colander, rinsed them and began to break off the tails.

"Arghh! You leave the tails on," O'Shea reprimanded.

He reached over, placed his hands firmly on her slender hips and spun her towards him. O'Shea's spontaneous move was far too intimate, too unraveling for a professional relationship. The touch of her soft skin against the texture of his muscular arms hit him like an electric shock. This was too close for comfort. They jolted apart.

"No tails ... I mean, keep the tails on," he insisted, *and keep away from me*, he thought.

"Yes, sir, Mr. Kitchen Nazi," she mocked.

After peeling the shrimp, the girl wandered over to the TV set and changed channels. Dan Anderson on CBS was moderating, or trying to moderate, a debate on gun control between Sheldon

Endecott, a Democrat Senator from Connecticut, and Roy Cotton, a Republican Senator from Alaska.

"You can insist, Senator, that the Constitution gives you the right to bear arms, but where is the well-regulated militia that the constitution demands? Where is it? What you've got are survivalists shooting up cans with assault rifles," complained Endecott.

"You cannot take away our right to bear arms!" snorted the plump, ruddy-faced Cotton. "Americans like to hunt."

"What has hunting got to do with this? What do AK-47s have to do with hunting? You can't bear arms against a rabbit," Endecott interjected.

"So you would take assault rifles off decent folk who just want to protect their families?" demanded Cotton.

"No one, not one person in this country outside of the services, needs an assault rifle!" yelled Endecott angrily.

"And that IS the very reason why the citizens of America need to be armed, in case our very own government decides to come and take our guns!" Cotton rejoined triumphantly.

"You'd shoot at our Armed Forces, our own National Guards, would you?" spat Endecott, aghast.

"Yes, Sir, we would. That's why we need guns! Because we cannot, I repeat, sir, we *cannot* trust our own government!" roared Cotton.

Suddenly, there was a loud crack followed by the sound of breaking glass. O'Shea looked around, grabbed Kee by the waist and threw her into the bathroom. "Get down," he hissed.

Someone had fired a round through one of the apartment windows. In an instant, O'Shea had his Glock 26 out of his zippered pocket and in hand. He turned off the TV and the main light, moved cautiously along the sidewall and carefully peered out the other window. He heard a car speed off in the distance. He couldn't see it. He was still standing well back from the window and peering into the swaying shadows of the lamplit street, holding his Glock in front of him, when he heard rummaging behind him. He didn't want to take his eye off the street, but ho he turned quickly and saw, out the corner of his eye in the ghostly blue light of the one lit gas jet on the stove, Kee going through his things.

"What the hell are you doing?" he stage whispered, nonplussed.

"I need a gun. I figured you must have more than one."

"Get back in the bathroom. I don't know what's going down here," he ordered.

"No. No. If some idiot is going to take pot shots at me, I'm going to fire back," she insisted.

O'Shea wasn't sure which way to focus his attention, on the street or behind his back. *It's bad enough having some lunatic with a gun in the street shooting at me, without having another lunatic with a gun behind me shooting at me.*

"Wow!" gasped Kee, opening the case of the Stag 3TL-M. "That's real firepower."

"Don't touch that," he snapped, trying to look out the front window and at the lunatic girl at the same time.

"How do you put it together?" she asked, seriously.

"You can't go firing up the main street of Ridgefield with an automatic Stag 3TL!" he shouted, all pretense of quiet crime scene surveillance abandoned.

"Have you got another gun?" she asked, reaching for a smaller case. "Perfect!" She had found his standard issue Smith and Wesson .40 cal. She pulled the gun out of its case and pointed it towards the wall.

"For Christ's sake, are you deaf? Put that down! I have no intention of being shot in the back with my own gun," he protested.

"Where are the bullety things?" the girl asked.

O'Shea left his surveillance post by the window and stormed over to the girl. He grabbed the pistol out of her hands.

"Hey!" she objected.

"Now shut the fuck up and do what you are told. Get your ass back into the bathroom," he ordered, seething.

"I was only trying to help," she sulked.

"When I need your assistance with a handgun or an assault rifle, Le, I'll let you know. Christ almighty!"

O'Shea returned to the window and waited for five minutes, but there was no movement in the street. This part of town consisted mostly of commercial properties. No one lived around here except the girl and old Mrs. Myers above the Happy Nails and Day Spa three shops down, and she was a little deaf.

O'Shea returned to the bathroom and switched on the light.

"Don't you get it?" he asked, irritated, as he slipped his Glock back into his zippered pocket. "This isn't a game. Someone just tried to warn you off. I'm going out back to see if I can get some plywood to block that window, and I would appreciate it if you kept *away* from the window and generally tried *not* to shoot anyone, including yourself, while I'm out back. Is that too much to ask? I felt safer on reconnaissance in Iraq."

"Hmmph!" she snorted. "I'm going to dry my hair."

"By all means. I've prefer a well-coiffed corpse, myself."

"Will you stop with the funny guy act? I'm sick of it."

For the second time that night O'Shea held up his hands in surrender.

"Yes, ma'am."

O'Shea returned to the apartment with a sheet of board he'd found blocking a hole in the back fence. It wasn't the best carpentering job, but between his Leatherman, a few nails he pulled out of an old crate, and a meat cleaver used as a hammer, he managed to patch the broken window.

"As a carpenter, I do believe your skills are lacking, but as a post-modern deconstructionist dadaist multi-media artist I am convinced you have potential," she announced.

"What does that even mean?" he asked.

She burst out laughing. "It's all bullshit, O'Shea. I just made it up."

They both laughed.

"Now I'll finish that meal I promised you."

O'Shea was good to his word. The pair sat at the rickety dumpster table eating their respective faux and real marinaras, which were both restaurant-worthy. Kee looked at her watch.

"It's only 7:15," she said, sounding surprised. "I thought it would be like midnight or something. It's been a full on day."

Her cell ringtone sounded. She looked at the screen.

"Freaking freak hell," she said, reading the text. "It's the AGB. Same serial number."

"Read out the message," O'Shea called from the kitchenette.

"I'm so over this. It was exciting for a day, but now I really don't like it. I'm trapped in this circus of freaks and maniacs, and I'm a sitting duck for any loony out there with a gun fetish."

"Just read the message," urged O'Shea.

"WE HAVE HACKED INTO THE NGSA RECORDS. WE HAVE THE NAMES AND ADDRESSES OF ALL NGSA MEMBERS. WE WILL RELEASE THE NAMES OF ALL MEMBERS STATE BY STATE STARTING TOMORROW ON WIKILEAKS VIRGINIA FIRST."

"Party's over. I'll have to ring Booker, then Gig DeKant," she sighed.

"I can do Booker," suggested O'Shea.

"No! This is my show. I'll call him," she snapped. "But why Virginia?"

"Probably because the NGSA headquarters are in Virginia," explained O'Shea.

"Of course, duh! I should have realized," Kee grumbled.

"How should I reply to the AGB, O'Shea? I mean, I don't want to sound like we're real pals now or anything."

"Keep it simple. Something like MESSAGE RECEIVED. WILL PASS ON TO DEKANT."

She sent the message verbatim.

Scrolling through her contact list for Booker's number, she noticed a Tweet from @PoliceBizz.

"Was in the vicinity. Saw shooter's car. Blue 1970s Ford Highboy Registration Number: 879 HYU @PoliceBizz

"O'Shea, are you watching this? I'm going to reply to @PoliceBizz. OK?"

"Yep! I've got it. Go ahead, Kee," replied O'Shea.

He was not conscious of the tectonic shift that had taken place in his psyche. The crazy catgirl under his protection had morphed in his mind into the lunatic girl, the workmate Le, and finally, the up close and personal Kee. She called him O'Shea and acted half the time as if she was oblivious to his presence, but in siege negotiator's terms, he had surrendered.

"Wow! PoliceBizz, what are you? My guardian angel?" @KeeHasSpoken

"Maybe" @PoliceBizz

"Thanks, PoliceBizz. You're a star, baby!" @KeeHasSpoken

"That's... amazing intel," said O'Shea, a doubtful look on his face. "What's this guy doing hanging around your place?"

"He's a good guy. Really," insisted Kee.

"I don't like it. Stalking you online, that's one thing. Hanging around your house, that's something else altogether," insisted O'Shea. He had the intel on the shooter's car up on his phone almost instantly.

"The car belongs to one DeAndre Chorinos, known to police. Last arrested for brawling at Billy Bob's Let 'em Buck Bar."

"He'd know Brodski, then. That bar was one of his haunts," explained Kee.

"I'll put the local cops onto him. That should put him out of action for a while," said O'Shea, scrolling through his contact list for the number of the local police. "And I'm going to have @PoliceBizz traced. It takes a little time. I'll need a warrant. Those social media nabobs think they are protecting free speech. Half the time they're protecting street gangs, drug cartels, pedophile rings, terrorists. You name it."

"O'Shea, are you watching? I'm going to update my Twitter account."

"Read out the Tweet. I'm looking for intel on @PoliceBiz."

"AGB threaten to release all names of NGSA members on Wikileaks starting tomorrow." @KeeHasSpoken #Target91

"Fine. Post it."

Kee pressed the Tweet button and then bent down to pick up Harold, who'd been sadly neglected in the kerfuffle and was still hiding behind the couch.

"Sorry, Mr. Harold," soothed Kee, "things have been a little hectic."

She sat on the bed and scratched him under the chin. He purred like an idling pickup truck.

Target 91

"I have to ring Booker, and DeKant," Kee remembered.

O'Shea picked up another Budweiser and wandered to the front of the apartment to carefully look out the one good window over the tattered Snip 'n Clip awning onto the street. He could hear the murmur of Kee's business-like conversation on the phone behind him, but outside a heavy stillness had settled in with the night. Dim lamppost light illuminated cones of haze down the dark street. A sliver of moon threw dancing, crisscrossing shadows of almost-bare tree-branches onto the sidewalk. O'Shea could hear a lone car in the distance and a dog barking. That was all.

Chapter 22

O'Shea

The Night Watch

O'Shea rang Booker.

"Yep!" answered Booker, brusquely.

"What do you make of the latest AGB threat?" asked O'Shea. "They are really ramping up the pressure on the NGSA."

"Let's hope our team can find some leads to break this open soon. You up to speed on the sniper theory?" queried Booker.

"Yep," retorted O'Shea. Perez was keeping him briefed via text message. O'Shea needed up-to-the-minute intel on the AGB to protect Miss Le.

When O'Shea told Booker about Kee deciding it was time to shoot back at the shooter, Booker laughed. He could hardly speak he thought it was that funny.

"You ..." chortle "better ..." snigger "be careful ... haha! Wear your flak vest to take a whizz. You never know ..." guffaw.

"Yeah, real funny," grumbled O'Shea.

Booker ended the call laughing.

"O'Shea," Kee called out. She wearing her standard night attire of grey hoodie and underpants, holding her cat in her arms and clutching her cell phone in one hand.

"You have to listen to this. I taped DeKant's response to the Wikileaks threat." She pushed Play.

DeKant's voice boomed out of her cell phone.

"We as a nation are facing a clear and present danger. This organization that calls itself the AGB, a group of deviant thieves and murderers, is putting the security of this entire nation at risk by publishing private information on the internet website Wikileaks. This abhorrent act, which begins with naming NGSA members, will continue until all the secret security information of this great nation of ours is handed over to the enemy. Protect yourself. Protect your family. Protect your country. Be armed. Be ready."

"Is that creepy, or what?" asked Kee.

"Once their names are out there, some of the NGSA will immediately assume that the 'bad guys' will turn up tomorrow to take their guns. It's a nightmare for law enforcement. Some officer arrives on some guy's doorstep to tell him his kid was in an accident or something and—Bang!—the officer gets shot doing his job."

"Are you going to bed, or what? Kee asked, yawning. "It's past ten. And I'm really knackered."

O'Shea sat at the wobbly table and began cleaning his Glock.

"I told you, I have to stay up all night. That last shooter was an amateur. Who knows what lunatic will turn up next? You go to bed. Get some sleep. We'll get you to a safe house tomorrow."

"Whatever!" sang Kee, as she dumped Harold on one side of the bed, pulled back the covers on the other side and climbed into bed. She fell asleep before she could even say "Goodnight."

She can be so irritating, thought O'Shea. *We don't get much thanks in this job. Here I am saving her ass and all I get is a 'Whatever.' Really?* He quickly turned his attention to the layout of the apartment as his sniper discipline kicked in. He had work to do.

O'Shea made himself a large mug of coffee and propped himself on a chair at the end of the kitchenette. His Glock rested on the stepladder/stool beside him. The L-shaped kitchen counter partly obscured his position, and he'd put a bedside lamp in the bathroom to throw some low-level lighting across the back door. He also tied a loop into one end of a length of thread with an old key attached to the other end and hooked it on the tip of the lever-style back door handle. If any one moved the handle the key would drop. It wouldn't make much noise, just enough. If someone was coming through that back door, he'd know. He would definitely know.

O'Shea waited. He'd done this before many times. He sat out the night with his own thoughts haunting him. It was so quiet and so still he was struggling to stay awake.

At 1 a.m. he woke with a start. Kee was pulling the duvet off her bed, complaining.

"You woke me up. You were snoring," she grumbled, half-asleep. "I'm going to sleep in the bathroom." Armed with the spare couch cushions and dragging the duvet behind her, Kee disappeared into the bathroom, followed by the cat.

"Leave the door slightly ajar," O'Shea yelled, "I need that little bit of light."

"Yeah, yeah. Whatever!" she huffed.

"And now I have to piss in a bottle because Madam has set up camp in the bathroom." At least O'Shea knew he wouldn't be falling back to sleep in a hurry. He sat and waited.

Target 91

It was around 3 a.m. when O'Shea heard the key drop. It was just a slight tinkling sound, but enough to confirm his reading of the situation. He knew, he just knew, some cartel prick would want to muscle in on the AGB media circus. If they could get to the young journalist, it would prove they could get to anyone. It'd be their way of warning off the AGB, and anyone else.

He picked up his Glock and watched the back door. The handle slowly turned, then relaxed. A key was pushed into the old lock. Slowly. Then it stopped. A newspaper was pushed under the door, and the key pushed entirely into the lock until the back door key dropped silently onto the paper. The handle turned slowly once again.

The intruder, in black fatigues and a black ski mask, entered the apartment with a purpose, with stealth, and with a Viridian green laser-sight clipped to the Picatinny rail mount on a Smith and Wesson pistol. He was also wearing night goggles. He took three steps into the apartment. O'Shea didn't hesitate. He fired a quick round, hitting the intruder and splintering his right shoulder at a point just outside of the flak jacket zone. O'Shea had loaded his gun with full metal jacket rounds, not hollow points; the bullet tore through the intruder's arm and out the back door. The shooter dropped his weapon, reached for his shoulder and took a lurching step forwards, gasping. O'Shea was setting up his second shot. He was going to kneecap the intruder, but he was taking his time. He enjoyed a bit of cat-and-mouse play, especially when he was the cat. And he wanted to get the second shot right: wing him enough so that he was no longer a threat, but not so shot up that he fell into a coma or bled out. O'Shea could collect some useful intel. All this action took place within a five-second time frame, but time always slowed down in the kill zone.

Kee had woken, screaming, at the sound of gunshot. Harold bolted and squeezed himself in behind the old-style freestanding bath. Kee quickly gagged her scream and crept to peek out the bathroom door. Someone shrouded in black had entered *her home* and was lurching forwards. Swiftly, she picked up the bathroom scales, pulled the bathroom door open, turned on the kitchenette light—completely blinding the shooter and O'Shea— and smashed the intruder across the back of the head as hard as she could. He dropped like a felled tree, smashing his face on his night-goggle gear.

"What the fuck?" yelled O'Shea, blinking as his irises adjusted to the dazzling blast of electric light.

"I got him!" yelled Kee, all excited, as she looked down on the limp body of the intruder. "I got the bastard!"

O'Shea, for possibly the first time in his life, was utterly flummoxed. The situation was not only moving off script, it was moving towards some bizarre new play he couldn't even imagine. He secured the shooter's weapon and stowed it under the couch. Then he walked over to the slumped body, rolled the intruder onto his back and pulled off the night goggles and ski mask. O'Shea patted down the body. No extra weapons.

As O'Shea moved away from the unconscious intruder, Kee moved closer and kicked the shooter in the leg.

"Don't do that!" yelled O'Shea, moving towards Kee. He pushed her away from the shooter.

"You're complaining about one little kick. He was going to kill me," protested Kee.

"I'm not worried about you kicking him. I've already winged the idiot. Now I have to kneecap him the hard way. By hand. That's a dirty business. But I need him out of action. His buddy could turn up any minute. And when this idiot comes to, if he comes to, and you haven't totally smashed his brains into another dimension, I can get some intel out of him."

O'Shea looked around the kitchenette and sighed. He picked up the old clock-dial style bathroom scales and felt them for weight. He held the scales longways in both hands, raised them in the air and smashed one end into the shooter's left leg. Right shoulder, left leg, out of action. The intruder was not going anywhere in a hurry. O'Shea rolled the unconscious intruder onto his front again, took some zip ties from his trouser pocket and secured the shooter's hands behind his back, then rolled him on to his back again. Kee watched, fascinated. O'Shea secured the intruder's ankles with another zip tie.

"You are not to Tweet or Text or write about this," he instructed Kee.

"I'm not going to do anything while you're within arm's reach of those scales," she joked.

"Seriously. Do you understand? We're in the field. We must make the operation zone safe and secure," he warned.

"I'm for it. Safety. Absolutely."

O'Shea stepped over the body to the sink, filled a saucepan with water, and threw it in the intruder's face.

"Are we going to heavy him? Get him to rat on his boss and all that?" asked Kee. She was standing on the other side of the trussed and prostrate intruder, who was now spluttering with each breath.

"It lives," said O'Shea, then turning to Kee, added, "and WE are not going to do anything. I will cross-examine the intruder without your very annoying assistance. You nearly got yourself shot before. By me. Sticking your nose in where it's not wanted."

Kee pulled an ugly frowny face. "Ner!"

The gunman started to come round. He was babbling incoherently. Kee looked down at the shooter and yelled, "You'll be sorry, Mr. Hitman, for trying to shoot me, you piece of shit."

She kicked him again, this time in his smashed knee. The intruder yelped.

O'Shea was dumbfounded. He leaped over the body, grabbed Kee by the waist and pushed her backward into the bathroom, kicking the door closed behind them with his left foot. He let her go, hissing, "*You* are not going to interview the shooter. You are going to stay *in here*, out of the way, minding your own business."

"This *is* my business," she huffed, reaching for the door.

O'Shea grabbed Kee by the wrists and pushed her back against the bathroom wall, pinning her hands above her head. He kicked her feet apart with one foot. They glared at one another. She started to say, "Under the UN convention of domestic truce ..." when O'Shea did something she absolutely didn't expect. He kissed her.

Kee looked shocked. O'Shea felt a kick of pain in his gut.

What am I doing? I've really fucked up this time, he berated himself. He stepped back and released her hands. She blinked. They looked awkwardly at one another. Time froze. He could see her breathing heavily. Finally, after the sliding past of centuries, she moved. She took one small step towards him, wrapped her arms around his neck and kissed him. Suddenly, time whipped into a frenzy. She was kissing him so passionately she was almost eating him.

O'Shea gave in, gave up, surrendered. Her smallness— petiteness, really—her rumpled black hair with the fresh smell of shampoo, her delicate, nymph-like face, the narrowness of her shoulders, her screw-you-O'Shea attitude broke through his tempered steel toughness, and he ached for her, felt the hard physical pain in his erection. He could sense her body responding to him. He pushed back her hair and kissed her neck breathing in the aroma of that wondrously intoxicating cocktail of girl scent shot with pheromones.

But getting her to shut up was something else.

"Is that a gun in your pocket, or are you just glad …" murmured Kee, adding, "freaking freak hell, it *is* a gun in your pock … et." She had slid her hand down to his hip. O'Shea kissed her again.

"But … but …" she interrupted, "what about the hit … man person in my kitchenette?" O'Shea kissed her throat as she leaned her head back. O'Shea whispered, "He can wait."

Suddenly, O'Shea grabbed her by the shoulders, holding her at arm's distance. He knew the look in her eyes. It was the live and dangerous current of desire, the fierce animal drive of attraction. Raw, voracious sex. But what did she see in his eyes, he wondered, indifference? No. Fear, maybe. Fight or flight? *Because that's what I do. Fuck and flee to another case, another girl, another state. You should keep away from me.*

"If we're going to do this, let's go slow," he urged. This was the sniper in him talking. He could wait out three days before full gratification.

"Fuck that," said Kee, pulling off his t-shirt and unzipping his fly. He hardly resisted. He managed to frantically kick off his boots, dancing from one foot onto the other, and then he hauled off his leathers, still dancing. Kee pulled down his boxers. Then she burst out laughing. Her laughter was like the tinkling of a wind chime, all free spirit and joy.

"Sorry," she sniggered, "you're not circumcised. All the boys I've been with have been circumcised." She started singing the Elton John classic, "Rocket Man".

"You know Elton John?" he asked, incredulous. Elton John was old school rock gold.

"I saw him on *The Simpsons,*" chortled Kee.

O'Shea grinned. She always, always, caught him on the back foot. As soon as he was sure-footed, knew what he was doing, she pulled the rug from under him. He wrenched her panties down and off. His desire was palpable. His body was racked by the gut-twisting pain of it. His cock was unbearably hard. He could barely talk. Kee kicked her panties under the bath. He pulled off her hoodie. Her camisole top was so slight it drifted to the floor like a feather. O'Shea didn't so much enter her as lift her up and slide his penis along the delicate flesh of her inner thigh until he was inside her. She clung to him. Wrapped her legs around him. She groaned. And he fucked her against the bathroom wall. This was furious sex. Up against the wall sex. He was in shape, but his thighs cramped with the strain of this sex. Her nails dug into his back and her back arched. She gasped as she came, lost in the musky sensuality of sex, swooped up in an exquisite high, then free falling with the dark angels of an orgasm. He could not hold out. He gave himself into the high-arching relief and ravenous nirvana of orgasm.

O'Shea gently lowed Kee so her feet touched the bathroom floor. They looked at each other, a little shell-shocked. What had just happened?

"Freaking freak hell," Kee huffed, reaching for her bikini briefs. "You didn't use a condom, did you?"

"Well, I ... you didn't ask," replied O'Shea, caught on the back foot again.

"Now not only is someone trying to shoot me ... NOW ... I'm going to catch some hideous boy germ," she sniveled.

"No boy germs. I promise. I'm cleared by the FBI," insisted O'Shea. This was, in fact, true. He had worked undercover for many years and had undergone regular health checks. He caught her hand, swung her around and kissed her on the neck.

"I hate myself," she moaned, "but this is sooo good. Freaking freak hell."

O'Shea put on his boxers and retrieved his tee and leathers; he could hardly drag himself away from this goddess-like creature, who had drawn him into the dark treachery of her underworld. He felt entangled, trapped somehow. He dated in the New York style, which, as one of his hook-up dates had explained, involved the 4 Fs: Phone. Food. Fuck. Fuck-Off. But this was different. It was not over. He could not take his eyes off her. She had turned her back on him to gather her clothes. She was only wearing her bikini pants. He stepped behind her and glided his hands up and over her pert breasts. He felt each erect nipple strum against his fingers. She wriggled free to get dressed.

"Chalk up another one, O'Shea," she said, smiling as she picked her camisole top off the floor and slipped into it.

"What?" he asked, puzzled.

"You've just earned your FBI Star Fucker's Badge." She laughed.

Reluctantly, he pulled on the rest of his gear, saying as he tied his laces, "Listen. It might be a good idea to leave the interrogation of a highly dangerous criminal to me, the FBI agent, trained in these matters."

"Maybe."

"And I'll get your sweatpants from the bedroom. I'll have to call an ambulance, and the local police. There will be quite a circus showing up any minute in your lounge room."

"Sounds fun," she enthused. But he didn't have to convince her to stay in the bathroom, for she remembered Harold. Poor Mr. Harold was stuck in his hiding space behind the bath, traumatized and refusing to come out. Mommy had her hands full.

Chapter 23
O'Shea
A Real Live Cop Show

O'Shea stepped over the barely-conscious intruder to retrieve the Smith and Wesson from under the couch. The Viridian green laser-sight could prove useful. He aimed the Smith and Wesson at the intruder. A green spot appeared on the shooter's forehead. He gave the limp body a shove with his foot. He took a picture with his cell phone and texted it to the night desk. Old Manny would do a search for him. O'Shea went through the intruder's pockets. There was no ID. So he was a professional.

O'Shea stood over the shooter, waiting. The intruder's eyes opened and darted erratically around the kitchenette. He was confused. O'Shea toyed with the Smith and Wesson, popping a green spot on the victim's forehead and mouthing the word "Bang."

The intruder moaned. He was in pain and panicked by O'Shea's behavior.

"Are you going-g to finish me off?" croaked the intruder in a, maybe, slavic accent.

O'Shea said nothing. His cell phone buzzed. He texted "Thanks" to Old Manny and read aloud the RAP sheet.

"Milos Dusanek Kostelac, 38. Czech. Drug dealing, small arms. Et cetera, et cetera. Armed robbery. So we know that you hang out with some mean badasses. Who sent you?"

O'Shea knew from the intruder's criminal record that he was most likely tied up with a drug cartel, that he was a gun for hire, a cartel enforcer and a nasty piece of shit. But why target Kee?

The intruder didn't speak.

"The thing is, I didn't shoot you with hollow points. The round was the full metal jacket. So you are not going to bleed out. You're not going to die quickly. I can just stand here asking you questions ... all night ... or I can ..."

O'Shea moved toward the intruder and pressed one foot on his busted knee. The shooter screamed.

"That's it. You've got the picture. Who sent you?" repeated O'Shea, looking down on the prostrate victim. The intruder didn't need any more encouragement.

"Ladislav Janecka."

"Good old Ladislav," remarked O'Shea. "So he's running guns now, and his retail business has run into a bit of trouble, with his sales team being offed like that! Must be bad for business."

The intruder just grimaced. O'Shea stood looking at the hired heavy with contempt. He could pop him off without a hitch. Self-defense. He was an intruder. *The question is*, thought O'Shea, *"is he worth keeping for questioning?"*

O'Shea walked to the back of the apartment and called the local cops. Four police cars roared to the apartment, lights flashing, sirens screaming into the still night. The local cops were putting on the best reality TV cop show on earth. The

Mayor/First-Selectman had told them to show the world "We mean business!" and the local cops were loving it. They even sent four cop cars, lights flashing and sirens blaring, to pick up their order of takeout pizza that night. They knew how to Barnum & Bailey a cop show cliché. O'Shea talked the Lieutenant through the night's drama. Crime scene photos were taken and the Smith and Wesson handed over as evidence. The busted knee was not mentioned.

Kee emerged from the bathroom wearing her cami-top and sweatpants. This proved problematic for O'Shea. He still couldn't take his eyes off her. Her presence burned into him wherever she stood. He was aware of every facet of her. Her swearing. Her sass. Her cute ass. Her taut belly and sweet breasts. Kee had surprisingly well-formed breasts for a slim girl. *A perfect handful,* he thought, then reprimanding himself, *Stop thinking with your dick and keep your mind on the job.*

O'Shea coughed. "Miss Le, this is Lieutenant ..." He couldn't remember the name.

"McLeish," replied the officer, holding out his hand to Kee.

"I'm Kitchi Le," she replied, shaking his hand.

"We all know who you are," he said, "you've been busy."

"Not by choice," she complained, adding, "Harold won't come out of the bathroom. He's terrified."

The lieutenant looked perplexed.

"Harold's my cat. Poor darling, he's not used to hired gunmen popping into his bedroom."

"I don't think anyone, human or cat, ever gets used to that sort of thing," replied the lieutenant.

"I don't know ... I seem to be getting used to all sorts of weird things happening these days," Kee complained.

Every member of this odd little crime scene cameo was looking down at the neutralized shooter on the floor. Kee, however, glanced up at O'Shea standing on the other side of the crim's semi-slab-ready body. He was looking directly at her. She tried not to smile, but a little grin flittered across her face as she looked up at him. O'Shea made a fatal move. He dropped his line of sight down to her chest. Maybe it was the recent sense memory. Or anticipation. But his eyes fixed on the vision of her erect nipples clearly visible through her slinky top. His rational human brain may have been saying *No. No*, but his body was rebelling. He had an instant erection. It wasn't just the hard-on that was the problem. It was the degree. It was painful. It hurt hard. He was feeling exposed. Still thinking in sniper talk, he turned toward the couch and grabbed his leather jacket for concealment.

"Should I come ... um, down to the station?" O'Shea asked. His brain was scrambled, but he had to have a reason for picking up his leather jacket.

"I don't think that will be necessary," replied the lieutenant, still concentrating on the shooter. "We'll have him out of your hair in no time. Just give us a few more minutes."

"You mean I can get back to sleep?" Kee cheered. "Thank goodness for that!"

O'Shea's mind was a long way from the shooter. *If the FBI psychs ever found out that I had a hard-on standing over the bleeding body of a crim I just shot, they'd have me sectioned, certified, cuffed and locked in the can for the criminally insane in a New York heartbeat.*

Photos were taken. Evidence collected. Then the paramedics arrived with a stretcher and carted off the would-be hitman. The circus quickly and efficiently packed up its act and rolled out of

Kee's apartment. So thorough was the circus exit, the carpet runner the shooter had bled onto in Kee's kitchenette was rolled up and carted off as evidence. The police even wiped the floor. They were looking for more evidence. God only knows what they thought they might find. A bullet hole, perhaps.

When the last officer left and closed the door, Kee and O'Shea burst out laughing. It was too bizarre.

"I feel as if a TV cop show just popped up in my apartment. Shooters. Cops. Flashing lights. The works. And now it's over. Weird. And how about you, Rocket Man?" Kee asked.

"You, Agatha," complained O'Shea, "have caused me no end of grief."

He walked her backward towards the bed, threw her down and fell on top of her, pinning her down with his body and holding her arms over her head.

"Don't call me, Agatha," she protested. "I hate Agatha. If you say that in public, I will have to kill you."

"So that's sorted. Now, Ms. Le, you are not moving until you say a proper thank you for my saving your rather lovely ass," breathed O'Shea, his face only four inches from hers.

"No," she said, squirming.

"Not moving," said O'Shea.

"I'll scream," she threatened.

"Soooo ... that ... old Mrs. Myers with the gimpy leg can come running to save you."

They managed another bout of sex. But this time slower. On the bed. Him on top of her, mostly. The sniper delaying the gratification with tenderness and caresses and kisses down Kee's stomach. And that silver tongue worked its magic too. Afterwards, Kee, lying on the bed with her eyes closed and one hand on her forehead, murmured, "That was freaking Glor-i-ass!"

"*You've* got the glory ass," said O'Shea, picking his boxer shorts up off the floor. *It should be over*, he thought. *The deed's done. Move on.* But he had a problem. He still couldn't take his eyes off her. Her presence seared into his psyche, into his skin. He wanted a clear head, but she had awoken a need in him that he did not understand, or like. He traveled light. He needed to be able to disappear at any time without explanation, without trace. He did not like this bullshit parasitic neediness she stirred up in him. Just thinking about her aroused him. He loathed this weakness.

"What happens now, O'Shea? Is there anything in the FBI code that says you can screw any member of the public you are guarding as long as you leave your gun in your pocket?" she joked.

He sat on the end of the bed naked, bent over and holding his head in his hands.

"This is so unprofessional," he sighed. "I cannot believe I did this. I cannot believe I screwed up like this." Kee found herself consoling O'Shea. He seemed quite distressed.

"We're still alive," she said, kneeling behind him and putting her arms around his chest. He could feel her naked breasts and suffused nipples pressed against the bare skin of his back. He just closed his eyes, opened his mouth and silently moaned.

"I see that as a positive. I mean, we have been shot at today. And there was crazy Tucker with his shotgun. It's Weird Shit Day 3. No, it's 4.05 a.m. on Weird Shit Day 4. You might as well screw yourself crazy today, for tomorrow ... who knows?" she said.

"You can sue the FBI for this inappropriate behavior," he said solemnly.

"Oh! I thought you were going to say I'd have to pay them for the extra service!" she replied, snorting with mirth.

They both laughed.

"Do you think you can get some sleep? I have to ring Booker and pass on the intel about the shooter," he explained.

"Wha? Wha? Wha? Come on, give me the dirt," Kee insisted.

"The intruder works for a drug/gunrunning cartel called The Mrazek Organization. It is run out of the Czech Republic with operatives in the US. They are not happy because their gunrunning retail outlets are being murdered. These gun runners that have been shot by the AGB might not even know that they are selling arms for a mob, but that's what they've been doing. And the cartel is not happy."

"It's not my fault," complained Kee.

"They don't care. They want the interference to stop, and you're an easy target," O'Shea explained.

"Great! I'm caught in the middle of a dick swinging contest."

"Something like that," agreed O'Shea.

"Can I publish this? Can I write that there is speculation that the XC1 victims have all been gunrunners? That's so cool!"

"I'll ring Booker and get back to you. You could offer me, your hero, a coffee or something," he pleaded.

"So this is how long it takes," Kee huffed. "You hook up for one night and the minute the whole shebang goes domestic, it's 'Will you make me a nice cup of coffee, dear? And wash my socks,'" Kee mocked.

"You! Wash socks!" scoffed O'Shea. "The moon will drop from the night sky first."

Kee was offended.

"It has been a little hectic of late, Mr. Neat and Tidy Man. Haven't you noticed? My whole laundry program has been upset by crazies with guns trying to shoot up my home," retorted Kee.

"Coffee? If I say please?" begged O'Shea.

"This once," Kee allowed.

"I did save your ass," pointed out O'Shea.

"And I will save your ass by not ratting on you to Booker. Lips. Sealed." She illustrated with hand actions.

"Booker knows," O'Shea gloomed. "He has a sixth sense. He will know as soon as I say hello. Believe me."

O'Shea rang Booker, but his gaze followed Kee's every move as she made a cup of coffee and flicked on *The Late Night Tonight Show* on NBC with Mickey Hannon. It was a replay of the earlier live broadcast. She laughed. She snorted with glee. Mickey Hannon was reading out a list. O'Shea was talking into the phone but watching Kee:

The booming voice of the TV host filled the room as he announced:

"The 10 Reasons Why You Do Not Want to Be in the NGSA.

"Number Ten: You must have a bad haircut. The greasy mullet seems to be in favor this week." Ugly snaps of the recent XC1 victims appeared on screen. *"And a police record."* Grim mug shots of the victims flashed on the screen.

"Number Nine: Your lawyer is a convicted murderer. Yes! The current lawyer for the NGSA was convicted of shooting his girlfriend's mother. He spent one year in jail, then the conviction was overturned on a technicality."

"Ladislav Janecka," said O'Shea into the phone. Booker repeated the name and asked some pertinent questions. O'Shea, half-listening to his boss, replied hoping he was making sense.

"Yep, he is a nasty piece of—oh, thanks." Kee handed O'Shea his begged-for coffee and threw herself on the bed to watch the *Late Night Show*.

The TV host continued:

"Number Eight: You shoot cute bears. One of the board members the NGSA has been convicted of illegally killing a Black Bear.

"Reason number Seven: You are an idiot if the reason you have a gun is to shoot black bears."

The audience applauded.

Kee laughed again.

"That's what I said, Chief," O'Shea said into his phone. "I've had a lot to do with Ladislav Janecka in the past. Drugs, mainly. But ... pause ... ah, gun running is a nice little sideline earner for him." He hoped he was tracking the conversation. If you wake someone at 4 a.m., it is an unwritten rule of phone etiquette that you are obliged to listen to their side of the conversation. But O'Shea was distracted. His eyes kept sliding towards Kee.

The TV host announced:

"Number Six: You think Hollywood kills people. Your CEO Gig DeKant says guns don't cause mass shootings, films do. You kill folk by throwing DVDs of American Psycho *or ..."*

"Booker wants to know if you're okay," O'Shea called out, holding his cell phone in her direction.

"I'm fine, thanks, Booker," she called back.

"And he wants to know if, ah, you plan on shooting or maiming any FBI Special Agents in the next week or so. He might have to change the roster."

Kee looked puzzled. Then she twigged to the conversation.

"Give me the phone," she snapped. "Hello, Mr. FBI. I'm road testing this one. If I find any faults I'll trade him in for another one."

O'Shea looked horrified, but a subdued chuckle sounded over the phone. It would have been louder, except it was 4 o'clock in the morning.

Kee handed the phone to O'Shea and turned her attention back to the Mickey Hannon show. O'Shea's gaze followed her.

The TV host joked, "*Or maybe the mass murderer just made those poor folk sit down and watch one of those movies.*

"*Number Five: You think the media causes mass shootings. You be careful, or one day the media might turn up at your door and beat you to death with a hamster on a stick.* Hannon showed a picture of a sound crane.

She laughed again.

O'Shea continued the conversation for some time half-listening to Booker adding, "Yep! ... Right!" when appropriate, he hoped, and then ended the call.

The TV host proclaimed:

"*Number Four: You hang with mass murderers. Yes! Timothy McVeigh, the Oklahoma Bomber, was a paid-up member of the NGSA.*

"*Number Three: Your grandma is in jail. Today, in Littleton, New Hampshire, a man bought his 86-year-old grandma a gun to protect her from the Lebanese family who moved in down the road. The plan backfired when Grandma ... I kid you not ... opened fire on the postman. She is now in custody, awaiting trial for the illegal discharge of a firearm. Of course, she can always claim self-defense. Some of those bills in the post are killers!*

Kee pig-snorted. "Too funny," she said.

The TV host waited for laughter to die down, then continued:

"Number Two: You think teachers should be armed. Don't laugh. It sure would encourage kids to do their homework."

Hannon turned his hand into a gun and acted out the role of an armed teacher. *"Did you do your homework? Are you feeling lucky, kid? I know you are saying to yourself, 'Is this a 3-times-4 clip or a 4-times-7 clip? And how many bullets is that? And how many did I fire? Shoulda done your homework, kid!"*

O'Shea pushed End Call and started to talk to Kee.

"Shh! Shh!" she said, "I want to hear the last one."

Finally, Mickey Hannon turned serious. The camera moved in for a close-up.

"And Reason Number One Why You Do Not Want to Be in the NGSA: You are happy that, in fact, you insist that convicted stalkers should have the right to buy guns. But how does it feel now, bitch, now that they are stalking you?"

Kee flicked off the TV.

"What happened to the sealed lips?" O'Shea asked.

"Just joking. Booker knows that," Kee insisted. "Wait. I forgot to ask, what did Booker say about the gun cartel link? Can I publish the 'speculation' about the victims running guns?"

"I forgot to ask," said O'Shea.

"You didn't *ask!?*" huffed Kee, outraged.

"Just joking. All good," replied O'Shea.

"Yee ha!" hooted Kee. "But I still might trade you in. I want to see the FBI Special Agent Brochure. See what's available," she laughed, adding, "What's the time? I really should get some sleep."

"It's ... ah," O'Shea looked at his cell phone, "4:20."

She called her cat. "Come on, Harold. It's bedtime." She yawned. The cat padded quietly into the room and jumped on the bed.

"Are you going to get some sleep?" she asked O'Shea.

"Nah. I'll sit this one out. Protect your cute ass," he joked.

"Thanks, Big Bang Boy," she crooned. She always had to get the last word in.

She is so annoying, and yet .... O'Shea's thoughts ran to the end of the track. He had no words for this weird situation. He shook his head. So the day began.

And Weird Shit Day 4 totally lived up to expectations.

Chapter 24

Kee

Monday, the 18th of September

Kee woke with a jolt of terror, fear gripping her heart. Her mind was blank, her memories blurred. She couldn't even pin down where she was. Slowly, the previous night's events materialized into a movie loop running in her head. It was part horror movie, part revenge drama. *I could have been ... like, one bullet. Phtttttt!* she thought, then, *Don't Phttt! with me, you morons!* Next minute she realized she'd been woken by her foghorn text ID. She picked up her cell from the side of her bed and read it lying down. It was Bradstreet.

GET YOUR ASS IN HERE ASAP. TV CREWS HAMMERING DOOR DOWN. WANT TO SPEAK TO U. WHAT'S GOING ON? WILL IT SELL NEWSPAPERS?

Kee: REAL WEIRD SHIT THIS TIME. WILL BRIEF U SOON. KEE

She heard humming. O'Shea was in the bathroom, shaving. Kee pushed Harold off her head with some difficulty and climbed out of bed. She was wearing her sweat top and undies.

O'Shea walked out of the bathroom with a towel tied around his waist.

Fuckable Frank, that one, thought Kee, saying out loud, "Don't talk to me. Don't even breath at me until I've had some coffee. I gotta pee." Harold followed her into the bathroom.

"No, baby. You stay out here with FF," she sighed. Harold stuck with her. "Okay, okay, whatever you want, Sir Harold."

When she returned from the bathroom, carrying Harold, O'Shea was dressed in a t-shirt, his leather biker pants, and bare feet. He'd placed a mug of hot coffee on the kitchen counter waiting for her.

"Awww! FF all gone," said Kee, disappointed.

"What do you mean by FF?" asked O'Shea.

"Never mind ... caffeine. Give me. Give me."

"And good morning to you, too, Little Miss Sunshine."

O'Shea was rustling about in the kitchen.

"Breakfast?" he asked, adding, "I was thinking of trying some of that Gourmet Cat Food on toast. Real lamb and rosemary sounded tempting ... you'll have to settle for eggs, scrambled, I'm afraid. We're on rations here. You only had three eggs left."

"I don't know how you can be so ... so cheerful in the morning, especially after someone tried to assassinate me."

"Is "assassinate" the right word? Can you assassinate a journalist? I think you exterminate them," he joked.

"Very funny. Seriously, how do you get over someone trying to 'exterminate' you? I should feel scared, but I feel crazy angry just thinking about it," she complained.

"You get used to it. You can get used to almost anything," he added.

"I'm not used to goggle-eyed hitmen turning up in the middle of the night. Not even a little bit. What I need is a gun," she retorted between sips of coffee.

"You mean a gun with bullety things that shoots ... like, peopley things?" he asked with more than a hint of sarcasm.

"No, just one that shoots smart ass FBI agents," she grumbled.

O'Shea grinned. "I think your weapon of choice is the bathroom scales. Accurate. Deadly. I'd stick with them, if I were you."

Kee smiled. *I am pretty handy with bathroom scales*, she thought.

O'Shea placed scrambled eggs dusted with cinnamon on the kitchen counter in front of her, adding, "A peace offering."

"That's more like the FBI home service I expect. Ooo! Smells good, too."

"Seriously," queried O'Shea, "how are you holding up on Weird Shit Day 4?"

"If an alien spaceship landed in the middle of my apartment and a Klingon put his head out the door and asked me for directions to K-Mart, I wouldn't be surprised."

Kee perched on the stool/stepladder, scrolling through Tweets on her phone. She called out to O'Shea, "Are you watching?" I'm about to post some Tweets."

"Type the damn things. I can't monitor a blank screen," O'Shea replied.

"Shooter turned up at my apartment last night." #XC1murders #Target91 @KeeHasSpoken

"Okay," approved O'Shea. Kee pressed the Tweet button. She knew how to stretch out the drama. O'Shea was, apparently, in a buoyant mood. He gave all her Tweets the thumbs up.

"Hitman came to my apartment in the middle of the night. Pistol, night goggles, green laser scope." #XC1murders #Target91 @KeeHasSpoken

"Read how hitman got hit. Tomorrow's *New England Gazette*." #XC1murders #Target91 @KeeHasSpoken

PoliceBizz replied.

"You OK? No buzz on the hitman from here. I'll look around. Completely missed that one." @PoliceBizz

Kee sent a personal Tweet.

"Hi, PoliceBizz. Am OK. Bit shaken." @KeeHasSpoken

"Latest intel. 7th body found. Carter McColl, 48, Lackawanna State Park, Pennsylvania." @PoliceBizz

"Copy that." @KeeHasSpoken

I'm talking FBI speak, thought Kee, as she tackled scrambled eggs with a vengeance.

"How will I manage when I lose my live-in chef/bodyguard/ sex slave?" she called out.

O'Shea was uncharacteristically silent.

"You didn't answer that question," prodded Kee. "What happens now? Do we have one for the road and that's it? You disappear forever? Or do we go on a real date and do—do what normal people do? Go to our favorite Italian restaurant, look into each other's eyes and talk all night."

O'Shea said nothing.

"I'm serious. Come on. Give me some intel on Mr. O'Shea. I know you're single. Divorced. But what about your MO?" she queried, pointing her knife at O'Shea as she devoured the last scraps of her scrambled eggs.

"As much as I'd like one for the road ... I ... can't," sighed O'Shea.

Kee stood up and walked over to her bed. She pulled off her sweat top and began rummaging on her bed, looking for cleanish clothes. She had on her silver silk camisole and black lace panties. "You mean not even one for the road?" she pouted, looking up at O'Shea.

"It's not ethical. You probably have—uh—Post Traumatic Shock. I can't take advantage of you. That would be un—ah—unprofessional," he replied, choking out the words.

Kee laughed. "I'm not going to pay you for your professional services. And post-traumatic sex sounds so good, just another FBI service from your friendly special agent."

He did not respond, not even with banter.

"Oh well, I'll just have to get dressed then ..." she said, returning to rummaging through her dirty laundry.

O'Shea walked up behind Kee and ran his hands underneath her camisole top, up her bare stomach, and across her erect nipples. He kissed her neck and she swayed, groaned. She was lost.

Previously she'd been with boys, had sex with boys. She could boss boys. Reece had been four years younger. it has been, *Sex. Now. Sex? Not now.* She'd controlled him. It had been like sex in high school. But this was different. This was out of control. She was overwhelmed by the maleness of him. The smell of him. The salty-sweet taste of him. The broadness of his shoulders. The strength in his arms. The tough guy talk. The mysterious otherness of him. She was so hungry for sex with him that her guts churned and her body ached for him.

O'Shea turned Kee to look at him. He threw her on the bed, pulled off her panties and unzipped his leathers. He ripped off his t-shirt, but he couldn't get his leather pants off fast enough.

He cursed, wobbling on one foot. She chortled. He kicked his leathers aside.

As he entered her, she wrapped her legs around his waist. His fists dug deep into the pillow by her head. He arched his back, his straightened arm muscles tense and taut. The sex was quick and desperate. Urgent. Pounding. He cried out with the exquisite pain of orgasm. She curved her back and gasped a low, relieved sigh. They were spent. Gloriously, rapturously spent.

"You... you fuck up my brain," stammered O'Shea, rolling off her. "I shouldn't have done that."

"Thank you, too," she said, insulted.

"No. NO. This sex is ... I haven't slept. I'm sleep deprived crazy. This sex is ... I ... I ..." O'Shea was lost for words. He'd never been so unprofessional. So undisciplined. She had put a spell, or maybe a curse on him, or maybe he had never known the total brain-crazed state others call "falling in love."

"As the only one here with sufficient brain capacity to communicate by the spoken word, I order you to come here this minute. And kiss me," she demanded.

He slithered his naked body across her soft naked curves and smothered her in kisses. She could have stayed entangled in their "lerv nest" for hours, but his cell phone rang. Scrambling to his feet and hopping around in the nude, he finally located his cell phone in his zipped-up leathers.

"Shit. It's Booker," he said. He pushed the green Accept button on his cell.

"O'Shea?" snapped Booker.

"Yep!" he replied, trying to sound like an official FBI special agent while standing naked, reeking of pheromones and dripping with post-coital sweat.

"Are you behaving yourself?" demanded Booker.

"Of course," replied O'Shea.

"Hello, Mr Booker," Kee called out, adding, "he's being a darling of a special agent."

"Shut up," mouthed O'Shea.

"He wants to talk to you," said O'Shea, handing her the phone as he hunted up his boxer shorts.

"Hello, Miss Le. I hope O'Shea is looking after you properly," said Booker.

"No complaints here," she replied, grinning over at O'Shea.

"Glad to hear it," said Booker. If either of them could have seen Booker's face, they would have squirmed. He had rolled his eyes skyward in a gesture of "I knew it."

"Now Miss Le, we have to get you out of Ridgefield, I'm afraid. Yesterday, you were the messenger for the AGB. Today, after last night's incident with the shooter, you are the news. We can put you in a safe house. But it is better if you go somewhere safe with the people you know."

"I can—ah—go and stay with my dad in Tribeca. Would that work?" she asked.

"New York. Good. That's ideal. And I want you to leave now," he insisted.

"What time is it?"

"9:15," said Booker.

"I can't leave now. I have to go into the office ... I promised Bradstreet ... then I'll have to pack."

"Don't pack, Miss Le. Just go," he ordered.

"Then there's Harold," she objected.

"Who's Harold?"

"My cat."

"Take him with you," urged Booker, "I want you out of your apartment, now. Then out of Ridgefield by midday at the latest.

Do you hear me? I'll get some extra police stationed outside your office. O'Shea will escort you to New York."

"Yes, Mr. FBI. Got it," she answered.

She handed the cell phone back to O'Shea who was, by this time, dressed.

"Harold is not going to like this," she muttered, "will you, baby? You'll have to spend hours in your little Harold prison."

O'Shea listened to some detailed instructions from Booker.

"Yes, Chief. Of course I will escort Miss Le to New York. Thing is, I've only got my bike here. I'll need a company SUV and some clothes," said O'Shea. He took more instructions, said "Right, Chief. I guess that will work. I'll text you the details."

"Explain something before you go. We've been looking at this sniper scenario from every which way. You were a sniper in the Rangers, so you know these guys. Tell me what they're like. What makes them tick?"

O'Shea hesitated.

"That's a tough one, Chief. That's like me asking you to describe what makes an FBI special agent a special agent. I can't group them. They're all different. They're all a little crazy in their own way, I think. The one thing they have in common is that these guys are disciplined and stay the course. They're relentless. They have to be, to sit there for hours, days at a time."

"So they can get themselves into position when no one is around and wait as long as it takes. Hmph! Unless we get very lucky, we probably won't turn up any witnesses. Well, if you get any other insights, call me right away." Booker sounded glum.

"Will do, Chief," O'Shea promised, and ended the call.

"I tell you, Booker is telepathic," complained O'Shea. "All I said was 'Yep' and he asked me if I was behaving myself."

Kee, still naked, climbed out of bed. She was rummaging through a pile of clothes when O'Shea walked in close, turned her to face him, put one hand on each of her bare buttocks and lifted her up off the ground. He kissed her on the throat.

"Behave yourself, sir," she giggled, wriggling free.

O'Shea made a few more phone calls while Kee was in the shower. She came out dressed in a plain navy suit, a white shirt, a yellow and navy scarf casually knotted at her neck, and high heels. She looked, despite all her casualness, as if she'd just stepped out of the cover of Vogue magazine.

"The Klingons have just landed," announced O'Shea.

"What?"

O'Shea nodded his head towards the one good window.

"There are some news vans outside your apartment."

"What do we do now?" she asked.

Chapter 25

Kee

Hackers Attack

Kee arrived at the office at 9:45 a.m. on Monday with a police escort. Three local police cars had been ordered to her flat. The news crews outside her apartment were held at bay as Kee, carrying Harold in his portable Harold prison, climbed into the middle vehicle, then the convoy sped off toward Bailey Ave with sirens wailing. She couldn't help but enjoy the drama. She felt like the President of the United States of America. All that was missing were the little flags on the hoods of the convoy cars. Assorted locals and camera crews were held back by a police cordon at the *New England Gazette* front door as Kee sprinted past an agitated crowd into the office, carrying Harold.

"What the bejeezus have you done now?" asked Bradstreet.

Kee quickly explained the shooter sent by the drug cartel to "off" her because of the interference with their "informal" gunrunning trade.

"No one is offing you until I get an opinion piece out of you," insisted Bradstreet.

"Thanks for the there-there-are-you-all-right warm-and-fuzzy concern," Kee joked.

"Of course I'm concerned," snorted Bradstreet. He patted her on the cheek. "You're my little cash cow. We can't let nasty drug cartels shoot you."

Hollis, Aron, and Chivonn were watching a news report on Aron's computer. Hollis, undoubtedly anticipating a TV appearance, had ramped up her Pop-Art Charity Shop couture to an entirely new level by wearing an orange jacket, bright blue and lime green plaid skirt, brilliant pink stockings and orange knee-high boots. Hollis's outfit was so luminous it made everyone else in the room look as if they were dressed for a funeral. In fact, the expressions on their faces seemed more in keeping with a funeral. Even Chivonn's round face looked cadaverous in the reflected blue light of the video screen, drawn and sad.

"What's happened?" Kee asked.

"I still can't believe it. Angel Lorca De La Vega shot dead," explained Hollis, wiping a tear from her eye.

"What? How? When? asked Kee. *I completely missed that news,* she thought. *I guess crazy Tucker, the hitman, DeKant's rants and the AGB were a bit of a distraction.*

"In a drive-by shooting in Dallas," explained Hollis, her eyes fixed on at the computer screen. "Such a beautiful boy. And he was only trying to stop folk shooting one another. Hardly a crime."

Kee watched with the others as the news bulletin played old footage of De La Vega speaking to the camera. He had the sophisticated looks of a young Spanish aristocrat.

"This government has relaxed the laws on concealed weapons to sell more guns. It has repealed bans on sales of assault rifles to sell more guns. This government has turned our 2nd Amendment into a marketing tool for guns."

The news bulletin crossed live to the head office of PAAW in downtown Dallas. A small crowd was milling around outside. PAAW kept a running tally of the number of Americans killed by guns displayed prominently in their front window. The score so far this year was 24,300. Someone had crossed out the last zero and added, above it, a hand-written "1".

Scrolling underneath this news bulletin was the tally for the XC1 murders. "7th victim in AGB murders found in Pennsylvania. 84 to go."

Even with Bradstreet earnestly trying to shoo them all back to their desks to produce copy and round up sponsors' ads for the next edition, their eyes remained glued to the screen. The following bulletin was hideously bizarre. The news footage panned across an installation produced by an artist known as Kranski in New York. To demonstrate sympathetic support for animals killed as hunting trophies he had mounted 7 shop mannequin heads on trophy display boards. He had called this artwork THE HEAD HUNT. Pictures of his installation were promoted online by the AFF, the Animal Freedom Front. The most gripping part of the installation was the one blank trophy board with the name "G. DeKant" printed neatly on the accompanying brass plaque.

"I know what it feels like to be hunted," commented Kee.

"Yeah! What's it like?" enthused Aron, the computer game addict.

"What do you think, Aron? It's TER-IF-Y-ING!" spat Kee.

Aron looked disappointed, as if he thought it would be awesome fun.

"Come on, my little wage slaves," urged Bradstreet, clapping his hands. "We have a paper to publish. You can't shake copy out of an angel's ass, you have to do the tippy-tappy work yourself! Kee, you write your drug cartel/hitman story and update the website. Hollis, you ring around our sponsors. Chivonn, what have you got?"

"I was writing a piece on gun sales, which have gone up since XC1 murders, but here's the thing. The top sales are to older women. I'm calling the piece Grannies with Guns."

"Love it!" cried Bradstreet.

"Hey, Boss," she continued, "you remember when Truda Downing, 48, from Key West, Florida, woke up in the middle of the night and mistook her gun for her asthma inhaler and shot a hole in her jaw? It was ages ago. Well, I was thinking the grannies might mistake their hairdryer for their gun and blow-dry an intruder. Or put a permanent wave in their own skull."

"Go easy on the grannies," called Hollis. "We're armed and dangerous. Don't cross us or you are asking for trouble!"

"Get that young art student … what's his name? Jamie Ford to do a cartoon. He'd nail that theme."

"Right, Boss," called Chivonn.

"Aron, what have you got?" Bradstreet called out.

"An Instagram meme," Shidfa replied.

"And what the hell does that mean in grown-up language?" snapped Bradstreet.

"It is a picture that everyone is passing around online. It's gone viral," explained Aron.

Bradstreet walked over to see. "Oh! That's nasty. Come and have a look at this, Kee. You need to see this."

The meme was a revamped edition of the Christmas card sent out by Gig DeKant when he first took office as NGSA CEO, with DeKant and his family dressed in red t-shirts and all holding guns. This time there were 5 bullet holes through the picture.

"Do you want to ring DeKant and get a comment?" asked Bradstreet.

"Awkward," replied Kee.

"Come on, someone had a potshot at you ... you can sympathize with him," urged Bradstreet.

There was a thud on the front window.

"They are not going away, are they?" moaned Kee, looking out at the news crews gathered outside the office.

"I don't think so. You have to feed the baying hounds some little scrap. Read them another statement. Get that out of the way first, then do the rest."

"Okay," replied Kee.

Fifteen minutes later, Kee stood with Bradstreet on the front steps of the *New England Gazette* office surrounded by flashing cameras, radio microphones and "hamsters on sticks", reading her statement. She was far more confident this time. As O'Shea had said, "You can get used to almost anything."

"My name is Kitchi Le. I am a reporter with *The New England Gazette*. This morning at around 3.00 a.m. a professional hitman, believed to be working for the Mrazek Organization drug cartel, broke into my apartment with the intention of eliminating me. He wore night vision goggles and carried a pistol with a green laser scope. The Mrazek Organization is also known for gunrunning. All the XC1 murder victims so far are believed to be involved—intentionally or unintentionally—in gunrunning for this cartel. These murders have, needless to say, been bad for cartel business. For some reason, the AGB, the group responsible for these murders, has chosen me to pass on messages to the NGSA. In the mistaken belief that I am therefore encouraging these execution-style murders, the cartel came for me. Fortunately, the FBI had already offered me protection, which I gladly accepted. A special agent with the FBI shot the intruder in the shoulder. The intruder was taken by ambulance to a secure unit at a nearby hospital and is being questioned by FBI agents.

"I also have one more message to pass on from the AGB. It claims it has hacked into the NGSA computers and will publish on Wikileaks the names of all members of the NGSA, state by state, starting with the list of names for members in Virginia. I have no more to add to this statement at present. Thank you."

"No questions," insisted Bradstreet, holding up one hand to the crowd as he shepherded Kee back in the office door. It was 9:50 in the morning.

"You know I can't stay, Mr. Bossy," Kee sighed. "The FBI want me out of here by midday. I'm going to my Dad's apartment in Tribeca. Oops! I suppose I shouldn't tell you that."

"I know," replied Bradstreet, sounding resigned to the loss of his star reporter. "Your very own personalized FBI agent has been keeping me briefed. He'll be picking you up at noon. Just get your hitman/cartel piece done. And then go." Happy-clappy man looked forlorn.

"I'm sorry about this, Mr. Bossy ... it all got a bit out of hand."

"Weird Shit Day 4!" called Hollis from her desk.

"One more thing. The National News editor of *The New York Times* rang me. He wants to do a profile on you for their Weekend Magazine. It would be tied to an Op Ed piece written by you. That's big-time exposure. You've got to think about it," Bradstreet urged.

"You know, Boss, it is what I wanted. Exactly what I always wanted. But I don't think I'm ready yet. I'm terrified that I'll blow it," she confessed.

"In this fucked-up world, it is very hard to hear opportunity knocking. But in your case, it is loud and clear. Here is his name, and number. When you're in New York, drop in and say hello. Or give him a call. It couldn't hurt," encouraged Bradstreet.

"Do you really think I should, Boss? So far I've ignored their texts and tweets. I wasn't sure what to say."

"I really do," said Bradstreet. "And seriously, I think you will walk out our door today and never come back. But it has been helluva lot of fun, hasn't it?"

She leaned in towards her ornery old boss, and he gave her a mammoth hug.

"And," added Bradstreet, 'now I almost know the difference between a Tweet and the ass end of an ostrich."

Chapter 26

DeKant

Monday, the 18th of September

Gig did not sleep well Sunday night. The 6 shots of bourbon had not dulled his irritation. He flopped one way in bed, then another. Time passed slowly in the early hours of Monday morning, as if Sisyphus were trying to roll the dead weight of it up an impossible hill. He looked at the bright red digits of the digital alarm clock on his bedside table for the umpteenth time. It was only 3:15 a.m.

DeKant had returned home following the Street Performer incident, irritated and unnerved. The 4 security guards who escorted him home had bunkered down on the DeKant estate, doing 2-on-2-off shifts through the night, patrolling the premises. He was glad to have Mick, Mac, Mike, and Muck—that's how he thought of them—on hand covering the night watch, even though they ate like a half-starved army and filled the house with brainless banter. But he was finding it hard to have faith in a bunch of macho-clowns who had gang-pressed him through the NGSA front door after his "Who is the

Murderer?" speech. *It was only a firecracker, for god's sake! Fucking morons.*

What irritated him the most, ate into him and twisted in his gut, was the fact that he had, without thinking, ducked. He saw himself as the gunslinger who stood his ground. Guns didn't worry him. He'd been around them all his life. But when the time came, he didn't stare down the guy in the black hat. He flinched and hit the deck.

He was also annoyed, no, not annoyed, he was almost blind with rage about the media cock-up. He was the Media Maestro. That's what they called him in the office, and he knew it. For the first time—ever—he had lost control of his media message. But today, Monday, he would reclaim lost ground, guns blazing … metaphorically speaking, of course.

He heard Beverley get up at 6.00 am and get dressed. He pretended he was still asleep. After a small eternity, his alarm clock sounded. "Thank God," he sighed. His day could begin.

"You look tired, Gig," commented Beverley, as she placed breakfast in front of him on the table. He looked down at the plate of fried bacon, fried eggs, and home-made hash browns. Bev had reverted to no-frills mess chow cooking. She had an army to feed. Gig was disappointed. He couldn't stomach a fry up today. He ate some buttered toast with his coffee.

"Don't forget, I've got the Bridge Fundraiser here this afternoon," Bev reminded him. "If you get time, pop in and say hello. The girls always love to see you."

"It could be tight, but I'll see what I can do," Gig said. "I won't be late. And the security detail will be back tonight to eat us out of house and home," he complained.

"Don't worry," replied Bev, "I've got that covered."

Two black BMW SUVs were waiting for Gig at his front door. The 40-minute trip to the office was uneventful. Gig was getting used to having Mick, Mac, Mike, and Muck follow him everywhere, even to the john.

At 11:30 a.m. precisely, Gig DeKant—flanked by his four lieutenants wearing flak jackets and sunglasses, and carrying assault rifles and side arms—stood on the steps of the NGSA head office to make a statement about the shooting of Angel Lorca De La Vega. Thanks to the gun carry laws of Virginia, DeKant's goons had the right to carry semi-automatic rifles or handguns in public, as long as the gun clip held less than 20 rounds. Was it legal to carry a semi-automatic with a 30 round clip if it was loaded with less than 20 rounds? This was a grey area of the law. But DeKant knew how to work the gun laws in his favor.

Meanwhile, thanks to the power of social media, a sizable movement had sprung up around the country overnight to pay homage to Angel. The vigil had begun outside the PAAW office in Dallas the previous morning. Supporters showed up with flowers and candles. T-shirts were quickly printed and sold to raise money for PAAW's ongoing campaign. These t-shirts pictured an AK-47 with the barrel rammed into the ground and a small American flag on the stock. The words BAN THIS WEAPON were printed on the front. The back of the t-shirt simply read I AM ANGEL. So popular were these t-shirts that PAAW rushed to extend the reach of the fundraiser and emailed the graphics template to every other PAAW office in the USA. Soon t-shirts were being printed by the hundred.

About 40 protesters had gathered outside the NGSA head office overnight. Grandparents. Families with children. University students. Musicians. Anti-gun lobbyists. By mid-morning, the numbers had swollen to more than 200 protesters. Most of them wore the I AM ANGEL t-shirt. When Gig DeKant appeared on the NGSA head office steps, the crowd started chanting, "I am Angel. I am Angel."

"What do those Leftie Losers think they'll achieve?" Gig asked one of his guards when he arrived at the office. "And don't any of them have proper jobs to go to? Isn't that typical? They're parasites who do nothing but sponge off society. Why would anyone listen to them?"

Gig stood at the lectern with the NGSA logo, surrounded by members of the media. He waited. The chanting continued. The Media Maestro was rattled. He looked outwardly calm, but a spasmodic tic in his left eye told a different story. When the chanting died down—even the protesters wanted to hear what DeKant would say—he read out his statement. He was his usual unapologetic, blustering self, but this time his performance hit the wrong note entirely. The news that the XC1 victims had been, even if unintentionally, gunrunners had shifted the public mood. Generally, when it came to Mafia executions, gangland shootings, or drug cartel killings, the public was of the opinion that a cull was a good thing. A few less criminals in the world did not hurt anyone—except, of course, the criminals—and death squads were not to be feared as long as they shot at each other and kept away from the general public. Some commentators even saw execution-style killings as a service to the community. "Gets rid of the scumbags," they remarked.

The XC1 murders had grabbed the public imagination and sympathy, but now the victims were much less sympathetic. Of course, supporters of the NGSA were still angry, but the general zeitgeist was expressed in comments collected from citizens across the country by CBS news crews:

Old guy, Los Angeles, California: "Folk shouldn't get murdered, but you not gonna lose sleep over those bums."

Young mother, Salt Lake City, Utah: "Live by the sword, die by the sword."

Middle-aged Woman calling herself Mystical Athena, a Psychic from Volusia County, Florida: "I can see 91. The number 91 reveals that those making these threats believe in their cause. I can see it. 91 will die. The numbers ordain it."

Vigil participant, Dallas, Texas: "Angel Lorca De La Vega fought to reduce gun violence in this country. He would not support gun deaths, even of gunrunners. But none of us are safe with so many guns on the streets."

Radio reporters, newspaper journalists, and TV news anchors gathered around DeKant and his goons, pushing microphones into DeKant's face. The protesters collected behind the media scrum to better hear DeKant's comments. He began:

"The XC1 murders are an open attack on sacred American values and the people who cherish them. The perpetrators show ruthless contempt for and downright hatred of ordinary Americans who believe in the right and might of our constitution, who want to exercise their right to own guns to defend their families and their property. Believe me when I say that the Whore of Babylon, the Mother of all Prostitutes and Abominations of this Earth has given birth to these enemies of the United States of America, who want to take our freedoms from us. Our fathers fought and many died protecting the freedom we enjoy today. We must not waver now. We must continue to fight for our right to bear arms."

Calling the anti-gun movement the "spawn of Satan" was typical DeKant. Most audiences loved biblical allusions. When DeKant read the next line, however, the crowd became agitated.

"The death of Angel Lorca De La Vega was a tragedy. But fools who do not own guns will get cut down like lambs to the slaughter. Anyone who does not carry a gun is stupid, and they are making an irresponsible, suicidal choice that will get them killed. Be safe. Arm yourselves."

The implication that Angel had committed suicide by not owning a gun had an effect like throwing petrol onto the peace candles. A few reporters shook their heads. But it enraged the protesters. They started booing. Some threw objects at hand: half-eaten apples, drink bottles, a few shoes. Kids, who thought they'd join in the game, picked up sticks and yelled "Bang! Bang!" A teenager pulled a cell phone out of her pocket—everyone agreed later that this was an incendiary act—in a black gun-shaped phone case. It looked like an FBI standard issue Smith and Wesson pistol. One of DeKant's goons fired. The bullet did not hit the teenager, but ricocheted off a trashcan and hit a 10-year-old boy, who happened to be black. A riot broke out in front of the NGSA offices. Windows were smashed. Cars were torched. One member of the public, who had turned up to watch the spectacle wearing a GUNS SAVE LIVES wind cheater, was knocked to the ground and kicked in the head. He ended up in hospital with a fractured skull. Riot squads were called in from as far away as Washington and Richmond. Tear gas canisters were thrown into the crowd. Protesters were arrested, dragged off the street and beaten by riot police. Eventually, an uneasy peace was restored, but only because riot police in full riot gear with helmets, batons and riot shields stood in a line protecting the entrance to the NGSA building. But the protesters did not go home. Instead, their numbers grew.

The riot had erupted so quickly no one could be exactly sure how it happened. DeKant made it safely back inside the NGSA headquarters with a gash to his lip. One rioter had hit him from close range square in the mouth with a retro glass coke bottle.

Within minutes, wobbly but viewable footage had been posted on You Tube, showing one of DeKant's lieutenants reaching for and then firing his sidearm. Separate footage showed the 10-year-old boy bleeding from the stomach and lying on the ground. These clips went viral, and protesters started arriving outside the NGSA headquarters by the busload, and they all wore BAN THIS WEAPON t-shirts. It was a stand off. DeKant could not leave the building, and the protesters weren't going anywhere else in a hurry. One hour after the riot, Booker rang through to DeKant.

"Mr. DeKant, I'm sending an FBI team to get you out of there and take you home," said Booker.

DeKant, defiant as always, refused help. "I can protect my family and myself. I do not need the assistance of the FBI!" he shouted.

Booker, however, insisted. And despite this decision undermining the very foundation of DeKant's belief in self-reliance, he was forced to accept Booker's offer. This was not an easy decision. The boy who' promised himself that he would always be able to protect himself and his family because he would at all times carry a gun, could not, would not admit that such protection had been taken out of his own hands. Many of those born at the end of or after the 2nd World War shared DeKant's outlook on life. These generations of Americans had inherited their parents' belief that the qualities that define a man—women did not need of definition—were independence and self-reliance. Yet these post-war generations had not lived through a depression or a long war. They had not endured what their parents had endured, and they did not experience the vital communal support fostered by extreme poverty or the non-discriminating threat of war. They grew up in a time of American prosperity. They grew into adulthood when Americans did not need each other. And these generations believe to this day that their own prosperity was due to their self-reliance and hard work and not, as some would suggest, good luck, the sheer good fortune of being born during the good times. It is one reason, for instance, that these generations do not want to look after the elderly. They don't want to pay taxes for aged care. The elderly should look after themselves is the endless mantra of the post-war generations who never knew Roosevelt's New Deal or remember there was a time before Social Security when the elderly starved to death. Now DeKant had to rely on his country to protect him rather than the other way around. He refused to acknowledge this reality.

At 2:20 p.m., a laundry van entered the NGSA building via the service entrance. The service entrance door was quickly shut. At 2:30 p.m., the vehicle left the NGSA headquarters to take DeKant and his lieutenants to DeKant's estate.

DeKant refused the FBI's offer of further protection. "This is my home! I have all the weapons I need. I can protect myself and my family from those left-wing loonies!" he howled at the FBI agents who had home-delivered him. These agents were glad to get rid of the agitated NGSA boss and his jumpy lieutenants.

At 3.05 p.m. the FBI laundry van stopped outside the gated entrance to the DeKant estate. There was no way DeKant was going to be delivered to his front door in a laundry van. Once he set foot on his home turf, DeKant felt a wave of calm flood his sleep-deprived body. He and his four armed lieutenants climbed out of the back of the van and passed between the wrought-iron gates and up the drive, striding out like a Lincoln County sheriff and his posse itching for a showdown with Billy the Kid. The driveway, which appeared to be banked in deep red clouds from the Claret Ash trees, was cluttered with cars, mostly new pickups and SUVs.

Beverly DeKant was throwing a fundraiser for members of the NGSA Women's League at their house. About 20 women ranging in ages from 45 to 75 were sitting at card tables in the vast living room of the DeKant estate, playing bridge. Hair, mostly grey, was permed and cut short. Younger women had ponytails. The preferred dress code consisted of jeans, red or blue checked shirts, black or grey puffy sleeveless vests and branded silk neckerchiefs. The plaited gold chain motif of the classic Chanel scarf was very popular. Nails were manicured. Shoes were brown designer ranch-hand boots for the ponytails. Sensible shoes with 2 inch heels with peep-holes for the toes were worn by the grey-haired brigade. Appropriate footwear for the occasion. There was a lot of heavy gold jewelry. The money raised was going to the Shooting for the Disabled initiative. This was a favorite cause of the DeKant's, whose disabled son Logan benefited from trips to shooting ranges and wildlife parks with other disabled members of the NGSA.

Beverley immediately made a fuss of her husband. She left her bridge group and ran to open the front door, saying, "Oh my! We were all watching your speech on the television. They've been playing that footage all day. I was so worried that one of those lawless heathens in the mob was going to throw a rock and really hurt you, Gig. It really is appalling. Where are the police when you need them? They have guns. Why don't they use them to enforce the law?"

Gig kissed her on the cheek and walked with his guard into the living room. There was a universal round of applause. Gig felt it was necessary to give a little speech.

"Thank you, Ladies. As you know, today has been a challenging day for all members of the NGSA. Our privacy is being violated. Our civil rights are being violated. Our lives are threatened. I hope all of you fine women of the NGSA here have finished your self-defense training course and are carrying guns with you today. You cannot be too careful. We have enemies. Ruthless, violent enemies who will not stop until they destroy each and every one of us."

There was another round of applause, but a more muted version this time. Gig's words terrified the women. They were simply having an afternoon out playing cards. Not one of them wanted to be co-opted into an NGSA women's militia or end up in a coiffured gunfight to defend their rights. They preferred, to a woman, the Hollywood experience of a gunfight where everyone eats popcorn, heaves a satisfied sigh as the bad guys fall to the ground and the hero emerges triumphant, and goes home unencumbered by bullet holes.

Gig left the bridge ladies and led his posse through the house to the kitchen where his son Logan sat in his wheelchair at the table. "How are you, Boy?" he asked, ruffling his son's head. Logan managed a twisted smile. There was one thing certain about the ladies of the NGSA Women's League: they knew how to put on a good spread. The extra long, black granite topped kitchen counter supported plates of cold cuts, coleslaw, green leaf salads, potato salads, dips, tomato salsas, corn chips and various breads. Dessert was apple pie and vanilla ice cream.

Gig's lieutenants had missed lunch. They didn't just help themselves to the spread on the kitchen counter, they fell on it like a plague of locusts. Gig watched in disgust as Mick, Mac, Mike, and Muck sucked up cold cuts and the like as if a tornado had hit the kitchen. Meanwhile, Gig sat at the kitchen table drinking coffee and reflecting on the strangeness of his day. It had not gone to plan. His media performance had sparked a riot. A baffling riot. "What was their problem?" he kept asking himself. He should have felt angry. But—the trip in the laundry van aside—he felt elated. He was determined to give the media a good show, and a riot was hard to beat on that score.

More significantly, he had been telling "this great country of ours" for years that citizens should be prepared. He had been saying the same thing over and over. "Arm yourself. Protect your families. Protect your children. Protect your property." *Well, now they' seen it for themselves. Now they will understand.*

"This is war."

Chapter 27

Booker

Monday, the 18th of September

Monday began early for Booker. He was asleep when his cell phone buzzed on his bedside table. That simple buzz was all he needed to wake him. He opened his eyes with a start and reached out for his cell phone to check the caller. It was O'Shea. *The devil gets no sleep*, was the first thought that tumbled through his brain. He let out a long breath. "I'll have to take this one," Booker muttered to himself. "What's the time?" It was 4:10 a.m. *Sweet Jesus*, he thought, *don't criminals ever sleep?*

As Booker half-crept, half-creaked his way into the kitchen, he listened to O'Shea describe the intruder incident. "Ladislav Janecka," Booker repeated, "you know him, don't you, O'Shea? Weren't you working undercover with his competition?"

"Yep," said O'Shea, "he is a nasty piece of—oh, thanks."

"What's happening?" demanded Booker.

"Just got a coffee ... it's been a long night."

"Hmmph!" Booker snorted.

O'Shea briefed Booker on the Ladislav Janecka operation but, as the conversation continued, Booker felt he was talking to a malfunctioning robot.

"And how is Miss Le handling all of this?" Booker asked. The faulty robot tripped over a few more sentences then handed Kee the phone. Booker decided, after a quick few words with Kee, that she was in remarkably high spirits for someone who had just been stalked by a hitman.

Then the artificially-unintelligent robot was back.

"It seems to me," continued O'Shea, "this whole XC1 murder thing is linked to ... sorry Chief, I'm a bit sleep-deprived ... the gun cartels. There is a lot of, umm, familiar stuff happening here. And, ah, Miss Le wants to know ... pause ... know if ... pause ... if she can put this Gunrunning link out there."

"If she can stir up some trouble with the cartels that would work for us. But warn her that this is dangerous. And I want her out of there first thing tomorrow ... today!" snapped Booker.

"Okay. I'll, ah, brief you later. Gotta go," replied O'Shea.

"I wouldn't want to keep you from your ... coffee," grumbled Booker.

Booker looked at his cell phone. 4:16 a.m. He thought he might catch a little more sleep if he went back to bed. He padded softly into the bedroom and slipped as quietly as he could between the sheets next to Phillis. He lay awake staring into the gloom for another 30 minutes before he gave up. He sat up in bed and—creaking as usual—slowly swung his legs onto the floor. "I can take my sweet time," he said to himself. The truth, however, was another matter. He only had two speeds. Creaking slow, and move it, move it, move it.

He looked at Phillis gently sleeping, blew her a kiss and padded to the bathroom. "62 ain't old," he reminded himself, recalling his youthful body when he was the running boy from Kansas. Once when he was 11 years of age, he'd snuck into Old Mr. Alldredge's apple orchard to "borrow" an apple on his way home from school. The cantankerous old coot, who couldn't see past the end of the barrel of his gun, came blustering out of his back door, fly wire screen slamming, holding a single-barrel, break-action shotgun. Booker chuckled at the thought. Old Mr. Alldredge had been the living personification of the cartoon character Yosemite Sam, except he wore a red and black checked shirt, had long matted grey hair and sported permanent grey stubble on his skeletal cheeks. This ensemble was completed by a battered hat, which bore a closer resemblance to roadkill than a product of the hatter's craft. Old Mr. Alldredge was all loud snorts and cussing bluster, possibly because it was a tradition among local kids to sneak onto his property and use slingshots to land stones on the side of his water tank or onto the tin roof until Old Mr. Alldredge came blustering out the door.

It's amazing, thought Booker, *how kids can have so little compassion for a lonely old man.*

But that one day, for some reason, Old Mr. Alldredge pulled the trigger. A spray of shot clipped the top of some nearby apple trees, and young Booker took off running for his life. He cleared the orchard fence in a leap and didn't slow down until he was two farms away. He could have been two states away, his legs, arms, and lungs were pumping that hard. But when he stopped running, he was still holding that apple. It was as sour as a swig of aging pig's swill, but he ate it. After all that effort, the apple wasn't going to be wasted.

Now, when he approaches a fence, he has to plan his attack. Hold down the barbs, get one foot over and swing the other. Of course, these days he is also wearing a suit. A sharp suit, too.

Would he swap the suit for all that youthful exuberance in a mean, nigger-lynching land? Some days, definitely. And Kansas wasn't as bad as Georgia. Or Mississippi. Booker started humming "Mississippi Goddamn" to himself.

He walked barefoot into the bathroom. There was a sharp shriek. His heart did a backflip. He'd stepped on a squeaky toy. Phillis was doing a manically-devoted job of making the apartment baby friendly. She'd scattered a few squeaky toys around the bathtub ledge. Booker had stood on a giraffe. *A squeaking giraffe*, he thought; then again, Booker couldn't be sure what noise a giraffe made. If any. "I must Google it," he said to himself. Charlotte had whispered to him, "Mom has gone totally baby mad. Like she's got a cot and toys, jumpsuits and crap. She thinks Nikki is going to pop out a baby 2 1/2 minutes after she's married. Do you think Mom should see a shrink or something?"

"Don't worry, baby," he'd replied. "You know your mom. She's always talking to babies in the street. She just can't help herself."

"Crazy," Charlotte had replied. It was crazy, indeed. Charlotte, who was obviously pregnant, though being a girl with substantial "oomph!"—oomph! was her mother's term for a full-bodied figure—she carried the baby well. Yet Charlotte still would not admit her condition. The whole family played along with the baby-love theme. Young Jarrel was particularly good at ramping up the baby hysteria. He wandered around the apartment singing, "I'm gonna be an uncle. I'm gonna be an uncle. Uncle Jarrel. I'm the man." Booker hoped the family's effort to send positive vibes to Charlotte would work some strange magic. Ironically, Charlotte seemed, with the pregnancyin-denial exception, to be the sanest member of the family at this moment.

The previous night—*Yes! It was only last night!* thought Booker—he'd arrived home early for a change, in time to have dinner with the family and watch some TV. Dinner was a comedy of mishaps, with Charlotte complaining that "the butter stinks" and Jarrel, in his eagerness to get it off the table, knocking over a carton of juice that Charlotte had left there. Later, Charlotte sat in a beanbag in the lounge room complaining intermittently that the film her parents had selected—*Jumanji 2*—was like for 5-year-olds. Booker didn't watch shoot-em-ups at home. "I see enough corpses at work everyday. No way am I going to sit at home looking a more of them," he insisted. Mid-film, Charlotte announced to the room and therefore the rest of the family "My boobs are growing! Do boobs keep growing? That's, like, really gross."

"Sometimes that happens," Phillis replied cautiously, "when your hormones get out of balance."

Charlotte shrugged. It seemed a reasonable explanation.

Then Charlotte, who was obviously pregnant to everyone but herself, tried to get out of the bean bag, but she couldn't get enough forward momentum to stand up. She was stuck bottom first in the purple vinyl monster, floundering like an upturned beetle. "This bean bag is broken," she complained, "No, really, it doesn't work anymore. I'm stuck."

Jarrel and Phillis pulled and hauled to get her to her feet.

"I'll get it fixed in the morning," Phillis reassured Charlotte.

"You should!" exclaimed Charlotte, as she shuffled in fluffy bright-blue scuffs into the kitchen for a drink.

Booker had his face buried in a newspaper, but his shoulders began to shake.

"Don't ..." said Phillis, but Booker couldn't help himself. He snorted with laughter, which set Phillis and Jarrel off, too.

"It's such a funny film," snorted Booker, wiping tears from his eyes when Charlotte came back into the room with a glass of orange juice.

Charlotte looked at the three sniggering members of her family and shook her head.

Booker showered and dressed as his thoughts riffed on the idea that, at times, the crazies on the street that he came across daily often seemed pillars of rational thought compared with his own family. Take the XC1 killers. They were cold-hearted killers. But they were taking out gunrunners, or gunrunners of sorts. There was a cruel logic to these shootings, and they probably reduced the workload for the FBI's Gunrunning Task Force. *I must ring them today,* he thought, *tell them about the arrest of Janecka's henchman in Ridgefield. They will be interested in having a few words with him in the secure unit at the Danbury Hospital.*

Dressed and ready for work, Booker walked into the bathroom to check his tie-knot in the light. He stepped on the giraffe again. It squeaked again. "Damn thing," snarled Booker. The thought crossed his mind that he was carrying his Glock 22 in his shoulder holster. Maybe he should shoot the damn thing. That would put it out of its misery.

The drive to the office gave Booker time to reflect. This was Day 4 of their investigation into the XC1 murders. The body count was 7. Snipers were involved. And now, at least, one gunrunning cartel had shown its hand. Could the snipers be hired guns for the opposition cartel? No, they'd sell the AK-47s and not leave them sticking out of bodies. He greeted old Manny at the night desk and proceeded to his office on the 23rd floor. It was 6:25 a.m. He had time to sift through some data. Ballistics. No new information. DNA. No unexplained DNA. There was barred owl DNA on the South Carolina victim, some ant species with long ant names, but it seemed critters in the forest had little appetite for gun-skewered human kabobs. "Be serious," Booker told himself.

At 9:15 a.m. he rang through to O'Shea, giving orders to get Miss Le to a Safe House. That O'Shea, he was a reliable undercover operative, but put him near anything in a skirt and Booker had his doubts. All that Irish blarney. It was rumored in the office that O'Shea could charm the copper panties off the Statue of Liberty. The problem was O'Shea had worked too long undercover. Those guys were lone wolves. They didn't take orders. They broke the rules. They slacked off on all admin work. A 3 sentence report was 2 sentences too long in their view. They just didn't fit the professional brochure—read FBI website —image demanded by upper management of FBI corp. Booker sighed. It's time for O'Shea to step up and shut up and represent the Firm.

Just after 10 a.m. the phone rang.

"Booker ... Yes, sir. I appreciate that ... I understand ... absolutely. Yes, sir."

Booker hung up the phone, mumbling, "Asshole. The top brass are as bad as the general public. They expect the case to be solved between the ad break and late night news. They wouldn't care who you threw in the cells as long as they can announce 'Arrests have been made in connection with the XC1 murders.'"

"Asshole," he said out loud again, and returned to wading through the paperwork.

Just after 11:30 a.m. Cogliano dashed up to Booker's office door and yelled, "Turn on the TV! Quick! You have to see the latest news. There's been another shooting. Not an XC1 murder. A street shooting in Virginia. Guess where? Right outside the head office of the NGSA. It's turned into a riot, Chief."

Booker's team collected in the Incident Room, along with the four rookie agents who were manning the phones, and watched the Riot Squad arrive on a live cross from a Fox News van outside the NGSA headquarters in Fairfax, Virginia.

"But, Chief, you also have to see this," insisted Cogliano, pulling up the YouTube clips of the shooting on his computer.

"Now ladies and gentleman," announced Booker, "we have an urgent and challenging task at hand. Before any reporter gets a hold of this story, we have to find out the names of DeKant's goons, who they work for and if any of them have a criminal record. We have to do this fast. I don't know what we might turn up, but if anyone within shouting distance of the NGSA headquarters thinks Riot Police have been sent in to protect criminals, then this riot could blow up in our faces and destroy a city. It's happened before."

Within 10 minutes Volkman nailed the intel. He went through the YouTube footage on his computer and enlarged a screenshot of DeKant's goons. They each had a small logo on their flak vest. Volkman enlarged the image, got the name of the security firm, and Booker rang the Commando Personal Security Inc. CEO. He was very cooperative. In no time the team had collected the names, birth dates and criminal records of each goon. They also had their military service records or, at least, those records available to the public: personal records including health, mental health, and disciplinary proceedings, except for dishonorable discharges, which were not accessible to the public or even, too often, to the FBI without a warrant. The armed services orbited under their own rules. They could rewrite the laws of gravity if some star-studded general deemed it necessary.

Booker rang DeKant and told him he was sending FBI agents in a laundry van to remove him from NGSA headquarters for his own protection.

"Thank you for your concern, Mr. Booker. But I have my lieutenants. They've been through situations like this before," DeKant objected.

"Mr. DeKant," Booker retorted forcefully, "the situation is slightly more complicated than you realize. Firstly, we now know that snipers are responsible for the XC1 killings. You will not see them. You will not hear them. Do you really think you can outwit a sniper?"

"That hasn't been reported in the press," huffed DeKant.

"These matters are a part of an on-going investigation. But there is a second problem," boomed Booker. "We have done a background check on your so-called lieutenants. The one who fired the round that hit that 10-year-old boy has a history. He shot and killed a teenager in Alabama. Two 14-year-old boys were tagging the back fence of a building supply business with spray paint cans when your lieutenant, who worked for a security company at the time, yelled at them to get out of there. When one of the teenagers threw a spray paint can at the security vehicle, your lieutenant shot and killed the boy. The victim was an unarmed black teenager. Your lieutenant was charged but found not guilty by a white-majority jury in a very controversial case. If this news gets out, you would be in extreme danger. A big crowd can easily overwhelm a police line and break into a building. The local police are keeping the crowd as far back from your headquarters as possible, and the riot police can protect the entrance to the NGSA building, but there is a time limit on this holding position. I must strongly advise you to leave when you have the opportunity."

Reluctantly, DeKant accepted the offer. One of the agents deployed from the Richmond office of the FBI in Operation Decant DeKant reported back to Booker, "DeKant's lieutenants were so trigger happy they kept fiddling with their handguns in the back of the van until we ordered them to holster their guns or we'd dump them by the side of the road. And the NGSA chief is so crazy-eyed jittery he was making no sense. He thinks the FBI is after him when we saved his ass. I think he's going all Branch Davidian. Get ready for another Waco standoff."

Booker had just hung up the phone when Perez appeared at his office door.

"Read this," she said, holding her cell phone in front of Booker's face.

At 4:28 p.m. the President tweeted:

"It is time for you militia folk to get your guns ready. May need you in this war against AGB." @TheRealPresident

"Sweet Jesus, that's all we need. Self appointed militias armed with God only knows what taking over the streets on the President's orders." Booker shook his head.

"Perez, have you had any intel back on ex-snipers with form?"

"No, Chief. Our friends in the armed services have not been what you might call cooperative. They said they will send us intel if they identify a suspect."

"So if they identify someone they are not looking for, they will let us know."

"Something like that," sighed Perez. "We are cross-checking Vet records against the registered assault rifle list with arrests in the Occupy Wall Street Movement. It is a long shot, but if the shooters have street-protest form it may turn up something."

Later that day at 6 p.m., Booker, his team, the 4 rookies working the phones, and a few strays from other departments gathered in the Incident Room to watch TV. Booker believed his team had to understand public sentiment concerning any case. This was a vital key to co-opting their support during the investigation. So they sat with coffee mugs in hand, except for Skule who drank tea, and watched the tragi-comic drama unfolding in the war zone debris of broken glass, temporary riot barriers, smashed street furniture, scattered trash and burnt out cars outside the NGSA headquarters. The riot had not deterred multiple sightseers, more protesters, assorted street entertainers and various media hounds from peopling the riot zone. There were fire-eaters and jugglers, hippies strumming guitars, and chanting protesters. Some buskers playing pan flutes, others romancing saxophones. One market-oriented busker sang "You Can't Get a Man with a Gun" from the musical *Annie Get Your Gun*. Coins were dropping like silver rain into her cowgirl hat. There were seniors with fluffy poodles, mothers with babies in strollers, and protesters in BAN THIS WEAPON t-shirts handing out pamphlets.

Katie Frapper from the *Today* show on CBS was walking through the crowd interviewing participants.

"So what brings you here today, ma'am?" or "... sir?" Katie asked. The answers varied.

"I like a party ... and there's a good vibe happening here. You can feel it, man," said one slightly doped-out, aging hippie wearing a sheepskin vest and a Keith Richard's style headband.

"My little grandson ... he was only 7 years old ... was shot and killed by his 9-year-old brother when he found their mama's boyfriend's gun. She didn't even know he owned a gun. I've joined Grandmothers Against Guns. And I'm going to protest until the day I die," said a 62-year-old teacher from a local elementary school.

"I've just driven over from Iowa to join this protest," said a 25-year-old law student with a pony-tail. "This is how stupid the gun debate has become. Polk County Officials in Iowa have issued gun permits to people who are legally blind. Refusing a permit would, apparently, violate the Disabilities Act. Is this why the 2nd Amendment was written? So blind people can own guns? Do we really need a blind militia to protect this country? We are all legally blind if we cannot see the stupidity of handing out guns to just anyone: drug addicts, the mentally ill, criminals with a history of violence, the blind!"

"We have a live cross to another protest across town," said Katie into the camera. "Can you hear me, Su?"

The television flickered, then Su Sin-Soo appeared on the screen. "Yes, I can hear you, Katie. I am standing outside the PAAW office in Fairfax, Virginia. While the PAAW supporters were all protesting outside the NGSA headquarters, it seems that an armed group calling themselves the ..." (Su Sin-Soo looked at her notes) "Nathanael Greene's Minutemen or The Oath Guardians, we're not quite sure which at this stage, has taken over the PAAW offices here in Fairfax, claiming that PAAW is trying to destroy their 2nd Amendment Rights. They say they are defending their rights and are there by Presidential Edict. The protesters that you can see behind me are holding rifles ... they are refusing to leave the building. They have set up a table and chair barricade and staked an American flag on a pole through the barricade. Armed members of the militia are patrolling this blockade."

"Do you know anything about the history of this group or groups, Su?" asked Katie.

"They may be associated with similar protests, one against the federal government in Nevada and one in Oregon. In the Baggett Ranch Stand-Off in Nevada, an armed militia faced down police who came to arrest Clay Baggett for refusing to pay fees for grazing his cattle on Federal land. The protesters said they were patriots defending Mr. Baggett against tyranny, and they threatened the local police and the FBI with assault rifles. If this militia here today is a part of the same group, police may be looking at a long standoff. The federal government eventually backed down in the Baggett Standoff. Has this militia found another cause so they can point their assault rifles at federal agents again? This is Su Sin-Soo reporting for CBS news from Fairfax, Virginia."

"Thank you, Su." Katie Frapper faced the camera. "It seems there is no end to the drama and melodrama involved in these pro gun—anti gun protests here in Virginia."

Katie Frapper continued to move through the NGSA protest crowd. The camera zoomed in on a black preacher with tightly curled grey hair, wearing an old brown hound's tooth patterned suit, white shirt, red polyester vest and a blue and green tartan woolen tie and cloth cap, who had set up his soapbox in front of the police cordon on the steps of the NGSA headquarters.

"Remember that in the eyes of the Lord you sinners are ten thousand times more abominable than the most hateful, slithering serpent is in ours. The Lord Almighty says ... in Samuel. 15:3 ... go and strike Amalek ... Do not spare them, but kill both man and woman, child and infant, ox and sheep, camel and ass."

"So there you have it," said the CBS reporter, "you better watch out for your camels and your ass. This is Katie Frapper reporting for CBS news outside the NGSA headquarters, Fairfax, Virginia."

Booker picked up the remote control and flicked the TV onto another channel. This time a news bulletin was showing live footage of a SWAT team leaving a Walmart entrance in Athens, Georgia. It was, as the breathless young news reporter gushed at the camera, a false alarm. One Ron Tranter, a 68-year-old pensioner, had driven his electric scooter into Walmart with his AR-15 assault rifle sticking out of the basket. The store manager panicked. But it turned out that Mr. Tranter went to the store simply to buy some Dr. Thunder diet soda. "Open carry," announced the serious young reporter, "is legal in Georgia, and that includes semi-automatic assault rifles like Mr. Tranter's. This is Raddon Paulk reporting for WUVG, Georgia."

Booker shook his head. "So we have a Tweeting 2nd Amendment pro-militia President, an armed militia holding out in an anti-gun activist office, unarmed anti-gun activists protesting against the armed National Gun and Shooters Association, an Anti-Gun Brigade shooting pro-gun gunrunners, and a volunteer battalion of armed invalids on motorized scooters exercising their constitutional right to Dr. Thunder diet soda. And, sadly, we also have the tragic death of that rare being, a real Angel. Have I missed anything?"

"You've missed the highlight of the day, Boss," chimed Perez. "78-year-old Tulsa man, Fletcher Finn, took DeKant's warning to heart, apparently. He spent all night guarding his house with his .22 Winchester rifle. When he heard a disturbance early this morning ..." Perez could no longer keep a straight face. She let out a snort of a laugh.

"... Mr. Finn shot and killed the neighbor's cat, one Mr. Figgins."

The team laughed.

"Poor Mr. Figgins," said one of the rookies. She was serious.

"An image on Imgur has gone viral," Perez continued. "It allegedly shows a mug shot of Mr. Figgins with the caption, 'Mr. Figgins was a convicted feline known to police.'"

Booker had to stop, take off his glasses and wipe tears from his eyes.

"I think we're done here for the day. I might just go home and look after my camel and my ass."

The team laughed again.

"Go on. Go home. We'll start fresh in the morning." There was, however, something bothering Booker. He couldn't quite put his finger on it. Something was not quite right. The problem would soon become painfully apparent. The problem was DeKant.

Chapter 28

O'Shea

Monday, the 18th of September

O'Shea had set the expected time of departure for Kee from the *New England Gazette* office at 12-hundred hours. He had briefed Booker, Bradstreet and the local police chief accordingly. But this was Weird Shit Day 4, and if it started raining marshmallows and chocolate syrup, he wouldn't be surprised. O'Shea arrived on time just before 12 noon, flashed his FBI ID to the officer guarding the back entrance to the office, and entered through the back door.

When he appeared at Kee's desk, she looked up and burst out laughing.

"You're wearing a suit!" she giggled, "I didn't think you'd own one."

O'Shea was, indeed, wearing a suit. Booker had ordered O'Shea to drive Kee to New York in a black company SUV. Since O'Shea needed to get a couple of hours' sleep, a rookie agent had been sent from the New York office to deliver both the SUV and a change of clothes (O'Shea kept an FBI-clone—he might have said "clown"—suit in his office locker for the odd face-to-face

274

with upper management) and also, much to O'Shea's distress, to ride his Yamaha YZF 1000R1 motorbike back to the office. The young agent was more than happy with this assignment. He delivered the SUV to Kee's apartment at the specified time and demonstrated excessive enthusiasm for his duties by almost ripping the Yamaha keys out of O'Shea's reluctantly proffered hand.

"Don't you drop my bike under any circumstances," warned O'Shea. "And don't lean too low into the corners or you'll just slide off out of control."

"Don't worry, sir," the young agent assured him, "it's all under control." *The kid*, thought O'Shea as he watched the slim, helmeted figure push his bike out through Kee's side gate, *looks all of 12 years of age.*

So O'Shea turned up in a navy suit. This was Booker's idea again. "You are no longer shadowing Miss Le," Booker had explained, "you are escorting her. You might be seen on TV representing the FBI, so get yourself looking decent."

"Not a problem, Chief," O'Shea had replied; but it was a problem. What was Booker trying to do? Hang him out to dry? O'Shea had spent the last 10 years in the FBI in undercover ops. Anonymity was vital. Now, in an instant, he was outed. Not just outed, he would be a front man for the FBI, a poster boy for the firm. O'Shea didn't like the idea one little bit.

Then there was the problem with the suit. He always felt ill at ease in a suit. His shirt collar was choking him. He had to undo the top button. The navy tie, his only tie, came from some official event with the 2nd Battalion, Ranger Regiment, dress uniform, from 10 years ago. And the suit didn't quite fit his muscular but no longer youthfully slim body. Kee tried to keep a straight face. Then she broke out laughing again.

"Everybody," she said, "I'd like you to meet my very own personal FBI special agent, Denney O'Shea."

Naturally, Aron wanted to know where he kept his sidearm. O'Shea, rolling his eyes, showed Aron the Glock 26 nestled in his leather shoulder holster under his suit.

"Wow! That's like, so cool!" enthused Aron, "I'm going to get one of them. You can hardly tell you are wearing a piece under your suit jacket."

"It'll be a totally screwed-up world if that ever happens," remarked Bradstreet, walking out of his office to shake hands with O'Shea.

"OMG!" screamed Hollis, "I want one-a them. My very own hot-babe FBI agent." The darkest clouds of Hollis's gloom had burnt off with the heat of the XC1 murders. She was the total fun-lovin'-party-pack Hollis these days, with or without vodka and orange soda.

O'Shea looked ill at ease.

"I'd rather be tortured by Taliban insurgents than go through a meet and greet like this," O'Shea hissed at Kee through clenched teeth.

"We better get going," said Kee, helping O'Shea out of his slow-death-by-awkward-social-intercourse.

"Not yet you won't. I want a picture of your FBI eye candy," exclaimed Chivonn, tripping toward O'Shea on high heels and holding up her phone.

"Get a picture of Kee and her FBI guy," insisted Bradstreet. "We can use that."

The deed was done. Booker had warned him. A picture was taken of a smiling Kee and wary O'Shea looking through stray strands of his unruly blond hair.

"Bye bye, Mr. Bossy," said Kee, giving Bradstreet a final hug.

"Get going," he huffed, "and keep sending me copy. You're still on our staff payroll."

"No worries, Mr. Bossy," replied Kee, collecting her laptop, phone, a few pens, and poor, incarcerated Harold in his Harold carrier prison.

"Don't worry, baby. Your ordeal is nearly over," she cooed at Harold. He had on his grumpy cat face.

"Bye, Kee," sighed Hollis. "It's going to be a bit dull around here without lunatics with guns storming the front door and camera crews thumping on the window." She added in a stage whisper, "I swear, Miss Le, that FBI agent of yours has taken lessons in how to make girls go weak at the knees."

"Oo-ah, yeah!" agreed Chivonn, hugging Kee.

The little band of *Gazette* staff stood in the office and watched O'Shea usher Kee out of the office and, perhaps, out of their lives.

Kee and O'Shea walked briskly out the back gate, O'Shea giving a nod of acknowledgment to the officer on duty. They climbed into the black SUV with the tinted-glass windows, which O'Shea had parked nearby, and hit the road heading for New York.

"I have to stop at a supermarket on the way," insisted Kee.

"What for?" asked O'Shea.

"Are we married now?" demanded Kee, "A girl needs things a girl needs. And I have to get some kitty litter and some cat food and blah de blah."

That is how O'Shea ended up pushing a cart around a Pioneer Supermarket in the West Bronx with Kee and the cat. Kee wouldn't leave Mr. Harold in the car. It was cruel, apparently. It was also the moment O'Shea ran into one of his buddies from his Ranger unit from his second tour. It was Jarret

Glass, one time Bronx street gang kid and petty thief, now a respectable store manager. That Ranger training did put a clean-cut finish on the roughest diamond.

"O'Shea. What ya doin', man? Are you a suit now? A desk jockey? I don't believe it?" joked Glass.

"Hey, bro, how ya doin'?" asked O'Shea. They did the one-hand-shake-other-hand-back-slap-man-hug. It was a bro thing.

"You? Manager of a supermarket? I remember when you lived off Big Mac Combo meals for 21 days in a row in Iraq. Maybe I should tell your boss about your Big Mac addiction."

"Thought each one might be my last meal," confessed Glass, "wanted to make it my favorite. And you?"

"FBI. On assignment. That's my charge there," he pointed at Kee and the cat.

"Man, oh man, O'Shea. You always fall on your feet. That piece of ass is work? You dumb ass, introduce me."

So O'Shea, feeling awkwardly uncomfortable in his suit, feeling so out of place in a supermarket he could have been a butcher in a blood-smeared apron at a vegetarian picnic, and feeling uneasy at introducing Kee to a loud-mouthed old buddy, found himself stumbling over the basic requirements for standard social introductions.

"Kitchi Le, this, um, this person here, who talks nothing but, um, bullshit and, um, more bullshit, is Jarret Glass, store manager."

"Oh, good," said Kee, "I'm looking for gourmet cat food."

"Aren't you that journalist girl from *The New England Gazette* who's always on t.v.?" replied Glass.

"I guess I am," replied Kee, surprised by her high currency in the fame frame.

"Follow me, and I'll tell you a few stories about O'Shea here," crooned Glass, as he and Kee disappeared down aisle 6.

All O'Shea could hear was Kee's laughter. It was enough to send O'Shea to the knife shelf to slit his wrists. No. He'd slit Glass's throat first. No. He'd finish off that smart ass Kitchi Le in one fatal strike. But what an ass. What an ass. O'Shea found himself thinking about Kee. He couldn't get her out of his mind.

Kee returned, chatting away to Jarret without a care in the world, while O'Shea stood holding the cart looking as fractious as a wild fox in a cramped cage. He felt useless and trapped in the minutiae of everyday life.

"So you were a bit of a tough guy in Iraq. A gambler, too. Cards. Arm wrestling. Pissing contests," she recounted with glee as she swung alongside O'Shea. He looked so out of place.

Glass left to help a customer, saying, "We've got to catch up, man. Have a beer sometime."

"Yeah, right," replied O'Shea.

"Don't worry. We only have to act like a happily married couple for 3 more minutes while I put this lot through the checkout," Kee said, as if to a sulking teenager. "You really haven't done this before, have you?"

O'Shea shook his head. "I'd rather swallow a bucket of razor blades than play ... Mr. and Mrs. Suburbia."

"Not so domesticated after all," Kee said with a sigh, paying the checkout clerk.

Kee teased O'Shea mercilessly until they pulled up outside her father's apartment in Tribeca.

"I know I'm being mean," she said, "just because you're ... (she burst out laughing again) ... wearing a suit. And you look so sweet. I'll make it up to you."

Just as O'Shea parked the SUV in front of the bakery-now-deli in Tribeca, Kee leaned over to O'Shea, ran one hand across his shoulders and kissed him on the neck. Slowly, very slowly, she slipped the other hand down his shirtfront, undid his suit waist button and slid her hand inside his boxers. O'Shea gasped.

"See ... I can be a real charmer myself sometimes." She paused. "I hope no one can see through this tinted glass. We don't want headline news FBI AGENT ACCOSTED BY JOURNALIST." Kee was conducting an entire conversation with herself while holding his balls. O'Shea couldn't speak. He didn't want to talk. He didn't want her charm offensive to stop either.

"And now for the real torture," announced Kee. "You get to meet my father."

O'Shea held his breath. He could hardly introduce himself to her father with an extreme erection ready to tear open the front of his suit pants. *She is so fucking irritating ... she puts me through extreme boot camp for sex partners, and she doesn't even notice.*

O'Shea sat behind the steering wheel until Kee opened the driver's side door and handed him the supermarket bags. That worked. Domesticity neutered him every time. "Move your tight ass," she said. "Time to meet Daddy."

So O'Shea got to meet Mr. Le.

Chapter 29

Kee

Monday, the 18th of September

Holding Harold in his carrier prison in one hand, Kee turned the latch and pushed open the heavy wooden door to her parent's apartment. It was 3:55 p.m. A thick, musky smell of stale incense assaulted her "Pops, I know what you've been doing," she called as she entered. "Where are you, Pops?"

The apartment stood two stories above the old bakery, facing Reade St, Tribeca. It had hardly changed since her parents first bought it in the seventies and furnished it with sturdy secondhand furniture. The living room was furnished with a cumbersome dark wood settee and matching armchairs with dark gold velvet cushions, wooden legs and wooden armrests with woven cane infills. Heavy green velvet curtains covered the windows in every room. Her mother had cut them down to fit from a theatre curtain going cheap. There was a standard lamp with a stacked brass and amber crystal ball stand and a gold damask shade with a six-inch fringe that would have last been considered a stylish piece of furniture in *Home Beautiful*, 1953.

Old sepia photographs of several generations of the family cluttered the surface of a vintage Stanley credenza. Prominent among the photographs on the sideboard was a silver-framed studio portrait of her mother taken in 1980, before Kee was born. She smiled when she saw it. Her mother had been a force that moved mountains. Several lit incense sticks protruded from the fretwork lid of an antique bronze incense burner. The overall effect was of a decaying lifestyle museum of the sixties. It reeked of stale cigarette smoke too. The living room was empty.

"I know you've been smoking, Pops. The incense doesn't fool me," Kee called down the hallway. She tried the study next. She gently pushed the door open. Her father was asleep on a chair, with a book in his lap and his glasses dangling off his nose. But what a chair. It looked like a beige-vinyl sitting robot wrapped around her father. Her father's legs fitted into the robot's legs. His arms were slotted into the robot's arms. But the robot had its left arm and its right leg raised as if it was a seated-robot frozen mid-dance.

"Pops," she called gently through the open door, "I'm home."

Her father woke with a start, knocking his book to the ground.

"Little Moon," he said, beaming, "you here!"

She walked over and kissed him on the forehead, quizzically inquiring, "Where on earth did you get this chair?"

"She buy it for me. Now she want money for it. Two thousand dollar," explained her father.

"Who?"

"Ba."

"You shouldn't let her buy you stuff," admonished Kee. She really wanted to add, "Don't trust that evil-eyed witch," but it was pointless. Whenever she criticized some crazy scheme of Ba's or Pham's her father just replied, "they kind to me."

"What is it anyway?" asked Kee.

"It a massage chair," her father explained, pushing some buttons at the end of one robot arm. Her father's head started vibrating really fast.

"That can't be good for you!" gasped Kee, thinking the vibrations might dislocate his neck or rattle out a few teeth. "Slow it down or turn it off."

"I try," said her father, pushing more buttons.

His left arm rose higher, and his hips started to wobble too. Kee laughed.

"It g-g-good-d for you," said her father in a wobbly, vibrating voice.

"This robochair looks dangerous, Pops." She walked over to the wall socket and pulled out the plug.

"I think we'll send it back before it vibrates you to death," said Kee. She turned to look at the old Sony analog television that sat on a vintage tea chest. It was gone.

"Oh my god. You've bought yourself a flat screen TV at last."

"That Pham. It very good. I like a lot."

"I've been telling you to get with the program for years, Pops."

"You come home now?" her father pleaded. This was a dagger in her heart.

"No. Pops. I can't come home just yet. But I'm here for a few days. And I was hoping you would look after Harold for me."

"Harold. Where Harold?" he asked, trying to get out of the Robochair. She had to help hoist her father to his feet.

"Here, Pops. I'll let him out and put the kitty litter tray in the kitchen."

A figure appeared in the doorway to the study. It was O'Shea, holding several supermarket bags. Her father looked surprised

"Who this?" he asked. "New boyfriend? I hope he better than last one. Who couldn't even decide if he want to be lawyer or doctor ... so he stay at university for 10 year living off his poor parents."

"Pops, this is Denney O'Shea. He is an FBI special agent who is escorting me..." explained Kee. She paused, floundering, then she had a brain flash. "... for an article I'm writing." Her father didn't keep up with current affairs.

"Hello, Mr. Le," said O'Shea, putting down the supermarket bags and holding out his hand.

"You lawyer?" her father asked O'Shea.

"No, Sir. Just an FBI special agent."

"She very old. You marry her?"

"Oh, Pops, stop it this minute," snapped Kee. "We've got to go out soon. You look after Harold. We'll be back later. Mr. O'Shea will sleep in Vincent's room."

Vincent was Kee's 29-year-old brother, who was an IT guru running some sort of start-up company in Seattle. He was making a sizable fortune but, naturally, had no time to enjoy it or visit his father. His father naturally approved of this situation.

"I'll just go and look in the fridge for a minute, but before I do I'm going to put your old chair back where you like it. Where is it?"

"It down there," he said. Not very helpful directions.

Kee requisitioned O'Shea to help her look for her father's favorite wing-backed chair. She told him about the Ba-Pham war as they searched the apartment.

"I wish I had two women fighting over me," O'Shea sniffed.

They found the chair in Kee's room.

"Grab one end!" sang Kee.

"I'm your furniture shifting guy now? That doesn't happen until after the third date?" O'Shea whined.

"Shut up and lift," Kee ordered.

The chair was an awkward shape and heavy. With its fleur-de-lis embossed and buttoned deep-green velvet upholstery it did look rather majestic. They both bumped and tripped and complained as they lugged the chair along the hall. O'Shea walked backward holding the legs. Kee made faces at him. He stopped dead and dropped his end to the floor. Kee had no option but to do likewise. O'Shea sat on the chair in protest.

"I'm not moving it with you sitting on it, you slacker," she complained. O'Shea didn't budge so Kea used the leverage of the chair's high back to tip it forward with O'Shea on it.

'Alright. Alright. I surrender' huffed O'Shea climbing out of the chair and resuming his role of furniture-moving guy.

They wrestled the old chair laughing into the study and pushed the Robochair out of the way. Her father was visibly pleased. He sat in his old chair, beaming.

"This very good. Thank you FBI," he said.

"It's just part of the service, Sir," reassured O'Shea.

Kee's father thought this was hilariously funny. He hee-heed, stopped for breath, looked at O'Shea and began hee-heeing again.

"It wasn't that funny, Pops," protested Kee.

"Tomorrow I have President come and vacuum house," he chuckled. They all laughed.

"Can I make you some tea, Pops?" Kee asked.

"Yes. And some Almond cookie. And some Hash Brownies."

"I think it's just Brownies, Pops. Hash Brownies are ... don't worry. I'll sort it."

"You'd think after all those years in the bakery he'd get that right," Kee murmured. "But, then, he worked out back. Má worked front-of-house."

O'Shea picked up the groceries and trailed behind Kee to the kitchen. Her first job was to check the fridge and throw out all the past-their-use-by-date jars and the food-turned-to-poison boxes rotting on the shelves.

"Oh my God, that's disgusting," she gasped, as she threw out one mold-sprouting takeout container after another.

"I've arranged a house cleaner twice a week. I truly don't know what she does. Last time I came home, I found her smoking with my father out on the fire escape." She grimaced. "Don't just stand there. Put the kettle on," she commanded.

"Yes, Ma'am. Where would you like your groceries, Ma'am? Anything else I can do for you, Ma'am?" teased O'Shea, holding out his hand for a tip. She slapped it. He grabbed her slapping hand, pulled her away from the fridge and pinned her with his body pressed against hers into the far wall with her hands over her head. He also used one foot to kick her legs apart so she could hardly move. Kee knew the maneuver, but she couldn't wriggle free.

"Now Miss Le," he demanded, "what is your next move?"

She kissed him on the end of the nose, whispering, "Not here. No funny business here. I can't do it with my dad in the next room."

"You'll have to do better than that, Miss Le," he insisted. "I think you should beg for mercy."

Kee tried to squirm. She couldn't.

"You've been badass mean to me. You said so yourself. So how are you going to make it up to me?" insisted O'Shea.

They kissed. Passionately. Too passionately. This was dangerous. O'Shea leaped back into the room.

"No. No. NO ... this isn't good," he said. "You go and sort out your father. I've ... got to make plans."

An hour later at 5:15 p.m. Kee was still sitting at the kitchen table checking her emails, texts, and Tweets, with O'Shea slouching on a chair with his arms crossed and one foot resting on the edge of an adjacent chair, looking like a bored school kid. He was dozing off to sleep.

"Have a look at this," she said to O'Shea. It was a Tweet from PoliceBizz. O'Shea could have checked the Tweet on his own cell, but he had been scrolling through his cell phone feed for over an hour, and now he was bored.

"What?" said O'Shea, startled.

"The AGB has published the first list on Wikileaks. Here's the link. But what's with this asterisk thing?" @PoliceBizz

"Thanks PoliceBizz. I'll have a look." @KeeHasSpoken

"I had PoliceBizz traced. That was easy. No dark web there. No virtual phone numbers. His name is Joseph Michael Lyman. He lives in Ridgefield," yawned O'Shea.

"Oh my God! That's Ironman. He works for the Mayor." Kee was astounded. Ironman. "Why all that secrecy?" she wondered.

Kee and O'Shea pulled up the Wikileaks post on her laptop. There was a list of 16,000 names under the title: NGSA Membership, Virginia. Some names were notated with an asterisk.

"So what do you think that means?" Kee asked O'Shea.

"It could be the AGB hit list, or something from the NGSA file like, oh, unpaid fees. Or it could be something the AGB is doing to intimidate the NGSA membership," O'Shea suggested.

"I better call DeKant, and Booker," Kee announced. O'Shea snorted.

"There, there," she sympathized, patting O'Shea on the cheek. "What are you getting all huffy about?"

"I had a plan," he replied.

"So?"

"We're in New York. I was going to take you on a date," he sniffed.

"Ooooh! A date! A real boy-girl date! You're on! I'll be quick," she enthused.

The doorbell rang. Kee moaned. She answered the door with O'Shea right behind her. A short, elderly woman stood at the door. She had a round face, crows-feet wrinkles extending from sharp eyes, and tight grey curls. She was wearing a maroon velour top, black pants and sneakers, and she held a plate of warm Vietnamese rolls. They smelled good, too. It was Ba.

"Hello, Ba," said Kee with a chill in her voice, "I would like you to meet Mr. O'Shea"—She kicked O'Shea so he'd go along with the ploy—"from the FBI. Show this lady your badge, Mr. O'Shea." He automatically flipped out his badge. "Now, Mr. O'Shea is here investigating an alleged scam involving a massage chair that my father did not order, but now demands are being made for payment. Do you know anything about this scam?"

"No. I don't know this," replied Ba.

"If this chair is not collected and returned to the shop tomorrow, Mr. O'Shea here will have to go to the shop to investigate, and charges will be laid. Isn't that so, Mr. O'Shea?"

"Correct," said O'Shea.

"And what's this? Spring rolls for my father? Lovely," cooed Kee, taking the plate out of Ba's hands, adding, "Thank you so much," as she closed the door.

"Now I'm your enforcer, am I? What the hell next?" sighed O'Shea. Kee took no notice.

They ran into Kee's father shuffling along the hallway in his slippers.

"You make tea. You said," he complained.

"Sorry, Pops. Got things to do for the newspaper. Go back to your study. I'll bring it in a jiff," Kee reassured him.

"You play Vietnamese chess, FBI?" her father asked O'Shea.

"Sorry, sir. I don't. I play poker," replied O'Shea.

"You not much use," grumbled Kee's father, as he shuffled back to the study.

"My thoughts exactly, Pops," said Kee, smiling at O'Shea.

The doorbell rang again. A short, elderly woman with a round face, crows-feet wrinkles extending from sharp eyes and tight dyed-black curls stood at the door. She was wearing a Royal blue velour top, black pants and black socks in leather scuffs. She was holding a plate of freshly baked brownies. The fresh bakery aroma flew Kee's memories back to her childhood in the bakery, they smelt so good. It was Pham. *If I had to back the winner in the get-your-claws-into-Vihn-stakes it would be Pham*, thought Kee.

"Hello, Pham," enthused Kee, O'Shea at her side.

"Your father he like brownies," said Pham.

"Thank you, Pham," replied Kee, whisking the plate out of her hands.

"Did you buy my father a flatscreen TV set?" she asked with an ear-to-ear fake smile.

"I did this."

"Does he owe you any money?"

"No. He pay cash," answered Pham with a questioning look.

"Good. Now if you buy him any more gifts, he will not be paying you money because it will be a *gift*. And Mr. O'Shea here from the FBI"—she kicked O'Shea. He flipped out his badge again—"will be my witness if there are any legal proceedings. Am I clear?"

Pham nodded.

"Thank you, Pham. My father will love these," Kee cooed, closing the door.

"Am I your bitch now?" grumbled O'Shea.

"Here, have a brownie, bitch," she said, holding the plate up to his nose. He took one.

"You are so easily bought," she smiled.

"But those brownies are worth it," mumbled O'Shea through a mouthful, adding, as he filched another Brownie, "Do you think your standover tactics will get your father's girlfriends to back down?"

"Maybe, who knows? At least he gets a few decent meals out of it."

Back in the kitchen Kee asked O'Shea, "Do you think DeKant will talk to me with all the hysteria going down in Fairfax?"

Kee knew DeKant's day had not gone well. His speech, the shooting, and the subsequent riot were being played in almost a constant loop on various news streams around the world.

"Maybe," replied O'Shea. "Booker got him out of the NGSA headquarters to defuse the situation. He's at home now."

"Perfect," replied Kee.

She made green tea in a pot, put it on a tray with a small bowl-shaped cup and some brownies, and carried it to her father in the study while talking to DeKant on her cell phone.

"Hello, Mr. DeKant. It's Kitchi Le. Sorry to intrude, I know you've had a hectic day."

"Hello, Miss Le. Those media vultures. They twist your words. Make it sound like I'm the one who is guilty. I have done nothing wrong."

That's true, thought Kee. DeKant may have inflamed the situation, but he hadn't thrown the match.

"I've just rung to tell you the AGB have posted the first list of NGSA members names. It's a bit weird. Some names have an asterisk. Does that mean anything to you?" she asked.

"Those pricks!—pardon the language," he said. "This is an infringement of our privacy. These AGB terrorists are trying to strip our constitutional rights every which way."

"Mr. DeKant, do you want to make a statement?" Before DeKant could answer Kee had a better idea. "Actually, Mr. DeKant, may I come down to Fairfax and interview you? It might give you a chance to put your side of the story without all the hysteria."

"Well, Miss Le ... I have to say you are about the only journalist I trust these days. You have been fair with me. That's more than I can say of the others. The scumbags. So it would be a pleasure to do an interview with you. When can you get here?" he asked.

"I think tomorrow at 2 p.m. should give me enough time. You know, I've been targeted too. Some gunrunning drug cartel goon tried to shoot me last night, and I've done nothing. So I think I know how you feel." She added, "I will bring my FBI escort with me."

"Do you want the address?" queried DeKant.

"I'm with the FBI, so they've got it. I'll fly to Washington and hire a car. You're not that far out of Washington."

And, thought Kee, pressing the End Call button on her cell, *I know who will pay for this trip.* She pulled the note Bradstreet had given her out of her pocket and rang the National News Editor of *The New York Times*, Dean Sifton. She had his private cell phone number. Few, very few, raw-recruit reporters had that number.

"Hello, Mr. Sifton, it's Kitchi Le from *The New England Gazette.*"

"Well, well. Hello, Miss Le."

The conversation went well. Very well. *The New York Times* would be delighted to pick up her travel expenses if she wrote an Op Ed piece on DeKant for them, and a longer piece for the weekend magazine on the perils of being caught up in a national gun crisis. Kee told Dean Sifton that she would only submit a piece if she felt it was up to *The New York Times'* standard. Sifton did not think she'd have a problem in that regard.

O'Shea snorted. He'd fallen asleep sitting in the kitchen chair. Kee let him sleep. She rang Booker.

"Hello, Mr. Booker, it's Kitchi Le."

"Miss Le. How is our special FBI personal protection service working for you at the moment?" he asked.

"He's asleep on a kitchen chair," she said, giggling.

"You've worn him out, have you Miss Le?" asked Booker.

"I will say nothing that could be used as evidence against me later in a court of law."

Booker chuckled.

"You are a smart one, Miss Le. I think O'Shea has met his match. What gets you on the phone?"

Kee told Booker about the Wikileaks post. She offered to text him the link. And she explained that she was going to interview DeKant the next day, in person, at his house in Fairfax.

"Now, Miss Le. How can I say this? Mr. DeKant is under a lot of pressure at the moment. He is, my agents tell me, a bit crazy. You watch yourself there. Take O'Shea. But use your own judgment, too. Get out of there if the situation looks threatening."

Kee said she would. She sat at the kitchen table, updating *The New England Gazette*'s website. She emailed a quick report on the Wikileaks post to Bradstreet and updated her Twitter file with links to Wikileaks.

"AGB post NGSA membership names. Virginia first." @KeeHasSpoken #Target91 #XC1murders

"Some names are marked with an asterisk. What does this mean? NGSA unpaid fee list? AGB intimidation? Death list?" #Target91 #XC1murders @KeeHasSpoken

That should get a bit of attention. She had 140k followers on Twitter. Kee walked into the living room and pulled back the heavy velvet drapes.

"It's so stuffy in here," she mumbled, then calling down the hallway, "Pops, you should open the curtains more and open a window once in a while to get some fresh air."

"Oh no!" she groaned, looking out the window at the crowd gathering on Reade St. Kee returned to the kitchen to write a website post.

She let O'Shea sleep until 6:30 p.m., then woke him, saying, "Nana nap time over."

"Wha? Ah! Oh, we of the short attention span," he retorted, "I needed that, I was awake protecting your ass all of last night if you remember." Then he reached over, placed his hands on her ass and pulled her towards him. He buried his face in her stomach.

"Girl scent," he sighed, "the most sensual smell in the world."

"Guess what?" Kee enthused, "we're going to Virginia tomorrow. Booker said you have to come with me to interview DeKant."

"Can we just go on our date now?" asked O'Shea.

"Argh! There's a problem," said Kee. "The Klingons have arrived. There's a news van parked on the street opposite the apartment."

Chapter 30

Kee

A Night Out in New York City

Kee was in the study with her father. She had changed into some fashionably torn-at-the-knee jeans, a high-necked cable knit sweater, and some gold sneakers. Her father was sitting in his old chair, happily munching on the snack food so "kindly" provided by the dueling witches. They both turned towards the new flat screen TV as the broadcast moved to the White House for the Presidential Address.

"Ba cook good rolls. You want one," urged her Father.

"No thanks, Pops. We're going out. But, really, Pops, you shouldn't let those crazy witches take over your life."

"Sometime crazy. Sometime good meal," explained her father. He looked up at her and grinned.

Not so stupid then, thought Kee, reassured.

The President continued:

"We, as a nation, must not back down, retreat or lose our nerve in this war against the anti-gun criminals who are terrorizing this country. We must stand our ground and hold our resolve to protect our 2nd Amendment Rights. Okay. I sent out a message calling on all patriots, the fine men and women in militias across this great nation of ours, to get ready. And I meant it. But I am asking you, the patriots of the United States of America, do not act yet. Do not take the law into your own hands. Put your faith in our law enforcement agencies. I call on you to help your local police and the FBI find these criminals. Pass information on to them. They are the men and women on the front line now. Give them your full support."

A slight change of tune, thought Kee. *Someone had a word in his ear. Like crazy militias running all over the place with guns was ever a good idea.*

"That's sorted," said O'Shea, bursting into the study with such energy his arrival was like a shockwave from a nearby explosion. "Come on, we've got to go now."

"Bye, Pops," Kee called out to her father. "Take good care of Harold." Her father nodded. He was patting Harold, who sat purring on his lap. Kee hardly had time to grab her shoulder bag and puffy maroon coat as O'Shea bundled her out the door.

"What's happening?" she queried.

"Come on. We won't have any trouble with the Klingons. I've ordered Chinese, Japanese and Korean take out meals to be delivered to the broadcast van. The last delivery guy just turned up and joined the others, arguing with the broadcast crew. It's chaos city down there. Let's go."

Kee and O'Shea were able to slip past the news van that was besieged by the 3 delivery guys and, ironically, amateur news hounds with their cell phones raised recording all the drama. They walked down Reade St. unimpeded and caught the subway at Chambers St. West Broadway to Penn Station on 34th street. As Kee stood holding the central chrome pole and swaying in the clackety subway carriage, she was drawn back to something she had almost forgotten: normal everyday life. She watched O'Shea. He looked distracted. Distant. But he also looked very much at home in the anonymous crowd of the big city. O'Shea had said he wanted to walk some of the way to the restaurant. So they ambled down 7th Avenue and onto Times Square, stopping to absorb some of the dizzy-dazzling video hysteria of the multiple big screens on the buildings facing the intersection. They held hands.

"Is holding hands allowed?" Kee asked, "I mean, is there some FBI Code we should follow?"

"I'm in a suit, and we're on a date. That's fucked up. We may as well hold hands too. I can't see how we can further fuck up an already fucked-up situation," he remarked.

"You have a lovely way with words, O'Shea. It must be the Irish poet in you," she joked.

"I love the M&M men," said Kee, waffling on, "they're always so happy. My friend Annalise, Oh my God, I must call her. Anyway, she calls New York the Capital of Capitalism and Times Square it's epicenter because it draws thousands of tourists to stand here taking pictures of ads. That's a bit mad. Like, mega-mad!" She was prattling and she knew it.

"Are we calling today Mega-Mad Monday now, or are we sticking with the classic Weird Shit Day 4?"

"Is it only four days? Really? It's still Monday the freaking 18th of September!" exclaimed Kee. She stood mesmerized by the flickering neon-brilliance of the video screens. Suddenly her image flashed across a news feed screen. It wasn't a very clear image, but a chill of horror ran down Kee's spine. She felt she was being stalked by her own ghost.

"Freaking freak hell," she muttered, adding with some urgency, "Let's get out of here. Come on, we'll walk up 44th Street to the Algonquin Hotel." When they arrived at the grand old hotel, Kee stood on the pavement outside the historic building to breathe in its significance.

"See that hotel? That is Mecca to writers, critics, playwrights, the lot. *The New Yorker* roundtable used to sit there. Dorothy Porter. Tallulah Bankhead. Noel Coward. Harpo Marx," she explained, "and they've even got a cat called Matilda. Any hotel that likes cats has to be a fantastic hotel."

He took her into the bar of the hotel for a drink. A pianist was tinkling away on the baby grand piano. "Of all the bars in all of the world," teased O'Shea as he carried a ridiculously expensive cocktail over to Kee, "you had to pick one with a cat." Kee was still in the lobby cooing to Matilda, who luxuriated on a small chaise lounge.

"You want your ears rumpled too, do you?" she joked, taking the Noel Coward Gin Sling cocktail out of his hand.

They finished their drinks watching well-heeled guests being greeted by the theatrically dressed doorman in top hat and tails. The young, svelte doorman looked as if he had recently escaped from a Fred Astaire movie and harbored the untapped potential to tap dance up walls. They left the hotel and walked through the man-made canyons of New York City with diffused light cascading down from the skyscrapers and the red glow of car taillights shimmering off the damp black asphalt surface of the rain-wet street. There was the constant background noise of car horns honking, police sirens wailing, and steam hissing and shushing out of road vents, and the endless stream of determined pedestrians, always determined, it seemed, to be elsewhere. They arrived at Cara Mia restaurant on 9th Ave.

"Here you are, M'lady, a table for two at a small Italian restaurant so that we can look into each other's eyes and talk crap to one another all night."

Kee smiled.

She and O'Shea spent an hour enjoying the relaxed atmosphere of the unpretentious Italian restaurant. From stuffed mushrooms and pancetta to baby artichokes with a citrus dressing, Cara Mia offered a surprising range of vegetarian options for an Italian restaurant. Kee wasn't stuck, as was often the case, with the Margherita pizza.

"Ahh," said O'Shea approvingly, "they've got Carpaccio di Manzo. I love a good serve of bloody raw meat." He looked up at Kee. She had screwed up her nose in horror. O'Shea burst out laughing.

"I'm joking," he said.

"You could be part werewolf. I know nothing, absolutely nothing at all about you!" complained Kee, "and you know everything about me. You've even met my father."

"Nothing to tell," said O'Shea.

"Come on. Come on. How long were you married?" asked Kee.

"Not long. It ended. We don't keep in touch," answered O'Shea with a blank face.

"You've got to have some flaw, some vice. What about the gambling thing?" Kee persisted.

"Arghhhh! It's a vice. Poker. Blackjack. Some sports. Baseball …"

"I love baseball. We can go to a game. Who do you follow?" she enthused.

"I don't actually follow any team. I'm a gambler. You don't want your judgment clouded."

"That's a bit weird. Almost un-American," she said.

After the meal, they strolled down 8th Avenue hand in hand. The hodge-podge of shops were closed except for a few restaurants, a Subway and a McDonalds. At Capitol One Bank O'Shea body-pressed Kee into the door enclave and glided his hands up her back under her puffy coat and sweater. He pulled her in close to him. He kissed her. He kissed her so voraciously he could have devoured her.

"Wai ... wai ... wait," said Kee catching her breath. "We can't screw in a bank window. We've got to go somewhere. Not my dad's place. You live here. How about your place?" asked Kee.

"It's a bit of a dump," he said, "you won't like it."

"Come on, Mr. Neat and Tidy man, you wouldn't live in a dump," she countered. O'Shea just shrugged.

So it was back onto the subway, two line changes and short walk to a dilapidated, almost abandoned, graffitied apartment building in Bed-Stuy, in that part of Brooklyn that had not been, as yet, reclaimed by the monied classes.

"This has character," remarked Kee. She was putting on a brave face. They walked up three flights of the shabby, creaking, graffitied stairs—there was no lift—to Flat 22. It had a graffitied metal door. Kee assumed that, like many apartment blocks in New York, the stair and hallways would be characterless, but the apartment interior full of cozy creature comforts. She was wrong.

O'Shea's apartment boasted one room, one neatly made up mattress on the floor and one chair. Even the kitchenette was a starkly grim monument to frugality. One cup. One plate. She was stunned.

"What are you, a monk?" she asked.

"I travel light. And I'm not here much. You know that," he said, grimacing as he looked around his bleak apartment.

"Light! I thought I'd get an idea of who you are from your apartment. But there is nothing here. Nothing. You are a blank slate. That's sort of creepy," she said, aghast.

"I've got some clothes in the closet." He opened the built-in closet to reveal his clothes—shirts and leather jackets, jeans and motorbike leathers. "And there's the safe," he added. The safe was the size of a box set of a dozen wines. He punched in the passcode to the safe, which appeared as 6 blue asterisks on the digital display. He swung the door open. Her eyes nearly jolted out of their sockets. It was full of cash. Serious cash. Thousands and thousands of dollars in $100 bills.

"Are you a drug dealer or something?" she gasped.

"I told you. I'm a gambler. The FBI doesn't approve of gamblers. Too vulnerable if they get in debt. Then they can be easily corrupted, blackmailed, used by crims to get intel on investigations. That sort of thing. So I don't bank the money. I gamble in cash. And I'm very good at it." he closed the safe door again.

"You know, this is weird even for a Weird Shit Day," she concluded, "I think I'd better go." O'Shea, the gambler, gave a tell. He looked disappointed. He tried to laugh it off.

"Oh, well," he said, "I never have sex on a first date."

She began to laugh. She laughed so much that she had to sit on the lone chair, which turned out to be wobbly.

"Even the chair is a piece of shit," she gurgled, and collapsed on the mattress, laughing. Kee looked up at O'Shea, the man-boy who looked lost even in his own apartment, and a surge of sexual electricity racked her body. Her mood shifted instantly. Again. Her body ached for him. Why was it that good girls fell for bad boys? And fell hard. O'Shea, she knew, was dangerous. He had that predatory cunning of a lone wolf. Yet she was overwhelmed by the sheer maleness of him. His unknowable past. His rough 5 o'clock shadow that cut into her soft skin. His untamable blond hair. The breadth of his shoulders, so much broader than her own. The not-so-blond trail of hair that ran down his chest to his navel. His taut, muscular body. The texture of the hair on his tanned arms. The male smell of him. All musky sweat, testosterone and bad intentions. She was utterly seduced, the suicidal moth irresistibly drawn too close to the bewitching flame.

O'Shea didn't join her on the floor. He pulled her to her feet and began to undress her slowly. Deliberately. Caressing her soft skin as he removed each item of clothing. He tugged down her tight ripped-knee jeans until he heard a ripping sound. He froze. Kee had to ease them off. He pulled off her bikini panties, slowly very slowly, kissing her stomach and, finally, she was entirely naked. He stepped back and ran his eyes down her body from her ruffled long black hair and impish-face to the curve of her buttocks to the small tuft of hair at her crotch.

"So beautiful," he husked.

"It's all right for you," she complained, "but I'm freezing." He threw off his clothes in a rush, kicking first his shoes and then his suit trousers across the room. She pulled down his boxers and held his erect penis in her hands.

"Hello," she cooed, "We met earlier in the day."

He moved in on her. Kissing her mouth, her neck, her breasts, stroking her hair. He wouldn't let her talk. Every time she tried to say something, he kissed her or put his hand over her mouth or did something unexpected like spin her around so that his erect penis rested between above buttock cheeks as his hand ran down her stomach to the soft, tempting folds of her female form. He found and massaged her clitoris. The conversation attempt died a sudden death. She put one hand on the back of his neck and arched her back. Her body tensed. She was almost strangling him. He waited. She gasped and cried out, shuddered and climaxed before he'd even begun. Suddenly, she went all limp like a rag doll. He tipped her forward so that she had to hold onto the back of the chair and took her from behind. Gently at first. Just gliding his penis between her thighs and inside her with his hands holding her hips. Then powerfully, if briefly. He gave into the excruciating exploding ecstasy of full desire and came.

They both fell on the mattress, exhilarated.

"Now you know," he said between puffs of breath, "why I need a chair."

She hit him on the head with the pillow, laughing.

"I think I will sue the FBI. This Fuck-Me-Palace is substandard."

Her cell phone foghorn sounded.

"Leave it," said O'Shea, his naked body entangled with hers.

"I can't," she insisted. "I've got to check it."

He wouldn't budge. So she reached down with her one free hand and grabbed him by the balls.

"Do I twist now?" she threatened, "Or are you going to move your butt?"

"You play dirty," he complained. She slithered her naked body across his and reached for her cell phone in her shoulder bag.

"Freaking freak hell!" she gasped, "It's the AGB."

The text simply read:

TELL DEKANT WE'RE COMING FOR HIM

Kee climbed over O'Shea with difficulty, swinging one foot and then the other over his nose. As Kee rose to her feet and looked down on O'Shea, he reached out and grabbed her left ankle.

"Let go," she huffed.

"Nope," replied O'Shea. Kee stood wobbling in the nude, balancing on one foot.

"If I kick you, you'll be sorry," she threatened, nudging him with her free foot.

"Try it," he said.

She drew back her foot to kick. Then, as she swung her foot forward, O'Shea managed in one movement to let go of her ankle, spring to his feet, scoop her into his arms and swing her around in a circle. She laughed.

"Acrobat, too. That secret FBI training unit sure covers a range of skills!" she joked. "But the fun's over." Slowly, very slowly, he set Kee down on the cold floor and sighed.

Kee dressed quickly and called DeKant. While she was on the phone, O'Shea hung his suit back in the closet and took out his biker leathers. He also took out two pistol cases and quickly packed a backpack and duffle bag from the closet for the trip the following day.

Chapter 31

DeKant

Monday, the 18th of September

After the indignity of the laundry van trip, following the very late lunch provided by the good ladies of the NGSA Women's League, Gig sat at the kitchen table looking at a map of the estate. He was surrounded by Mick, Mac, Mike, and Muck. They were discussing estate security. They were still eating, and one of them, possibly Mick, kept adding suggestions through half-chewed mouthfuls of cold meats.

Gig checked the date on his phone. 18 September. What day was that? Monday. He was losing track of time, but not his sense of commitment to the cause.

"I will be going back into the office tomorrow morning, same as usual, so you boys must be prepared for that," instructed Gig. "In the meantime, we have to prepare to defend the estate tonight. Some lunatic may get it into his head to pump a few rounds at the house just to scare the bejeezus out of us. So we have to be ready for that possibility."

It was unfortunate—they all felt—that the estate was so heavily wooded. Beverley did like her trees. But the one factor in their favor was the floodlights. Gig had had them installed when he was being stalked by a religious nutter. This lunatic, who seemed to think he was a pastor for a congregation that didn't exist, would set up his portable lectern outside the NGSA office to declaim hellfire-and-brimstone passages from the Old Testament. When the preacher/lunatic turned up at Gig's front door one night and started lecturing him on his own doorstep, Gig had had enough. He installed floodlights that lit up the immediate vicinity of the house like a baseball park. This dissuaded many an unwanted visitor.

Once the meal was over—meaning, thought Gig, that Mick, Mac, Mike, and Muck could not squeeze in another slice of ham even if they shoved it in their ears—he called each of his children, asking them to come over with their families that evening. This was the calling in of the clan, and his children always answered the call. *They're good kids*, he thought, *loyal to the family*. The fact, that Gig supported each of them financially didn't enter into the equation, in his mind. He needed his family around him. And they would come.

Gig was still annoyed about the way the events of the day had unfolded. The riot had been an inconvenience, but a brilliant media event. The shooting was unfortunate. The issue, however, that stuck in his craw like a spiked fishbone was his exit from the NGSA head office. He had run like a yellow-bellied coward. Rather than face his foe down the barrel of a gun, he'd skulked away, hidden in the back of a laundry van. He felt like one of those soldiers in a war movie who breaks down, sobs and splutters, slumped into a useless fetal-ball in some trench or foxhole when under fire. He wasn't that kind of guy. He stood his ground.

Beverley was waving off the last of her guests at 5:20 p.m. when the call from Kitchi Le came through informing him of the Wikileaks post. Gig pulled the post up on his laptop and sat with his lieutenants looking at the list.

"Is it real?" asked Mike, or maybe Mac.

"It looks real enough," replied Gig, "but this asterisk business is downright obscene. I'll be calling it the Death List tomorrow. That should get some media attention away from all that loony Left bullshit put out by the anti-gun fanatics."

Beverly began sorting out the meal schedule. "As the family is coming over we'll have a barbecue on the paved terrace just outside the kitchen. The salads are covered," she murmured to no one in particular.

Despite the best effort of Mick, Mac, Mike, and Muck, there were plenty of salads left over from lunch. Then again, they were serious carnivores. They didn't just eat meat, they hunted it, killed it and drove triumphantly through the forest with the bleeding corpse of a 400 lb. Red Deer stag on the SUV hood.

"I'll just throw some plates in the dishwasher and thaw out some steak in the microwave, and that should be enough." Beverley was used to entertaining, although Gig knew that at 64 she might have preferred to kick off her shoes and put her feet up. But, as she told her husband, "You have an important job, Gig. And I'm here to support you."

The clan arrived in dribs and drabs. First to appear were Emily and the boys, Hunter, 7, and the twins, Brayden and Carter, 6. They were usually a handful. As soon as they rushed in the door, the house became host to a miniature barroom brawl. There was yelling and fighting and toppled furniture and crying and entangled bodies rolling on the floor or running past at full speed. This time the boys ran in the door yelling, "Grandpa! Grandpa! We saw you on the TV."

"Where's Cliven?" Gig asked Emily.

"He had some work to finish at the yard. He'll be over later."

Gig's son-in-law Cliven worked at the Molt family lumber yard just outside of Fairfax. He was part-manager, part-gopher, part-kicking-post. Gig knew Cliven hated his job. The problem was Cliven's father, who constantly berated the boy, often for no reason. Emily had told him as much. *But the boy isn't stupid,* Gig thought. *One day he'll inherit that lumber yard. That's worth putting up with some grief.* But he could still remember his daughter screaming, "Inherit the yard? That old goat is going to live to 105!"

Amy and Hank turned up next with Kelsey, 6, and Carlson, 4. And finally, Brad, Logan's twin brother, pulled up in his pickup with his girlfriend, Melodi, 22, who made blonde bimbos look like Einsteins. She'd once said, "I've never been to Canada or any other country in Europe." But she wore plunging necklines and had the biggest breasts in town, breasts that were especially large for a girl who was rather short. Whenever Melodi entered a room every male eye in the place followed those breasts like hawks watching their prey. Gig often wondered why young girls today had such big breasts. He couldn't remember girls being so "up front" as he called it in his day. Could it be all those hormones they pump into food these days? Or have the bloodlines selected for big-breasted girls?

"Hey Dad, nice work!" Brad grinned. He was wearing his usual outfit of jeans, a lumberjack shirt and a baseball cap on backward. "Everyone will want to own a gun now with those anti-gun motherfuckers losing it like that. Ha! Now people will be scared of the anti-gun lobby."

"Language," corrected his mother.

"Sorry, Mom," said Brad, holding up a can of beer to acknowledge his mother's scolding. "Got carried away with the good news."

"I have a constitutional right to state my views," Gig expounded, "and they denied me that right. Freedom of speech, boy. You have to be vigilant. Fight for it."

Gig's lieutenants were doing a sweep of the property, while back at the ranch, beers were opened, wine bottles uncorked, and conversation flew around the news bulletins appearing on the flat screen TV in the kitchen. A PAAW representative was talking to camera, complaining about the militia occupying their office in Fairfax.

"Suck on my machine gun, you motherfucker gun hater!" Brad yelled at the screen. He'd had three beers already.

"I'd have to agree," snorted Gig, "but watch your language, son."

"Muv a fukka" yelled one of the twins as they raced through the kitchen and out onto the patio.

"See what you've done," complained Emily. "They'll parrot anything."

"Sorry, Sis. I keep forgetting."

"Tell them he said Mother Trucker," suggested Melodi, but nobody listened to her.

Gig went outside to man the six-burner, hooded barbecue. It was the Big Mama of Gourmet Grills. He cooked steaks to perfection. There were hamburgers for the kids. Mick, Mac, Mike, and Muck did a thorough sweep of the food table. After the meal, the family sat watching a debate on a special edition of *Face The Nation* on CBS. The usual protagonists faced-off once again.

Roy Cotton, Republican Senator for Alaska, was steaming with fury.

"You cannot, sir, change an Amendment. That 2nd Amendment is sacrosanct. Written for all time. And it states unequivocally that American citizens have the right to bear arms."

"He's good," said Brad on his 5th beer.

"Real show pony," said Gig.

"Sacrosanct, rubbish. We got rid of the 18th Amendment. We kept it for 14 years, and then we tossed it out," countered Sheldon Endecott, Democratic Senator for Connecticut. "This is a democracy, sir. We can change Amendments. If we could not vote out Amendments, Prohibition would still be on the books today. It was voted out in 1933."

"That's bull crap," scoffed Brad, "you can't vote out an Amendment."

"Now you see what we are up against," warned his father. "They will go to any lengths to get our guns. It is my constitutional right to bear arms. I have a duty to defend my family. No one takes my guns from me."

It was 9 p.m. before they tackled dessert. There was apple pie and ice cream enough to feed a small army, armed or otherwise. Gig's cell phone rang.

"Hello, Miss Le," said DeKant.

"I'm sorry to disturb you again. But I have a message for you from the AGB."

"Yes?" replied Gig briskly.

"It said, 'Tell DeKant we're coming for him.'"

"Je-sus Christ," he said, "those goddamn assholes."

"Sorry," said Kee, adding, "I'll see you tomorrow."

DeKant's manic blinking started up. It had been a long and unnerving day. Sleep deprivation was disrupting his thought processes like flashes of lightning in an electrical storm, pushing him to cling desperately to a few rock-steady phrases. *It is my constitutional right to bear arms. I have a duty to defend my family. No one can take my guns from me.*

His daughters were busy putting the children to bed. There were plenty of bedrooms, and all the kids liked bunking in together, "To get up to more mischief," as their grandfather claimed. While the women tidied up after the meal, the men, including Logan, withdrew to the gun room. Gig had a special gunroom with security bars on the windows to store his arsenal. He had an old oak desk in the room where he'd sit at night to clean and oil his guns.

This was the moment Gig, the half-drowning, troubled teen shot at by his father, had been waiting for all his life—to be armed, stand his ground and protect his family. Gig unlocked the gun cupboard and ordered Brad to open the ammo draw.

Gig owned six pistols: a colt lightweight Commander .45, a Sig Sauer P226, a Glock 9mm, a Smith & Wesson .40, and the two Lugers from his father, both P08 pistols, one from the Luftwaffe and the other from the Reichsmarine. He also had a Smith & Wesson Model 29 .44 Magnum revolver, a real Dirty Harry handgun. He kept three assault rifles: a Colt AR 15 with tactical scope, a Heckler & Koch HK 417 and a Barret M107. He had one sniper rifle, a Remington XM 2010; a Remington 870 pump action shotgun; and one working vintage rifle, a 30-30 Winchester Lever Action, a real cowboy rifle.

"Listen up. There are eight of us"—Gig always included Logan in any count—"and we are heavily armed. We will draw up a night watch roster. If you see or hear anything, anything at all, flick on the floodlight master switch and take them out."

Gig was pleased with his DIY special ops speech. They were all keen. Armed. Ready to rock and roll.

Two of the lieutenants, Brad, and Logan were given the first watch. Gig liked to team the boys up, to let Logan feel as if his father did not discriminate between his sons. Brad didn't mind. Hell no! He was the lucky twin. Brad pushed his brother to the front of the house and they sat under the porch light, one in a wheelchair and the other on the porch seat.

The other men went off to bed, with the two spare lieutenants bedding down in the living room. These were fairly cushy digs for a security detail. These guys could sleep in a gutter or the back of a tray truck if necessary. Gig, however, still felt uneasy and was struggling to get to sleep. His mind riffed spasmodically through the repetitive mantra: *It is my constitutional right ... to bear arms. I have a duty ... to defend my family. No one ... can take my guns ... from me.*

At 1 a.m. there was a commotion. Brad had finished his 9th can of beer. This was not unusual for Brad. He could hold his liquor. But he wasn't paying attention and handed Logan the Sig Sauer with a loaded clip. Usually the family just handed Logan a pistol with an empty magazine so that he felt part of Team DeKant. He'd never held a loaded gun outside of the shooting range and on those occasions the instructor placed his hand over Logan's to help him safely aim the pistol. He didn't know this gun was loaded. Brad had dozed off and Logan, after some effort, managed to get one finger on the trigger and squeeze it. The pistol discharged. The .40 cal hollow point bullet hit the porch ceiling and discharged a cloud of plaster dust and chips. The floodlights switched on. Armed security guards came running just at the moment that Cliven came motoring down the drive. The clapped-out heap of a 1992 Dodge D250 pickup that he drove had broken down 3 miles from the yard. He'd called a tow truck and gotten a lift back to work. Some of the boys at the yard had been sitting around a metal wood burner fired up with offcuts, drinking a few beers at the end of their shift. So Cliven had stayed for a while, quite a while, then drove one of the yard's even more beat up pickups to the DeKant estate. Its registration number was not on the Known Vehicles list.

The lieutenants had all seen military service in Iraq, and they knew unidentified cars posed a clear and present danger. They fired a brief warning burst into the air. The pickup continued to approach along the drive, weaving erratically in a way that looked like evasive maneuvers to the trained, professionally paranoid eyes of men who'd been on the receiving end of heavy fire on more than one occasion. Cliven, cold, tired, inebriated, and longing for a warm bed, was used to hearing target fire at the estate. Now the lieutenants realized that the weapons they desperately needed in this situation were still in Gig's gunroom: the AR 15 or the Barret assault rifle. The AR 15 could take a 60 round magazine—hell, a 100 round box clip if you wanted—and it had a range of maybe 500 yards. This was similar to the weapon they'd used in the army. These two lieutenants on duty were not even carrying AK-47s. They were armed with Uzis because Uzis are cheap and the security company bottom-line had to be considered. Their Uzis had 32-round magazines, and they wore spare clips on their belts. The Uzis were set on fully automatic. They had the gun power, but the Uzi range was only 200 yards. They had to wait until the pickup was closer to the house. The security guard in command of the situation held one hand out to stop his fellow lieutenant from firing. They had to get the timing right. They waited, aimed their guns, and on his signal proceeded to shoot up the advancing truck.

The lieutenant in command hadn't fired off a full clip of rounds for some time, and in his haste and excessive enthusiasm for a real—not just a video game—Uzi bullet spray, he forgot to maintain a firm gun grip. The problem with Uzis is that they ride high when set on automatic. His gun kicked upwards. He put a few bullet holes in the eaves and knocked out some spouting before he wrestled in his weapon. His fellow goon thought they were under fire and dropped to the ground while holding his Uzi in the air with one hand. He took out more spouting around the DeKant house. Once they recovered, DeKant's lieutenants quickly changed clips, took aim and demolished the car.

This action sequence took less than 20 seconds. By the time Gig arrived the pickup had careered out of control, hit the fountain in the middle of the turnaround and rolled. The two lieutenants ran to the vehicle, pointing their guns at the driver, who was unconscious, while the other two lieutenants, fresh on the scene, scrambled to cover them. Brad joined the party at the shot-up pickup.

"Christ!" he yelled, "it's Cliven."

The guards dragged the unconscious Cliven out of the vehicle and laid him on the lawn. He was still breathing. The women had woken up by this stage and came running outside in their pajamas.

Emily screamed, "You've killed my husband!" just as the boys ran out the front door in their pjs and started screaming at the tops of their high-pitched voices. Gig sprinted inside for the medical kit and dialed 911. Emily was sobbing over the body of her husband. She kept repeating "You've killed my husband," and sobbing. Beverley tried to console the little boys, but they were hysterical. Gig returned with the medical kit and examined his son-in-law more carefully.

"He's still breathing," announced Gig, his eyes watering from the stale liquor stink on Cliven's breath. "I can't see any bullet holes. Plenty of cuts. But he'd have half his head missing if he'd been shot." For some reason, this failed to comfort his daughter. The paramedics arrived, siren screaming into the still night, and declared Cliven free of major wounds. His face had been cut by shattering glass, and he'd been knocked unconscious when his head hit the steering wheel. The pickup was too old to have airbags.

The security guards had not, in fact, been aiming at the driver but rather taking out the car by ripping out the tires. The reason for such precautions is always the same. The paperwork. If, as private operators in the line of duty, they had cause to shoot anyone the paperwork was exhausting. So they aimed at avoiding paperwork or other legal entanglements wherever possible and aiming their fire at tires. They had been aiming low and shot up a lot of dirt while punching only a few holes in the bodywork of the pickup.

DeKant had to do some quick talking to convince the paramedics that no one had been shot so the police need not be involved. Cliven was taken to the ER of the nearest hospital for some head scans. Back at the DeKant ranch, Brad wasn't about to admit that he'd handed Logan a loaded gun, so the origin of the first shot remained a mystery for the time being. Everyone was jumpy and more than a little distressed.

The girls made the first move. "We're going home, Dad," insisted Emily between gritted teeth. "I'm not staying here with the boys. They might get killed. I'm not staying for that."

"Stay. I can protect you and the boys. It's my duty to defend my family," insisted Gig, walking towards his daughter. But he tripped over the medical kit and only managed to stay upright by grabbing the arm of one of his lieutenants. He fought hard to mask his anger. His eyes blinked erratically.

Something snapped inside Emily at that moment.

"STAY?! You nearly shot my husband. Their father. I'm not staying until it is too late. I love you, Dad, I really do, but I'm not risking the boys' lives. No. No. NO. Come on boys; we're going home."

Amy was next. "I agree with Em. There is no point us being here risking the kids' lives. This is your fight, Dad. Not theirs. Come on, Hank. We're going home."

Hank, wearing striped pajamas, looked at his father-in-law and shrugged. The shrug meant, "She's the boss, what can I do?"

The final party to leave was Brad and Melodi, who was the most hysterical member of the gathering. She was sobbing with such might her famous bosom was heaving and rolling like a rogue ocean wave. It was amazing that she could remain upright with all that momentum whooshing around the top of her body. Brad and Melodi said their goodbyes and left, heaving bosom and all. Gig was unnerved and disappointed but he could understand his children's points of view. He couldn't insist that they or their children stay in a house already damaged by bullets.

The DeKant camp now consisted of Gig and Beverley, Logan and, "those 4 clowns, Mick, Mac, Mike, and Muck. The M&M squad." Gig briefly inspected the gunshot damage to the house eaves and guttering muttering 'Those fucking clowns. It's all their fault." Bev put Logan to bed; then, as she had utter faith in Gig's ability to control events, happily threw off her dressing gown, put her head on her own pillow and went soundly to sleep. Gig decided to sit out the rest of the night, his fourth night in a row without sound sleep. His lieutenants didn't drink. They were on duty. But Gig sat in his study with his Glock, Colt Commander, Smith & Wesson, and Sig Sauer on the desk and open his bottle of A.H. Hirsch Reserve 16-Year-Old Straight Bourbon Whiskey from Kentucky. It was a gift he'd received that day from an arms manufacturer.

The neighbors are a good lot, thought Gig. There'd be no trouble from them. When he'd first moved into the estate over 18 years ago, he told one neighbor, "Don't worry if you hear the odd gunshot, as I will be setting up some targets on the trees out back and firing off a few practice rounds from time to time." The neighbor had replied, "I'd be worried if I didn't hear gunshots." This was Virginia, after all. (Unbeknownst to Gig, his neighbors were very alarmed about the gunfire they heard that night, but they were not about to buy into that particular gunfight. They'd seen the news bulletins.) The Cliven situation was a fiasco, but Gig knew deep down with utter certainty that he could defend his family and himself.

The AGB said they were coming for him. Let them come. They had no idea who they were messing with. If they thought he'd be an easy, isolated target they'd get the surprise of their soon-to-be-terminated lives. No cause for worry, he assured himself, their latest rhetoric was a hollow threat. But he was wrong. Very wrong.

Chapter 32

DeKant

Tuesday, the 19th of September

At 5 a.m. Gig sat at his replica green leather-top Victorian desk in his study and opened his computer to check his emails. His work email account had hundreds of requests for interviews from around the world. His personal account reflected a normality that grounded him in everyday life. He cleared out the spam—for erectile dysfunction pills, mostly, plus a few Nigerian scammers who found a way past any filter—and looked down the list of emails from staff, select NGSA members, gun shows, gun magazines, manufacturers and the politicians that called him "friend". The front cover of UrbanEnforcerMagazine.com showed a middle-aged male kitted out in brown, green and khaki camouflage fatigues, cloth hat and face paint squatting behind a tree holding an AK-47 with the caption: DEFEND YOURSELF IN AFGHANISTAN, IN IRAQ ... IN YOUR LIVING ROOM.

StrikerFireMagazine.com boasted articles on "Tits & Targets: Hot Girls at the Range" and their latest "What do I feel when I shoot a terrorist? Recoil" t-shirts. Girls&AmmoMagazine.com

had a pretty-in-pink cover featuring the hot pink .223 cal AR assault rifle and the Flash Bang (pistol) Holster that attaches to your bra. It was good, mused Gig, to see the girls getting right into gun ownership. The numbers were very pleasing. He clicked on the YouTube link to the ad for My First Rifle. He was glad of the reminder. He'd already bought a .22 caliber single-shot Crickett rifle for Hunter for his 7th birthday. Kelsey would be 7 soon. He'd buy her a Crickett rifle too, a purple one; she was crazy about unicorns and the color purple. "It was a damn shame when that 5-year-old boy shot his 2-year-old sister with his Crickett Rifle. But guns aren't toys. Children should be taught how to handle guns in the same way we teach young folk to drive cars," Gig argued to himself.

Gig looked through a few ammo ads in americanguns.com. Even though he wouldn't admit it, Gig did get a little confused of late by the caliber of bullets. His Glock pistol fired 9mm rounds, but that was a 40 cal pistol, wasn't it? His AR 15 fired .223 Remington or 5.56 NATO rounds. Was that 22 cal or a 55cal? A 55 cal bullet was serious ammo. One shot would blow the brains out of an elephant. He used to know calibers for all his guns by heart like the Lord's Prayer. But there were times, these days, when he stumbled over some of the numbers. It made him angry. He just had to work around these lapses. That's what they were. Minor lapses. Nothing more. The main thing was to read the ammo packet to check which ammo went in what gun, load the clip, lock it in place and pull the trigger.

Gig opened the HAPPY FALL HUNTING ad from AR-15.com. The AR-15 was a mighty fine weapon. Lightweight, reliable and, like the AK-47, it had the capability of pumping out 600 rounds a minute when set on automatic. Of course, it would overheat and seize after a minute or two, but the rifle can be easily reset as a single-shot or four-round burst semi-automatic. It had served Americans well in combat. And now the Russians had cut the costs by manufacturing steel case bullets by the ship container load. 500 rounds still cost $129.95 at gunbroker.com so playing with an AR-15 or an AK-47 set on automatic wasn't cheap. Multiple bursts for say, 10 minutes, could run you $1,500 and send you broke, especially if you bought the ammo on your credit card. Now that was a trap. He'd heard stories.

But the urge to hunt is a basic instinct. It has nothing to do with economics. *Look at fishermen,* thought Gig. *They can spend $50,000-plus on a boat, trailer, rods, bait, magazines and beer and go out for days at a time to catch, if they're lucky, a fish worth $9.99 a pound. Then they have to gut it, scale and fillet it. It's quite a thing just for a man to say, "I caught this fish. I am hunter-gatherer man."* But men just don't get the same kick out of gathering. Gig had to be more or less dragged screaming to the Happy Hills You-Pick Strawberry Farm each year.

Around 6:40 a.m., as the light was slowly crawling through the triple-glazed glass of his study window, Gig closed his laptop lid, picked up his Smith & Wesson pistol and his crystal tumbler refreshed with bourbon, and walked to the front of the house to get a security update from his lieutenants. He was wearing a paisley-patterned navy silk dressing gown over his grey sweatpants and sweat top that served as his pajamas. He could make out the silhouettes of small shrubs and distant trees. And he could see the outline of Cliven's pickup still overturned in the garden bed.

"Anything to report?" he asked the lieutenant standing by the front door peering down the drive.

"Nothing, Sir. All quiet. Can't even hear any traffic moving yet."

"Good," said Gig. He stood by the lieutenant, staring into the murky morning gloom.

Two retorts sounded in quick succession. One hit the lieutenant in the right shoulder at the edge of his flak vest. The other smashed Gig's crystal glass, spraying expensive whiskey and shards over the silk dressing gown. Gig managed to drag the wounded guard in his front door, leaving a trail of blood across the front porch and onto the rug in the entrance foyer with the polished pinewood boards and large planter box full of spiky green plants. The lieutenant on guard at the rear of the house came running, as did the two lieutenants who had been sleeping in the living room to the right of the front door. Not one of the lieutenants used the two-way radios clipped to their flak jackets. They were trained for this, but deep down they simply didn't expect to see any action on a cushy private security assignment, not after the earlier "threat" turned out to be a fiasco. Even when the three operatives saw their wounded comrade lying in the entrance foyer, they could not get the reality of the situation into their heads. They were in shock. Combat wounds and upmarket wood paneled foyers didn't go together. So Mick, Mac, Mike, and Muck missed the opportunity for their big Hollywood moment of radioing "Man down" to the rest of the team. As one member of the team put a temporary pressure bandage on the wounded lieutenant, the third guard closed the front door and flicked on the floodlights. The fourth lieutenant rang their manager's personal cell phone number. This was, after all, an emergency.

"Right. Yes. Copy that," said the lieutenant on the phone.

Beverly arrived in the foyer and screamed. She was, in fact, more concerned about blood stains on the carpet than having someone with a gunshot wound lying in her entrance foyer.

"Don't take him into the living room. That's new carpet. I'll bring a pillow and a blanket here," she ordered. She disappeared for several minutes while she searched for an old pillow and a sufficiently worn blanket that could be thrown out after this ordeal.

"Sir," said the lieutenant, pushing the red end call button on his phone, "I have to inform you that those rounds were fired as warning shots. There is no doubt that the sniper who fired those rounds could have taken you and our man out if he'd wanted to. We have been forced to reassess the situation. I must inform you that we can no longer secure your perimeter or guarantee to provide personal protection for you or your family. The security level is extreme/evacuate. Head office is sending a chopper. It will land at the rear of the property away from the firing line. It is important that we get immediate medical attention for our wounded team member. We can also send a chopper to evacuate you and your family if you so choose."

Gig was stunned, then livid. "Go! Go!" he raved. "I can defend my property and my family! You lot turned out to be a bunch of fucking clowns, couldn't guard an outhouse. In fact, you caused nothing but trouble. You nearly killed my son-in-law."

Beverley returned with the blanket. It was only 20 minutes before they heard the thudding of the chopper blades cutting into the air above the DeKant estate. It landed without incident just beyond the paved back patio as the sun was rising.

The lieutenant who had taken command of the operation did not disclose the full reason for their sudden evacuation. It was the bottom line again. Getting security guards shot cost the company a lot of money. Getting them killed could sink a business that provided personal security in non-standard conditions. No company would provide insurance for their personnel. They also had to get their man to one of their staff doctors. The shooting would not be reported to the police or made public. Being on the losing end of a security detail was not good PR. Commando Personal Security Inc would keep its unblemished record. The NGSA would bear the medical, rehabilitation, and chopper costs. It was all in the contract.

The three capable lieutenants carefully lifted their comrade onto the blanket and carried him, bent over and running to the chopper. Within 2 minutes they were gone. They would send a detail later in the week to recover any weapons left on the premises.

Gig was furious. Rattled. Unhinged. He couldn't find his Smith & Wesson pistol. He had shoved it in his dressing gown pocket when he dragged the wounded lieutenant in the door while Beverley busied herself cleaning the carpet.

"Cold water is the best thing to remove blood," she muttered to herself, "and peroxide. A lot of cold water when there is a lot of blood. Then sponge it dry." She was wearing a pink brushed-nylon dressing gown and yellow rubber gloves, and was surrounded by several buckets and multiple rolls of paper towel.

Gig retreated to his gun room to rethink his strategy. He could barely contain his rage. To steady his nerves, he poured himself another bourbon in a cut crystal tumbler with the NGSA engraved logo. He couldn't be sure if the sniper was still out there waiting for him. It seemed unlikely. It was the day their garbage contractors emptied their dumpster; surely a sniper does not like trash collection trucks entering their kill zone. He paced back and forth. As he did so, he became aware of a weight that swung with the momentum of his turn. He discovered his Smith & Wesson in his dressing gown pocket.

"Motherfuckers!" he bellowed at the ceiling. "If you think you can intimidate me ... you don't know shit." Reflexively, he drew his Smith & Wesson out of his pocket and waved it angrily in the air as he walked around his desk. He tripped over a duffle bag left on the floor by one of his goons and accidentally fired a round into the ceiling. He was enraged by the stupidity of those clowns. He was also seriously rattled by the relentless, nerve-jarring and violent threat of being stalked for days by cold-blooded killers. Gig released all his pent-up fury like a World War 2 bomb that has lain dormant for years until it is unearthed by an excavator. He exploded. Gig fired several rounds into his gun room ceiling, yelling, "You assholes! Come and get me." This was a poorly judged move. He hit an electrical wire in the ceiling; it shorted and triggered the electricity trip switch. The switch turned off all power. The electricity power box was located at the front of the house, and he felt disinclined to stick his nose out the front door, let alone walk to the power box, turn his back to the drive and switch on the power.

He carried his drink and his Smith & Wesson back into the living room. He thought he might turn on the television, then he stopped himself. He couldn't; there was no power. Just at that minute, Beverley bustled into the room, saying, "The fridge is off. I have so much meat in the freezer. This is a disaster. Why isn't the fridge working?"

He loved her. He really did. But she had no goddamn idea about the pressure he was under at the minute. She was worried about blood on the carpet and a few pounds of steak when his life was in danger. He snapped, and yelled at Beverley, "Are you a fucking moron? We are under attack here, and you are worried about some frozen hamburgers!"

She burst into tears. "I've stood by you, Gig. I've stood by you for 42 years. Sickness. Health. Everything. To be treated like this!" She ran out of the room. He was really disappointed with himself for yelling at her. She was right. Goddamn it. He turned to go after her but tripped and banged his shin on the edge of the coffee table. A sharp current of pain ripped into his bone and up his leg. This was the last straw. With veins standing out at his temples, red in the face with rage, Gig looked up and saw the glassy-eyes of the bezoar ibex staring at him.

"What do you think you're looking at, asshole?" he yelled as he raised his pistol and fired several rounds in rapid succession. He neglected to follow standard handgun practice. Grip, stance, line of sight and trigger squeeze went out the window, as did one round. Other rounds hit and ricocheted off the brick chimney. He was lucky he wasn't hit. He couldn't say the same of the flat screen TV. It now had a perfect bullet hole slightly to the left of mid-center.

Gig took his failure to hit the trophy beast as an insult to his marksmanship. He marched to his gun room, refilled his Smith & Wesson clip and picked up a loaded Glock, so that he now had a pistol in each of his dressing gown pockets along with some extra clips, then returned to the living room with his AR-15 and shot that ibex right between the eyes. He took out the red wildebeest too, blowing off its nose. He'd never really liked that trophy. The wildebeest was a miserable looking creature. Not at all majestic like the bison.

Fifteen minutes later Beverley returned to the front of the house, dressed and pushing Logan in his wheelchair. Her handbag was hooked over a wheelchair handle.

"I'm not staying here one minute longer. I'm leaving, and I'm taking Logan with me. We'll go to Emily's. You can come with us, but you can't bring any guns."

Gig was too knotted up with frustration and disappointment to answer. His eyes blinked erratically.

"Well?" she demanded. He couldn't let Beverley see this weakness in him. He turned his back on her.

"I'm not worried about the AGB," she sobbed to his back, "I'm frightened of you. You won't call the police. You won't leave. You think your some sort of hero. I think you're losing it. Look around you! Look what's happened. You are mad."

She found her Ford Flex SUV keys in her handbag. It had been modified to lift and fit Logan's wheelchair. She pushed Logan out the front door. It would be quite some time before she returned to the house.

After Beverley drove off, DeKant aimlessly roamed around the house. He kept a firm grip on the pistols in each pocket. In the bedroom he changed out of his dressing gown and put on a black, puffy vest, carefully placing his Glock in one pocket and his Smith & Wesson and extra clips in the other. "It's too big a house to be defended by one man," he mumbled, as he made his way back through the living room. He fired another shot at the ugly motherfucker wildebeest but missed by a mile. He didn't even know where that round went. "Stance. Grip. And the rest. Must remember that stuff," he muttered to himself, shoving his Glock back in his pocket. *Beverley has done a fine job of cleaning blood off the carpet in the foyer*, he noted as he walked past. He really should be more grateful. But blood smears still ran down the front steps and along the front of the house. He had no will to go out front and inspect the blood stains or reconnect the power. He didn't even have the energy to call the tow truck firm and have Cliven's overturned pickup removed from the front drive. Later. He'd attend to these little details later. He withdrew to the gun room to consider his options.

DeKant sat at the old oak desk surrounded by his guns planning his day. What day was it? He couldn't think straight. Maybe it was the weekend, and he wouldn't have to go to work. He checked his cell phone. It was Tuesday, 19 September. He felt as if he'd lost 2 days of his life completely somehow. He couldn't remember those two days. Only fragments.

He'd have to go into work. It was late. At 8:25 a.m. his cell phone started ringing. First Beverley. Then Emily. He didn't answer their calls. Then the office rang. His second-in-command informed him that angry anti-gun protesters were still staking out the NGSA head office. DeKant should delay his return to the office. He could work from home for a day or two. The cell kept ringing. He put it on silent and ignored most of the calls, but he kept an eye on the phone just the same. He didn't want to miss an important call. Beverley. Brad. Emily. Beverley again. Emily again. DeKant ignored their calls.

He wandered out to the kitchen and made himself a coffee. He did this by boiling a saucepan of water on the barbecue gas burner outside the kitchen. DeKant began to feel more himself and less concerned about the sniper after that coffee. As a nod to his home defense plan, he pulled out his Glock and fired off a few rounds across the lawn into the woods behind the house. The manufacturers claimed the Glock had a range of 50 yards. Factoring in accuracy, however, it was probably closer to 25 yards, tops. So the living creatures and, indeed, any stray snipers inhabiting the woods a good 80 yards away were, more or less, safe. A 9mm round, however, could travel quite a distance; so, ironically, while a nearby sniper might be safe a neighbor mowing their lawn half a mile away might not be so lucky. He fired 8 rounds from 10 yards at the china donkey with a cactus in each side basket that Beverley kept on the patio table and missed each time. Finally, he walked over to the donkey, put a gun to its head and took it out. "This single life isn't so bad," he announced to the "dead" donkey. Then he laughed. Giggled, in fact. Anyone who heard that giggle would not think it the utterance of a sane man. Then again, sanity is only relative. You need an outsider, a line-caller to blow their whistle when you've crossed the line into the crazy-man zone. But could you trust the whistleblower? He reloaded both handguns and emptied their clips into the garden and felt the better for it. He returned to his gunroom carrying another cup of coffee and some homemade chocolate chip cookies left over from the Ladies' League luncheon. He checked and rechecked all his guns, including his handguns, making sure they were locked and loaded. DeKant liked that term. "Locked and loaded," he muttered as he inspected each gun again. His cell kept buzzing. Brad. Emily. Beverley. The family was worried; of course they were worried. Brad again. Senator Cotton. He'd have to take this call.

"Senator. I understand. Yes! Yes! The NGSA is right behind you. We appreciate the expenses involved. It will be sorted." *You slimy asshole*, thought Gig, pressing End Call on his cell.

"Not much on the agenda for the rest of the day," Gig noted, as he poured himself a bourbon and leafed through some of his gun magazines. He rarely had the time to read them. Home Defense World Magazine had a fascinating article titled "Don't Register Your Guns". The standard argument in the gun community was, "If you register your guns, the government will know what you own and come and get them." This article put an economic spin on the issue. "America's insane national debt could turn the nation into a third-world country under martial law, a situation in which good law-abiding folk will need to be armed for their own protection."

"It could happen tomorrow," mused Gig. "Tomorrow? What am I thinking? It happened yesterday right outside my own office."

DeKant was losing track of time. He looked at his phone. 2:08 p.m. But he'd forgotten what day it was again. He poured his third—or was it his fourth?—bourbon and rechecked his phone. "It's Tuesday," he said to himself. His cell buzzed again. This time it was Kee saying she was at the front gate.

Chapter 33

Booker

Tuesday, the 19th of September

At 7 a.m. on Tuesday, Booker gave Perez strict instructions over the phone. "Do not, I repeat, do not call me under any circumstances unless the situation is strictly life or death. Do you understand? Tell the others."

"Right, Chief," replied Perez.

Charlotte had gone into labor at 4 a.m. that morning. She was currently in the New York Presbyterian Hospital after three hours of labor. Booker would have preferred to leave all the fussing to Phillis and Nikki, who had escorted Charlotte in the ambulance, but he had to be there, not only to support Charlotte but Phillis and Nikki too. He wasn't at all sure what he could do, but he had to be there.

The labor lasted eight hours, which wasn't too bad for a first baby. Booker popped in and out of the birthing ward. He couldn't bear to see Charlotte in such pain. It was emotional pain too, he suspected. She kept saying, "I'm having a baby," part in shock and part in amazement. Booker spent most of his time pacing in the tacky waiting room with the threadbare carpet and worn chairs, buying coffees from the dodgy machine in the hall, which he then failed to drink. He was on edge.

The Organized Crime team followed his instructions to the letter. There was not a cell phone beep from them. Just after midday, a chubby, healthy baby girl made her appearance in the world. She was 7 pounds, 6 ounces, which was a remarkably good weight for a first baby, and she was the image of her mother. Everyone in the birthing unit was crying.

Charlotte had been offered a private birthing room because of her unusual history. Everyone in that unit knew her story, and when her baby was ejected out of her body with that final gigantic pelvic-floor straining push, everyone in the unit—apart from Charlotte—held their breath.

"You have a beautiful baby girl," declared the midwife, placing the little mucus-covered froggy creature between Charlotte's bare breasts.

They all waited.

Charlotte looked down at the little bundle, and then looked up at her own mother and grinned.

"She's beautiful," she said, and everyone in the birthing unit cried. Charlotte would never know that most births are not accompanied by a general outbreak of crying and eye wiping and nose blowing.

"What do you want to call her?" asked Phillis.

"I think, um, Destiny," replied Charlotte, which was a lovely name, especially for one thought up on the spot, and tearfully poignant too. Phillis called Booker into the birthing suite, and he got to hold his little granddaughter for the first time.

"I don't know how this works, Miss Destiny. But I'm in love with you already," Booker cooed to the baby girl. That bought another flood of tears from those in the birthing suite. He rang his mother. He didn't know if she'd understand but he wanted to include her in the excitement. "Mom, Charlotte has just had a baby girl. She's named her Destiny."

"You've had a baby?" has mother asked.

"Not me, Mom. Charlotte."

"Who's Charlotte?" his mother asked. He talked for a little longer, promised to bring the baby out to visit her soon, and ended the call. He slipped the cell phone back in his pocket. It buzzed immediately.

"Only a matter of life or death," he'd told Perez, so he had to assume someone had died. He handed the baby back to Phillis, who was cooing and oohing and ahhing, and walked out of the birthing suite door to answer the phone.

"You have to come, Boss," insisted Volkman. "There's been a development."

"What?" queried Booker.

"I can't tell you on the phone, Boss; you have to come to the office."

Booker jumped in a cab. He was in the lift heading for the Incident Room on the 23rd floor within 20 minutes of that call. Booker looked at his cell. It was 1:15. Where had the day gone? He'd been awake since 4 a.m. His internal circadian alarm clock had reset. He was waking every morning now at the godforsaken hour of 4 a.m.

"What is it? It better be good, Volkman," snapped Booker, heading to the bank of computers at the end of the Incident Room. The entire team was gathered around Volkman's computer.

"You a grandpa yet?" asked Perez.

"Yes, a beautiful little girl named Destiny."

"Good name," said Skule. Everyone congratulated Booker and patted him on the back, but there was tension in the air.

The team reconvened around Volkman's desk. Volkman's computer had the biggest screen possible so that he could view several windows at once. He also had windows open on his laptop and tablet. Volkman was the master of combing through the fine detail. He nitpicked the small but significant pieces of evidence others missed. When Wikileaks published the names of all members of the NGSA who lived in Virginia, it was Volkman who'd worked out that the asterisks did not signify a Death List.

"Why not?" Booker had asked.

"Because I counted them," explained Volkman. "There were 259 asterisks. If they represented a Death List, there would be 84 or fewer. Most likely fewer. 91 is the magic number here. The AGB threatened to shoot 91 members of the NGSA, around the entire country." This time, Volkman didn't just throw a spanner into the investigation engine, he derailed the train.

"I'll step you through this, Boss. First, this guy rings. The officer who took the call flagged it. He thought it might be worth a follow-up. The caller doesn't want to leave his name but says he wants to help. He had sold an AK-47 three months ago. Now the buyer wants the gun handover to take place in some remote spot at the Zerta Landfill near Zion. He says it's about an hour out of Chicago and is mostly abandoned ship containers and piles of building rubble. The seller gets there. It's dark. Wet. He gets cold feet. So he sets up this deal. He'll leave the gun in a railway locker at Union Station in Chicago, and when the buyer posts the cash to a PO Box, he'd text the locker combination. The buyer agrees. The money arrives, and sometime within a 24 hour period the buyer turns up and collects the gun. Now, Boss, the seller gave us the exact date of this transaction. I've called in all the CCTV in the area ... some has been over ridden ... 90 days is on the edge of most storage limits, but there is still some good footage. So see ... there ... there is our guy. He pops up out of nowhere. He knows what he's doing. Baseball cap. Dark clothes. It's nighttime. He keeps his head away from all the CCTV cameras. Picks up the gun and disappears again. We cannot find how he leaves. Nothing."

"I went over and over this footage ... then ... Gotcha! I get an image on a side view mirror of a car. This mirror is turned up for some reason facing the CCTV camera, and we get a split-second look at our buyer."

Volkman clicks on a window and up pops a picture of a white male in a baseball cap.

"Sweet Jesus," Booker breathed. "It's O'Shea. What the hell is he doing? Do you all agree? It's O'Shea."

They did. "Right. Perez, get the IT team here, now. All of them. We're going through everyone's computers. We have to get a handle on this. Skule, you check his flight times. He's escorting Miss Le to Fairfax. The rest of you have to look into O'Shea's history. Cogliano, you do his military service. Godbold, you do his FBI history. How did he end up in the Organized Crime squad?"

"He was working undercover to crack some drug-running/gunrunning cartel back then, wasn't he? It's probably a part of a field op. Then he wanted out. So coming to Organized Crime made sense?" suggested Cogliano.

"Maybe this was a field operation. Even if it wasn't, O'Shea hasn't done anything illegal," argued Skule.

She felt loyal to O'Shea. She couldn't help herself. They all felt they should defend O'Shea. But no one had any answers.

The IT crew arrived and searched all their computers for the names of the XC1 victims on dates before their execution-style murders. O'Shea's computer had 7 hits out of 7. Perez's 5, Booker's 3, Cogliano 7, Godbold 6, Volkman 4 and Skule none.

"They were suspected of gunrunning, Boss," said Volkman.

"So we should have them on our radar. Still, we have enough intel to flag O'Shea as a person of interest. He is not on the board. He is not a suspect. But we need answers. What does he know that we don't?" demanded Booker. "And keep in mind, those undercover guys, they are strange creatures. True chameleons that adapt to suit any environment. They're hard to read. I've always thought they'd be perfect poker players. Their opponents would never see a tell with one of them. Not even a flicker of an eye. Wait. Wait. Before we get any theories up and running, I've got to alert Miss Le."

Booker was about to call her cell phone when he remembered that O'Shea's cell phone had been tethered to hers.

"What time is it?" he asked no one in particular.

"2:45," replied Volkman.

Booker looked intently at his cell screen as if pleading with it to give him some ideas. Then he had an idea. He rang DeKant and—Hallelujah, saints be praised—DeKant answered.

Chapter 34

Kee

Tuesday, the 19 of September

Kee and O'Shea landed at Dulles International Airport, Washington, DC, at 12:10 p.m. In the cab on the way to Newark International Airport, Kee had remarked to O'Shea, "It doesn't feel like Weird Shit Day 5, nothing much has happened today." She almost sounded disappointed.

"Wait a bit," he replied, climbing out of the cab. "You haven't experienced the full FBI airport silver service yet."

She paid the cab driver as O'Shea opened the trunk to take out a backpack, two handgun cases, and another large duffle bag. Kee was on the gravy train. *The New York Times* would pick up her expenses. She hoped.

"Why have you got all that luggage?" she asked. "We're only going to be here for 3 or 4 hours. I've got a laptop, my phone, and that's about it."

"I'm always prepared for World War Three" he replied lightly. O'Shea directed Kee to an unmarked door behind a security desk at Newark Airport. There was one guard on duty.

"Hey ya, O'Shea, come on through," said the guard.

There was no ID check, no baggage check. Nothing. They walked through the poorly lit, echoing corridors of the airport underground security system.

"To your right," explained O'Shea, "you will see some interrogation rooms. Further down that corridor is the prison system. There are always prisoners on the move, being extradited to another state, another country."

"You mean, they put criminals on ordinary flights?" Kee asked, amazed.

"What else? You can't send them by courier pigeon," joked O'Shea.

"I never thought about it before," said Kee.

"Generally, you don't know. We load the prisoners on the back of the plane. We don't wear uniforms. And often they aren't cuffed. Commercial airlines, quite a lot of them, won't allow prisoners to be cuffed during a flight. It's different for J-PATS, the prisoner transport division. They have their own Con Air planes. Their no frills service includes belly chains, handcuffs and leg irons."

"Wait, wait. So we can't take a nail file on a flight, but you can take on a murderer, who gets to walk around the plane?" she demanded, agog.

"They don't walk around. They have an escort or two sitting beside them. And there are armed marshals on flights," he reassured her.

He guided her into a private, windowless FBI lounge to wait for their flight. As a silver service it lacked the trimmings, but there was free coffee, free wifi, and TV. O'Shea threw his bags onto a lounge chair and turned towards Kee.

"Aren't they going to check our baggage?" she asked.

"They will. Later," he said, grabbing her by each buttock and lifting her up.

"Put me down. This behavior is very unprofessional," she half-joked.

"Who for? You or me? You're the one on expenses," he replied.

He put her down and immediately ran his hands up inside her white blouse. She was hopeless. She just melted like chocolate. He kissed her. *I know what's happening here. I'm such an idiot. I was a goner the first minute I saw him. That boyish grin thing. The surfer hair. The tough guy leathers. Now I'm aching in my gut to jump on him and screw myself crazy and I can't.*

"Mmm," he said, undoing her top blouse button.

She slapped his hand. "Behave yourself." But he kept pestering her, and she didn't trust herself. In the end, she ordered him to sit on the other side of the lounge.

"I'm only doing my job. I'm protecting that ass, And those breasts, and ..."

She gave him her mama's-not-happy frown. But she was deliriously happy.

Soon enough they were called for their flight. They walked down more echoing corridors and flights of concrete stairs until, finally, they went through a minimal FBI security check. O'Shea talked with the security officer during the screening in that clipped men-on-a-mission style speech. O'Shea's gun cases were set aside to be put in special security lockers on board the plane.

"You on that XC1 case?" asked the security officer.

"Yep," said O'Shea.

"You got any intel on this AGB group yet?" asked the officer, viewing the bag scans.

"Nothing to get excited about," sighed O'Shea.

"You think they'll follow through all their threats to NGSA?"

"Maybe," responded O'Shea.

"Weird one, that," commented the officer, handing them back their bags.

"Weird as fuck," agreed O'Shea.

Kee thought, *Honestly, at times the male of the species seems incapable of conducting casual conversations. They might as well still be grunting at one another.* She attempted to break the grunt talk mode and be sociable by asking the officer how long he'd been in the FBI. He replied, "Long enough."

Kee just shook her head.

They were shunted to the back entrance of their flight on a golf cart and walked up the back steps just as the flight attendant began her safety talk. O'Shea's luggage was secured in a special locker in the steward's pantry. They sat in their seats at the back of the plane as the doors closed.

At Dulles International Airport, Washington, the arguments began.

"We're taking an SUV," said O'Shea.

"I'm paying, so I get to choose," she retorted.

"SUV, please," he said to the car rental agent.

"Well, I'm driving," she insisted.

"I'm driving," countered O'Shea, "because you will spend half your time fiddling with your phone and being a general nuisance on the road and a danger to all traffic."

"Yerrrrr! Okay," she conceded. Kee started fiddling with her cell phone as soon as they left the flight and walked into three pedestrians, nearly knocking one passenger with a broken leg off his crutches. The next argument was over the route. O'Shea prevailed again. "I've been here before," he argued. "These highways can be murder. We'll take the 226, then the 286 to Fairfax."

Kee sat in the passenger seat, scrolling through her emails and Twitter feed as O'Shea negotiated the heavy traffic. It was 1:30 p.m.

"How about this," she said, "@PoliceBizz says there's been trouble at the DeKant residence. No further news. I wonder what that means. Did you hear anything from Booker?"

"Nope," said O'Shea.

Kee sent a Tweet back to @PoliceBizz.

"I'm heading to the DeKant house now. Any more intel let me know straight away." @KeeHasSpoken

"You still owe me a drink." @PoliceBizz.

"Sure. When I get back. I had the FBI trace you. Know who you are IRONMAN." @KeeHasSpoken

"Damn. Was fun while it lasted. Be careful BB." @PoliceBizz.

"Will do." @KeeHasSpoken

"Let's put some music on. We'll be there in 30 minutes."

So they cruised down the highway listening to "Mustang Sally". It seemed to fit the mood. O'Shea stopped the SUV just outside the DeKant estate at 2:10 p.m. "You better ring through and tell him you are coming. Something looks out of whack here. I'm not sure ... I can't quite see past those trees lining the drive."

"Hello, Mr. DeKant. It's Kitchi Le. We're at the gate. We'll be there in a minute. Are you okay with that? ... Right... Yes. Good."

"He's a bit drunk," she said. "Slurring his words. What are the ethics here? Is it okay to interview someone when they're drunk?"

"I don't like this. I don't like this one little bit," said O'Shea, as he slowly drove down the DeKant driveway.

Kee saw Cliven's overturned car and said, "Holy crap. What's happened here?"

O'Shea could recognize bullet damage. The house had been shot up.

"You can't stay here," he said. "I'll take you back to the gate."

"No way. I'm going in. This is my big break, and you aren't my boss."

"I wish I had a flak vest for you," muttered O'Shea.

"Weren't you prepared for the 3rd World War with all that luggage?"

"Apparently, I've turned up at the wrong war. Look," said O'Shea, retrieving his bags from the car trunk, "I've got one flak vest. Here. Put it on. But you stay in the car and let me knock on the door and see what happens. If you hear a gunshot, leave."

"Jesus! Fuck! Are you trying to scare the freaking daylights out of me?" she demanded.

"I have to be realistic," he warned. "We don't know what's happened here."

O'Shea, dressed in his leathers and carrying his Glock in a zippered pocket, knocked quietly on the front door. DeKant opened the door. He looked twitchy and a little the worse for sleep deprivation, but not depraved. He was wearing a grey sweat suit and a black zip-up sleeveless padded vest. His grey hair was unruly, and his feet were bare. DeKant actually looked pleased to have guests. O'Shea called Kee over to the house.

"Hello, Mr. DeKant," she said, holding out her hand. "What the hell happened here?" *That wasn't very professional,* she thought, but then again, she felt she was in a war zone at that precise moment, so she didn't give a damn! *War zone? Freaking freak hell. I forgot to put on the flak vest.*

"Just a misunderstanding," DeKant replied

"With a couple of machine guns, by the look of it," O'Shea remarked.

"And this is FBI special agent, Denney O'Shea."

The two men shook hands.

"Sir, I have to ask you," said O'Shea, "who is on the premises? Are you armed and do you have any armed guards patrolling the grounds?"

DeKant shook his head.

"I'm the only one here. They've all left. It wasn't safe for the children, and we've been under sniper fire."

"Oh my God!" cried Kee. "Are you all right?"

"Are you armed?" O'Shea persisted.

DeKant showed them that he was carrying two handguns shoved, in defiance of all gun-safety rules, in his vest pockets. He kept his hand on the pistol in his right pocket as they talked.

"Come in. I'd offer you coffee or something, but Beverley usually does that sort of thing, and there's no power."

DeKant took them for a tour of the house. "I see you've killed the ibex," noted O'Shea in the living room. DeKant ignored him, mainly because he'd tripped over the coffee table again. He grimaced, grabbed at his wounded leg, stood up stiffly and then limped for several paces as he continued the house tour. Kee managed to get in a few questions en route.

"How do you feel about being a target of the AGB? What message do you want to send to them? What are your future plans?" DeKant managed to reply in below-par mode. He was, he explained, an innocent man. He had broken no laws. Cared for his family. Wanted to protect them. He was a true patriot of this country. He didn't understand why he would be the target of the AGB.

Gig showed his guests his gunroom. Various guns were laid out on the desk, loaded and ready for action. Kee and O'Shea were suitably impressed, although O'Shea's reaction slanted more on the wary side.

"I have to inspect your handguns, Sir," said O'Shea, "to make sure your safety catches are on. I'm protecting this young woman. I must insist."

"Like fuck you will—"

As DeKant moved around the desk to face O'Shea, he tripped over the abandoned duffle bag again. He grabbed for the edge of the desk with his left hand to steady himself and fired a round, by mistake, with his right hand. It tore a hole in his vest pocket and ripped through the leather upholstery of his favorite desk chair. Muttering a garbled curse, he turned to glare at the FBI agent.

"Sir, I must insist," demanded O'Shea.

DeKant took out the pistol he'd just fired by mistake and pointed it at O'Shea. He also gripped the handgun in his other pocket firmly with his left hand.

O'Shea took one step forward, and DeKant fired a round over his head.

"Shit!" gasped O'Shea. He pushed Kee backward with one hand, signaling her to leave. Scram. Get out of there. But he did not take his eyes off DeKant. Kee just froze. With all her recent dealings with DeKant, she didn't feel unsafe.

O'Shea held his hands up palm-out in front of him—a part of his FBI non-aggressive behavior training—and proceeded to negotiate. "Trust me. I'm not trying to take your gun, Sir. I'm just checking the safety catch. Just put it on your desk. We'll talk about it."

DeKant refused to comply. He shot another round over O'Shea's head, but the agent did not stand down.

"Trust the fucking FBI?" DeKant yelped. "Those fascists?"

It was 2:45 p.m. DeKant's phone rang. He picked up his cell phone from his desk and looked at the screen. He answered the call.

"Hello, Mr. Booker. Yes, they're here. And you can tell your son-of-a-bitch agent to back off. It's my house. He has no right to take my guns."

"I'm not here for your guns, Sir. It's a safety measure," said O'Shea.

DeKant handed his cell phone to Kee, saying "He wants to talk to you."

"Booker here, Miss Le. Just say 'Mmm' now and then and listen. It looks like O'Shea could be involved with the XC1 shooters."

"Mmm," said Kee.

"We have some intel. It's not much to go on."

"Mmm," said Kee.

"But you must leave immediately. Just say you forgot something, and get out of that house and drive off."

"Mmm," said Kee, "good."

She handed the phone back to DeKant.

"I left my recorder in the car. I'll go and get it," she announced. O'Shea didn't respond. Nor did DeKant. *Too busy swinging their dicks*, she thought.

As she galloped through the front door, she heard another round go off. Kee ran as fast as she could to the car and climbed into the driver's seat, but she didn't drive away. She couldn't. O'Shea had the keys.

She waited. Five maybe, ten minutes. She had no plan if a demented DeKant came through the front door with both guns blazing. There was one more gunshot, and then silence. Total, utter silence. She waited. And waited.

Finally, O'Shea walked out the front door, zipping his Glock 26 into his leathers' side pocket. He walked calmly to her side of the car and signaled Kee to lower the window. She couldn't; he had the keys. So he opened the door, put the keys in the ignition and dropped the window himself. Then he closed the door.

Kee sat in the SUV, clutching the steering wheel and looking straight ahead.

"You used me," she said.

"A little."

"You knew the cartel would come for me that night."

"I thought they might."

"You used me to get to DeKant."

"Hey, who used who? You get your *New York Times* article and a career out of this. You should thank me."

"But... why?" Kee turned to look him in the face.

O'Shea sighed. "It was simple. We're off fighting a war, and kids at home are being shot. Our kids. A niece, a neighbor's kid, a stepson. A group of us were sitting around talking the same old shit one night when someone says, 'Why don't we shoot the fuckers who push those guns onto the streets? You know, assault rifles, automatics?' Everyone thought it was a good idea."

"You kill people."

"Not me."

"They kill people."

"You can't call those gunrunning fuckheads people."

"But they're American citizens. What about their rights?"

"What about the rights of the kids, kids who are shot and killed? No one, absolutely NO ONE stands over their graves saying, 'These children should have the right to grow up.' There is no amendment protecting them."

"Why DeKant and the NGSA?"

"You interviewing me?"

"May as well."

"DeKant is not what you think. He and the senators on his payroll are into some serious shit. Believe me. No one can touch them. They use the media to block investigations, saying Left Wing politicians are taking away their constitutional rights."

"What about the NGSA?"

"The NGSA has one worldview: Everyone should own a gun. No restrictions. But what happens when the guns are pointed at them? How cocky are they then? The shooters are not after ordinary members. Just the assholes pushing illegal guns onto the streets."

"But how can killing gunrunners help?"

"To get the public to see what's going on. To get their attention. To break through the media silence that their money buys."

"They kill in cold blood. How can they do that?"

"That's how we were trained. By our own government."

"And the coordination?"

"Red Team, Blue Team. That's also how we were trained. They're on the Blue Team now."

"But you shot Americans."

"Not me. My hands are clean. Not even DeKant. He shot himself. You saw what was going on. He was crazy. I tried to talk him down. No way. He's such a shit shooter, he couldn't even do that job properly. He clipped one ear. How can anyone miss their own head from point blank range?"

"Booker will track down every sniper in the country."

"He won't find them, and you know why. Snipers know how to disappear."

"Booker had some intel on you. You'll be their number one suspect."

"I'm clean. You wait and see. Booker doesn't know everything. He doesn't know why I joined his team or what I was doing there. Now I need a little vacation. A few days at the beach, I think. I'll let Booker know I won't be in for a few days."

"Will there be more shootings?"

"Maybe."

"But we could have had such a good time."

"We had a good time."

"That's it? You just vanish now?"

"Come with me."

"I ... can't."

"I know. You've got your career to think about."

"And Harold," she said. They both laughed, a bleak laugh.

"But where will you go?"

"I have friends," said O'Shea, opening the trunk of the black SUV to grab his luggage.

"But none of them," he admitted, as he returned to the car window and threw his cell phone onto the back seat, "have an ass as cute as yours. Sorry. Gotta go before the circus rolls into town."

O'Shea turned towards Kee for a moment and smiled. And still, despite all of this, her pulse jumped and her body ached with the longing for him. But her heart was a mess, knotted and twisted with real heartache. Kee felt such a crushing pain in her chest she thought she might be having a heart attack. She watched him walk down the drive in the rear view mirror. He didn't look back. *He didn't even say goodbye*, Kee thought. O'Shea ambled out of the DeKant Estate and disappeared.

Kee was gripping the steering wheel of the SUV so fiercely her knuckles were white. Now she relaxed her grip, put her head forward on the steering wheel and cried. Her tears rolled down the steering wheel rim and dropped onto her lap.

The SWAT team arrived 15 minutes later. Kee was ordered out of the car. She didn't care. She felt numb. Utterly empty. Once the SWAT team had secured the premises, the officer in charge, wearing full black SWAT fatigues, black helmet, black gloves and carrying a Colt AR 15 assault rifle, came over to her. He pushed his face-shield to one side.

"The FBI wants to interview you, Miss Le. They're flying in a special agent from New York by chopper. I have a message for you. 'Be careful who you trust, Booker.'"

She just nodded.

Chapter 35

Kee

The Cross-eyed Wildebeest

It had been a long day for Kee. She was physically and emotionally spent. She just wanted to go home. But she was stuck at the DeKant Estate outside Fairfax waiting for Booker. After the SWAT team checked the car for weapons and gave it the all clear, Kee wasn't sure where to put herself. So she climbed back in the driver's seat of the SUV and cried herself half stupid until she was all cried out. Then she sat in the car staring blankly ahead. She saw an ambulance arrive, collect a patient—*DeKant,* she thought—and leave. She watched more police vehicles arrive, crime scene SUVs and local police cars. Kee had been sitting for almost two hours when she heard the thud-thud of chopper blades. The chopper landed gently on the lawned area to the left of the shot-up pickup truck.

Booker climbed out of the chopper, said a few words to the FBI agents outside the house, then walked over to Kee and signaled to her to drop the car window.

"Hello, Miss Le," he said, bending to talk to her through the window. "How are you holding up?"

She just burst into tears.

Booker walked Kee past the SWAT team outside DeKant's house. At this stage, they had their helmets in hand and their rifles pointing down in the rest position. They were smoking, joking and drinking cans of coke. The CSI team were carrying bagged guns out of the house. Booker, as she explained to her friend Annalise later, was kind. That's the only word for it. He sat her down. Made her a cup of coffee. The agents collecting evidence in the house couldn't work out why it was so dark. One of them found the fuse box out front and turned on the power. Nothing exploded, so they figured there was no real problem.

"Now Miss Le, you have to step me through this. When I spoke to you on the phone, what was happening? Did you leave the house as I requested?"

Kee took a deep breath. She needed this. She needed the debriefing. It stopped all those crazy thoughts flying around in her head, at Warp Speed 10 this time. It helped her think straight again.

"We were in DeKant's gun room. Me, O'Shea and DeKant," explained Kee.

"Okay, Miss Le. Let's go there."

They walked the short distance to the gun room. Kee continued.

"DeKant was drunk. Drunk as whatever you get drunk as. A skunk? He was tripping over furniture, slurring his words. He was wild-eyed crazy. Blinking non-stop. He was holding two pistols. He fired one by mistake. Here, into the chair. You can see the bullet hole. O'Shea was standing there, and I was behind him. O'Shea asked DeKant several times to put his guns down so he could check the safety locks. DeKant goes psycho. Like, 'Nobody's taking *my* guns.' DeKant points one gun at O'Shea.

He fires over his head. That's about when you rang. I left, sat in the SUV for, maybe, ten minutes. Hard to say. There were two shots. Then O'Shea walks out. Throws his cell into the SUV and walks off down the drive."

"Did he say where he was going?" inquired Booker.

"Didn't he tell you?" she asked.

"He left a voice message." Booker scrolled through his phone and played the message.

"Hi, Chief. O'Shea here. Kee, I mean Miss Le, is safe. I've just got to tidy up some business out of town. Back Friday. Maybe Monday. Need a break."

"Do you think he shot DeKant?" Booker asked quietly.

"O'Shea told me that DeKant shot himself, and he said that DeKant was such a bad shot he didn't even do a good job of it. He couldn't hit his own head at point blank range. He only took off a bit of one ear."

"Do you believe him?"

"I don't know. Maybe." She fell silent. Booker waited.

"Come on, Booker. You've got to tell me. What do you think?" Kee queried.

"I think... if O'Shea wanted to shoot DeKant at that range, he wouldn't miss," Booker replied.

"So, what's going on here? What's O'Shea up to?" implored Kee.

"I really don't know, Miss Le. I really don't know. What about you? Do you think he's involved with the XC1 murders?"

"I think he knows more than he's letting on," Kee replied.

"You'd be right there," Booker sighed. "These undercover agents are—what?—you're the writer."

"Screwed up?" suggested Kee.

"Yes, that is one way of describing them. I would say, not team players. Others have to clean up their mess."

"But, but you rang me. Warned me about O'Shea."

"That was a gut feel call. O'Shea pinged on a gun purchase. I couldn't be sure what was going on, and there was no time. So I rang DeKant, hoping I'd reach you. It was the right call."

"I've got a question for you, Booker. All of this is such a freaking mess, and I have to write a piece for *The New York Times*. What do I write? What part of this story can I include and what parts are off limits?" pleaded Kee.

"Tell the truth," urged Booked, "always tell the truth, because people can catch you out on a lie. That's how we get you. You lie, we've got you. But you don't have to tell the whole truth. Now I know you and O'Shea got on... too well, I suspect. You might not mention that detail. I'm not protecting O'Shea. I'm concerned about you. Readers will distort that story. As for DeKant being drunk ..."

"I've got that one covered," explained Kee. "I say an empty bottle of bourbon was on the desk. Leave the readers to work it out for themselves. It's the shooting that has me stumped. Who shot whom? Or whom shot who? I'll have to Google that grammar."

"Mmmm," murmured Booker, "I'd say... 'shots were fired.'"

"Yeah! Yeah! Thanks, Booker. I couldn't get my thoughts clear on this. The thing is, the house was all shot up. O'Shea said there was gunshot damage on the outside, and—this is funny—two stuffed animal heads, a gazelle thing and a—what is it?—a wildebeest, hanging on the wall over his fireplace, were all shot up too. Hanging is not the right word. Mounted, that's it." She was getting back into Reporter mode. "The eyes of the gazelle thing hung out, stuffing everywhere. The wildebeest had been shot in the mouth, nose blown off. Its glass eyes had sort of slumped together in the hole. Oh my God. I've got to write about seeing a cross-eyed wildebeest." She snorted with laughter. Booker laughed too.

"Miss Le, what will I do when this case is over? It will never be the same investigating a mass murder again, without you being involved," Booker sighed.

"I'll volunteer to be involved as long as I'm not a victim," she said with a smile.

Booker laughed again, adding, "I pity a mass murderer who takes on you, Miss Le."

"Glad to hear it, Mr. FBI."

Booker had one of the FBI agents from the Virginia office drive Kee to the airport in the SUV. He also arranged for one of his team to meet her at the Newark Airport. Kee was pleased to see Perez standing in the airport lounge waiting for her, but, she thought, *It's not at all like the FBI silver service.* Her heart twinged at the thought.

Kee arrived outside the Tribeca flat well past 8 p.m. Perez escorted Kee to the door. Kee thanked her, shoved her key in the front door latch and turned it. She wanted desperately to flop on her bed. But she could hear voices in the study. She opened the door and saw Pham massaging her father's feet.

OMG, I so don't want to see that, she thought. She called out, "Hi, Pops. I'm home. I'm done in." Covering her eyes, she turned her head and bolted to the kitchen. Harold wrapped himself around her legs as Kee rummaged through the fridge for food.

"Hello, Mr. Harold. I've missed you. Mmmm! Spring rolls. Yum! And what's in the cake box? Chocolate chip muffins. Lovely."

Target 91

Kee posted a few Tweets.

"Exclusive interview with Gig DeKant. Details tomorrow's *New England Gazette*." @KeeHasSpoken #Target91

"CEO NGSA Gig DeKant shot in his own home. I was there. Details tomorrow's *New England Gazette*." @KeeHasSpoken #Target91

She sent an updated text to her boss. He replied:

THAT'S MY STAR REPORTER. TRY NOT TO GET YOURSELF SHOT. BRADSTREET

Kee had totally forgotten that she was actually writing for *The New York Times* now. She would, she decided, still provide *The New England Gazette* with updates.

Once showered and with her hair washed, Kee felt semi-human again. "I thought I would roll up into a fetal ball and sit in a darkened room sobbing into a 16oz carton of Ben and Jerry's Chocolate Therapy ice cream, the one with chocolate cookie swirls and puffy chocolate pudding clods. But I feel okay. I feel like working," mused Kee. She opened her laptop and began typing up the recorded bits of the DeKant interview that made any sense. Then she began writing the Op Ed piece for *The New York Times*. She would check it in the cold light of morning. She found writing was much better therapy that eating chocolate ice cream, though she was willing to keep the second option open.

Kee heard the front door close and her father shuffling along the hallway to her room. He knocked gently on the door. Kee called out, "Don't tell me. None of my business. Don't want to know."

Her father put his head around the door and said, "I just come to say goodnight, Little Moon. And tell you not worry. Tomorrow Ba massage my back by walking in bare feet, chanting." He tried to keep a straight face. He couldn't. He saw the horrified expression on Kee's face, and the laughter bubbled out of him.

"I joke," he said. "Goodnight."

"Night, Pops. You worry me sick sometimes," Kee chortled.

Kee fell asleep after midnight with Harold sitting on her head.

Chapter 36

DeKant

Tuesday, the 19 of September

Gig DeKant woke into the worst nightmare he could imagine. He was lying on his gun room floor with his head twisted back and resting on his right ear. Rivulets of sticky-thick blood trickled from his left ear across his face, under his nose, and onto the floor. Some blood had dripped into his mouth. His tongue was so parched, so rough, it felt like a desiccated roadkill lizard from Death Valley. He had a piercing pain in his head as if an electric drop saw was screeching and slicing its way through his frontal lobes. His muscles were locked stiff. His bones ached. He could hear faint noises like schoolyard chatter. He opened his eyes.

A SWAT team operative with his face-shield pushed aside and assault rifle slung across his chest was crouched beside him demanding, "Sir, can you hear me? Can you hear me, Sir?"

He tried to speak, but his throat was too dry. DeKant nodded his head.

"Paramedics will be here soon, Sir. The ambulance is waiting outside the front gate. Once we have secured the area, they'll be here. Your injuries do not appear serious. You are bleeding from one ear."

Gig could not protest. He could not speak. He could hardly move. If there are nine circles of hell, then Gig had woken up in the innermost circle. His house, his sanctuary, his home and hearth, had been invaded by storm-troopers in black SS uniforms. Those corrupt fascists in the FBI were in his home. Gig wanted to scream "Stop!" at the top of his voice, but the words died in his dry mouth. He could hear other FBI agents—it sounded like a battalion of them—invading through the front door, opening and shutting bedroom doors, calling "Clear!" to one another. Even as Gig found himself prostrate and stranded in the inner circle of hell, a portal opened beneath him, dropping him into an even more torturous Hades. Circle 10.

The SWAT officer leaned over Gig and patted him down for firearms. He found the Smith and Wesson .44 jammed awkwardly in the vest pocket beneath Gig's slumped body and picked DeKant's 9mm Glock off the floor.

"We, have to take these guns. They are evidence in a shooting. Ballistic tests need to be—"

Gig choked out, "No!"

"Sir, there has been extensive criminal damage to property involving guns on these premises. There are unexplained pools of blood on your doorstep. There is an overturned truck with bullet holes at the front of the premises. Gun damage at the back. You appear to have a bullet wound. And this incident is a part of the ongoing FBI investigation into the XC1 murders. These weapons will be confiscated and tested."

The SWAT officer, clad in black from head-to-toe, in an outfit that was all Velcro-ed pockets, spare clips, knee pads and flak vest, wore black gloves and a black balaclava under his helmet. The words FBI were printed in white block letters across his chest. Gig could only see the operative's eyes.

The officer's helmet headset crackled and spluttered into action. The SWAT team operative placed Gig's guns on the oak desktop and, holding his right gloved-hand on his right earphone, spoke into the microphone arm attached to his helmet.

"Yo ... Right. I have searched the victim and confiscated all firearms ... Okay. Got it." Then turning to DeKant he said, "The property has been cleared. The paramedics are on their way. FBI officers and crime scene investigators will be here soon."

Two paramedics arrived with a collapsible stretcher. They quickly checked Gig's blood pressure and shone a flashlight in his eyes. "Shit!" one of them hissed, and immediately began prepping and then attaching an IV. As they lifted Gig onto the lowered gurney, FBI agents, wearing flak jackets and blue disposable gloves, followed by crime scene investigators, enclosed from foot to head in puffy white disposable suits, entered the room. They started opening and closing and rifling through the gun room draws, cupboards and filing cabinets. Color was returning to Gig's face as blood surged through his veins, pumped by the explosive, hell-driven additive of raw anger—and Glucose 5% Solution. But Gig was trapped in a low response body with jittery mad-monk eyes.

At the front door, however, he tried to get off the stretcher. He fell to the floor. He was wrestled back onto the gurney by the paramedics and restrained. He couldn't tell them what was happening, he couldn't explain his utter desperation. They were taking his guns. FBI agents had bagged and tagged the guns in his gun room, plus a stray Uzi found out front. They were carrying these weapons to a police vehicle parked further up the driveway. The bags were made of thick, clear plastic. Gig could see the bag contents clearly. They were taking his guns. This was everything Gig feared the most. This was the very reason citizens needed to be armed, to defend themselves from a home invasion by the tyrannical, callous, corrupt and corrupting government agencies.

DeKant was taken to the Fairfax Hospital where he was kept overnight for observation. He had lost the top of his left ear to a gunshot wound. The FBI had swabbed his ear for gunpowder residue. His head was bandaged to protect the raw flesh of the truncated ear. Word quickly spread. News crews collected outside the hospital. This was a big story. The CEO of the NGSA had been shot.

Had the AGB done it?

Had they intended to kill him but missed?

Had he fired back?

And what DeKant rant would he fire off next?

At 4:00 p.m. precisely, Gig's second in command visited him in the hospital. J. Bob Dow was in his fifties, short, round, and bald, and full of NGSA-approved resolve. He had been the second in command at the NGSA for over ten years. In his opinion, that was at least five years too long.

"Hello, Gig. How are you?" he asked.

Gig was, by this stage, sitting up in bed, eating stock-standard rubbery refrigerated hospital sandwiches and drinking warm, brackish hospital coffee. He was hooked up to multiple monitors and the "bip ... bip" beat of his 72-year-old heart could be seen and heard, strong and true.

"Those fucking tyrannical assholes at the FBI took all my guns. Can you believe that? I'm the victim. I'm the one in the crosshairs, and those motherfuckers take my guns."

"I've spoken to the board, Gig," announced J. Bob, "and they want you to take time out to recover. As long as you like. So they've asked me to step up while you are on leave. I thought I'd tell you this in person to put your mind at ease."

"Well, thank you for your concern, J. Bob, but I'm fine. I'll be back in the office tomorrow."

"Thing is," boomed J. Bob to his one-man audience, "the board are not happy with the situation."

"That's ridiculous. That riot was media-provoked."

"The riot is not the problem. Nothing like a good riot to get the public interested in guns," sniffed J. Bob. "The real problem was the shooting. Shooting a kid is lousy PR for the gun lobby. The Board wants you to lie low for a while. Take some time off. Take Beverley on a cruise. Have a break from all the gutter fighting push and shove of gun politics." Gig just nodded his head. He couldn't smell a whiff of tear gas, but he definitely could smell the strong, putrid stink of a corporate coup in the air.

At 4:15 p.m., even as J. Bob's footsteps could still be heard echoing down the hospital hallway, Gig DeKant called his son, Brad.

The family had been shocked, outraged, bewildered when police informed them about the incident. Beverley and Emily were on their way to the hospital. Brad was going over to the DeKant estate to check on the house. Amy was looking after all of the children.

"Yeah!" replied Brad after Gig explained the situation. "Yeah! Yeah! Got it. Shove it up the fuckers' asses," he urged.

At 4:45 p.m., before Beverley and Amy arrived and against doctors orders, Gig DeKant stood outside the front door of the Fairfax Hospital lobby and addressed the cameras. He was wearing a grey suit, a fresh shirt, and an NGSA logo tie. Gig had wisely decided not to face the media wearing a wind-catching, butt-baring hospital gown. Brad had brought him the suit. Gig was also wearing polished black shoes, without socks. Brad had forgotten the socks. He'd volunteered his own socks, but his father preferred no socks to wearing socks that, possibly, had been marinated in toe-jam-ripe Brad-sweat for over a week and had a Tweety Pie motif.

"I stand here to bear witness to an insidious and extreme danger faced by each and every one of you, the good and decent men and women, the patriots, of this great country. They are coming for your guns. Your government cannot protect you during hurricanes, floods or blizzards. They cannot protect you from rioters, looters or street gangs, or from house invaders who want to rape your women, tie up your family and extort money from you. These are the life-threatening perils we all face today. These threats are not imaginary. They are real. It's not paranoia to own a gun. It's common sense. It's survival. It's responsible behavior, and we encourage law-abiding Americans to do just that.

"I know the President is dedicated to the 2nd Amendment. But evil forces exist within government agencies. Those pea-brained, yellow-bellied, doped-out, tree-hugging, faggot Leftards have sympathizers working in each and every government agency and, mark my words, they are coming to take your guns.

"Last night a lone sniper tried to take me out at my own front door. He missed. This afternoon, an FBI agent came to my home to take my guns. I stood my ground. I defended my God-given right to own and bear arms. When I refused to hand over my guns, he aimed at my head from point-blank range. By God's intervention, he missed," Gig lied. He knew he was in command of the narrative, and he knew whoever spoke first and loudest would be believed by the majority of viewers. This was his arena.

"Now I am the victim here. This afternoon an FBI SWAT Team and other agents invaded my home and took all of my guns when I need them to defend myself. This could happen to you. Fortunately, the board of the NGSA understands this grave threat. They want me to be very clear on this issue.

"Read my lips. NO ONE HAS THE RIGHT TO TAKE YOUR GUNS.

"I am lucky. I'm not defenseless. I have friends with guns. But be warned.

"The Survivalists, the Preppers, the Doomsdayers were right. The Rule Of Law is collapsing. God help us, the End of Days has arrived. You are all in grave danger. Go to your home, your bunker, your silo. And get ready.

"You can be sure of one thing, and one thing only.

"They will come for your guns too."

Chapter 37

Little Boy

Tuesday, the 19th of September

Desean Boykin, known as Little Boy, read the text message and yelled to the small group sitting in the improvised kitchen "Cop Watch. Corner of Sacramento and Lake. Near a vacant lot." They were on their feet in an instant, scrambling for cell phones and jackets as they headed for the door. Little Boy got the engine of the battered maroon 1992 Chevy pickup revving. With one hand hooked around the steering wheel and looking through the rear window, he backed the truck in an arc away from the fence, stopped and changed gear as two bodies piled into the pickup. They were at the Cop Watch site within minutes.

Racial tensions run through the streets of Chicago like exposed electric wires which can, at any moment, spit and spark, or explode and kill. Little Boy's crew was mixed race. This had its strengths. Today's crew, however, were all reimagined Black Panther bros, dedicated to continuing the cause as born and bred Chicagoans. No planning was involved in this mix. This just happened to be the Cop Watch crew that jumped into the truck. Each member of the crew on this day was carved out of the same leanness that comes with a harsh life and a vegetarian diet. Not that they agreed on the exact terms of the Vegetarian philosophy. Some ate dairy. Some didn't. Some ate eggs. Others scorned egg consumption. The crew, except for Ish, wore black pants—jeans or sweatpants—black zip-up hooded jackets and black sneakers.

The leader of the crew, Little Boy, was 42 years old, with cropped receding hair, round face, full black beard and tribal tattoos across his body and up his neck. Flonard Lasike, or Vile, was 29 years of age, had fine cheekbones, dreads held back with a black headband, a pencil-thin mustache and a struggling beard. The others teased him about his inability to sprout a properly virile crop of facial hair. He argued that *his* hormones weren't spent on the wasted effort of growing facial hair. The youngest member of the crew was J Jackson, or Junior J. The 19-year-old wore a camouflage zip-up top with fur-lined hood, camouflage pants, and a baseball cap on backward. His passion for army camouflage gear was ironic, as he'd been dismissed with a Dishonorable Discharge from Army Boot Camp for smoking dope in the latrine when he was still 18 years old.

The only Black Panther bro missing was Diondre Acho, or Roach. Roach was currently out of the house on an assignment. He had waist-length dreads, thick eyebrows, a thick, closely cropped beard, and attitude. He was the one Little Boy had to watch, as he could flare up at a scene of unprovoked police violence. He couldn't take it.

Two of the crew had smartphones, Little Boy and Vile. The Cop Watch crew weren't there to record police violence, but to stop it. Videoing arrests did have an effect. There were, after all, written rules of police conduct in Chicago. Some cops had never read them. Little Boy turned his phone towards the cop tackling a black youth with short dreadlocks, a loose blue and grey check shirt and baggy sweatpants. The boy's two friends stood back from the scene, fidgeting and shuffling on their sneakered feet, not knowing what to do.

"It's 8:30 p.m., Tuesday, 19 September. We're located at the corner of Sacramento and Lake." Now the youth was bent over the police car with his arms spread on the hood. He tried to turn to tell the cop something, and Little Boy's crew caught this exchange.

Cop: Did you fucking make a move on me?

Youth: I got stabbed. It's my shoulder. I got stabbed.

Cop: You made a motherfucker move against me. Do that shit again, and I'll take you to the station and throw you in the cells.

Youth: No officer. I'm tryin' to tell ya. I got stabbed. My shoulder. It hurts bad.

Cop: Make another fucking move like that again, and I'll show you what I can fucking do.

Youth: I won't officer. My shoulder. I got stabbed.

Cop: You move again ... and I wish you fucking would ... that's assault. Do you hear me?

Youth: Please, Officer, I've been stabbed!

Cop: Any of you on parole? Right. If I see any of your fucking asses again tonight I'm going to lock you up ... understand that, Shit?

He wrenched the youth's hands behind his back and cuffed them. The boy screamed.

Youth: Arrrghhh! Officer, my shoulder hurts.

Little Boy yelled to the police officer, "Let him go. We've got this. You have no grounds for arrest."

Cop: You fucking keep your fucking nose out of other people's business. He made a move on me.

Little Boy: Moving is not grounds for arrest.

Cop: It's grounds if I say it's grounds.

Little Boy: You're right, Officer. You can make the arrest.

Cop: You're goddam right I'm right.

Little Boy: But this recording will be used as evidence against you, Officer 37211.

The officer grabbed the boy by his cuffed arms and yanked him into a standing position. The youth screamed. The officer undid the cuffs.

Cop: Now fuck off.

The youth, holding his shoulder with the patch of blood, and his fidgety mates scrammed. The police officer climbed back in his car, did a U-turn and left the scene.

"Did you get that, Vile?" asked Little Boy.

"Yup! But I've only got 5 minutes left on my cell. Not enough to email it or upload it to YouTube. You got more time?" asked Vile.

"Yeah! I got plenty. Use mine," replied Little Boy, as the group climbed back into the extended cabin of the sturdy pickup, a maroon with parallel white stripes along the bottom of the chassis S-series Chevy. The great Sonoma.

"I hate them. I hate those motherfucker cops!" yelled Junior J, punching the back of the pickup seat as he climbed into the truck.

"There's a lot to hate," replied Little Boy, as he settled himself behind the steering wheel.

The group returned to the mini-mart and adjacent auto repair shop on the corner of an unnamed lane and Walnut Street in West Garfield Park, Chicago. The buildings had broken and boarded up windows, unreadable graffiti of the ugly tag-variety on the walls, and some reggae music festival posters circa 2009 glued along the sidewall of the minimart facing the lane. Some leaves, dirt and aged junk mail accumulated under the minimart security door at the front of the store. The graffitied rolling door to the auto repair shop had not been opened in years. These were zombie properties. The banks had foreclosed but not reclaimed the properties for resale.

The premises, however, were not abandoned. Little Boy, as Desean Boykin, had offered to pay the bank a nominal rent to occupy the property, thus taking the pressure off the bank to make a quick decision, and giving Little Boy and the rest of the crew a semi-secure residence. The bank might not have been so enthusiastic about the deal if they'd known the nature of the group who now occupied the derelict buildings. They were anarchists. Anti-capitalist, anti-central-government, black flag waving—and wearing—anarchists. The Black Flag tattoo was more or less compulsory for an anarchist, but it was hard to know if this was in support of anarchy or a tribute to the legendary seventies punk rock band of that name. The members of Little Boy's crew, wearing black, only had to add a black neckerchief and pull up the hood to complete the standard anarchist uniform. It is ironic that anarchists conform to a standard dress code. But the Black Bloc uniform made one anarchist indistinguishable from the next at (sometimes violent) anti-NATO, anti-G8 protest rallies.

Little Boy turned the pickup into a driveway that ran the length of the auto repair shop. Junior J, the youngest, got out and pulled the wooden gate shut. There was no hierarchy in the anarchist handbook, but being the youngest in the crew was still the lowliest rank. Little Boy parked the pickup in the backyard among the patches of overgrown grass and weeds. The yard also entertained some polystyrene fruit box planters full of earth waiting for next spring, two wooden and aged outdoor tables, several weathered plastic outdoor chairs, and assorted derelict machines from rusting bicycles to a wheelless bus.

There was a plywood-lined corrugated iron lean-to at the back of the minimart. The graffitied wooden door of the lean-to acted as the official entrance. A pink, battered, seventies-vintage female shop store dummy stood guard at the entrance, naked and wearing an army surplus gas mask. The sliding-bolt gate lock was secured with a padlock. Apparently, Carcass, the other crew member currently in residence, was out collecting supplies for his white powder habit. Sugar was his addiction in all forms, but mostly as soda. Vile undid the lock and opened the door onto an open cement floor area, stacked on the left with such equipment as amplifiers, sound systems, anarchist banners, boxes of books and old clothes, other boxes of old china and saucepans. The anarchists ran a free exchange market and vegetarian soup kitchen every second Saturday of the month. A wood framed opening in a plywood wall to the right lead to the kitchen.

Turning a mini-mart and auto repair shop into a residence was something of an *ad hoc* affair. The kitchen had an old-style round-topped fridge, a table-*cum*-stove with three portable single-jet butane burners on top, milk crates as shelves, a dull green kitchen counter plucked from a dumpster with a microwave oven in situ, a plastic bowl on milk crates as a sink, and running water supplied by a hose poked through some louvre windows. A hole punched through bricks on the far party wall led to the auto repair shop. A plastic sheet could be dropped to cover the hole and protect the kitchen when spray painting was in full swing in the repair shop. The lounge room space at the front of the minimart housed some old orange corduroy couches pulled out of hard trash, a door on bricks as a coffee table, an old, slightly-out-of-tune piano, and an old projector-style TV and set-top box. It was home, if you can put up with a no-frills-and-hello-winter-chills existence.

All the anarchists worked. They had to. Anarchy was neither a full time nor a paying job. Car washing, laboring on building sites, window cleaning, busking, dishwashing, furniture removal and selling stuff on eBay were all occupations that brought in a trickle of cash. Past their use-by date cans and packets of food were often scavenged from a nearby supermarket dumpster.

Little Boy threw the pickup keys on the table, saying, "POD should be here sometime after 6 a.m. tomorrow morning." The crew only used nicknames, even in the house. This was best practice anarchy. There would be no slip-ups on the street, no ID giveaways for the cops at rallies when crew members were wearing their neckerchiefs as face masks. Anonymity was a vital part of the anarchist toolbox.

"We better have a bed for him," said Little Boy, thinking out loud. POD stood for Prince of Darkness. It was the nickname they gave to O'Shea. The bed situation in Chez Anarchy required an extremely flexible view of what constitutes a bed, along with some applied imagination. Chicago's winters are bitter and cruel. Hell frozen over. The minimart became the master bedroom when it wasn't being a lounge room. It had an old seventies oil heater. It still worked, but oil was expensive. Vile, Roach and Junior J slept in sleeping bags on couches in the master bedroom/lounge. Little Boy had a mattress on the floor of a pool cabana—treated pine siding with an aged shingle roof— that'd they'd trucked into the workshop from downstate. It had power and an electric oil column heater. Very snug. The other members of the crew—the honorary bros—were 36-year-old Pedro Le Blanc, otherwise known as Carcass; 66-year-old Jeimer Jay Jr., or Triple J; and 34-year-old Lavette Biaz, the only female crew member, aka Ax. Carcass, Triple J and Ax slept in different vehicles parked in the workshop most of the year, but infiltrated the minimart in winter. Triple J and Ax were returning from delivering a nondescript grey sedan to Fairfax when Little Boy rang with another assignment. Roach was also returning from a separate assignment in nearby Indiana.

Vehicles were often flipped and replated in the workshop. These activities were illegal, but anarchists do not believe in the "capitalist system" or "hierarchical, authoritarian institutions". But vehicles make warm beds, depending, of course, on your definition of the word "bed".

The handguns were stowed for quick access under cushions, pillows, and bedding where the crew slept. The sniper rifles were meticulously stored in aluminum cases concealed beneath the repair-shop oil drainage pit trays.

Chapter 38

Little Boy

The Crew

Little Boy, a charismatic, self-educated but disenfranchised vet, had carefully recruited each member of the crew for their willingness to take on a specific anarchist goal. The destruction of the American industrial/military complex was on the Anarchists Wish List, for sure, but it was not realistic. Anarchists believe that "war and military occupation are an obscene exercise of state power"—that is, of course, if you can get anarchists to agree on anything. Little Boy's crew aimed at a more modest and manageable goal than the complete annihilation of the worldwide war-mongering machine. They, adopting Little Boy's personal manifesto, aimed to disrupt the corrupt association of politicians, gun manufacturers, gun dealers and gunrunners in their country.

Little Boy had found Carcass, an Iraq vet and body man—that's auto body man—at an anti-NATO rally throwing his medals, one by one, at the riot police guarding the conference center. Carcass had a tattoo of an eagle on his left bicep that was such a botched job, the others had declared it deceased, dead, a carcass. That's how he got his nickname. Carcass wasn't lean like the other crew members. With his broad shoulders, his thick neck and a No. 1 buzz cut of his head and facial hair, he was more nightclub bouncer material, handy to have around if a protest turned sour. But his bulky build was viewed by some in the house like strokes of pink highlighter on the page flagging excess consumption, a vegan Fail. Carcass had to put up with constant lectures about his diet, his high fructose corn syrup intake in particular. He was a true addict. He needed multiple cola hits each day.

Little Boy had found Triple J, a Vietnam vet, drunk and homeless just up the road in Garfield Park, in the actual park. Little Boy brought Triple J back to their pad for a good feed and a hot shower. They had a bathroom with an improvised shower in the mini-mart. Triple J just sort of stayed. He eased off on the booze and didn't say much. He was an active member of the group.

Little Boy had run into Ax at one of their Free Market days. She was muscular, with short-cropped hair, and she wore Army fatigues. Her straight Romanesque nose and intense gaze gave her a regal look. Others might describe her as scary. It was her abrupt manner that drew Little Boy's attention.

"You a vet?" asked Little Boy.

"Yup," replied Ax.

"You serve overseas?"

"Yup," replied Ax.

"You a Marine?"

"Yup," replied Ax.

"Ranger?"

Well, that started a conversation and a half. Ax had always wanted to be a Ranger. She hadn't realized, when she'd enlisted, that women were not allowed to join the Rangers. They weren't even allowed to try out for the squad. This was the first time Ax had run into the glass or, more accurately, the brass ceiling. She was still angry five years after leaving the Marines. It was the violently pro-feminist angle that attracted Ax to the anarchist movement. She thought the anti-war Codepink feminism was bullshit. "Wear pink?" she snorted with contempt. "You want to get their attention, shoot their balls off." Ax had also favored the anarchist movement during the Occupy Wall Street protest. "How can assholes that sit at a computer worrying about decimal points all day earn one hundred times the income of a Marine facing months of hostile enemy fire? It's a fucked up world." Little Boy could only agree. But Ax had achieved one goal as a Marine. She'd trained as a sniper.

The crew had found Junior J during a Cop Watch. A cop was savagely swinging his nightstick into the defenseless, doped out teen. At the sight of cameras in Record mode held high, he cursed and left the scene, covering his face and name tag. Little Boy offered to drive the kid home, but as Junior J explained, "I got no home, man." So they said he could stay at the minimart house for a while. Triple J took Ash under his wing, hence the name Junior J. The older anarchist organized regular excursions to a landfill site near Zion and trained Junior J up as a sniper. The kid had a gift. He was uncanny in both stealth and accuracy.

Little Boy had found Vile and Roach as leathered-up members of the Black Death Motor Cycle Club, an all-black biker gang. The policy of many biker gangs is to recruit white supremacist thugs. The only difference between these gangs and the KKK is that the bikers wear badged sleeveless denim jackets instead of white hooded bed sheets. So an all-black gang had certain appeal for the two vets, who had served in "wars you couldn't win", Vile in Afghanistan, and Roach as a military prison guard in Guantanamo Bay. Little Boy knew that returning to civilian life posed a huge challenge for many vets. Often when combatants returned home their ordinary life fell to pieces. They missed the camaraderie, the got-your-back support, and the unspoken but deep connection that grows out of the intense shared experiences of combat. Some vets joined biker gangs because these groups mimicked the armed services. Biker gangs have ranks, uniforms, camaraderie, firearms, missions, enemy gangs, assault raids and shootouts. The latter were often staged in a burger restaurant car park, to the horror of folk who'd dropped in with the kids for a quick bite on a Saturday night. Unfortunately, biker gangs also run drugs and guns, with racketeering and contract killing on the side in between turf wars. Vets can end up tangled in "Death before dishonor" loyalty to murderous, maniacal, greed-driven drug lords. Vile and Roach were held hostage by their membership of the Black Death biker gang with no way out. They were also facing jail terms. Little Boy scraped together enough cash to pay their bail bond and fund a cheap lawyer, who, miraculously, managed to get the gun running charges dropped because the police had lost the guns. No evidence. No conviction. Some cops' pockets were lined with cash that day, and the guns sold for a sweet profit. Vile and Roach had to disappear. Joining the anarchists provided good cover. There were no links between biker gangs and anarchists. Both Vile and Roach were trained riflemen.

The links between Little Boy and O'Shea were long standing. They had met in Iraq in 2005. Talked the usual shit. Little Boy had read Marx; but, he said, "Communism was just a dream that never came true. Capitalism is the real threat." As Little Boy explained to O'Shea, "Think of it this way, man. The American

Dream is based on ripping off the poor." (A position Little Boy understood long before the "We are the 99%" cry of the Occupy movement.) "If someone, say a drug manufacturer, makes a 1000% profit on—what?—an asthma medication, is that fair? And if someone who cannot afford the medication, one they desperately need, if they then break into a drug store and steal it, ask yourself, 'Who is robbing who? Who is the bigger thief?' That is the new morality. Theft from thieves is a morally justified act. Once you could trust the establishment—doctors, bankers, power suppliers, drug manufacturers, presidents—at least, you could trust them a little. But not now, man, no way. Sure, businesses made a profit in—what?—the fifties. That was fine. But today they make the biggest profit they can squeeze out of you without actually killing you. They are, all of them, parasites, leeches and scammers." Little Boy hardly took a breath.

"I could go for this anarchy shit," said O'Shea at the time, "but gang violence and theft hurts small businesses more than it bothers the big pharma companies. And there have to be rules. Someone has to decide, say, which side of the road you should drive your car. Or Jesus, there would be total fucking chaos."

"The anarchy movement isn't about everyone doing their own shit, man. It's not 'I do what I wanna do, fuck you!' It is about consensus. Everyone agrees we drive on the right-hand side of the road. Right. No one—except for a few British tourists —has ever complained. But everyone is equal. None of this private estate, private road shit. We're all equal, man. No central control. It's a grassroots run community."

"I grew up in a grassroots run community in Belfast. The IRA ran it. That was fucked," replied O'Shea.

"Not like that, man. In a grassroots community, you care for the people. You don't stand over them. And you shoot the assholes that use politics to screw the poor and line their own pockets, the assholes that get into positions of power so they can make more money. As if, like, having $1 billion isn't enough already."

When the conversation wandered into the on-going tragedy of young kids being shot and killed back home while they were away fighting a war, Little Boy had an answer. "That's what I'm saying, man. Shoot the fuckheads who make money pushing guns onto the streets and putting guns into the hands of idiots. Once gun manufacturing was a sort of honorable pursuit, you know. Back in the fifties they made guns for the army and for hunters. Now they make obscene profits putting guns into the hands of criminals. And selling to countries that use the fucking weapons to kill us! You know for damn sure some of the bullets that take out our boys here are Made in USA. No one talks about that shit. It's not just gun manufacturers. Politicians, corporate media, gun dealers and gun runners, they're all in it up to their necks. I'd shoot the lot of them."

"So what turned you into an anarchist?"

"Jesus, O'Shea. What ya doin', man? All these questions. You gonna waterboard me next?"

"I'm interested."

"Okay. Like, it's not one thing. It's everything. The banks foreclose on people's homes. I've seen it. They send in the heavies to evict them. The sheriff and shit. This family is out on the street with all their belongings. Then the empty house sits there rotting into the ground for years. But the government provides welfare for the banks, pours trillions into their corrupt coffers. The Federal Reserve Bank is not run by the government. It's run by bankers. That's fucked, man."

"If you are a core anarchist and not just full of bullshit, LB, why enlist?" O'Shea asked. It was a fair question.

"Two reasons," explained Little Boy. "Firstly, you can learn a lot about coercion, brainwashing, power structures and running covert and overt ops from inside the military. And secondly, I needed the money. But I hadn't counted on the control they have over you once you enlist. They control *everything*. What you wear, how you speak, where you live, where you eat, what you eat, where you crap, where you work, where you sleep, how long you sleep, what your job is, if you live, if you die, what meds they pump into your arms. They have total control over you. They dehumanize you, so you can't think for yourself. Man, when I'm outa this shithole, I gotta get my brains back."

Little Boy and O'Shea went separate ways once their deployment ended. But they met up again eight years later at 11 p.m. in a 24-hour burger chain car park in Chicago. Little Boy was kitted out in standard black. O'Shea wore his unruly blond hair tied back in a ponytail, a long-sleeved black tee, and a torn and worn short sleeved grey tee over the top. Each had shed the clean-cut Marine sheen. Now they both looked like civilians at the opposite end of that spectrum. Undisciplined and disheveled.

Little Boy was looking to buy a couple of sniper rifles on the black market. He wanted weapons that could not be traced. O'Shea was selling. Neither of them could work out what the other was doing. O'Shea claimed he had won the guns in poker game against crazy gun running wackos. He wasn't into that shit, but he needed the money to pay another gambling debt. Little Boy knew O'Shea was a big-time gambler. Bet thousands.

Scary shit. It was a wonder the mob wasn't after him or something. Little Boy told his old buddy that he was an anarchist.

"So why the guns?" asked O'Shea.

"Just in case, man. We are rattling the chains of the local cops. They'll come after us one day. And cops aren't just cops anymore. They're militarized now. They have military firearms. They run raids against their own citizens like a marines' op. You'd swear we were back in Iraq, man!"

The story of seller and buyer didn't quite fit the operative. Little Boy eyed off O'Shea like an attack dog warily sizing up the opposition. He decided O'Shea's poker-playing, gun running wacko friends might provide some useful information. He took O'Shea to Chez Anarchy to meet some of the crew, and then invited him along on a few Cop Watch assignments.

"Jesus fuck, Little Boy. You have lived up to your creed," marveled O'Shea after one particularly violent Cop Watch incident. "Have you started on your master plan to destroy the industrial/military complex yet?"

"Thinking about it," replied Little Boy.

"What about you, man? What brings you to Chicago, for real?" Little Boy asked.

"This and that. Gambling. Fishing," O'Shea replied with a grin.

"Jesus, man. For all your funny-guy shit, you don't say much," complained Little Boy. "We should call you POD. The Prince of Darkness."

O'Shea laughed. But Little Boy knew what he was saying. O'Shea always held his cards close to his chest. And Little Boy had seen O'Shea operating up close in Iraq. He was a designated sniper but volunteered for nighttime ops as well. After raids on houses hiding some local insurgent cell, he was the one who tidied up the enemy "mess". Of course, cleaning up depended on how you defined the word "mess". O'Shea's idea of cleaning up was brutal, but effective. If there were any victims left groaning or even pleading for mercy, he finished them off. No loose ends. No mercy. Others in the squad didn't have the stomach for it. But O'Shea, it didn't worry him. "They live, we die," was his call on the situation.

"Maybe you can contribute to our destroy-the-industrial-military-complex-plan, POD," suggested Little Boy.

"How so?" O'Shea asked, sounding off-hand.

"You play cards with the gun running wackos. You must know some of the names of the scumbags operating around here. We could do a tidy up," suggested Little Boy.

Months passed, then late in 2015 Little Boy got a text message. Two names. Mugshots. Addresses. Signed, POD. Little Boy's crew decided it was time to do a gunrunner cull. But they took their time. Watched the crazy dudes, stalked them, worked out their MOs. Set up a sniper overwatch position. Bang. One target. One shot. Job done. Ditto the second victim. But this was Chicago. The victims were gangbangers. Everybody, including the police, assumed they were taken out in a drive-by shooting. The police didn't even bother to look at the angle of trajectory. Nothing. Two less scumbags on the street was seen as a good thing. The shooting death of two known gangbangers didn't even make front page news of *The Chicago Sun-Times*. The story made the 6th page. The photo of a lost dog called Barnie— the mutt had walked twenty miles home to Orlando Park—being hugged by his 6-year-old owner, Maddison, made page 1.

The next time O'Shea was in Chicago, he dropped in on the anarchists.

Little Boy made full introductions. "Everyone, this is POD." The anarchists knew POD's role in their little project and greeted him like a long-lost member of their anarchist crew. It was time to talk. O'Shea explained that playing poker at his level meant he moved in organized crime circles. He picked up intel all the time. He'd pass on any that was relevant. What they did with that information was up to them. He didn't want to know. Couldn't know. Keep him out of it. But one thing he could use, from time to time, was a driver. He did get himself into tricky situations, "up shit creek without a paddle or a canoe."

"If I could call in a driver, that would save my ass and keep the intel coming," suggested O'Shea. Junior J volunteered to be a driver. Ax too. Junior J would leave a car for O'Shea at some out of the way spot. Junior J would hitch a ride home, or Ax would fetch him. O'Shea then drove it back to Chicago. All the time, O'Shea was sending them gunrunner intel. But nothing happened for months.

After their media silence that attended their first foray into gunrunner extermination, Little Boy was disappointed.

"You know, what we have to do is make the assholes that run the military/industrial complex, we have to make them sit up and take notice. We want the big bosses to be scared, not dismissive of some lowly scumbags," he lectured.

"Pissing themselves!" snapped Roach.

"But how do we do that?" asked Junior J.

"Remember the Black Panther salute?" queried Triple J.

They all remembered the salute. Roach held a clenched fist in the air. The Blank Panthers were gods to these anarchists.

"Remember the salute at the Olympic Games?"

They didn't.

"God help us. You were all born yesterday," complained Triple J. "It was the best publicity stunt ever."

"I think I remember it," said Little Boy. He googled the event. "Okay. 1968 Olympic Games. Before I was born. Gold medalist Tommie Smith and Bronze medalist John Carlos stand on the podium with their medals and hold their fists in the air in a Black Panther salute during the fucking National Anthem. Have a look."

"Awesome," breathed Junior J.

"It was the biggest news of those games. It made the front page in newspapers around the world. We should do something like that."

"So we've all gotta beat Usain Bolt now to win a gold medal," joked Vile. They laughed. The seed was planted, but not quite ready to sprout. In the meantime, they were busy enough keeping up with Cop Watch duties and exchange market days.

The crew was sitting outside on assorted outdoor chairs and milk crates around a picnic table later that year. They wore an assortment of sleeveless t-shirts with bare flesh exposed to the sun, sweating and swatting mosquitoes, enjoying beer and a veggie and Haloumi cheese cookout on the improvised drum and wire mesh barbecue. It was summer. Suddenly, Ax, moving with the blade speed of a flick knife, staked a cockroach to the wooden table with a steak knife.

"Hey, Roach," she jeered, "just skewered one of your relatives." She left the little tableau on the table for everyone to admire. Then she had an epiphany.

"What we've been looking for," Ax thought aloud, "is a publicity stunt that scares the shit out of them. Right?"

The crew had practiced their sniper skills, but the day Ax came up with the final AK-47 flag stunt was a strategic breakthrough. It took them several months to put the entire MO together. They couldn't stalk victims. It took too much time and wasted effort. They had to draw the "vics" out. They needed weapons to leave in the body. Use the vics' own weapons. AK-47s were a finely tuned, ironic choice. It was coming together. Times. Locations. Sellers websites. Sniper hides. All set in place. They trained like combatants. Vile was their go-to IT guy. Once he'd joined Little Boy's crew, he used his hacker skills to push the anarchist cause. He had the smarts to create online chaos under the tag Anonymous, but the resulting turmoil only prompted a flicker of inconvenience for the corrupt authoritarian capitalist system. This time his hacking skills would be targeted, and Little Boy knew whose computers to attack.

The reporter girl was a bonus. She had turned up at the crime scene of the first "vic" and started blogging, tweeting and generally creating a media storm. The perfect storm. They found her cell number on *The New England Gazette*'s website under Editorial Feedback. All they had to do was ring and say "wrong number" to check that it was hers. It was.

The riot was an unlooked for publicity coup. POD had told them months back about the secret club within the NGSA, a gun-promoting network of top execs. POD's informant flagged the address where this network met: 91 Central Park West. Threatening to kill 91 members of the NGSA proved very effective at grabbing the headlines. But it was just that, a threat. The list of names in that asshole network was their goal, but they wanted the media's attention first. And their bodies-skewered-with-guns "media stunt" was a great success.

"We're really going after those capitalist scumbags now!" chimed Little Boy, rubbing his hands together with glee when the crew gathered at Chez Anarchy after their separate missions, "I think I'll break open a bottle of extra malt capitalist whiskey tonight."

Chapter 39

Little Boy

Wednesday, the 20th of September

Junior J ran out the back door at 8:15 a.m. and down the drive. He pulled and tugged the old wooden gate open. A nondescript grey sedan drove through the entrance. Junior J closed the gate. The baseball hat-wearing driver swung past the maroon pickup and parked the car in the workshop for replating and respraying. It was O'Shea.

"Man oh man. FBI ... fucking FBI. Why didn't you tell us?" gasped Little Boy, as a what-the-hell-is-going-on? greeting to POD.

They gave each other a bro handshake/hug and climbed through the hole in the wall to the kitchen. O'Shea was carrying his evacuation bag, backpack, and two pistol cases. Little Boy sat him down and started making breakfast. Coffee. Eggs. Toast. The coffee had been pulled out of a supermarket dumpster two days earlier. Twenty-four 12 oz packs of ground coffee. Nothing wrong with the packs. The cardboard box container was broken. That was all.

"I'm whacked. Totally whacked," complained O'Shea. I need a few hours sleep."

"Let me get my head around this, man. You are FBI. Right?" queried Little Boy.

"Hey, Junior J," called O'Shea, giving the young anarchist a high-five as the boy squeezed past on his way to the fridge, "Good to see you, man. Who did the Fairfax sniper work?"

"Ax," Junior J answered.

"It was sweet work. Cleared out the security guards. Gave me access to the whole place. Where is she?" O'Shea asked.

"Ax and Triple J are out. Roach too. They'll be back later," explained Little Boy. It would be some time later. Ax and Triple J had delivered a nondescript silver grey sedan to a discreet parking spot outside the DeKant estate with the keys stowed on top of the front left-hand tire and were on their return trip, with a side mission.

Once O'Shea was well clear of the estate, he'd sent the first two names, addresses and cell phone numbers via text message to Little Boy. The anarchist "leader"—*facilitator* might be the term anarchists would prefer—had diverted Ax and Triple J to one address, Roach to another. Having cell phone numbers was too easy. Vile could track the targets and relay the information. Little Boy looked at his watch. 9:05 am. Their assignments should be done and dusted by now.

"Junior J here did some beautiful work in South Carolina, then forgot to leave the AK flag. He's halfway across Tennessee. Had to send him back. Then he couldn't find the vic. 'Was near a tree,' he said, ... in a fucking state forest. Light's failing. Three hours later he trips over—"

"Don't tell me. Don't want to know," cut off O'Shea, holding his hands in the air.

"I sorted it," snapped Junior J.

"FB-fucking-I." Little Boy shook his head. "Why didn't you tell us?"

"How did you find out?" O'Shea asked.

"You're the fucking front page pinup boy for the FBI. Haven't you seen it?"

"Nope. I've been on the road."

"Vile will get the picture up on the computer later."

"Hey, Carcass!" called O'Shea, giving the big guy a high five/hand clutch as Carcass moved to the fridge. Carcass took out a can of cola.

"You drink too much of that rat poison," Junior J warned. Carcass shrugged his shoulders and drawled, "Yah choose yah own poison. It's mah right. It must be in the Bill ah Rights somewheres." He grinned. He was used to dodging this flak.

"The media loved that story," continued Little Boy. "The girl rescued by the cool guy with the gun who shot the hired hitman. They totally love that shit. And you were wearing a suit." Little Boy laughed.

"Not you, too!" groaned O'Shea.

"Who else thought you looked like a monkey in a suit?" asked Little Boy.

"The girl ... she ..." O'Shea didn't finish the sentence. Little Boy sensed there was a story behind those lost words.

"She going to be a problem?" he asked.

"Problem! Staking bodies to the ground with AK-47s is a problem. That's the sort of shit I investigate. I didn't want to know what you were doing, arms distance, just pass on some intel here and there, see if you could get to the untouchables. Then you pull this stunt, and the entire world is watching, and

I'm stuck in the middle of this fucking show. I've been in tight spots before, but this ... this is ... Jee-sus!"

"What about DeKant? He says he was shot by the FBI agent guarding the girl. That would be you, POD."

"He was shit-faced. Stumbling around. He tripped and shot off a bit of his own ear. Passed out on the floor. It gave me time to rifle through his files."

"Did you get the entire list?"

"Yep. And my informant was right. The group meets once a month at 91 Central Park West, NY, the penthouse once owned by William Randolph Hearst. That's everyone who is anyone in the gun business. And they actually call themselves Club 91. It's on the front cover of the folder."

O'Shea reached down and took a folder out of his duffle bag.

"Why didn't you take photos of the list? Easier," asked Little Boy.

"I want DeKant to know it's missing. That's where the threat lies. I'm handing it over to you. I don't want it on me. I did a count. 50 members exactly. Do whatever you want to with it. Don't tell me. Don't involve me."

"Sure, POD," said Little Boy, opening the folder and looking down the list.

Little Boy still wasn't sure about POD. He couldn't work out whose side he was on, but he was in so deep now it didn't matter one bit. If they went down, he went down.

"Club 91. Once you gave us that first intel I knew how we'd play our hand. Kill 91 NGSA members. We were never going to do that. But I figured, man, we will scare the bejeezus out of this lot, this Club 91. It was our coded message to them. We're coming for you," explained Little Boy, adding, "Look at this!" Even though he knew the system was corrupt, he was still amazed to see the evidence in black and white. "Three senators, two supreme court judges, five state governors, three White House advisers. And then the usual suspects. Arms manufacturers. Gun show owners. Pentagon procurement officers. Businessmen. Corrupt to the eyeballs. Look here. XXXXX. Member X. Who's that?"

O'Shea had nearly finished his breakfast. He stretched and yawned.

"Do I get a bed, LB?" he asked.

"Yeah! Sure, POD. You get mine. Nice little cabana. Feels like a resort in there. But aren't you in deep shit with the feds, disappearing from the scene of a crime and all that?"

"I'll be all right. I've worked undercover for years. It's what you do. Never hang around at the scene of a crime. I'll stay here for two nights and go back. No problem." He had earned the nickname Chanel when he worked undercover. Chanel No. 5. When ops went sour, everyone else's shit stank, but not O'Shea's.

Vile came wandering in from the minimart dormitory/lounge.

"POD, man," he said, giving O'Shea a bro handshake.

"Vile, great. I've got a job for you," announced Little Boy. "This is The List. The full list. This is what we've been after. I want you to set it up with Wikileaks for later today, okay? Under the heading CLUB 91. Put up the addresses, but not the phone numbers. We might be able to use them. These are the corrupt assholes we're going for. They are the ones who make money turning this country into one never-ending shootout."

"Sure thing," said Vile, whistling as he read through the list.

"And in a minute," continued Little Boy, "I'll text the girl. It's perfect timing. Ax and Roach can retext a message or two. That will ping the cell phone towers in different states. Keeps us out of the picture."

Chapter 40

Kee

Wednesday, the 20th of September

Kee woke with a start at 9:25 a.m. when her foghorn text call sounded. She had slept like the dead through the night.

"What day is it? I don't even know what day it is," she muttered to herself. She looked at her cell. "Wednesday, 20 September. Really? Wednesday." Her text message foghorn ringtone sounded again.

"Oh, no," she said, "It's the AGB."

Text 1:

MESSAGE FOR 3 SENATORS, 2 JUDGES, 5 STATE GOVERNORS, 3 WHITE HOUSE ADVISERS AND OTHER CORRUPT MEMBERS OF CLUB 91. WE KNOW WHO YOU ARE. WE ARE COMING FOR YOU. WE HAVE THE LIST.

Text 2:

TELL ORDINARY MEMBERS OF NGSA THEY WERE NEVER OUR TARGET. WE HUNT GUNRUNNERS AND CORRUPT OFFICIALS. WE HUNT THE MEMBERS OF CLUB 91.

Text 3:

TELL DEKANT WE KNOW WHO IS IN CLUB 91. WE ARE COMING FOR HIM. WE ARE COMING FOR THEM. NOW THE REAL COUNTDOWN BEGINS.

Text 4:

THE LIST OF NAMES IN CORRUPT CLUB 91 WILL BE PUBLISHED ON WIKILEAKS LATER TODAY.

Kee sat up in bed. "I thought this story could never get any bigger, but it has just gone ballistic."

The first thing she did was ring Booker.

"Hey Booker, you'll never guess what?" she exclaimed. She read out the text messages from the AGB.

"Sweet Jesus, you need protection. Now! First, you upset some crazy gun cartel, now you might upset all three branches f legislation. This is bigger than Watergate."

"You mean, I get my Pulitzer Prize and a few major gunshot wounds."

"Don't worry. I'll send someone for you. You met her last night. Her name is Perez. Her first name is—Goddammit! What's her first name?—Um, Lucia. That's it. I always call her Perez. You've got her number."

He hung up. He didn't say goodbye. That made Kee feel happy. "He's not THAT worried about me," she mused. That was Kee's irrepressible optimism kicking her mood up a few notches.

Kee finished polishing her *New York Times* article. She still wasn't quite happy with it. She hit the 1,000 word mark easily, but it was such a dark piece. She couldn't add any of the light-hearted moments, like seeing a cross-eyed wildebeest on DeKant's wall, or the FBI agent complaining that DeKant was such a shit shooter he missed his own head at point blank range. She had to write it straight down the line. No frills. Hardly any adjectives. She kept within the guidelines for a professional commentator. Keep to the facts. Avoid emotive rants. She emailed the copy to the Op Ed desk as instructed by her *New York Times* contact, then rang through to the Op Ed editor, who seemed pleased with the piece. Pleased in editor-speak means that editor kept Kee on the phone for 20 minutes as she read the copy, adding comments like "Mmm! ... Mmm! ... Did you double check the gun calibers with the FBI? ... Mmm! ... Are you sure the FBI SWAT team was from the Richmond office? Check that. You can email me. Mmmm! ... You haven't said if you were worried that you might get shot when you went inside DeKant's house ... Yes, that does mean you are putting yourself inside the story, but in this instance I think that is necessary. Add that detail. Fact check those other points. And I think you're done. email me the clean copy."

Kee finished the rewrite, held her breath and pushed Send on her computer. The door bell rang.

"Freaking freak hell!" Kee exclaimed. "What time is it? 12:45! Damn!"

She leaped out of bed as he father answered the door.

It was Perez.

"Perez. FBI. I'm here to, um, work with Kee," explained Perez tactfully.

"You play Vietnamese chess?" queried Kee's father.

"Sorry, Sir. Vietnamese chess is not one of my core skills. But I do play Mahjong. Is that useful?"

"That good. Yes! Good."

"May I come in?"

"Yes! You good FBI. Other FBI," sniffed Vihn, shaking his head, "useless."

"I'm glad I passed the test," Perez responded, following Vihn into the kitchen.

About ten minutes later Kee arrived, panting. Her hair was wet. She was dressed in a navy suit, holding her shoes in one hand and a scarf in the other.

"I thought I'd save you from the Great Chess Inquisition," Kee said to Perez, nodding her head in the direction of her father.

"She good FBI. She play Mahjong," explained her father.

"Don't admit to playing anything," warned Kee, smiling, "you'll get trapped for hours. Pops, a *New York Times* reporter is coming to interview me. He'll be with a photographer. Don't ask them if they play chess," Kee admonished.

Her father looked forlorn and chastised.

Kee sighed.

"I'll talk to them. And you can make the tea, Pops. Is that all right?"

He smiled.

"I do think you know how to manipulate everyone around you," she joked.

Her father put on a look of total innocence.

The door bell rang again.

"Perez, you put on the kettle. Pops, you put out the tea tray," ordered Kee, running towards the door.

"Wait! I've got to come with you!" yelled Perez.

Kee opened the door to a young man in black leather jacket and jeans holding a camera and an older woman, maybe 40ish, wearing a black trouser suit and white shirt.

"Are you Kitchi Le?" asked the woman.

"Yes!" replied Kee, "Come in."

Perez checked their press passes.

"Well," announced the reporter, stepping through the doorway, "you are the flavor of the month in at the *New York Times* office, I can tell you that."

"I am?" gasped Kee, grinning from ear to ear. She followed the press pair, ushered by Perez down the hall and into the kitchen.

Kee's article appeared on the front page of *The New York Times* the next day under the headline: "NGSA Boss Shot. I Was There." The article occupied a single half-column under Kee's byline and photograph with the footer under the text stating: continued on page 7. Her article would have been given more space on a normal news day, but an even bigger news story was breaking across the nation.

The full list of names of Club 91 had been published on Wikileaks the previous day about the time Kee was being interviewed by the *New York Times* reporter. More astounding still was the news that, later that day, two more bodies were found. One victim was identified as Billy Cotton, brother of Republican Senator Roy Cotton. An AR-15 bearing a small American flag was found rammed into the lawn at the front door of his woodland estate on Timber Rd, Goldsboro, Pennsylvania. The other victim was Greg Ahern. He was found lakeside in jogging gear on the beach near the Indiana Dunes. An AR-15 was shoved into the sand by the body. The victims were the first two names on the Club 91 list. Each rifle had a half-letter sized US flag attached to the stock. Printed on the back of the flag found by the first body was **CLUB 91 90**. Printed on the back of the flag by the 2nd victim was **Club 91 89**. The banner headline for the lead article that day in *The New York Times* read: THE REAL COUNTDOWN BEGINS.

The End

About The Author

Kerry Cue

Kerry Cue is a humorist, mathematician, journalist and author.

She loved *The Andy Griffith Show* on TV in the sixties, with Ron Howard playing the little kid. "Later I realized I was that little kid," explains Kerry. "I grew up on a police station in rural Australia where the police phone and radio sat on our kitchen bench and my father's Lithgow .22 rifle rested against the fridge. There were 5 kids, a dog, a cat, ferrets, a budgie, chickens, a sheep and total chaos. At 10 years of age I'd have a tray shoved in my hand by my mother and told to 'go feed the prisoner'. I had to pour the prisoner's tea from a pot through the bars." Kerry wrote 3 books about her hilarious childhood.

"It was far too crazy to study at home so I had the keys to the local court house, built in 1856, and I did my high school homework in the Jury Room." Later Kerry studied Science/ Engineering at Melbourne University and taught maths and science for 10 diabolical years before becoming a best selling Australian author of 20 humorous and educational books including *Life On a G-String, I Left My Heart in Chinkapook and my knickers in New York* and *MeLand, 10 Ways Self-Obsession Makes You Stupid.*

She has written columns for every major newspaper in Australia, with some columns running for over 20 years. "The best thing about being a humorist," says Kerry, "is that you get to give totally unreliable advice to absolutely anyone on any topic." She also travels around Australia enlivening serious but dull conferences with humorous presentations, such as her stress management talk titled "And When You Smile, Try to Look Sane". She is the maths blogger, Mathspig, with over 1 million hits. Following the popularity of her blog, she spoke at the International Congress of Mathematical Education in Hamburg in 2016 as that very rare breed, a comic math blogger.

Kerry has two adult children and step-children. She lives in Melbourne with her husband and her little dog.

JAKE FOR MAYOR
BY

LOU AGUILAR

Ken Miller is having a bad run of luck. After torpedoing his career as a campaign manager, he drives through tiny Erie, Colorado, when a homeless beagle named Jake causes a series of mishaps that lands him in jail. Ken is granted bail on two conditions: that he not leave town before his trial in three weeks and—much to his chagrin—that he not let Jake out of his sight until then. Stuck in Erie as it prepares for a mayoral election, he's drawn into the local politics by a waitress who vehemently opposes incumbent Charles Dunbar, the only candidate on the ticket.

Unable to resist political adventure, Ken gets a brainstorm. If he can exploit the dog's popularity among the townspeople and get them to elect Jake as a protest candidate, the publicity will put him back on top. But things don't go exactly as planned. Ken warms to the dog, falls for the waitress, and employs her teenage son and his gang as campaign aides in a madcap battle with Mayor Dunbar ... who has no intention of losing to a dog.

PENMORE PRESS
www.penmorepress.com

The Prick
by
DC Wales

Civil rights law, Harassment in the work place, Labor laws and lawsuits, Unequal conditions in the work place, law stories, legal legends, legal gossip

Jason Hunter's dwindling bank account is a daily reminder that Jason never should have left his job at a prestigious law firm to start his own practice, a solo shop located in uncomfortable proximity to a strip club. Hope arrives in the form of Maggie Moxley, a legal assistant who tearfully claims that Robert Spelkin III—her boss, and the office's most profitable partner—sexually assaulted her at work. Looking to transform Moxley's misfortune into profits, Jason takes on Spelkin and his powerhouse firm, Levitt, Bennett & Taylor, LLP. Spelkin, a man of unbridled ambition and aggression, demands not only victory but Jason's legal dismemberment. Levitt engages Rebecca Trent, widely regarded as the city's best employment litigator, to embark on a campaign that will annihilate Jason, his little firm, and his client.

Jason's only weapon is the truth of what happened that night. But the more he gathers evidence, the more he questions whether Moxley has told him the whole story. Meanwhile, Moxley's accusations initiate a series of events whose consequences extend far beyond accuser and accused, creating chaos for everybody in their orbit.

PENMORE PRESS
www.penmorepress.com

THE MAN IN THE SPIDER WEB COAT BY PHILIP ACKMAN

Titus Buchanan, a professor who runs a think tank at Williams College, believes he's figured out how to stage a successful revolution. When the United Nations adopts a historic vote spelling the end of colonialism, Buchanan seizes the opportunity to test his theory. His laboratory will be the Splendid Islands, a collection of palm-fringed cays scattered across three quarters of a million square miles of the South Pacific. Its inhabitants will be his lab rats.

But complications arise. The Splendids belong to New Zealand, and New Zealand has no intention of giving them up. The United States has its own secret "space age" agenda for the islands. The Queen of England is bound to support New Zealand, but she doesn't want Britain to fall out with the Americans, who favor independence. Meanwhile, the islanders, gripped with revolutionary fever, have ideas about self-rule. Reverend Geoffrey Brown, originally recruited by Buchanan to run the revolution, joins forces with an unlikely crew of locals and sets out to match wits with powerful opponents.

PENMORE PRESS
www.penmorepress.com

Rembrandt's Angel

by

Steven Moore

A Neo-Nazi conspiracy threatens Europe . . .

Esther Brookstone's life is at a crossroads. A Scotland Yard inspector who specializes in stolen art, she's reluctantly considering retirement. A three-time widow, she can't quite decide whether paramour and colleague Interpol Agent Bastiann van Coevorden should be husband number four. Decisions are put on hold while she and Bastiann set out to thwart a neo-Nazi conspiracy financed in part by artworks stolen during World War II. Among the stolen art is the masterpiece "An Angel with Titus' Features," a work Esther obsesses about recovering.

The case sends the intrepid pair on an international hunt spanning several European countries and the Amazon jungle. Evading capture and thwarting death, Esther and Bastiann prove time and again that adrenaline-spiked adventures aren't just for the young.

PENMORE PRESS
www.penmorepress.com

Penmore Press

Challenging, Intriguing, Adventurous, Historical and Imaginative

www.penmorepress.com

www.ingramcontent.com/pod-product-compliance
Lightning Source LLC
Chambersburg PA
CBHW032159180726
48284CB00001B/114